All-Night Visitors

Northeastern University 1898–1998

Other titles in The Northeastern Library of Black Literature edited by Richard Yarborough

LLOYD L. BROWN	*Iron City*
STERLING A. BROWN	*A Son's Return: Selected Essays*
WILLIAM DEMBY	*The Catacombs*
JESSIE REDMON FAUSET	*The Chinaberry Tree* *There Is Confusion*
ANDREA LEE	*Sarah Phillips*
JULIAN MAYFIELD	*The Hit* and *The Long Night*
CLAUDE MCKAY	*Home to Harlem*
J. SAUNDERS REDDING	*Stranger and Alone*
GEORGE S. SCHUYLER	*Black Empire* *Black No More* *Ethiopian Stories*
ANN ALLEN SHOCKLEY	*Loving Her*
WALLACE THURMAN	*Infants of the Spring*
RICHARD WRIGHT	*Lawd Today!*

CLARENCE MAJOR

All-Night Visitors

Foreword by BERNARD W. BELL

Northeastern University Press
BOSTON

Northeastern University Press

Library of Congress Cataloging-in-Publication Data

Major, Clarence.
All-night visitors / Clarence Major.
p. cm.—(The Northeastern library of Black literature)
ISBN 1-55553-367-1 (cloth : alk. paper)
1. Afro-American men—New York (State)—New York—Fiction. 2. Vietnamese Conflict, 1961–1975—Veterans—Fiction. 3. Lower East Side (New York, N.Y.)—Fiction. 4. Men—Sexual behavior—Fiction. I. Title. II. Series.
PS3563.A39A45 1998
813′.54—dc21 98-33492

Designed by Ann Twombly

Composed in Fairfield by Coghill Composition, Richmond, Virginia. Printed and bound by Maple Press, York, Pennsylvania. The paper is Sebago Antique, an acid-free sheet.

MANUFACTURED IN THE UNITED STATES OF AMERICA
02 01 00 99 98 5 4 3 2 1

We are short term visitors
engaging the heart
of each other's life
one another's body,
sometimes forever
yet so brief
the sad distance
of our all-night transit.

FOREWORD TO THE 1998 EDITION

Like Toni Morrison and Ishmael Reed, Clarence Major is a virtuoso contemporary African American writer who soars above social and literary conventions to realms where even angels fear to tread. His movement beyond black sites of cultural production and consumption, as well as beyond thematic and structural concerns with racial and political consciousness, to a preoccupation with exploring the boundaries of language and imaginative consciousness can be traced in his trajectory as a black modern and postmodern artist, especially in his eight novels: *All-Night Visitors* (1969), *NO* (1973), *Reflex and Bone Structure* (1975), *Emergency Exit* (1979), *My Amputations* (Western States Book Award, 1986), *Such Was the Season* (Literary Guild Selection, 1987), *Painted Turtle: Woman with Guitar* (*New York Times Book Review* Notable Book of the Year, 1988), and *Dirty Bird Blues* (1997). Except for *Such Was the Season,* they are primarily transracial, transcultural expressionistic narratives that thematize a self-reflexive process of the creation of a dynamic, multifaceted self and art. Also, except for the last three, each is more fragmented and discontinuous in structure than its predecessor; and finally, each engages in self-conscious linguistic play that blurs the line between the worlds of fantasy and social reality.

Comparing this second, unexpurgated edition to the earlier version of Clarence Major's first novel still evokes a myriad of feelings and thoughts, including Francis Bacon's familiar aphorism: "Some books are to be tasted, others to be swallowed, and some few to be chewed and digested." Like the heavily cut 1969 Olympia Press publication, this new edition of *All-Night Visitors* is a sensational, memorable narrative construction of contemporary black male identity for at least three major reasons: its desperate sex, deadly violence, and expressionistic journey into the depths of the body and soul.

Unlike the mainly male reviewers of the first edition of *All-Night Visitors,* some readers, especially radical feminists, may be outraged by what they consider the offensive, phallocentric objectification and abuse of women in this novel. Some, especially radical black cultural nationalists, will be equally critical of what they may perceive to be a celebration of the stereotypic black stud. And some, especially those allied with religious conservatism, may find this text further justification for the censoring of material that they consider immoral. But many others—especially literary critics, bibliophiles, and those general readers who take the time to chew and digest the book—will be intrigued by the Freudian and expressionistic construction of the identity of a black male of the 1960s and the linguistic exploration of sex as the paradoxical and perverse expression of the forces of life and death.

It is important to remember that the first edition of *All-Night Visitors* was a product of disruptive, turbulent times in the life of the nation and the author. On one hand were the boycotts and sit-ins by blacks in the late 1950s and early 1960s, the March on Washington in 1963, the Civil Rights Bill of 1964, and the revival of the feminist and sexual emancipation movements in the mid-1960s. On the other hand were the assassinations of President John Kennedy and civil rights leader Medgar Evers in 1963, Malcolm X in 1965, and the Reverend Martin Luther King, Jr., and Senator Robert Kennedy in 1968, as well as the massacre of Vietnamese civilians by American troops in 1968 and the urban black liberation revolts throughout these years. The 1960s was thus a decade that tried the souls and ruptured the traditional social order of white and nonwhite peoples while simultaneously challenging individuals and nations to reconstruct themselves and their communities into a more free, just, democratic, and transcultural world order.

In an interview in 1969 Major expressed his personal aesthetics. "What I've had to come to realize," he tells the interviewer, "is that the question of a black aesthetic is something that really comes down to an individual question. It seems to me that if there is a premise in an artist's work, be he black or white, that it comes out of his work, and therefore out of himself. Or herself. I think that it's also true with *form*. It has to be just that subjective." Elaborating further in a self-interview, he states: "Subject matter is usually directly from my own experience. . . . It becomes a question of balance—how I handle the interplay between what has gone into my unconscious and what remains controlled at a conscious level." Paradoxically, Major also believes that "the characters in a story are not real people. They cannot be based on real people. They are words and not simply words on paper. . . . All words are lies when they, in any arrangement, pretend to be other than the arrangement they make. On the other hand, what I try to do is achieve a clear and solid mass of arrangements, an entity, that passes for nothing—except flashes of scenes and impressions we all know. Again, the wedding of the conscious and unconscious." Major's initial efforts at writing novels were therefore more expressionistic than realistic.

The first edition of *All-Night Visitors* was the culmination of four frustrating years of apprenticeship in writing novels. Commenting on the construction of the book, he states: "*All-Night Visitors* was not written in any straightforward way. It was salvaged from four or five failed novels. The Vietnam section was originally a novel about Vietnam. I'd never been there, but I imagined this war story about soldiers in Vietnam and that didn't work. Then there was a novel about Chicago and there was this New York novel, a lower east side novel. . . . So, bits and pieces pulled from here and there came together to make up that novel. As it turned out, only half of that book was published and since Olympia Press was interested in the sexy parts, they published a distorted version. . . . I've always known that was not the true book and that the true book the way I wrote it should be published."

Almost twice the length of the 1969 book, this current text of *All-Night Visitors* is "the true book" and, in Major's words, "an epic collage poem." Unlike the first edition, it is not divided into two major parts, and its thirty-five chapters provide a more balanced, yet equally non-linear, discontinuous, frequently surreal, first-person narrative of the protagonist Eli Bolton's conflicted physical and psychological construction as a contemporary black American man. Abandoned, loveless, and neurotic as a child, Bolton is transformed by his experiences in an orphanage and the Vietnam War into a hollow man in search of spiritual, emotional, and moral regeneration.

Both editions open and close in the Lower East Side of New York in 1967, moving back and forth in time and space through reveries, dreams, reflections, and retrospective narrative from Eli's birth in 1940 and abandonment in an orphanage to his symbolic death in Vietnam and rebirth through lust, love, and compassion for women and children. On one level, "Tammy," the opening section, ostensibly reduces Eli's quest to a reconstruction of his fragmented identity through desperate, phallocentric, heterosexual adventures with all-night urban visitors. "My dick is my life, it has to be. Cathy certainly won't ever come back. I've stopped thinking about the possibility," Eli thinks retrospectively. "Eunice has of course gone away to Harvard, and I'm taking it in stride. My ramrod *is* me, any man's rod is himself." After contrasting Eli's lust for his current partner with the love he experienced with Cathy and Eunice, the implied author proceeds to engage us, the readers, emotionally and to distance us ethically from the narrator and protagonist by exposing us to a graphic first-person description of fellatio and sexual intercourse between a psychologically frustrated, callously exploitative Eli and a homeless twenty-year-old white Midwesterner.

The ecstatic rhapsody of metonymic names for his penis that Eli catalogues in this and other episodes in order to stress the tension between life and death in sexual activity contrasts with the playful variety of names he created earlier for Cathy when she became the agent for the recovery of his compassion for others and the reconstruction of his manhood. In one scene, for example, Eli expresses Cathy's impact on him in a series of names that register extremes of mood and feeling: "glorious Kathi, gentle Caathy, sacred Katheas, my empress, Cato Katheus, my princess, Catti my whore, divine Kathee, my angel Cathela!" On one level, then, the shift from defining himself and others by naming their body parts to naming them as whole subjects maps the changes in Eli's identity. In the opening episode, with its reduction of himself and his partner to sexual objects, the language of the implied author highlights Eli's emotional, ethical, and psychological relapse as a result of Cathy's departure.

In "Mama Mama," the final chapter in the novel, Eli is jobless and abject, receiving money from Tammy on two or three of her nightly visits. But Tammy's lying and her proposal that he pose with her in pornographic pictures shock him into walking out on her. More importantly and melodramatically, the crying of an abused and abandoned pregnant Puerto Rican mother of seven children outside his apartment door during a thunderstorm becomes the catalyst for a redemptive act of compassion, when he provides the family with shelter and food for the night. "*Her* dispossession was my responsibility, despite her husband. Who he was socially," Eli reflects while deliberating about opening his apartment to these refugees. "Though the Warden [the abusive director of the orphanage where Eli was raised] may have helped arouse within me a streak of cruelty, my bitterness was imperfected; I was no victim of complete inner blindness, subjective corruption." For some readers this postmodern resistance to narrative closure offers too little, too late for the redemption of the toubled narrator/protagonist.

The major difference between the two editions of *All-Night Visitors* is that more background, context, and coherence are provided in the current version. Before we hear by indirect interior monologue how Eli loved and lost Cathy, the implied author historically grounds Eli's story of social and psychological dissociation in contrasting narratives of his dual racial identity that are passed on to him by white authorities in Paulson School, the orphanage where he was abandoned by his black or white mother in 1940. In the orphanage, young Eli is terrorized by Warden, the brutal surrogate mother who cruelly lashes him with a heavy switch for reading in the dormitory after lights out, and by Leroy, who bullies Junior, a younger teenager, into vivisecting Warden's pet puppy, Gypsy. Later, as a foster child, Eli is initiated into the mysteries and pleasures of the body with Clara during sexual intercourse.

His horrifying experiences in Vietnam in 1961 morally, psychologically, and physically disillusion, desensitize, and disable him even further. In several dreamlike flashbacks, Eli bears witness to the shell shock of deafening, deadly, endless carpetbombing in

Vietnam. The soul-destroying atrocities, perversities, and paradoxes of Americans in an undeclared war that he recalls include "a kind of routine thing where we kinda dashed in and finished taking the beauty out of a couple of old harmless men and about six children" whom Master Sergeant Dokus Mokus shot instead of delivering to the battalion prison control detachment. When questioned about the murders, "Mississippi Moke said, 'Listen, you little sawed-off nigger, I don't have to explain a dagblasted thing to the likes of you!'" Eli reflects, "There's just no way on earth I can elevate a killer like Stars and Stripes Moke-anny to the level of a human divine creature when I think back on the drama of his battlefield history and how he's so tolerated by these upstanding officers and his fella countrymen."

In the flashback in "Grunts," which reveals how weed and coke highs do not dull Eli's psychic pain, readers encounter the most devastating trauma that he suffers in Vietnam and that is the major source of his personality disorder. In this sequence, Eli remembers his horrified disgust and disbelief when he and a fellow black soldier named Bud find the sadistic Moke and his sidekick Smith raping a young girl: "As light came around the corners of our journey we saw Mokus's big naked pink ass, beneath a bush, struggling updownupdown, humping what looked like a child with dirty knees, no shoes; her muffled groans trapped inside something massive like his fist and Smith holding back the bushes for him with his peewee hanging hard as a popsicle waiting . . . Bud and I were so numbed by the sadistic inhuman monstrous incident we couldn't react . . . for a moment; then we rushed in, our rifles down; still Smith threw his up directly in our faces. 'Just take it easy, Jackson,' which is what he calls all niggers. 'You ain't about to get none of this—I'm next.' And he actually thought *we* wanted to share in the activity in which he and Dokus Mangy were engaged. I moved my leg. 'I'll pull the trigger just as sure as my name's Smitty. I'll kill a nigger jus' as soon as I'd kill a VC. See that old man over there—bet you *he* believed me.'" In the grass thicket, Eli sees the bloody body of the frightened old man whom he had earlier passed on entering the village. "'I cut his heart out like he wuz a chicken,'" Smitty boasts. Bud, in turn, tells Eli,

"'The sad thing, my man, is it wouldn't do a damn bit uv good to inform—.'"

The inhumane, cruel nightmare continues in Eli's mind, "Moke finished, stumbled back out and fell on his ass laughing his evil-eye laugh, dripping with the child's blood while Smith unhitched his belt saying to his ace, 'Take my rifle. These niggers think they gone get some, shoot 'em if you wanna, I don't give a rat's ass.' I turned away and Moke laughed. Bud walked over to the old man's body and stood looking down at him. How could we stand here like this and let this happen? Why couldn't I kill Moke and Smith? Why should I carry the weight of their deed with me forever? . . . Moke went over and stood beside Bud, pointed his rifle at the dead man's temple, pulled the trigger three times, grinning while Smith got his nuts got up and I jumped him with my fist sailing into his eyesocket busting the string loose, I hoped, but it didn't as he shot the girl in the chest. Her legs twitched the knees came together the silence the stillness and I hate myself I hate myself you—" After witnessing directly or hearing of the brutal rapes and killings of Vietnamese civilians, Eli mentally disintegrates. The cruelty of Moke in Vietnam, of the Warden and Leroy in the orphanage, and of his mother in abandoning him haunts Eli's consciousness throughout the novel.

As Eli struggles to rediscover and reconstruct the vital pieces of his humanity, he moves aimlessly through North America and Mexico, returning to Chicago and the orphanage in Amesville, Illinois, to visit the dying Warden after hearing news of President Kennedy's death. Bitter and desperately searching for love in Pittsburgh, Philadelphia, Detroit, and again Chicago, he "screwed many women." Through a surreal marijuana haze while working at a soda fountain, he remembers being challenged by Jimmy Sheraton, an old, white former comedian from Mississippi who was "raised by a colored woman" and who was frequently in and out of the mental hospital. Eli also recalls dispassionately how Jimmy, while harassing him on the way home, is attacked and killed with his own knife by "young splibs" whose subsequent confession to the cops Bolton corroborates. After Jimmy's murder in "Beef Kill," the final twenty-five surreal chapters of the novel are dominated by desperate, dissolute, lonely prostitutes, drunks, and drug addicts, as well as by destitute elderly folks whom he encounters as a night clerk in the Other Side Hotel and by regenerative sexual encounters with Anita, Cathy, and Eunice.

The implied author uses Eli's compulsively detailed descriptions of his erotic adventures with these three women to show how the protagonist attempts to rediscover his humanity in the capacity for love and compassion by rhetorically constructing a multilayered black male sexual identity. Eli relates to Anita, "a shapely Afro-American, the color of a Chinese," as an insatiable stud on one level and as a Priapic trickster on another, renewing an uninhibited sexual relationship with her in Chicago upon returning from Vietnam. "Anita was not a black woman who emphasized the *black*ness of her beauty," Eli tells us with mixed emotions about both her and his own racial identity. "I mean, she went to the beauty shop to have her hair fried, oiled, curled, or straightened to make it look like Lady Clairol; she was a shadow of a blonde, she believed blondes had more fun, once she even dyed her hair blonde; she used bleaching creams though she was already lighter than the average bear; she was a devoted reader of *Ebony*—she believed in its philosophy, especially its ads."

Although Eli hates her concern for "material luxury" and her attitude that "you're the man, *you're supposed to do for me! I'm the woman,*" her "natural fellatio skill" and "overwhelming self-confidence and spontaneous ability to enjoy lovemaking with the sense of fulfillment an artist knows through creating pleasurable art" accentuate his "essence in the world." In an extraordinarily detailed, ten-page description of fellatio that challenges his powers of linguistic creativity as well as sexual prowess in controlling his orgasm, Eli metaphorically reduces his identity to "a pompous dog ready to bark" and metonymically to such names for his genitalia as "Mr. ex-Perpendicular," "Mr. Prick," "Mr. Hammer's under-belly," and "Mr. Tail." In this expressionistic exploration of the extent to which sexual orgasm paradoxically evokes both life and death, the implied author is ultimately concerned with the psychic impact of the tension between lust and love, wholeness and disintegration in Eli's sexual passion and reconstruction of his identity. "It is only at these moments, of course," Eli reflects, "that this particular 'movement' of the symphony of life is so beautifuly important, all-consuming . . . Equal to the working moments when I am excited by the energetic, rich growth of a concept I am able to articulate! Or my sudden ability to construct bookshelves, or create a silly wacky lovely painting, equal to anything that I do involving the full disclosure of myself! I hesitate to say equal to my ability to handle those firearms in Vietnam, against those nameless human collages that fell in the distance, like things, but maybe even equal to that, too . . ."

Both Eunice and Cathy, who are white, are more sexually inhibited than Anita, who becomes a relic of Eli's past after he meets and falls in love with Cathy. Even though, like the narrator, Anita is desperately searching for someone to love her as well as someone to love, the reflexiveness of the language of the text reveals Eli's double consciousness as he emotionally and intellectually distances himself from her. This occurs in part because Eli sees Anita as biologically black but culturally white: "she thought the Hully Gully was a game invented by Jewish kids in Israel, that who Stagger Lee shot was his mama, that a Blood was an Indian, and that C.C. Rider was a civil service technician." The deep pain of a black woman who loses her man to a white woman is also dramatically captured in Anita's signifying attack on both Cathy and Eli. "That little young dumb country-looking bitch! I swear *I can't see* what *you see* in her. But you must see something . . . ," she tells Eli with a pathetic laugh at his betrayal of her and his race. "She walks like a fucking bear—and that raggedy coat she was wearing needs to be thrown in the garbage . . . I wouldn't use that funky coat for a dog to sleep on . . . But that's the way you colored men are, though: if it's *white* no matter how skunky it is it's *right*."

A young VISTA worker in Chicago, Cathy regenerates Eli's capacity for love. While drinking in a bar, she shyly trusts Eli with the story of her emotional distress and sexual frigidity as the result of two childhood traumas. The first was her birth in Rhode Island to a "brutally indifferent" mother whose family disapproved of her marriage to Cathy's biological father and who beat Cathy because she reminded her of the father. The second childhood trauma was her sexual molestation and physical abuse by a stepfather who was a tortured prisoner of war and whom she confusedly thinks that she "honestly loved . . . *in a way*." After Cathy and Eli futilely try to make love for at least two weeks, Eli's passion, patience, and pampering prevail. Reflecting on their lovemaking, Eli describes the psychological renewal of sexual fulfillment in rhapsodic vernacular language. "She held very tightly to me. Her legs clutching my back. Her mouth, dry, opened, like a bird in the sun all day and finally, our tongues together, we bit gently at each other's flesh. Warm, radical, delectable colors rippling through my mind. I felt the beginning of *delirious* fulfillment. Waves of excitement mounted in me as I buried my face in the valley of her full warm breasts; her softness, her absorbing moisture, her genital mystery engulfed the thick swollen loneliness of myself. Shooing away the bats, the scarecrows, the Warden and everything! And my false impression of white pussy! and frigidity!" Two days later they engage in mutual oral sex that culminates in Cathy's "first complete orgasm."

Eventually Cathy leaves, heading west. Eli's recovery of and reconstruction of his capacity to love are contrasted with the darkness of his feelings: "I am depressed, evil, I feel the crashing weight of her departure," he muses in the opening of the third and final section entitled "Cathy." "I hardly know what to say to her; it is five o'clock already, the superstitious hour of birth and death, and this bright electric luminous frenzy I feel, the ebb of my dishonorable condition, is too much! But I cannot let Cathy know that I am desperately insane with the sickness I feel at her leaving me; the bewitching entanglement of all the luxuriant feelings she has constructed in me leaves me charmed and ensnared in myself, ugly with craziness."

Later, Eli turns to Eunice. Moving from his apartment into a hotel room and walking the streets of the Lower East Side, he remembers: "I took the ashes of my soul, in search of some beatitude I had once touched, the intrigue of Cathy, to try to cultivate it again." Near the end of the novel, he recollects meeting Eunice, who "had never had a black man before" and who was the "most sophisticated unpretentious girl I had ever loved. . . . She occupied a sweet place in my mind, like Cathy. Like Anita, before both. And she was an intellectual, Eunice the Brain!" Eunice becomes his "life away from the Lower East Side's Other Side Hotel, and its strung-out people." Although they exchange vows of love, Eunice dreads that the possiblity of a pregnancy might disrupt her departure for a new life at Harvard on a scholarship to study Eastern religions. Dreading the imminent loss of her love, Eli leaves her and sinks into joblessness, loneliness, and, as the novel ends where it begins, the lustful visits of Tammy. Eli's shock at Tammy's proposal to participate in pornography and, in the concluding chapter, his compassionate identification with the abandoned mother of the Puerto Rican family are the small yet significant signs of hope for the spiritual renewal, if not the moral redemption, of his manhood.

The physical and psychological journey of Major's narrator as he seeks to reconstruct his identity as a black Vietnam veteran in this edition of *All-Night Visitors* is more chronological, coherent, and sympathetic than in the first. The dislocation of temporal and spatial order in this expressionistic narrative of desperate sex and deadly violence is a bold, imaginative effort to reconstruct the perversities and paradoxes of the struggle for black American male identity during the emerging new world of the 1960s. Because, like Toni Morrison in *The Bluest Eye* and Ishmael Reed in *The Free-Lance Pallbearers,* Major boldly explores the boundaries of language as well as of spiritual and moral consciousness in this uncut edition of his first demanding novel, *All-Night Visitors* should, in Bacon's words, be "chewed and digested" carefully for a full understanding and appreciation of its ambitious achievement.

BERNARD W. BELL

Selected Bibliography

Byerman, Keith. *Fingering the Jagged Grain: Tradition and Form in Recent Black Fiction.* Athens: University of Georgia Press, 1985.

Fair, Ronald. Review of *All-Night Visitors. Black American Literature Forum* 13, no. 2 (Summer 1979): 73.

Klinkowitz, Jerome. "Clarence Major: An Interview with a Post-Contemporary Author." *Black American Literature Forum* 12, no. 1 (1978): 32–37.

Lehmann-Haupt, Christopher. "Books of the Times: On Erotica." *New York Times,* 7 April 1969.

Major, Clarence. *The Dark and Feeling: Black American Writers and Their Work.* New York: Third Press, 1974.

McCaffery, Larry, and Jerzy Kutnik. "Beneath a Precipice: An Interview with Clarence Major." In *Some Other Frequency: Interviews with Innovative American Authors.* Ed. Larry McCaffery. Philadelphia: University of Pennsylvania Press, 1996. 241–64.

Miller, Adam David. Review of *All-Night Visitors. The Black Scholar* (January 1971): 54–56.

O'Brien, John. "Clarence Major." In *Interviews with Black Writers.* New York: Liveright, 1973. 125–39.

Reed, Ishmael. Review of *All-Night Visitors. Black American Literature Forum* 13, no. 2 (1979): 73.

Review of *All-Night Visitors. For Now* 13 (1973): 38–40.

Scharper, Alice. "An Interview." *Poets and Writers Magazine* 19, no. 1 (January–February 1991): 15–19.

Starrex, Allan. "Long Day's Journey into Sex." *Man to Man* (May 1969): 16–17, 58.

Tate, Greg. "Major Major." *Voice Literary Supplement* (September 1990).

Weixlmann, Joe. "Clarence Major." *Dictionary of Literary Biography* 33: 153–56.

Welburn, Ron. "All-Night Travelers." *Nickel Review* (August 1969): 15.

All-Night Visitors

TAMMY

I've just come in from the street. A few moments ago I was frustrated, almost unhappy, but Tammy is on the bed. Her name isn't really important. All I want her for is to fuck her. She has a kind of savage ability to fuck well—we screwed a lot last night, and probably didn't sleep until three o'clock. For some reason I suddenly feel very insecure. Her pussy hasn't helped. I had been at it as though it might in some way give me protection.

Everything will be all right, I tell myself. I know everything will be all right, and yet I am not quite sure of what I mean by "everything." I look down at the girl. In a way she is very sad . . .

I found her three weeks ago sitting outside, outside the door, on the stoop. She had no place to go. She got the address of the woman who has the apartment next to mine; she got it from the Diggers' Free Store. The message she had was: "Can you put this girl up until she gets on her feet?" Apparently, the woman next to me, who is really not bad-looking, kind of fat, a redhead, certainly no more than thirty but kind of mean-looking, had left word at the Diggers that she would be willing to let people sleep on her floor. This kind of thing is being done a lot in the East Village.

But I came up the steps and said, "Hello," and that was it. She was more than friendly, more than willing; she accepted every invitation I made.

Inside my place, she ran her mouth, a Midwestern cracker accent, a mile a minute. She was telling me about how she hitchhiked from some dinky little town in Illinois, got arrested in Ohio, got out of jail when they checked back by phone with somebody there at the reform school where she practically grew up, and discovered that she *was really* twenty years old like she had been telling them all along, from the moment they picked her up.

She wasn't pretty to me and she doesn't even begin to "shape up" now, though I feel sympathy for her. I mean the sometimes-warmth I feel for her doesn't make her look better, but she knows how to fuck. She is a master at it, and works her ass off.

I realize that I am simply evading so many things by lying around all day like this, letting her play with my dick, sit on my lap, suck it, get down on her knees, upside down, backwards, any way you can think of. I can do nothing else right now. My dick is my life, it has to be. Cathy certainly won't ever come back. I've stopped thinking about the possibility. Eunice has of course gone away to Harvard, and I'm taking it in stride. My ramrod *is* me, any man's rod is himself.

This thing that I am, this body—it is me. *I* am it. I am not a concept in your mind, whoever you are! I am *here,* right here, myself, MYSELF. I am not *your idea.*

Yes, this *is* distraction. I sit down now on the side of the bed, I am about to wake her, *because* I am depressed, frustrated. Her round, innocent-looking face is hard, deep in the pillow. Her pink cheeks are red, her hands are folded beneath her face, and there is a frown between her eyebrows. I know she is really a very fucked-up, unhappy girl, but somehow basically strong, rebellious; I touch the wet edge of her scalp, like black women. Jokingly I say, "Damn, baby, I think you been lying to me! You *really* a secret nigger!—" She is nude beneath the sheet, I know. I pull it all the way down and stroke her little girl–size body. Each tit is no bigger than half an orange. I turn her little white wrists over and look at them. They are healing, where she cut them with a coke bottle that first night here, after getting drunk from wine I offered her. Now I have beer here, this is the first booze I've had in the apartment since the end of the wine three days ago. I want to fuck her, like she's a *thing.* The overpowering rapture of just grinding gently with her, without compassion, because I know there is no future for us, no real reason why we should protect each other's feelings. I don't want to see her eyes when I screw her, because sometimes they are *too* sad. I feel I can almost see a pig looking at me from her eyes, at times. I touch her pussy now, the dry hair. My sperm dry on it. Little streaks of dry *cum.*

She rolls over automatically without waking up, and it is easy to spread her legs. I am in a very uncomfortable position: I want her to wake up and suck me, but it must be done in a very subtle way. I must convince her that I am really passionately intent on making love to her, that I want to turn her ass every way but loose! This is a ritual. I'm sure. She knows I'm lazy. That I will make a big showing, maybe for a few seconds, with great ambition, in a kind of hungry struggle to rip her open since she likes it rough, then I'll stretch out on my back, on this tiny cot we have here, and take a deep breath. And she is asking, "You like my pussy?" And I am saying, "Yes, yes, it's good." She is adjusting herself over me, so that she's sitting astraddle my hips, with the mouth of her pussy just at the tip of my meat. The female smell of her these three days hasn't been unpleasant at all, though she's had only one bath. Strange that she doesn't smell sour. But there is something about a twenty-year-old girl that simply doesn't get too odious. Maybe I shouldn't say that because it probably isn't always or even generally true. This morning I don't want to go through the ritual of even pretending I'm going to be very manly and supervise her, so to speak, sexually. I want her to wake up right now and get to this proposition; I am beginning to feel a streak of evilness creeping in me. I want to *force* her—I can almost see my hands lifting her, opening her mouth, as though she were some kind of doll, and choking her with the splatter of my dick.

The dried sperm on her hair turns me off. I don't want to bother with getting that stuff on me. It's old, dry, and the stuff inside her, this morning, from last night, is thick by now, like some kind of cheese, so it is understandable, or should be, that I now want the relatively clean receptacle of her mouth. I know that she won't want to, but I can't put my clean ecstatic dick into her, not right now. Not while I'm depressed. Sometimes I can do it, no matter how sloppy the snug, sumptuous hole is. I am stroking the insides of her thighs, and unbuttoning my shirt.

I stop fooling around, stand up and strip down to my birthday suit, my butterscotch body, my half of the feast of life!

Suddenly I am straddling her, my knees on either side of her head; I feel playful *and* evil. I am holding my supernatural enravisher, and just thinking about her tongue, the pressure of the walls of her mouth—how they could work together to get it all out of me (flowing, endlessly flowing, waves and waves of enchantment, voluptuousness, and it seeming so scrumptious all the while *to her,* and she never gags)—and the tickling sensations of rubbing the tip of it against her half-opened mouth, is causing it to swell, the veins in it standing up, the bulbous head, purple and spongy against the sleep-dry small lips; I'm watching all this. And her eyes are coming open, but she is not fully aware.

She is yawning now, turning away from my playful dick. She's rejecting it, and I feel only more frustrated. Well, I'll fuck her, just to wake her. She's always willing to fuck, even while sleeping. She'll fuck in her sleep anytime, keeping the rhythm, everything going, just as though she were conscious . . .

I suck the hard, small red nipple of the left tit, it tastes of sweat, but not really nasty sour sweat; just as I am beginning on the other tit, I can feel her eyelids blinking against my arm, which is somewhere up there against her face. I have one hand gently moving over her bush.

Then, I feel the gentle pressure of her small delicate expert hand beginning to stroke Mr. Ill-Bred. He begins to get vulgar with his uppity big head swelling bigger, ready for an engagement. But he has a definite nobility, and she respects it. I feel her tight, firm stomach, beneath me, move up deliberately against mine. She is trying to be physically closer. It is enticingly pleasant.

It is genial; I feel a healthy Henry Miller kind of vitality toward it all; her hands—she's now using both of them. The pleasure of it almost equals the early stages of a good, drawn-out blow job. She has a kind of rhythm, but the position I am in is complicated, and a strain . . .

I take my hand from her cunt, knowing instinctively that this will increase her focus on what *she is doing to me,* not on what I am doing to her. The attraction of my hand, my fingers at her clitoris, only distracts from her skill on my dibbler. I slowly lie down beside her; she's moving a little to make room for me, the cot is so small. Lying down, the odor of her alluring body is stronger, but I do not want to hassle with it, only to let it seep into my psyche, to stretch out in the huge comfort of this luxury . . .

She hasn't noticed the beer sitting on the sink yet; I am leery—if she sees it she'll surely want to get drunk. She's so easily distracted. And even beer will make her drunk. Or so she says. No reason not to believe her. Meanwhile, she sits astride me, easing her honeypot down around the throbbing upstanding round rod. She watches my eyes in their rapture—I know I must have this kind of look. The muscles in her cave of life suck with real strength at the prepuce.

The wet sound, I listen to it; I am enjoying the exiguity of her doing her thing. It surprisingly does not worry me that the hole is not clean, not much anyway, and even the little worry that is there, around the hairs of things, is leaving. This is agreeable. Life seems so large and natural, like it should be. The way I feel, the navigation of her hips. The SLAP, slap, *pop* slap, SLAP, slap, *pop* slap! the luxuriance of her walls around my bluejacket, the scudding hammer looking straight up, its one eye, up into Life, the Beginning, raceless beginning, of everything deeper than anything social. And her words come back to me: "Do you hate me because I'm white?" "I don't hate you—what makes you think I hate you?" "I don't know—this colored boy I used to go with in Chicago used to make me get down on my knees and blow him, he said I was a no-good white trampy bitch and the only place for me was on my knees sucking him. *Boy!* did he hate white people! I just thought maybe all colored guys were that way." This conversation took place yesterday. The edge of it comes back because I am thinking of asking her to float my *coc* in her skilled slimy wet pink cave, but I know my reason isn't the same as that other black dude's. I would dig it just as much from a "sister," morals aside; as a matter of fact the best head I've had came from the knowledge box of a beautiful, down, black chick, long-standing; but I now pop the question in the middle of all this intense gratification: "Some head, baby?" "But isn't *this* good?" I'm lying here on my back, and she's working with the faucet like a champ; sure it's great, but I want the extra punch of those magic heights—her tongue, teeth, walls, lips, the mobility of the whole thing, the sucking, biting, pumping, that performance itself! The slick walls, the hair, my twin wrinkled and frolicsome balls being carefully caressed all the while, and the other hand busy gently gliding over the babyhairs up and down my stomach. "Yeah, it's good—you know you're good, but—" "*But* you want me to give you a blow job! I think you just like the idea of having a *white* girl give you a blow job!" There is this sideways half-assed grin on her face, it's a jest and not unkind, saying tacitly, "Huh?"

"I really think you're sick with all this racism, baby, every minute you're into *that* bag . . ." I hear myself saying, also fearing that I'm blowing my chances. "I bet that's why you woke me," she says, ignoring my statement against her mind. She's now simply sitting there dumbly on my *kok,* with a dreamy expression, looking down into my face, but not seeing me, probably seeing something, somebody, some sad scene in downstate Illinois. She knows that I'm "from" Chicago, which impresses her, but I have refused to talk about Chi with her because we obviously don't have notes to exchange. She came through the city, but was in the hippy intrigue, driven and pestered by cops on the near North Side; I know the area, but in a different time element—I'm seven, eight years older than she.

I really begin to give up, thinking surely I've blown it; the dicker will simply have to settle for the appetizing second choice of warmed-over stale pussy with old *cum* still in it, gooey valley with *so* much profusion—when she surprises me by lifting all the way up, the draft of warm air striking the wet milky nakedness of my *dik,* which begins now to become flaccid, and I'm not as ashamed of its sudden enfeebled face at a moment like this as I used to be, say, at sixteen, because unlike then, now I understand MY MIND, and trust its relationship with this experienced *cokke* of mine; and not even a broad can *runmedown,* you know, like this hippy here once or twice jokingly has tried to do with something like "You're so ol' you can't fuck no more." It doesn't get to me, this kinda thing. I just want her to understand *her function,* that this isn't *romance* for me either, she sometimes seems to forget *that,* though she ain't fooled about her *own* position . . .

I'm about to give up when it happens: the caress, the hand, its strength embraces my reclining soldier; I can now close my eyes, no need to fill the insipid psychological space between us because this womanish "treat" will revive my gun to its frisky textured life, I trust. With the firmness of my big toe I wiggle her clitoris. It is a small man-in-a-boat—she obviously hasn't masturbated a lot; I remember now, that first night, during her wild, frantic, endless monologue, slowly it became clear that she has been humped, been working the hardness out of roosters since she was ten or eleven years old . . . The wrap. Her lips wrap around it, the wet usage. The "root" feeling, deep down feeling, the pressure—up. She is beginning slowly, these gateways into simple beauty, these slabs of life, these tissues wrapping around each other, the texture of this plant, growing bigger in the spit-slick walls of mother nature. Growing John is growing so mighty he does not need the shims of her hands, the gentle strength of those fingers, the weight of it. The pulling goodness, tugging at the nerves beneath the skin, the root, at the base of my nuts, the tickle in my ass, running up my spine, the weightless rivers running all through me, into the ends of my scalp; my back, flat, though still, deliberately not tense—though I am tempted to tighten up—seems to ripple. My stomach ripples.

Her mouth cascades, the tight grip lifts, drops again, lifts higher this time, almost pulling up to the tip, almost losing the meat—air felt moving around its wetness. My eyes are closed. Why is this as beautiful to me as writing a poem? As *important* as philosophy, or anthropology, or music? BECAUSE IT IS. Her fingers—of both hands—tickle, caress, flutter it, add to the total flourishing of the act! She is percolating me, and I can lie here in the extravagance of it. No, it doesn't matter *who* or what she is now, I do not love her, I do not hate her, her skin is not white, is not black, is not skin, necessarily. Drenching me with the sweet tidal rides of her mouth! I *deliberately* fight the tendency to *stiffen* from the excitement of it. I am fighting it so hard, the soft membranes slapping, *slush slush,* she tightens up, then, *slush slush* again; the plush washing tides of it, into me, into the waterfalls of my mind, my psyche, my fingertips, my deep canals, the silent nerve dark blood riverbeds of my human self responding to the gesture, the wave of her velvet tongue, the "chewing," gentle chewing, permeating action. I am coming, coming slowly, just very very slowly, a draining, that she nurses carefully, licks at, rolls around on her tongue, teases, washes down; her tongue stabs one or two times playfully at Mr. Perpendicular. He does not react with fluid, he is so stunned in the paradox of being *relaxed* under the command of my body, this black castle, its intelligence, and logically wanting to, needing to *explode in orgasm* a steady serum of overflowing, sopping-life—the spurt of life! but cannot gush forth, its need for a climax, to *keep* existence itself, the deepest definition of its agony, to keep it going, *going*.

My mind begins to wander when she bogs. I am so content, arrogantly almost, that I need not be alert. I even allow Mr. Ill-Bred to get soft in her so she'll have to wonder about her skill, doubt herself, feel threatened, do better, work harder at the dibble of him. I know her neck is very tired by now; she complained about it last night and the day before. The position is very uncomfortable, but so is anything of value that is in the—

Ahhhh, in gentle appreciation I lazily reach down and stroke her hair. It is moist. Suddenly, like a character out of Batman Comics being sprung out of captivity, her head shoots up, her mouth, a wet radius, closes; she catches her breath, I see the Adam's apple move almost imperceptibly, like the neck of a tense lizard filtered through the brilliant electric technological media of Walt Disney, and she asks, "Say—by the way, were you in Chicago last Christmas, during that grand hoax, when everybody thought God was coming down from the clouds to save us poor sinners?" I am completely thrown into a state of emotional and mental chaos and deep lassitude by this untimely question. I simply whisper, "Yeah, yeah—but come, please, don't stop *now!*" And I force her head down. She begins again . . . I know she will soon stop, though she knows that *I* want her to continue until I complete the circle. The "aching sweetness," a phrase commonly used, does not describe it precisely. She has made the dome by now spit-slick and it is sliding easily.

The softness, she begins to work at it, for the hardness. Dead tired, I know. I feel some anxiety, pity, fear. But please don't stop, not yet, I say silently. This can go on for over an hour "if" she is strong enough. With my toe I examine her split, and discover that it is very marshy (*she* has been coming all this time, enjoying it?), the gooey stuff drips down around my toe, between the cracks (I am able to work at her vagina like this because my knees are bent, and my feet are together meeting directly beneath her bottom), it is watery-fresh, so definitely not from last night's making. The head is throbbing and jumping in her thrifty enclosure, when she suddenly disconnects, lifts her face, red as a tomato, her eyelids droopy with tiredness; she's holding herself on one arm, still sitting on her knees; she brushes her hair back from her face. "Fuck! Ain't you never gonna come?" This increases my anxiety, my frustration. I hardly know what to say, but I say, "I'm coming, now, baby—I was almost *there* when you stopped." Like on the edge of wisdom, but I was always there, at the point and *that* was the dark rich joy of it, being stunned in a pivot . . .

She starts this time, *really* working for a quick explosion from me. I'm holding back as much as possible. I relax, fighting the excitement she is pumping into my limbs, throughout the channels of myself! Her pink grip is tighter, the pumping is automation! It washes me! Giant waves shock my skull, to my fingertips, my lips dry up, my throat dries up, I feel my head lift and fall in hydraulic waves, I can hardly keep still. Everything in me is pushed to the point of a silent—stillness, on the edge of a massive flesh*kok* human storm—on the edge now, as she pumps it (and I still fight her!)—she means to finish, to shrink me! Mr. Rooster slides madly in the pink walls, her fingers dancing everywhere from nuts to staff, helping the mouth at its work; the serpent is stern in her depths though, holding back, expressing its sweet happiness by emitting a superficial little stream of false sperm into her hard-working membraney cave, as though to pacify her, give her hope, make her think she is getting somewhere. And she is! She really is! I can't *hold on* much longer; the emission is pushing against the many bevels of the dammed-up walls of myself. *Oh shit,* I think, *oh shit,* this is *too* much! I really begin to submerge, sink down into levels of self as I feel it lift—I am dying, flowing down as the *splash!* enters the first stages of its real career issuing out of the gun; it is coming—now—out—of—the—firearm *valve,* its ordeal beats me back into ancient depths of myself, back down to some lost meaning of the male, or deep struggling germ, the cell of the meaning of Man; I almost pass into unconsciousness the rapture is so overpowering, its huge, springing, washing infiltration into Her, an eternal-like act, a Rain, I am helpless, completely at her mercy, wet in her hands, empty, aching, my ass throbbing with the drained quality of my responsive death . . .

And she stays at it gently, knowingly, not irritating it unnecessarily, but just long enough to glide it to security discreetly, to empty it of every drop that might leave it otherwise pouting, to suck, suck, suck, suck, pull the very last crystal drop of *cokke* lotion out of me, into this specific cycle of herself, beautiful! beautiful! to the last drop, and I'm in a deep sleep again.

It is three hours later. She is not here. I have been sleeping, I feel fine, very good, like I felt this morning, on the street, going to the bank, thinking of the city's pollution, happy with being—just being, watching Catholic kids going to school, the hippies, passing the vegetable stands—I feel now happy like that, again. What she said, just before she left, it is vague in my mind, but it comes back. Something about going to the Diggers to see if she could find a kitten. I know that I must not get attached to her, so I must get rid of her soon. It can become a sick thing . . . So she must go soon.

CAPRICORN

I was born under the sign of Capricorn, the tenth sign of the Zodiac, and was faced for a very long time with the huge mystery of not only my cultural and historical past but also with the deep, elusive, seeming unjustness and enigma of my immediate familial and lineal history. Naturally, very early I began furiously to probe anything—method, technique, science, religion—I could come by, searching for clues to the meaning and reality of myself on earth. Of course I became disillusioned many times: during basic training (1961) in Texas, for example, during my first off-base leave, I had my fortune told by an old gypsy, who obviously was a great judge of character. She told me, "You're too troubled about yourself. I also see a girl; you love her very much. But you don't trust her love for you. You're afraid that you are losing her." Yes, that was Anita, and this was the proper message for any American GI. But when I discovered astrology—and I discovered it very reluctantly—I had a lot to work with. The excitement of trying to learn enough about the subject and method of analysis to cast my own chart occupied me for a long time, off and on, from long before I left the orphanage until I was shipped to Vietnam. In the ancient world, the Hindu considered the Goat the most important of all the signs. Discipline. The sun passing through Capricorn; ruled by the mighty Saturn, exalted; threatened by Mars, etc. I discovered that I had, astrologically speaking, a mixed destiny: disaster early in life and exaltation later. And so much that would be negative, because I had several empty houses, so much that would be nocturnal; and in me, a certain coldness, a sternness, a distance, but most of all an obedience to myself that would be astonishing! But this wasn't enough. I had to know more! What about the name grafted to me? This white name, in this Western language, the *e*, the *l* and *i*; *El* in a Hebrew dialect means god, the primordial one, the father, *il*; or *Elli*, a female goddess of old age, mighty and a great physical champion, according to Norse mythology; or in pure Americanism, *El* for elevated train, as in my big hick town, Chi; or *El* Paso; or the mighty *el*ms, their vivid color; or the e*el*; the *el*bow (*el*enboigen); or *el*ectricity (*el*ektrik); or in every language in the world: *el*fogad (accept); the *e* in Portuguese and Romanian, the *i* in Polish, Russian, for *and*; *el*ain in Finnish for animal; the *i'*me in Greek for be, or *e*ma for blood; or the *e*n in Japanese for circle; *el*zar in Hungarian for close; or the way the number 11 is spelled in Dutch, German, Swedish, Danish, Norwegian, English, and Yiddish; *elli* in Turkish, for fifty; or the *eli* in *eli*mination; *Eli*sa, *Eli*jah, the prophet of Yah, the Jewish god, who began the destruction of Ahab, making way for Amos (another cousin of mine, without Andy); or *el*ul, for the twelfth month, in which I was born; or *Eli*seos, *Eli*sios, *eli*sion, *eli*tro, *eli*xir, *eli*de, *eli*cit, *eli*te; the Spanish *el* for the and he; and even *Eli*zabeth (my mother's first name) was a name southern white women used to refer to black women in general, who were, for the most part, their domestic servants. And if none of this research made sense *li*nguistically, if none of it had any profound bearing on the essence or physical property of the *me* or the *I*, then, at least it was great fun and it fed my usually starved ego! All kinds of techniques added to the jigsaw puzzle of my heritage. For instance, according to the Warden, who was never famous for accuracy, on the day my beautiful black mother was born—same date of my birth, the twenty-eighth of December, but in 1908—eighty-five thousand people were killed by an earthquake in Messina, Sicily; the town was completely wiped out; thirty-two years later, Elizabeth Mamzazi, I call her, left Chicago to vacation in Europe, during April 1940, and was fucked long and hard, deep and long, on top of a pile of hay under the midday sun, by a swarthy Italian gambler, a member of the notorious Mafia, and I was instantly conceived; however, nine months later *el*la dropped Eli at the most public hospital in the world, swooped for Mexico, where, it is said, she continues to live in disguise, married to a wealthy landowner. That is just one of the many versions of how I came about. Mrs. Paulson, descended from the founder of the school, once told me a brutal, long story of my origin, the gist of which was: my mother, a white girl, was raped in

Mississippi by a giant black field nigger, who was burned in kerosene while white men watched and jacked off in the town square; afterward my mother, under the protective shadow of night, left for Chicago, where she lived in hiding with a German butcher on the near North Side until she gave birth to me and gave me to the county.

HONEY LOCUST

The Warden comes into the bay where I sleep, blood running down the strands of her hair; she does not seem conscious of her desperate condition; something else is odd about her, she's walking funny, and she's carrying a candle; also for the first time, I see her in her nightgown. Other boys, Junior, for example, accidentally saw her through her window, changing into her lace, her flabby pale face inert with cold cream. That was before the dog Gypsy was "assassinated." The candlelight has her face lit up in a curious way: her scowling, the wryness, is comic, theatrical. She has a massive forehead, with long, impressive wrinkles going horizontally, but between her eyes, where her big nose begins to build a foundation for itself, there are only two moody little creases that seem to have their origin more in thoughtfulness than bellyaching. But what is she doing here this time of night? Spying on the boys again? Trying to catch some masturbating—her type of game. She can't sleep, so she comes over to assert herself. Under the cover I am holding myself. I still have my bedside light on; yes, she's coming toward me. Calvin's light was on too, but the moment she hit the top step, his went out, like the short in his brain. I'm a heap big bad brave distressed night-reader, with a copy of Chester Himes's novel *The Primitive* open in the tangle of my propped-up knees. The floor is squeaking under her, against the other wall, she's a huge weary bear making tracks. Some shadow! Ain't nobody really sleeping, I'm hip to that, even with their hands covered they can smell or probably see the Warden. No oversight possible when she's navigating the spaces of our lives. And before I can get my mouth open to explain why my light is still on—

WHAM WHAM WHAM WHAM

I look up into her brown speckled eyes, I see lachrymose she-wolves jumping insanely up down in them as she lashes me across the head, face, arms with a long heavy switch, torn from a honey locust, the big tree of the area, the three-pronged dagger, that strange, otherworldly tropical odor of the foliage, the lightness, the clusters of locust thorns that are now snapping quick scars into my flesh—though I quickly jump out of bed, away from her, she lands several fresh blows, dropping her candle, the sheet of my bed catching fire, flames crawling swiftly to the headboard, the paint curling, cracking under the blind energy of the fire, and the Warden spilling seeds from the honey locust weapon, jumping on my bed, following me, tearing into my back, as I run down the aisle, the daggers going WHAM WHAM WHAM WHAM on me and I can hear the fellas snickering, I can already hear the jokes tomorrow, I'm going down the steps, and she's following in heat, irksome, beating me with the four-inch needles of the honey locust, the curling pods, the thorns, and I'm screaming bloody murder.

CLARA

Clara waits outside, I am coming up the steps, it is hot, dusty, I am still vaguely excited about having twat every day, like this, it isn't every boy's luck! School begins to lose even the dull finish, the false glossy fabrication it has, but Clara's cunt is so lovely. We don't come up the steps together because somebody in the building might tell my foster parents. (I've just begun to feel kinda relaxed here, with the Jake Williams family. Mr. Williams, a Baptist preacher; she's an active sister in his church; their daughter, Charlotte, is *high yella,* it puzzles me, 'cause both of them are jet black, he's tall, slow, a man of huge pride, and she's an unusual black woman, quiet, a kind of deeper shadow of him . . . Mrs. Williams is in church every afternoon. I admit I like having the place to myself. Charlotte goes to rehearsal at the same church almost every evening after school. Mr. Williams is almost never here. He stays very busy, in his devout, slow way. I think *Mrs.* Williams must know he's doing it to at least four or five sisters devoted to his church and him. But she pretends not to know.) I put the lock off so when Clara comes up, in a minute from now, she can ease in . . .

First thing I do is call, "CHARLOTTE!" I wait, no answer, the coast is clear. Clara, naturally, won't come in until I stick my head out the door to say it's OK. So far we haven't been caught. Once we almost fucked up, though. Mr. Williams came in five minutes after we had started, but we heard him coming up the steps (there's this long squeaky stairway), and since we were still fully dressed we had only to dash out the back door; he never heard a thing, and we stood under the back stairway until we heard his car go away from the front, which was only five minutes later, at the most; but now the *possibility* of this *anytime* drags me, at the same time it makes every moment of Clara's cunt like a *narcotic* that I'm illegally exploring, exploiting, gorging myself with—

"*Come on!*" She is standing, thin, sixteen years old, a creamy mixture of brown hues, black eyes, dark greasy hair pulled back from her face in a ponytail, the dull tension of an extreme, but unfinished-undefined panic in those black eyes. "It's OK! Come on!" Now she comes forth, her books—a math, an English text, a notebook pretty much unused—held against her small breasts. I have never seen them. I know they are tiny. She won't show them to me. She always keeps on her bra. I suspect there's a scar or something ugly; maybe it's the smallness she's ashamed of. Clara's face is round, no, more oval, I notice now, as she comes . . . She's wearing a wide-tail cotton print skirt, like all these chicks this summer wear—I like her in it. The big flowers, green, red, yellow, the large spaces of white; I hardly notice that her blouse is white, seems she always wears white blouses. She's clean, but the home she comes from, those brothers and sisters, her old spiritually dead, evil-looking father, her *yella* mama, walking into all of that, her home, shocks me—it's all so dreadful, the squalor! It pinches my eyes, scowling at me, even the walls . . .

Tiptoes, we're on tiptoes though there's no reason to be—*is there*? I close the door, lock it from inside. "Don't do that," she says, "best to leave it so they can get in—" Yeah, she's right. I take her books and drop them on the couch. I'm still kinda gnawed by tension, uneasiness, feeling clumsy just before the delirium of such a fuck . . . She is peeping out the window. "Can we see Mr. Williams's car when it comes?" "It's not coming; don't think about it—" I am standing behind her, as she is bent slightly, her face hidden enough behind the curtain, not even a passerby could detect this combustible-female oval mask. My hands are busy on her long, narrow legs, where they bend; in rapid succession I stroke them, all the way up to the warm polarity of her butt. She is nervously talking, still pretending to look from the inside out. But *I* know she's seeing nothing out there; she's here, her mind *in* the action of my hands. "We should stay close to the door," she says, "so we can hear anybody—" She is turning, almost looking at me, as she speaks. "Yeah, good idea . . ." If I catch her focused directly where her eyes meet mine, hers quickly fall away; we're still walking, as we move over to the door of the apartment, on our toes.

She is not as bashful as I am. I defeat myself too often, getting out my gristle, rushing it into the wet, juicy bed of her mound with a slit . . .

I am filled, *stuffed* with fear, the deep threat of Mr. Williams, or anybody, beginning to climb the steps. Clara's back is against the door. I can feel her heart romp, my hand forgetting for a moment as it begins to explore her breasts. Her eyes are round, evasive holes, waiting; her vacancy is a gentle, open abstraction.

Some opening in my mind, slashing the idea of my ego with the shuffling magic that my youth is eternal, *beautiful,* everlastingly *young,* strong, and I will always *be like this,* a very delightful destiny, that I do Clara a favor by putting my ramrod into her—but I secretly admire her thing. I feel so much virility I ache with it. My hands crawling now down into her skirt, this wide skirt. I lift it, unable to enjoy the full texture of her . . . otherwise. She pushes the pink panties from her golden sardine-lotion-powder-smelling lower body. I want so much to really get down there and examine her cunt. But I am ashamed to do it. I might be called a "Cunt Eater," for even getting that close. I have too many affectations. I fear she might tell someone at school and I can just imagine eyes on me, whispering faces, "He eats pussy . . ." and I worry about it now, though I know there's nothing wrong with eating it. It's just the stupid taboo. And Clara is *stupid* after all. Just good for a fuck. A furrow for my new way of masturbating—a shelter, a link, *tunda shimo ma*—that takes the edge off the *oneness* of one's self.

Her belly is really bright, creamy like very light rich heavily milked chocolate, I am stroking it, she's breathing surreptitiously. I probably am too, this furtive act itself *is* so much the diversion. I wish her thighs were fuller, even her ribs show, but I tell myself she's not really gaunt, though I can't find any plump areas. The silence of the daytime "darkness" of the apartment hangs behinds us. My fingers are working up an irrigation in her whirlpool. The juice is slight, clean. She is always clean. Douches every night, she says. "Clara," I whisper into her, "lie on the couch for a minute—I think I feel something *odd* up in you. I better take a look—" Her eyes stretch. *"Like a lump?"* I see so much fear I hardly know what to say. "You know women have cancer a lot in their pussies," she says. "God, I hope it isn't—" I drop the skirt.

Meanwhile I am leading her to the couch; I wait until she's stretched out. "How d'you want me to lay?" "Open your—yeah, like that." I push the wide skirt up around her chest; her narrow ass is wide open to me for the first time in about seven weeks of gory screwing, not just here, at her place, anywhere we can find privacy. I am not anxious to plunge into her and scout around with my fresh hardheaded extra-long black dick. We have been leading such swervingly sneaky lives that even as I get down to examine her, I am more clinical and furtive than I mean to be. I want to look at it with passion, to run my fingers into the lukewarm mugginess of it, with affection, without haste. But this is a problem I have had, this haste. I'm trying to control my urge to do it so fast . . . but it is not easy with the strain we're under. Like in the next five minutes it may develop that I'll miss out on fucking her altogether today, anyway, because footfalls might start up . . .

Frankly it is a big porous hole; the light from the window is a sentry on it, though it is a fading afternoon light with little enthusiasm in it. With the thumb and index finger of each hand, I hold the mouth open by pulling the outer lips apart; the interior begins deep-purple where the black wiry hair ends but it fades brighter into pink shades at the vestibule, getting red, deep inside. I have never before examined a vagina. I have always dreamed of doing so. I now lift the tepid inner lips to see what these layers and various textures, nooks, crevices are all about. Here in the anterior are overlapping lips that fascinate me, I wiggle them, look up to see Clara's expression; she's looking up, blankly, at the ceiling, now asking, "See *anything* yet?" "No, not yet . . ." I wet my finger by sticking it into the mucous-membraney interior, bring it out, and with my other hand carefully clear back the hairs from the top of this sheath; I begin to feverishly but strategically undulate her clitoris. I know from pictures where it is. It's very large on her; she's probably played with it a lot. Swollen and very sensitive as I continue to sway it, changing my method of stroking it with this sloppy finger. She is saying, *"What're you doing?"* alarmed, but I evade her question. "Just be still!" I command. She begins to respond, first with a few cascading movements of her ass, then more and more, in a pumping, motivated manner . . . Already the marshy suds are coming out. They are always coming out of her, she comes all the time. Just sitting in school, she says, listening to the teacher talk; if he's "fine" like Mr. Woods, for example, she has an orgasm.

I stop tickling her clitoris, and the layers of moist skin close over it; I pull open the main passageway, looking into it, now, as far as I can see, the walls are slimy with mucous membranes and juices but the back of it looks like the roof of her mouth. This mysterious "whole" thing—on such an attractive hillock of hair, with muscles, its internal orifice, all the copious secretions coming from it, membranous depths of wonder! And I'm also aware that I come originally from here, smeared with this gore, this grayish or yellowish-white fluid.

And I'm compelled to keep returning to it, my melancholy hammer searching for female bonanzas! I wonder what it is really all about?

"We better hurry!" she is whispering. "I don't see anything," I say, in her bewitching spell, taking out my length *cokke,* standing over her, I ease down, firmly finding positions for my knees, I say, "Put it in," I like the *feeling* of her hand on it, inserting it, the muzzled-guiding effect, the lips stretching, as she crams it into her inlet, adjusting her posterior to it . . . the weight of my body, my position. I am not really comfortable. I wish I could take off my pants, but I don't dare, and yet I'm tempted to do so . . . "Let's get on the floor—this is uncomfortable . . ." As I talk I stand up, my sentry drenched with her fluids, the bubbles of her, and without a word she stands. "I wanna show you something new," she says, grinning. "What?" "Let's get close to the door so we can hear." We move, and she says, "Why don't you take your pants *halfway* down? You can always pull 'em up quick that way if somebody comes—" I stand there dumbly, not understanding anything suddenly. "Lie down," she says, "I'm gonna sit on it and give you yumyum you'll never forget—it'll be so good you can remember it to jack off to—" She giggles. But her shallow, almost comic, lightweight eyes still evade mine, as I search her face, now.

I stretch out on my back on the hard tile and she is busy unbuckling my belt, unzipping my pants; she pulls them, with my jockey shorts, down and is careful to push my hard *kok* through the hole in the pants as she does so; now, she stands over me, one foot on either side, looking, with a silly grin, down into my astonishment, my puzzled skull. I can see under the wide skirt, as she fans it out by simply twisting her hips quickly in short, half body-turns, throwing the confused skirt out—the oral cavity nesting in that knoll of rough warm hair holds the attention of every sense in my body. Now she begins to squat directly over my huge desperate valve, her voice getting thick with her own sexy involvement. "You just *be still,* don't make a move." I don't know what to do with my hands. But for a moment I almost relax, forgetting the potential danger of having her here.

Her knees are bent. Her feet are flat on the floor. She is holding the skirt just above her knees, which means I cannot see her thighs, nor her trap, any longer, from this angle. I wait; now I feel the coarse texture of her slightly swampy hair scrape the head of my faucet. Her cunt seems to be mowing at the head, now, gently though, trying to force back the prepuce, and it is still secreted enough to easily respond, but she seems to be teasing the bulb, too. She is squatting like a dancer in the middle of some exotic performance; the oral bitchiness of her gut-mouth digs circles around my baseball-bat hardness, meaty encouragements; the wet lips of her hole shake greedily over the head until the mouth opens and drops down, engulfing Him in the chocolate depths of her pink orifice—her eyes stretch in surprise. Accident. Quickly she gives the by-now throbbing amorous head a vigorous muscular squeeze with her young rumba samba cha-cha, jive swinging—any kind of motion—yeye, this new life-crevice so overpowering for me I can hardly think anymore! Just one quick squeeze to milk it into huge anticipation—then up she goes. She now incites the head, prepuce again, persistently by a gyrating motion, the wet lips, the hair, the spasmodic prospect of the orifice gobbling down—taking in all of my acutely sensitive amorous love-rod—is the pivot of it all. My sword throbs under her guidance. "How does it feel?" "Good." As I come out with the word, I feel the eternal abyss, ma, the permeating symphony *to* my phallic beauty, this *tupu* flesh song like the magic honey in soul music or any goodness, confusing my King, stabbing, biting at him. Then, WHAM!

She sinks, Oh! heavy, wet, on the ample Chief, fucking him

copiously, the walls of her in spasms of vaginal gluttony; now bracing herself, with one hand on a nearby chair, the other flat on my stomach, she begins to use her gypsy agitating ass, all of her bottom, the "oven" too, to bring me to a violent orgasm. This *bonde* (valley) eats at me like I'm popcorn! Her pussy is like a skillful mountain climber who loves to climb to the peak and fumble around, loves this tumultuous point, likes to speed down, all taste buds vivid as color, reacting to every impression of the descent. She mows my dick. She elevates it. She climbs, sinks, squeezes it so—I close my eyes in the mounting rapture—I uncontrollably begin to come, my *upanga* gushing its hot tides of "ore" up into her, as she continues to milk the shaft, prepuce, and *swollen* spermy erupting head, as it kicks inside her, bathing the spasmodic spiral path of membrane comfort—

And I hear Mr. Williams's footfalls coming up now and I haven't finished, the *cum* still shooting up as she jacks the hammer of me with her butt-grip; the heavy feet coming closer, and I am crazy with ecstasy. *Fuck him,* I'm thinking, they only took me 'cause of the money they got from the state, *fuck* him . . .

And the socket of her pouts now; fear tickling forth from it, it lifts, at the same time, contracting, but still dripping my juices . . .

His key now gnawing at the hole in the door . . . Already I see myself on the way back to the orphanage, and it's all right, really all right with me!

Lately I've gone to the chow hall not so much because I'm hungry, but this *thing in me.* The harshness of her fingers as they form a fist, dumping the soup into my bowl, the steam, the odor of tomatoes, her sweat. Her eyes lift every time, like a measuring cup. She never looks at the white boys, though. It's me, she looks cordially toward me. Not even this much respect for Leroy, and she never looks up when Calvin comes through the line. Her coal-black skin, the tight dry lips, her sheltered dignity. Who am I looking for in her? I take my tray to the table, the barking, gruff and shrill chatter of our pessimistic faith all around, filling up the oblong barrackslike chow hall; but all I can hear is the click of her soupspoon, even down in the deep thickness of the pot one of us will be unfortunate enough to have to wash tonight before bedtime. Her giant tits hold my eyes hypnotically. I miss my mouth a couple of times with the spoon. I am falling into her big open wet pussy. Sweat-beads dripping off it as it throbs, the lips of it are rose with heliotrope color near the bottom, and in spots, near the top. She can make it move in a sucking motion. And tonight in bed I will cling like ivy, twine around her, sink into her, stick like a leech, her molasses consuming me; I will become fetus, deep inside her.

The last time Steve came back, after running off, he told me he had a dream about her while sleeping in a mission flophouse on State Street in Chicago. She was sucking him. I began to wonder how many of the others thought about my sapphire woman. But it doesn't matter. Loudmouth Calvin, I know for a fact, jacks off to a picture of that broad who used to play Jane in the Tarzan movies. I think Leroy thinks about fay chicks too, when he beats his meat. Me, I like that big titty black bitch!

GYPSY

Junior is trying to prove he's brave and heartless, just to be accepted. The shadows of the trees out here, maybe two hundred yards from the wall of the orphanage, drape us; the crickets in their endless creak burp burp they go keep things natural, the kaleidoscopic shades cling suck our whispering safely but a loudmouth motherfucker like Calvin might attract somebody; anyway he never can keep his slavery-time voice at a whisper. I can't see anybody's face clearly but Junior has the furry wiggly pup between his knees and he's obviously stalling like hell, but Leroy is right over him and I know that's scaring the shit out of him since he promised us he was going to take care of business, you dig; we form a circle as shields against the possible appearance of the Warden or some other jailer, but the little boys are asleep so it must be after ten, and the ol' hags are watching TV—the late show.

I feel a strange excitement, almost believing that Junior *really will* go through with it, he seems to have courage, and I'm a vicious beast myself, one of these variegated forms, standing here, beneath this ancient oak tree Mrs. Paulson is so proud of, she reads Longfellow under it, shit like that; now we are each umbilical connections, the night dampness, sounds of an occasional car going by on the nearby highway, or that motherfucking lonely-crying train whistle that comes by every midnight, then again at three in the morning, Oh shit sometimes I could—I won't say it . . .

"Junior is chicken!" snaps Leroy, his words forming abstracts in me. "He ain't gone do shit! Just fucking around! *Playing with the motherfucker and shit*—" "If you *don't* Junior," hissed Buddy—I can't see his chops but imagine his big lips spouting—*"you mama is a man!"* And little Junior, our age, but the size of a ten-year-old and acutely conscious of it, ashamed of it, feeling like a freak, always ribbed, laughed at, he's in a spot, and, "Man, what you gone do, Junior, stand here and play with the dog all night?" bites Calvin. "Yeah, motherfucker," I say, "it's cold. Give me that knife I'll show you how to do it!" somebody in me said, a conforming lineage god of insanity, with buckteeth. *"He ain't gone do nothing I'm going inside!"* says glorified Leroy, his lips pushed out, as though an oval plate has been placed flat lengthwise there. If he speaks like this, he means it. Nothing diminishes his firmness, not even the Warden, who I think is a little scared of him since he punched her in the gut that time she tried to beat him with a metal pipe. Junior is a little fuckface, Junior is a little fuckface, I say in my mind, trying to decide whether or not I should start singing it. Junior is the little fuck we always thought he was. Like earlier today, the way it all started: Junior was throwing a stick out as far as he could, sitting on the back steps, slothly. And a couple of us were just screwing around, like nothing, throwing a softball back and forth, and this dog, Gypsy's its name—the only creature on earth the Warden treats like a human—so there was this mutt running out, bringing back this stupid stick to Junior, who is heself a little dumbdumb prick, a faggot, bookworm jerk who don't even know his ABCs, can't add two and two, and stinks, but sometimes I feel very sorry for him, even though I can't let Leroy and Calvin and them know. They'd laugh at *me* and call me a punk and sissy, too! So half the afternoon this dull shit went on, until Leroy kept the ball in his hand, and in his most awe-inspiring stride, clutching the ball to his chest, looking at the ground like a great baseball pitcher, modestly taking his natural long steps to the dugout after a great inning, he went over to Junior and just stood there, looking down at him. All the splibs on the playground knew by Leroy's action that it was Fuck With Junior Time, which is one of our most respected rites. And nobody dares not take part, for fear of being turned into a scapegoat himself. Leroy is the dumbest, ugliest, biggest, baddest—I mean *really* malignant!—black mammyfugger on the playground. The dude can make zipguns, firebombs, anything! He'll stop a gray boy in a minute, bust his nose and take anything they mamas send them. A gray boy called him a "savage" once, Leroy drove a maiming fist between his eyes. The Warden found a home for that boy two days later just to get him away from Leroy, who had promised to kill him. So, earlier today, during Fuck With Junior Time, Leroy said, "Junior acts like he *looooooves* that little black and white mutt as much as he loves that stanky-smelling bitch the Warden." Everybody laughed; most of the laughing was forced, distorted sounds. Cowards sniffing bait. Our apparatus for survival. I can't let nobody know I think like this—I'd be fucked if it got back to Leroy. I've seen cats get their jawbone knocked alllllll the way down into da crevice of they ass, behind some shit like whispering in a corner to somebody against Leroy. The word always gets back, 'cause somebody's always willing to see somebody else get electrocuted! "I don't love *nothing!* man!" barked Junior, not so much to Leroy, but to all of us. "I'd just as soon *cut* that dog's guts out, as I'd cut out the Warden's." *"Prove it prove it prove it!"* sang Leroy. Calvin and Buddy echoed him, mischievously. "*If* you don't take your knife right now!—and do it—your mama's a coal miner with a funky assful of coal dust; for drawers she wears overalls, she got fleas in her crack, she stinks like a goat, she's as musty as a skunk, she shits rotten eggs, eats polecat meat—drinks my piss—sucks the diseased dicks of ol' cripples and bums on West Madison Street in Chicago, and for Kotex she uses Brillo pads—" Meanwhile everybody was falling out with bloodthirsty laughter, some of us running around in circles, holding our stomachs, malicious and deformed by our devilment. Calvin, actually rolling in the dust, Buddy, bent double coughing on the steps, were food for Leroy's ego, and fuel for his one-sided game of the Dozens. "Damn Leroy," shot Buddy, "you sho know how to signify!" Meanwhile Leroy was running it down: "*If* you don't do it—I swear 'fore God—your mama is a man! She got a dick bigger 'n the Warden's nose—and that's some job, boy! Your mama—she got two balls growing under each armpit, and for breakfast she eats ape turds creamed down low in rancid goat piss—drinks cabbage juice of skunk cabbage for coffee—she spreads stinkweed on her bread for butter—she lets the milkman fuck her in the nose, while she lets the grocery boy stick his dick under her eyelids!" I looked up, red-eyed, with the viciousness of *so* much unhappy laughter, to see a nearby group of white boys, who'd stopped playing horseshoes, looking at us like we is nuts, and at this point, Junior, who looked on the threshold of tears and violent trembling, said, *"See this knife—Wait 'til tonight—"* "Oh!" Leroy sang, imitating one of the white boys or a faggot, "Oh baby baby! Junior baby! Is gone prove to us he's *a man! like we is*—I can't wait!" And now, in this foggy moment, we're all looking down on Junior, helplessly turning over the dog with his left hand, the animal is making playful snaps at Junior's wrist; the hand containing the knife—a long switchblade—comes up, the dog groans from the strain of the awkward position Junior has her trapped in. *"He gone do it—he gone do it!"* sang Calvin, clapping his hands softly. Somebody says, "Shhhhhh!" Junior has the knife's blade at the dog's stomach and tears are swimming in his miserable eyes. He's looking helplessly up to us. Suddenly—the ripping sounds of *flesh* tearing—the quick spiteful confusion—the malevolence—action of arms; I miss some of it, but do see Leroy's plunge—hear his groan, smell him, the acid of his venom! The tears shooting from Junior's face—the ritualistic blood here, this rite, it gnaws at the pith of myself, though I may be nothing, I'm hung in it: Leroy's hands have gripped Junior's forcefully—he harshly guides Junior's hand down, the blade steadily opening a slit in the dog. He has Junior between his legs, and is, at the same time, holding the dog with pressure from Junior's knees, locked against the dog by the pressure from his—Leroy's—legs. The dog is opening the night sky with her diabolical sound: "EEEEEEEEEEEE!" Junior is sobbing unrelentingly. So horror-stricken—I'm out of it—the space of my mind, ill-disposed; I fall back to see the hellish, satanic glow in Calvin's eyes, in Buddy's face! Calvin holds his dick for comfort, a hypnotic air about him. I can't believe the world is real—that I'm real—that incidents are ferocious, that love is possible—suddenly—I know! I swear I know! Nothing is real! Nothing has any meaning! What have we done to each other? Leroy's savage strength is chief, as we all stumble back in our psychic bad smell! Everything—moving: what's happening? Blind circles!—Cats running!—The Warden coming!—Mrs. Paulson's voice, near! The blood, the dog's sounds dying. Before I split I see Junior, in shock, blood all over him. He seems to be frozen, his eyes as big as coffee cups, the knife glued to his hand. And he ain't even got no mama to be insulted nohow. We all run into wet shadows, the dew. Leaving Junior this way until he dies maybe in a madhouse. Still holding the innocent knife.

INDUCTION

I've been through so much hell, it doesn't surprise me that I receive this induction notice to come down to LaSalle Street in the Loop to take my physical; just because I wasn't in the first quarter (but the second) in my total college grade average, this is the shit that is slapped on me, while I'm trying to get "it" together, working like a *peon,* to incite the future of my breed and acknowledge the beauty of man, and the social and political ritual of what is said to be my national duty, recoiling in the light of who I am, suffocating as a black person at a nottoohip school, I mean a school that had a jive rating really, here I am faced with the prospect of dying, unready to commit homicide, engage in bloodshed, butchery, even infanticide, to carry the insignias and national words of the government I am born to that has in the bleak years of my short life seemed so unsympathetic, to say the least, to my cause on earth as a human being—so dig me! AFRAID, hung by fear, I have an overwhelming sense of dread when I think of spending two, three, or four years in prison; that rigid, cloistered kind of existence nips my senses, though I try to weigh against it the rigidity of army life, killing on the front lines in Vietnam. I try to taste the lethality of both situations to see which would poison me deepest and since I keep coming up a shambles ready to answer the call of the Great White Father to defend his Great White Nation I know I'm gory with cowardice; and I, unlike some black boys from Mississippi, Alabama, Georgia, and South Carolina, can't defend myself on the grounds of ignorance. I know about the organizations, groups, and committees that are more than willing to help me fight the draft, who are willing to offer me free legal aid—see, I am a member of SNCC; I *know* SNCC and others are assisting the young black inductees in fighting the draft! The papers have come and I am simply beside myself with anger.

For the first time in my life, I think I'm getting somewhere, working like a sonofabitch, washing dishes, mopping floors, packing boxes with shit I ain't got and never will have no use for, any kind of shit job you can think of, working to stay in, to try to become a kind of black knight.

Yeah, I want to really get sensitive to words, not just to get ready for some profession in a jive brainwashing academy of weak spirits! But to become more conscious of myself, of the dispatches of others.

But it doesn't matter now; *look at me*! standing butt-naked in line with all these other dudes! I notice the eyes of some cats here, openly and secretly spying, measuring the length and width of the next guy's dingdong! We are all in a slow-moving line, having our mouths, ears, assholes inspected! Finally dressed again, we sit down a moment and talk with a psychiatrist. "Name?" "Eli Bolton." "Date and place of birth?" "December 28, 1940, Cook County Hospital." I am already frustrated by the prospect of lying. Here it comes! "Father's name?" "Eli, same as mine," I blurt. "Then you are a Junior?" "No . . . I mean *yes* . . ." This is the first time I have given my "father" my *own* name. The illusion of him has been with me so long, perhaps I feel he *is* me. I am my own father, the lie does not separate us. I am the father *and* the son, the holy ghost. "Your mother's name?" "Mamzazi." "How do you spell that?" "M-a-m-z-a-z-i." "Hump!" he grunts. "Your mother African?" "Gee, how'd you guess?" I am grinning until he slaps me in the face with "Where'd you attend elementary school?" "The Paulson School for All Homeless Infants and Children." I am telling the truth for the first time, sick of lies. The doctor's banana-shaped face, that of a mild academician whose devotion to psychology seems ruined by a bloodthirsty interest in warfare, says, "That's the school in Amesville, Illinois, isn't it?" "That's right." "How long were you there?" "From 1946 to 1958." "Then what?" "I've lived in Chicago from '58 until now with a brief stay in New York." "If you have parents, boy, why were you in the Paulson School?" "I was there because I . . ." I am trapped. I am angry. "My mother and father separated; my father died. My mother was a very ill woman. She lived with her sister who, uh, took care of her. She couldn't afford to keep me." He is watching me suspiciously. After a long silence, during which he is looking at a transcript of my grades from Roosevelt, he murmurs, "Your grades are somewhat low." His blue eyes drift up toward me. "How do you explain this?" "LISTEN—" I almost explode, catch myself, say, "Forget it!" "When did you start attending Roosevelt?" " '58." "And you're twenty-two, now, right?" "Something like that." "You'll get that chip knocked off your shoulder in the army, boy! A good place to really get discipline. It'll be good for you. Even better than college. Some people just aren't cut out for college." His smile is plastic. He is signing his symbols to papers representing me. Then he shouts: "NEXT!"

And the next person who steps up is me. I say to the crazy doctor: "You mean I've got to go through that bullshit all over again?"

DOSSY O

Shit! I don't feel good no time, baby, not here in all this mess, and ain't no sense in me trying to pretend that I understand why I'm here or trying to bullshit somebody into thinking I know what all these generals mean when they demand "large-scale fighting" or that I understand and sympathize with a mammy-fucker like Sergeant Moke; yeah, the fathead rube with the sweat rings around his ass, his shirt collar, his nose, and his red neck; me and Cocaine call him Hootenanny the Flagwaver. I get so pissing disgusted I don't even like to talk; for days baby I don't say shit to none of these lame peckerwoods these discipline-drag-legs walking around here acting like they got as much invested here as some of them cats so waybackintheshadows you never see, hear their names who's for real da boss; yeah, all kinds of battlefatigue monkeys strolling around here, bad shots hitting psychological maggie drawers all day long; I just get tired *tired* I keep a big funky headache all the time; lately I ain't said nothing to nobody but Dossy O, that's Cocaine which is the way my man keeps himself together. I can't blame anybody here for getting high; if you felt like a battering ram, somebody's monkeytime doodlesquat which is what they had our man Bob Churchill into until we pulled his coat, told him damn baby how long you gone be a chump we been checking you out ever since we landed . . . I think the deep furrow of our message got to him. Sergeant Dossy O Bud Cocaine Lemon a little bitty dude but wide with big muscles coming at you from behind thick horn-rimmed glasses is my ace boon coon! Me and Bob Churchy sometimes call him Hoppalong Cane, or just plain Hophead or Hopstick or Hoss like keeping each other in stitches is one means of surviving this hubba-hubba flagwaving get-them-first thing—when I first shipped into this regiment my thoughts started moving along the lines of getting out. I heard so many brothers quiet as it's kept get washed up and put in prison for just thinking the way I thought to say the least. I lay in my sack night after night weighing the crucial matter fearfully carefully. I thought about it for possibly twenty-four hundred hours a day through tough extended trips into self; I knew a Vietnamese faker, a real expert, had an in with a lot of black-market people a lot of Victor Charlies—I suspected he was from Hanoi though he denied it, said he was a former officer in the Army of the Republic, even claimed he was tight with several very powerful smooth persons in Saigon who could get me straight into China with absolutely no hassle crossing the Bamboo Curtain, but how do you know a little grinning buckteeth sapsucker like that ain't trying to murphy you? You just don't. He seemed very sure he could ease me like a breeze for the right bread of course right into Sweden where I could get political and military immunity—just oodles of it—I never told anybody what was on my mind during the few days I met with him except right after the last time I met with him I found Bud under the half-roof of a hut in a captured village. He was nodding, his gear disposed around him. I sat down and eased mine off—we had extra-heavy loads being the only two medical tech assistants in the unit—it was always good to rest all that shit. When I first started wearing it the straps ate belligerently into my shoulder blades; now it's OK. I'm just like a jinxed jackass I can't even think about it no more Bud told me that day, "I'd be the last cat to tell you not to do it if I had the nerve—I'd get my simpleminded ass outta this mucketymuck jive Sylvester's whipping on me! But I think about my baby brother at home growing up in a bullshit city like Chicago and he ain't got nobody to look up to but me you dig; so I kinda owe it to the dude to make it back *there*, to answer as many questions for him as I can; if I didn't stay high baby I'd have probably run up to Captain George Rat Cheese Zedtwitz heself a long time ago and put a birthday cake full of surprises into his hands; and the same goes for Second Lieutenant Sal Magoo Ramono and faggot First Lieutenant John Madison Avenue Brinkerhoff too!" "Yeah," I said. *That* rap by Bud put my mind on strike to demand of my heart a logical enough reason to want to go back to the States; I couldn't get any homespun shit together on this score so I got some honorary convictions slightly boosted by logical respect for death you dig, 'cause anything as torrid as getting your hat right in the middle of military commitment is a highly repeat highly dangerous activity so this is why I'm still in Captain Zedtwitz's regiment, still responsible to Second Lieutenant Sal Ramono, still have to chance a look at Hootenanny's nasty red face every day—this is why too I never feel really gooooood you know deep down good never. It's been three days now since we had any action and that was only a kind of routine thing where we kinda dashed in and finished taking the beauty out of a couple of old harmless men and about six children—they were turned over to Master Sergeant Dokus Mokus for delivery to battalion prison control detachment some five kilometers behind us because no helicopter from the unit or higher up from company command could be sent in—well you know what happened to them Dokus who was returned by helicopter the next morning said, "By God, them crazy VCs ain't got a bit of sense; they plum ran away from me and I had to shoot 'em." Later after Captain Zedtwitz and his fun flunkies had the incident report written up and everybody tough theoretically had forgotten it Dossy O asked Rube Moke, "Did you shoot 'em in the back?" and Mississippi Moke said, "Listen, you little sawed-off nigger, I don't have to explain a dagblasted thing to the likes of you! You uppity nigras think you own the world! All the godblasted fuss you people raise back home proves that you're not true Americans and ain't got no respect for law and order if it was up to me I wouldn't have none of you defending the country you don't love it I would—" Coke cut him off: "You would jump into a tub of Cap'n Rat Cheese's shit and eat it if he commanded you to wouldn't you? You big mucketymuck slab of—" WOOPH! Fathead Moke's fist put a spell on Hoss, who quickly recovered his dignity from the ground obviously still quite dizzy and tired and tried to get to Mississippi when Cap'n Ratty Cheese came up from a nap in the surviving basement of what was once a well-built Indo-China house never touched by the French, who were here before we were, trying to do something like what we're trying to do. When Cheese came to the surface we were all about to take sides and waltz a war dance. There's just no way on earth I can elevate a killer like Stars and Stripes Moke-anny to the level of a human divine creature when I think back on the drama of his battlefield history and how he's so tolerated by these upstanding officers and his fella countrymen, how he gets affirms on requests a boot'd have a bitch of a time copping; I remember that time Bud and I accidented into the Butcher himself and his running ace Smith engaged in a act of their common sadism and killing that day the antiaircraft TAT TAT TAT TAT TAT TAT ratratrat-ratrat-rat-rat-rat shit sounding everywhere along the parallel we'd just reached, can't remember which one, like that's a month ago which now seems a year back in all this contradiction you notice I even stop trying to talk proper shit whatda fuck difference do it make dat's what I ask! Anyway, the air force drivers were laying eggs all over the designated VC installations zone we wuz s'pose to move in on and sop up being grunts which is what you do while you shit—that's the way they seed us—this action was not far from the Ho Chi Minh Trail, if memory ain't failed me. Dossy had busted a cap and got heself together never touched shit till Sam got him under all dis pressure he was ready to walk right in and fuck up Mississippi Moke if he could catch him, that's why we'd come, shit I can't remember boo koos of kilometers 'fore we began to really hear the mortar shells singing in the curves they take, the perfection of U.S. electric magic! You sometimes had to just stand back and look up there in amazement at those U.S. Discipline-Conformity cats and say Wow! they really could workout takecare-ofbusiness their particular kind, you dig; even if the war wasn't honorable like the Trojan War where a good cause was at the center where pussy always is suppose to be—anyway now these flying Trojan horses with all their traditional help had us and the Army of the Republic of Vietnam, which Coke Bud L. called "Marvin," while the rest of the U.S. Army settled for a less remote corruption "ARVN." Anyway mortar shells kept on tinging the sky all morning as we waited in our DMZ foxholes busting blood rivers into lives already trapped deep in hot frigid death, cracking our eardrums while most of us applauded the numbing skill of the U.S. drivers. For days man after a deal like that we'd go to sleep with our ears skunky from the decimation of it so when the pilots split back to the U.S. birdman (aircraft carrier) we'd hubba-hubba ah ambitious cadence in to mop up the rotten eggs and this particular time is when Wallace Sylvester Mokus and Smitty turned my stomach so profoundly I gag every time I see 'em—I could never before eat with 'em in my eyesight but afterward it became impossible to look at them; I never would have believed Moke'd cry though—that same day it was just as we were about to go in for the mop-up when the last bomber aircraft was splitting that we heard the one just before it crash into the cables on the carrier and boltered and killed the pilot instantly, that got Moke's tears, I heard that the captain patted him on the back like he was a baby and Madison Avenue tongue in cheek and looking at the captain said: "The best soldier we have in this outfit, sir!" And ol' stonewall agreed with him. I know nobody on earth would believe such an unmilitary act and statement coming from an officer I found it hard to swallow 'cause I never for a moment thought Georgia Cap'n Zedtwitz could ever pat anybody on the back anyway.

GRUNTS

After the Captain wouldn't believe our side of the story, Bud and I stopped talking to *those* cats. We were just there. The Captain even refused to believe that the mutilated child was the work of one of his men. It was impossible. No American would do a thing like that, Bud and I should've been ashamed of ourselves for such wild hazardous accusations!

During mail call there is never anything for me—not even from Anita. I sit here, waiting, listening to the names rattling from Sergeant Moke's murderous face. I sit here—I don't know why—like I expect to get something. I listen to the names. Bud's name is called, sometimes. His brother writes to him. His Ma works too hard, she's always too tired to write, but he understands; besides, she's not so keen on the craft of letter writing. I think about how silly my name sounds. It's like Bud Lemon backwards. And maybe me and ol' badman, my coasting high buddydud are really two sides of the same coin. But he gets mail—a big difference. I used to read Bud's mail until I got embarrassed: I mean, it was all right for him to cut me in to all his private positions and shit like that, you dig, but the *personal* aspects of some of his little brother's letters—well, were too much for me. But he used to bait me: "Damn, baby, you're a college man, and you ought to be able to help your best asshole buddy in the whole Sambo section of the U.S. Army by reading his little brother's questions and trying to help him! That ain't asking too much!" That's how I started. But I wasn't really helping Bud by telling him what to say in his next letter to his brother: Bud was helping me, in my loneliness, by laying the letters on me.

Moke and his buddy Smith vanished behind a little row of bombed houses. Me and Bud took the courtyard, the general store, the houses facing the main road. I found an old man who was trying to tell me something but we couldn't make out what he was saying and we let him exist and urged him to beat it across the field behind the house. Magoo and Rat Cheese and that faggot Madison Avenue came in last, after I shouted the OK signal. Nobody thought anything about Moke and Smith for awhile until the captain asked about them and ironically, Bud and I were sent to hound-dog them on the way, in the direction I saw them take. The moment we were out of sight we came on them, in the narrow clearing; as light came around the corners of our journey we saw Mokus's big naked pink ass, beneath a bush, struggling updownupdown, humping what looked like a child with dirty knees, no shoes; her muffled groans trapped inside something massive like his fist and Smith holding back the bushes for him with his peewee hanging hard as a popsicle waiting . . . Bud and I were so numbed by the sadistic inhuman monstrous incident we couldn't react . . . for a moment; then we rushed in, our rifles down; still Smith threw his up directly in our faces. "Just take it easy, Jackson," which is what he calls all niggers. "You ain't about to get none of this—I'm next." And he actually thought *we* wanted to share in the activity in which he and Dokus Mangy were engaged. I moved my leg. "I'll pull the trigger just as sure as my name's Smitty. I'll kill a nigger jus' as soon as I'd kill a VC. See that old man over there—bet you *he* believed me." The body of the old man indented a thicket of grass. His chest was coated with blood. Poor guy hadn't gotten very far. "I cut his heart out like he wuz a chicken." Moke was crushing, pounding, and cursing the child, her terror-stricken cries were so repressed they emptied down into the earth itself and caused eternal earthquakes all through the nature of the Western world nothing less; we couldn't see Dokus's face but heard him: "You little bitch be still by God you goddamn VC keep your little tail still you hear?" The sun was high, Smith's shiteating grin was plastic. Bud said, "The sad thing, my man, is it wouldn't do a damn bit uv good to inform—" Moke finished, stumbled back out and fell on his ass laughing his evil-eye laugh, dripping with the child's blood while Smith unhitched his belt saying to his ace, "Take my rifle. These niggers think they gone get some, shoot 'em if you wanna, I don't give a rat's ass." I turned away and Moke laughed. Bud walked over to the old man's body and stood looking down at him. How could we stand here like this and let this happen? Why couldn't I kill Moke and Smith? Why should I carry the weight of their deed with me forever? No bullshit, I hate that motherfucker with all the energy of my being, I could wipe out his creed, I could stick a time bomb in Smith's ass and blow him to his phony God. Moke went over and stood beside Bud, pointed his rifle at the dead man's temple, pulled the trigger three times, grinning while Smith got his nuts got up and I jumped him with my fist sailing into his eyesocket busting the string loose, I hoped, but it didn't as he shot the girl in the chest. Her legs twitched the knees came together the silence the stillness and I hate myself I hate myself you—

About twenty kilometers back we ran into a couple of real VCs, just trying to keep out of our sight. Moke said, "I thought they were trying to ambush us." Somebody else said, "Oh, well."

Word from company command is: "Everything is A-OK," says Captain Zedtwitz. I don't know why I even bother to listen to any of them, especially him.

Again, Smith and Moke ambushed some female children—three of them, I think, and wasted them when they finished. It wouldn't do any good to report it to anybody. I'm beginning to think I'm crazy, maybe Captain Zedtwitz is right: it didn't happen. Me and Dossy just stay high all the time and try to keep our eyes off *them*. We walk along. Heavy sickness. I can still hear Smith's voice: "HURRY UP MOKE YOU BASTARD HOW COME YOU GOT TO ALWAYS BE FIRST!" Just a few yards from the house Cap'n Rat Cheese had set up his temporary headquarters, and unwrapped his cheese.

Once Moke and Smith let Nigger Bobo Johnson finish off the end of a train on an older girl, according to Churchy Mule. Allegedly, Johnson shared it with his mutual Sambo friend, flaplips Serg Lowell, sometimes known as Raise Cane, because that's what he did before coming into the army, he grew sugarcane in Alabama, "the most honorable state in the union," he once inserted in a letter to his congressman, trying to win some time off for good behavior. Not here, but back there. And Lowell even called to Churchy, who was about to split: "Bob, hey, Bob! Boy, you better come on and get some of this Vietnam nooky! They letting *us* get some, this time—"

I had just finished fixing up Serg Lowell's arm, where he had been nipped, while we were waiting to go in for a mop-up after the drivers from the air force scrammed back to their birdman. I went into a shack to look around, and a VC, young, skinny, with painful, large, kernel-dark nut-looking eyes, threw a huge knife straight toward my head. But I moved too quickly for him.

Even my own presence, being in earshot of the little girls' screaming, as I patch up a wound on my own leg—really just a scratch from a fall—the screaming drives me deep into the reality of my helplessness. Why can't I go and kill Moke, blow out his brains? Why would I have to face the entire U.S. government and die for such a deed? White nigger Lowell is with them again. I don't see Johnson, so maybe he is too. Bud, under a tree, across the road, is sleeping. He's just had some nice shit.

I pass a sick dog on the road as I search for a spot to take a crap. The dog is throwing up his guts, his eyes are Gypsy's eyes. I wonder, Are any of the fellows from the Paulson school here, how about Buddy and Leroy? Once ran into Calvin in Chicago, he told me Leroy was doing time for armed robbery. Can't remember which state. But I know *where* Junior is. The last time I saw the Warden, just before she died, she said, "He's over in Kankakee, in the mental hospital."

Shit. I'm a serial number, a dog tag, a set of graceless cadences in this rude mud. I'm vulgar, high, and in the wrong atmospheric conditions; I am so high to keep sane I smell the radar electronic circuits all the way at the other end of the DMZ where another division of the battalion is fortified; my mind keeps flying up, up out of the legwork, the grunt work of this cadence. Shit! If I'm pulling guard duty sometimes after a couple of joints I can even see Mighty Mouse making it across the moon; once I thought I saw Alan B. Shepard, famous U.S. astronaut, one night, right after I first landed here. But it turned out to be nobody but old Superman himself, out for night practice.

This little guy is vomiting blood as Bud and I try to fix him. But he isn't going to make it. Moke runs his bayonet through the VC's chest, twists it a little before he pulls it out. I am beyond reaction. Moke is saying: "What fucking difference is it betwixt one slant-eye commie and the next, huh, answer me that?" But he doesn't really exist so how can I hear his question?

I've lost control of my muscles; I'm down in the mud; I see the dreary murky cadence of my blue-black strungout self in this hopped-up night, watching Leroy pushing Junior's hand; I'm Junior, killing, killing . . .

Emptiness, chromatic, hangs in my psychic clashing hold on the present; my ribs are moving up and down, defeated, I am a wet skull left in the mud; I started sliding through the mud at the top of that hill—I remember, I . . . *yes,* I remember that much! And Moke's laughter, the others. Do they plan to leave me? Maybe they should. But I feel them coming, they shake the bushes. The dark thick growth, the sounds of boots in grass. I think I'm laughing. Maybe I was shot. No, I don't feel any pain, a hole anywhere; I seem to be together, just out of my mind—yes that's all—I've always suspected this would come. *"Look look Sergeant Bolton done flipped out plum crazy!"* shouts Johnson. His voice, all right. I never reacted like this behind a reefer, what's the matter with me? Their feet, now. The spaces, the holes where the sky, black and blue ultramarine comes down. "What's wrong with you, boy?" asks Captain Zedtwitz; against the moonlight I can see the Jeff Chandler–style gray hair of his skull, and vaguely wonder why he has taken off his helmet. I've never seen him without it. We are always being cautioned about removing our helmets unnecessarily . . .

Bud's face is close to mine. I hear his voice: "I'll fix him up, Cap'n . . . He'll be all right." The others murmur. The Cap'n says, "What's wrong with him? Should he be in a hospital?" Bud answers, "Maybe a little *rest* would straighten him out, Cap'n, but if he ain't snapped outta it by morning, then maybe the hospital would be best . . ." The Cap'n sighs. "OK. You're the MTA." His gloves slap against his thigh, like he's seen Gregory Peck or somebody else in the movies do. "The last MTA we got . . ." And Bud's arms are digging beneath my shoulders, and he's calling "*Johnson!* Get his feet! And be careful, motherfucker!"

Though it's probably premature, already I'm thinking now maybe I'll get shipped stateside away from all these forests and bugs, shellings and bombings, these firefights and vicious henchmen zigzag running through nightmares of booby traps and spike traps, away from the dull killing sounds of my own dog tags around my neck, the few piasters in my pocket, the countersweepings the sounds of rockets or five hundred–round mortar barrages or caches blowing sky high or stumbling on VC stockpiles and watching the Cap'n's face light up—Oh to get out of these rice fields and marshes, to get back to my sweetpussy foxy Anita! To hold her close to suck her long-nippled tits. Oh shit!

GETTING OUT

The moment of pain didn't last very long—the bullet hit and darkness closed around me until I woke in the American hospital in Saigon; ironic that I was wounded a few days before I would have started processing out. The doctors, the nurses, everybody commented on the irony; I was sick of hearing it. They had me on very strong darvons and I read books until I was well enough to fly back to the States. I had never seen much of North America except during basic training, and while studying medical technology I moved rather swiftly through Texas, Colorado, Florida, Georgia, Indiana, and so on, but now, disenchanted to say the least, I didn't want to settle down anywhere—I wanted constant distraction. I had perhaps close to two thousand dollars, which I figured would hold me for a while. I landed in San Francisco and began drinking and running around in the area of Fillmore Street, being very careful not to spend too much, while I tried to make up my mind whether a couple of months in Mexico would be worth my time and effort. If so, I could knock around, coming up slowly, possibly by way of Tucson, checking out the motherland at eye level. After two days in San Francisco, I converted my money into American Express traveler's checks and somehow found myself in San Diego, waiting to board the Mexican International Railroad. It was a little after noon, I think, when I was loitering and stopped to get a drink from a water fountain. A group of white construction workers were dawdling around with their lunch buckets. They were laughing heartily about something in those voluble, raucous voices they're so famous for. A portable radio was reporting something that sounded very urgent. I will never forget the day: November 22, 1963. Finally, between their spurts of laughter I heard it: "THIS IS AN UNCONFIRMED REPORT: PRESIDENT KENNEDY HAS BEEN SHOT IN DALLAS, TEXAS . . ." One of the workers stopped his flow of mirth long enough to say, "They just reported that a nigger was seen running from the scene of the—" Another one said, "I never liked Kennedy nohow. No sweat off my brow." Another said, "They come and they go." A muscle-headed guy, who was looking from strained eyes at me, suddenly turned to his buddies and said, "Hay! yousguys! Looka the cullard kid over there! He's CRYING ALREADY FOR CHRIST SAKES!" They all burst forth, a tower of laughter. Meanwhile, reports were coming in that kids in classrooms in the South were cheering Kennedy's death. As much as I detested standing there, listening to the men in the train station, I wanted to hear their radio.

It was several days before I felt the full impact of Kennedy's death—I was in Mexico. Though the Mexican women were often very lovely and sensuous I never made love to any of them. Knowing that my money wasn't going to last forever and that I wanted to *see* a lot more, I moved on. On a Transportes del Pacífico bus I went west from Guadalajara and into Mexico City, which I found very disappointing—it looked like something out of a Texas nightmare! I knocked around there for a while anyway. So, going north with a sense of dread, I hit Tucson, Arizona, sat in a train station there for six hours before I could move on. I stayed in Wyoming for two days, knocking around with a cat I ran into and remembered from Vietnam. There was really nothing there except a big air force base and a small town thriving on it, but Brother Wimpy, who had been in food service in Vietnam, had settled here, opened a barbershop, and was married to a foxy woman who had a stone fox for a friend. The friend was humdinger!

When I got to Chicago I was so disgusted with the sight of the old streets I kept going. I ended up down in Amesville, Illinois, at the Paulson School and Orphanage. I stood out on the road, unable to make up my mind whether or not to go in; so, I said, after coming this far, why not. And I went in, only to learn that it really wasn't such a frightening place after all, and it seemed so much smaller than I remembered it. Mrs. Paulson, the granddaughter of the founder, told me that the Warden was deathly ill in the hospital. She had had a heart attack. I think she was once close to death long before but had recovered, and this was the second attack. I went to see her. I don't know why, but I did. I felt very strange, deeply troubled; I felt very bitter, and yet very sad, standing there listening to her talk, her eyes not ever meeting mine. She mentioned several of the boys I grew up with. I simply wished her good luck. It must have been about eight fifteen, very dark, and I was walking blindly down the street toward the train station, crying, and didn't know why.

I kept moving around; I screwed many women. I settled in Pittsburgh during the summer of 1964, but calmly soon swooped on to Philadelphia, where I loved and annexed the life of a sweet, quiet colored lady who had two kids—she thought they were illegitimate until I told her, "No such thing as an illegitimate human being!" But it turned stale and I landed in Detroit working as a welder in a steel plant during 1965; exterminated with racism—fired suddenly, at a time when I was flat broke; reason: the boss accidented on me in public one night; a white girl was holding my arm.

I'd been thinking more and more lately about Anita, remembering the best of her; also I played with the idea of returning to Roosevelt to get a degree in English. So, it was Chicago again, the land of depressed people, lonely people under pressure—the abominable city that is really just a clutter of small towns. So in August, 1966, I was walking around—still completely disoriented—in the Loop, looking for a job. And, by night, trying to locate Anita. Unfortunately I found the job—as a waiter in a restaurant—later I found Anita, rather she rediscovered me, and found that I wasn't the guy she had known.

BEEF KILL

A short jet-black man with powerful shoulders and a freakish processed head of long hair was sweeping behind the drug counter when I walked up and asked, "Is the manager in?" I felt I was a mouth, talking.

Jumpy eyes. "You're looking for a job?"

"Yeah, man."

"Well," he said, resting his broom, stepping from behind the counter, closer. "Listen," he continued as he lit a cigarette, "the boss's name is Mr. Marvin Goldburg. He's downstairs right now. They do need somebody to help at the fountain over there and if you play your cards right the job might be yours."

"Like what?"

"Address him as Mr. Goldburg, see? Introduce yourself, see? You ever do fountain work before?"

"No." He mustn't know I'm *Somebody*.

"Well, tell him the truth if he asks."

"I see." Never in his life, my circles. All of them: Vietnam, the animal Moke, the symphony of so much pussy, my circles in everything, the revolution we were pretending didn't exist. What truth to a formation of meat, chromosome, protoplasm blues, mystery . . .? NOT ME! Even standing there I was dying; Floods. And suffering, burned; the Fire.

"Here he comes now! Keep your cool!" My worried friend cautioned me, as he picked up his slave tool and continued sweeping. Brother was dead, killed.

He stopped near the cash register, so I walked over. I spoke: "Mr. Goldburg, my name's Eli Bolton. I'm looking for a job, and wondered if you have anything."

His eyes narrowed as he closely studied my face. Hesitatingly asked, "Did you talk . . . with . . . Ruth—Kowalczyk, yet?" Why does he occupy space?

"No." Couldn't he hear my CONSTRUCTS?

My friend was sweeping within earshot.

I was thinking, here I am a war hero and an ex–college student, really qualified to do something better, and yet, here I am in this jive! Wanting *them* to believe—

"Well, let's go over and see if she needs—"

I followed. I had come in here on a hunch; tired of checking newspaper ads, tired of being turned down by suave personnel managers. This store had a center section devoted to artifacts like plastic dolls, potted flowers, teddy bears, greeting cards, and relics of life. I glanced back at my mentor and winked one eye. On the way, Goldburg asked, "You ever do soda fountain work before?"

"No."

"Oh. Well, we'll see."

We stopped at the swing gate leading to the interior of the section, and without being called, a big-faced woman came "front and center." She was a very tired-looking, nervous wreck.

Standing before Goldburg she kept her sad blue eyes focused on him. Wiping her hands on her apron.

"Hi Ruth. This young man wants work." He hesitated, his eyes narrowed as he closely watched hers.

Out of the silence of her face she was asking him a question, or waiting for a *signal*. While he obviously wanted one from her. My part in the game was to play as though I noticed none of this. To be indifferent to it, wait for the verdict. It was a language spoken with the eyes; I looked away.

The deep odors of dishwater, breaded steaks, onions, veal, pork, stale liquids, and the pungent smells of pies, cakes, rolls, syrup for sodas; the busy horns of bumper-to-bumper traffic outside, the chatter of customers, all seemed to crowd in on me so that I hardly heard what was being said to me. ". . . So have you done this sort of work—!"

"No, I haven't." A straight face.

"Think you can do it?"

Are you serious? "Sure I can." Standing on my head, lady! It's a breeze, I'm sure.

This was a game! Meanwhile I rechecked the latest aquatic (aqueous) data in my electronic eye (mind) so I wouldn't end UP dead *and* dumb like these two obviously would!

"How do you know?" Goldburg asked.

"I catch on pretty fast."

"What do you think, Ruth?"

She shrugged. "Won't hurt to try him."

Goldburg looked at me. "When can you start?"

"Anytime." I had already started.

"Can you start now?" He smelled of Noxzema.

"Sure." I'm a Big Horse, I think.

"Good." Then he looked at Ruth and spoke to her: "I'll get Wayne to show him the dressing room downstairs." Then addressing me, as he turned away from her to leave, he said, "Come with me, Eli." ("Come with me, nigger," said Tick-Tock.)

On the other side of the store, Wayne, my mentor and friend, was still sweeping. Goldburg told him, "Show Eli where to get a uniform. He's starting now."

"Yes, Mr. Goldburg." And Wayne put down his broom and signaled for me to follow. Is he a eunuch, really?

Down the steep basement stairs, along a narrow hall, all the way to the back he led me to where a row of dingy lockers were. The place smelled of mold and fungus. The damp air of the depth!

"See you made out all right, cat!"

"Yes, thanks to you," I said.

He reached out to shake hands. "Wayne Fisher's my name." There was Trojan, sphincter, and something venereal about him.

"Eli Bolton's mine." I was lying. You will see!

"Yeah, man." And he brought out from a wooden locker in the far corner a starched white shirt and pants. "Here you go, cat." He smelled anonymous, like *coitus per anum.*

"Thanks." I heard Satchmo singing.

Wayne sat in a swivel chair and lit a fresh cigarette as I began to change into the uniform. He talked. "Goldburg isn't a bad guy, you should get along pretty good with him. Ruth, the big Pole, is just a hardworking, softhearted chick, she won't give you any trouble."

"I saw some women—other women."

"Yeah, man. Well, Judy is kinda funny but nice. She'll probably like you right away. Her husband, David, cooks. That plump, light brown–skinned gal is Jolene. Drinks. But a sweet person. The white broad at the cash register digs spooks, so beware! Name's Mari. There's another fellow who cooks on David's day off, an Indian. You working days or nights?"

"I don't know yet, but I was hoping I could work nights." Paused. "I've gotta start saving money pretty quick so I can get back in school." But really I was already thinking of saving to return to New York.

"Oh yeah, school, huh—where?"

"Roosevelt." I smoked Winstons and used Lifebuoy. Also I wasn't telling him the rest of it, neither. About me, the Muhammad Ali fan, me the eater in Salaam restaurants, the Black Panther, Mace sprayer (on cops, i.e.), me the ABSTRACT, me, who was beyond definition . . .

"Yeah, that's right around the corner."

"Yes. I was studying English there until—"

"Money ran out?" I heard water running . . .

"That's what happened," I said. By now I had gotten into the stiff white uniform.

On the way upstairs Wayne said, "I'll take you over and introduce you to everybody."

We went past Goldburg busy at his drug counter; Wayne led me back to where David was at the grill and deep-fry section. The grease was bubbling and the steam from the pots on the stove had the place as hot as Macon, Georgia. David was a small man, really about the size of a twelve-year-old boy. "David, Eli. He's going to be working with you guys." David and I spoke to each other. His eyes were very light, like a cat's. The protruding bones of his face.

"Ham and—" Ruth called out.

A pleasant-looking, plump, creamy brown–skinned woman came back to the grill and said, "Order fries and burger." (So much heat! Was the building burning?)

David said, "Eli, this is my wife, Judy."

She said, "I hear you're going to work with us."

"Yes." *A foolish move.* I was thinking. Here was a black broad, a Circle herself, even ripples and trying to be smooth. I could see the symphony of life in her beauty.

"Haven't I seen you before?" she asked.

"I used to come in here."

"Thought so."

The other woman, also plump and lighter in complexion, was introduced as Jolene Johnson. She gave me a big nice smile, without stopping her work.

There were three counters. One had no one working it.

Ruth came over, wiping her hands on her apron. "Ah, Eli, Mr. Goldburg told me to tell you your pay will be a dollar eighty-five an hour plus tips. It's five thirty now," she said, looking at the watch she had stretched up her arm. "Your work hours will be from four to twelve. All right?"

"OK. How about off days?"

"They vary. Can you work Saturday and Sunday?"

"Sure."

Wayne was talking in David's ear. The cook took out a racing form and pointed out something to Wayne.

Ruth said, "I'll take the 'Closed' sign off this section and you can start right here." She threw it under the counter. "Just wait on the people and give the order to the cook, or if it's coffee or a coke or something like that, I'll show you where to find it."

Later that night a short, fat, red-faced, raggedy-assed man came in. Looked very drunk. Head hung forward, as he shuffled along. Bumping into things in his mind.

He fell to the stool and threw his arms forward; his old jacket was torn at the elbows. Murky marbles sunk in oblong saucers for eyes. His chin tolerated a stubble, his mouth was filthy with tobacco.

He barked at me: *"Service!"*

He banged on the counter.

"Coffee!" he demanded.

He couldn't focus his eyes.

I brought the brew to him.

Reaching into his back pocket for something, he knocked over the sugar container. How did anybody get into this kind of shape? Spit dripping from his nose, snot from his mouth; next he would be shitting out of his eyes and shedding tears from his asshole—

such a sad waste, empty spools of the self, worthless, yet not thrown away; something fumbling around in such a tired, demented ritual even death had forgotten to be kind to it—

I caught a glimpse of Ruth's annoyed face, and she winked at me. The meaning I didn't get, but the old drunk at my section was blowing the coffee gently as he boldly poured in a portion of whiskey from a bottle.

Fuck it, let him do what he wanted to do. Since nobody apparently saw the action except me.

He was murmuring to himself. My only concern about him came under the heading "Tips."

"Hey!"

"Yes?" I stood elegantly before him.

"Did you know my mama was a black woman?"

"No, I didn't."

And he wasn't joking. He was hurting. But he was telling me because I was black. Maybe.

"Much blacker than you. Black black."

"Do you want anything else?"

"I fed at her breasts. My real, my white mother didn't—uh, she left. My mama was a Negro. I like Negroes. What's your name? My name's Jimmy. Ever hear of me? No? Comic—very good . . ."

It was almost clear then that I was going to see the dick of death stuck into him, the storm like the floodgates down at the far end of the earth where the tides already had started washing away the sands. He would simply become soft like Junior, kissing the dog, in his abstract . . . or continue to fall in space forever like me when Harold threw me out the window. That would go on, and on.

Ruth shot over and said, "Jimmy, shut up now or Brogan will throw you outta here like last time!"

I wondered who Brogan was. Must be a bad cat. Then I remembered that a short fat guy with a bald head had come in about two or three hours ago and relieved Goldburg. Then Brogan was the night druggist. Every once in a while I could see him, on the other side, pacing behind the drug counter with his big mean cigar clamped in his beefy mouth, his hands behind his back, fingers locked, plying the half-crazy image of the little general. When he answered the phone I could almost see a fist jump out and knock him in his mouth.

Jimmy said to Ruth: "You're white—don't wanna talk to you. Go away." Pointing to me. "He's my people. Black people." Voice scraping the air; eyes averted.

Sure enough, Brogan stepped up behind the drunk and stood still, peeping around him, looking at the side of the man's face. Brogan worked his cigar around in his mouth, then he coughed meaningfully.

Jimmy turned slightly at the sound behind him. He must have caught a view of at least Brogan's cigar and smelled the smoke. He noticeably straightened up.

The mighty Brogan spoke. "*What do I have to do?* Didn't I throw you out last week?—Told you not to come back!"

Suddenly Brogan had the little tough-guy stand-and-manners but quickly jumped from static into high speed. Bulldog-faced cat with *an attitude!*

He leaped on his victim, paused for a breathless second while he picked up the cup and sniffed insanely its contents. He wheeled back, offended. *"There's whiskey in this coffee!"*

"Medicine!"

"Crap!" shouted Brogan. He didn't go lightly as he tightened his grip on the drunk and literally lifted him from the rotatable stool, gripping his pants' legs and the collar at his red wrinkled neck. He dropped the heavy man on the tiled floor, not able to launch him. *". . . And never come back!"*

Jimmy was trying to get up but was having an awful time. Brogan kicked a sharp cry out of him. He got up and was going forward too fast to balance himself, but the ceiling beam stopped him. *Bong!* on the skull, and his wild arms brought down display artifacts by the hundreds. Before he could fall again, Brogan had him by the seat of his pants and was only a few seconds in throwing him out the front door. He put him in the revolving structure and pushed it around, to the beat of the mirth of teenage girls really cracking up.

The little hoghead weightlifter, Brogan, bulldogged it back to his kennel, the witch-doctor section.

“That’s a shame,” said Jolene.
And I’m starving!

I take a break to eat. I have just come up from the basement’s toilet where I cocktailed the last of a roach I had now three days in my wallet, smoked it, a mellow high, boss shit from North Africa, I think the dude said. Picked it up on 35th and Cottage Grove. This guy Goldburg seems not to be hung up, picky, you know. Anyway this joint has given me a mental speed that is driving huge throbbing cold voracious hunger pangs throughout me; pot always does this to me. From the first time, years ago at the orphanage. I sit down, almost embarrassed by all the dishes I’ve placed before me. My first day—night, rather—on the job, I’m stuffing myself like a hog . . . My dry retracting facial orifice begins to secrete saliva ready to wrestle with the foamy ornament covering a spongy yellow underbelly, some pie. It even looks *brighter* than it should. Maybe I’m losing my mind; I look around, no, nobody’s watching. Meanwhile the wet fumes from the heavy slices of richly gravy-lacquered steak drift straight up from the plate into my nose. I’m watching the little rivers of oil in the gravy run down through crevices in the meat, the bubbles, chunks, a green piece of something, spice; meanwhile the dairy taste of the soft white substance is weightless in my chopper. Two muffins, on a side plate, broken open, thick chunks of butter, pushed into them, drain out; the odor of corn, rich waves of it, drifts, blends with the steak smells; the *blood* of fattiness, which I won’t eat anyway, it doesn’t bother me, but I am automatically slicing the fuming flesh, seeing this big Mexican, with a gut that pushes out of his shirt, even unzips his pants, so that he has to keep zipping them up, as he sweats, I see this poor Mexican, with fifteen kids at home, dig, and here he is at the Chicago stockyards, department: BEEF KILL, he’s at the hatchet-door—it’s a gate, not a door—and these dumb cows keep coming, one after another, smelling of deep rich animal odors, the mystery of such smells! They are coming—in single file, through a very narrow passageway, up to the AX, which is above the gate, and this poor motherfucker, this Mexican, stands there all day, every day except two days both belonging to gods of antiquity, and polices their entrance into the gateway, beneath the ax; the blade comes down, and I am putting the tender, well-done steak into my mouth, the acutely sensitive interior of my mouth, almost throbbing with anticipation, I'm also sweating and melancholy, the blade comes down, WHAM! takes off the cow's head very neatly, the gushing rivers of blood shooting everywhere against the wooden walls, slimy walls so thick with blood that they are like the insides of living creatures, almost breathing, and I'm chewing now, chewing, grinding my teeth into the secreting meat, the porous deliciousness of it, so focused on it I've forgotten how beautiful the salad is with its polyunsaturated oil, the modest drop of sour cream; I'm feeling as vicious as a grizzly, in his huge *excess*, the Mexican tucks his bloody shirt back into his coveralls, pushes the button that opens the floor beneath the cow's stunned, still-standing-up headless body; it falls down, vanishes, the floor closes, another cow rushes in the moment the Mexican pulls the rope that lifts the gate; the gore of this dark meat smears across my mouth, I don't worry even if Judy or Jolene sees me, or anybody. I am as involved in this savage activity as any animal of gluttony would be, the membraney walls of myself reacting, responding to it. My time space, because of the high, is even shaped like a spiral path, I move in circles; the Mexican, poor Mexican, drifts back, he is going away, the cows drift back, their blood still jumps, but I find it hard to focus on it, the cows keep coming up, being axed, left stunned, standing on four legs, without a moo-moo, but it ALL falls back, back, drops to another level . . .

My mouth is tired. Cows, animals, anything dies. My fork is into the salad, picking up rich orange chunks of cheddar cheese, that cow is being milked, fucked every way you think, I'm beginning to smile. Why am I smiling? Is somebody watching me? I shouldn't get paranoid just because I'm high; nobody can really tell. These circles. My taste buds are weakening. I've been smoking too much, drinking too much booze. I feel the crisp lettuce slumbering in my tired mouth; it is cold, but as tasteless as the sour cream is sour! My overindulged stomach also seems to be paranoid, violently uncomfortable, ulcerous, maybe blood already flowing down into the chitterlings of my body, ready to come out, blackening my shit; but I continue until I'm crudely dragging the last of the last muffin through the last drop of gravy. I'm dumping it into my shaft, gorging my frustration, the slow, high, sensibilities of myself still craving EATS, as "we" say anyway, when I spy this long dish shaped like a canoe. It is clear what I will do now, I am not ashamed. I just won't look at their eyes. If they look, I ain't worried. Ruth might say something, but I doubt it. I take the "canoe" from the shelf, ah! like a good Indian, to the ice cream pits I come, and using the scoop, feeling their dress-tails sweep by, I dig up huge, nearly frozen, bright glowing balls of strawberry, chocolate, and butternut, expecting any minute to hear Ruth or somebody behind me say, *"How long you going to take to eat?"* But nobody says anything, and when I've put five scoops in, I hold the heavy canoe under the pineapple faucet squirting the thick, chunky juice all across the balls, the chocolate syrup faucet, same, the cherry-flavoring faucet, same, now I hold the mountain of sweet dairy-confusion beneath the whipped cream outlet and ooze it all along the terrain, and finally I drench the whole domestic-slayer-of-thin-waistlines with chopped nuts—all kinds mixed together.

"Who was that guy, anyway?"

"Jimmy Sheraton," Judy said.

"Who *is* he?"

"Just an old drunk with the manners of a southern sheriff, a pig, really."

I laughed.

She talked now out of the side of her mouth with one hand covering the other side, a shield from the view of the customers. "He came from some small town in Mississippi. Raised by a colored woman. Used to be a well-known comedian or something but he's a nut. In and outta the crazy house all the time."

Meanwhile Brogan was nervously going to the window, looking out like a restless caged animal.

Later that same night, on my way home, walking to the subway at Van Buren and State Street, the same man stumbled alongside me and said, "Well, to hell with him. I say *to hell* with him!"

I was a little peeved. I wasn't in a good mood anyway. I was tired. In fact exhausted, and mad at myself for having settled for a shitty job like that, when I might have found a better one with a little effort. I halfheartedly considered telling him, Go fuck off, fella!

"I know you."

I said nothing, only listened to the clicking of my own heels on the pavement.

I glanced at him. Poor guy, I thought. What must be going on in his screwed-up mind, I tried to imagine. The night smelled wet and oily. And it was still hot.

I paid the man in the booth and went through the toll gate and down the stairs, not really expecting to see the bum follow me into the subway.

But he was coming and making a noise like crazy, like giving the impression we knew each other.

An old man waiting for the train looked up with his twisted, ugly face, eyes of a snake, and leered. Two women, each three feet six inches tall, with heavy black dresses draped on their frames, turned huge eyeglasses upon the drunk comic figure tagging along behind me. A Negro in overalls and carrying a lunch bucket gave me a dirty look.

"Ah shit!" I said to myself and started walking the distance of the underground tunnel, hoping to lose him.

But I heard him behind me. He was calling.

The Jackson Park El came, and Jimmy was fumbling around the door for a second after I got on. For a moment I thought I had lost him, but he made it.

The subway was not crowded.

"I said to him, I said—"

I sat in a seat by a window, and here he was leaning over me. His breath stank.

"This seat, there's no reason—"

He fell down into it.

"His eyes," the drunk said, "mean eyes."

I was tempted to ask, "Whose eyes?" but thought I'd better not encourage conversation.

"You didn't know that, did you?"

The train was speeding along with the mad insistence of a bull.

"My act brought top billing . . ."

I couldn't resist. "What?"

He looked at me with dog eyes. "I was famous!"

I looked out the window at blackness jumping like tigers at the night. We hit Roosevelt Road and shot up out of the underground. A southern nigger sitting in front of me said, "Hot dog! Look at this bad motherfucker go!"

When I got off at bleak 47th Street, there he was still tagging behind. *Ah* fuck! I thought. What dismay and sympathy I had felt went out of bleak metal windows like wild strange birds. The fallen star was in the graveyard of frustration, the womb of a new life. Here in the South Side night I was uptight and moneyless, just a reference in the culture. The air of rancor! The copious odor of gases, poverty, desperation, black mercy!

"HEY!"

I kept going. The poor bastard.

"HEY!" he bellowed.

Before I knew it he was at my side. Something thick and yellow was running from the corners of his mouth. He seemed more narcotized than drunk.

I was walking east toward the ghetto apartment building (that hazardous structure of barbarous carelessness) in which I stashed away.

On the other side of the street were three sharp, tackheaded young dudes doing a mean but elegant strut. In tight-fitting suits, expensive shoes. The neon lights danced on their conked heads.

He reached out, touched my shoulder, bellowing, "Haaaay! JUSTAMINUTE JUSTAMINUTE!" The young men heard and saw him instantly. Dagger eyes, black visions!

I swung around, faced him. He was breathing with difficulty, and seemed terribly annoyed. Shook his thick finger in my face. A blast of splashy blood hit my mind; *Who* had done that to me, finger menacing . . .? I couldn't stand it. "Don't think I don't know! I KNOW!"

"Why don't you run along and sleep it off, fella?" Out of the sides of my eyes, I saw *them* now.

Staggered in their slow, deadly pace. Echoes of the Blackstone Rangers, of the Minutemen.

At the end of the dim block, creeping toward us also was a thin old woman in a shapeless dark garment, her hat glowing in nightlights. My mind shaped the scene.

Closer, she shouted something the instant the young splibs hit the sidewalk and rushed Sheraton, frisking him, throwing him against a wall. Sheraton brought out a surprisingly long knife and struck at the closest boy.

In an instant, they were on him. One got the knife. "Whitey bastard!" a boy cried. The old woman was calling madly. I couldn't hear what she was saying. The knife was plunged suddenly into the old man's heart.

ANITA

I had just gotten in, was tired and nervous—imagining all sorts of possible punishments or deaths for myself, but was going to read a little before going to bed. It was about two o'clock in the morning when the knocking came.

I went to the door and asked, "Who's there?"

"Anita."

I was overjoyed. She was a shapely Afro-American, the color of a Chinese. She was very together. I hadn't seen her since returning from Vietnam. She didn't look much different now than she had then, except she had gained some charming weight.

I remembered all those miles of delicious pussy, the *tupu* goodness of her! *Shimo!* Her thick, protruding clitoris, trimming her, her inner lips, but most of all—what an expert she was at handling my *cokke.* How she had milked, milked me, milked, milked me! And she wasn't as mean as some black chicks. She had a spongy goodness, she was getting into herself, last time seen, in a way, but . . .

But there she was!

"Come in, baby!"

"Thank you." Pause. "How are you?"

That last dark convulsive night, her sensitive voice: "I'll just have to get someone else," Anita said ingenuously. "Sure, I guess you will," I answered. "You see," she countered, "I can't go on like this, Eli. At first, I imagined you cared for me. I mean, I'm human, you know, I need certain things, and well . . . you're not giving me what I *need!*" The night was tinged with mist. A socialist poster was trapped on a brick wall, a kind of American infraction. I strolled beside her, silent, bestial. The heaping stink of this urban captivity wedging in like her words. Her mouth, a cove. Her red dress, black in the encroachment of night. Her heels slapping the sidewalk.

Unrequited love! What a *thankless* bastard I had been! Three boys went by with the word "Warrior" impressed on the cloth of their backs, a kind of justice for them. Some legacy! I saw a bat circling slowly around inside a werewolf's medieval dwelling of the mind. She was at a deep blue brink. "But, of course, we're still friends." "Somebody else?" "No, Eli." I frankly didn't accept *that.* I couldn't feel self-righteous, but I craved it this instant. Our footfalls. Her hands in her trench-coat pockets. Her long eyelids, still. And my hands, the tips of my shoes.

Anita's face was the kind that is difficult to remember because it possessed a kind of universal beauty, that is, by any standard. There was a film of white-yellow overtone to the deeper red-brown of her complexion, so that she came through, usually, depending on the light, as caramel creamy rich, a glowing darkness suggesting ancient rapture. Her eyes were deep brown. If I was angry with her about something, I picked on the stupidity in her eyes as justification for my violent moments of intense hatred for her whenever it was obvious that she wasn't devoting her entire life to boosting and accentuating *my* essence in the world. Her mouth was large, juicy. A few teeth in the back missing. Its wetness, hollowness, was excellent aid to her natural fellatio skill. She had no academic argument pro or con to inhibit her overwhelming self-confidence and spontaneous ability to enjoy lovemaking with the sense of fulfillment an artist knows through creating pleasurable art. Her nose was the only slightly offbeat component of her face: it was rather flat, with a kind of bulbous head, and the ridges were like Brazil nuts; she had a good high forehead, pronounced, high cheekbones, a firm, protruding chin—a softness altogether that detracted from the unfortunate nose.

She now stood facing me in my living room. I was, for the moment, speechless. I had thought of her quite a bit lately. A sad half-smile on her face. She lifted a finger, pointed it at me. (Goddamn! That finger—suddenly it came back to me: at the orphanage *that bitch!* The Warden used to push her finger into my face between my eyes, jabbing; her mouth going yakety-yak!) "You're really—Oh, forget it!"

"What's wrong, Anita?"

She had her face covered. I went to her. She was trying to cry; her shoulders shook. I held them.

Finally she lifted her face. "Have a drink with me, Eli?"

"Sure."

"Strange that I could later almost completely forget her.

Outside, the night air was thick and damp, but warm, like walking through a green pool of dark water. Peaceful because she *wasn't* the world to me.

Anita, beside me, was murmuring: "This time, Eli . . . I think I've found *him*. I'm really nice to him, too."

"You mean your man?"

"Don't say it *like that.*"

"What other way is there to say it?"

"Well, anyway, on Sunday, I cook him all kinds of wonderful meals. You should see some of the nice—"

"Why should *I* see them?"

"There you go, getting mad already!"

"All right! I won't say anything!"

"Well, if you're going to be made I'll just—"

"I'm sorry, Anita. Go on, tell me."

And she went on: "He loves salads! You never cared for them, did you? He loves all kinds of salads . . . You know, onion, lettuce, tomatoes, grated cheese—real salads."

"I'm guilty of a crime."

"You are, indeed."

"I tried my level best."

I detected in Anita's tone a high wind over a cellar of frustration. Just how deeply unhappy was she, and to what extent would she go to cover it? Why tell me? He would soon cause my fists to ache.

In any case, we went to a modest bar and ordered scotch on the rocks. Her face, in the great shadows of silky purple hair, seemed gently trapped in a furious unhappiness. And she was still a very lovely woman. But what was happening to any woman? What were they letting the world do to them? Not just black women, all women! That great hump rump bang ugh bang bag they were in, selling body. The idea of body, a commodity.

I didn't want a woman who was going to do too much moralizing about anything. At this time, I wanted in a woman complete femininity; this I found extremely necessary. Other times, my relationship to women had been hypothetical. (In Vietnam, I hadn't bothered them. They seemed so sad.)

". . . I have a nice place, now. He helps me—Harold, I mean—with the rent and groceries."

"Do I hear wedding bells?"

"I doubt it. He's—well, I won't say . . ."

"Live with you?"

"No, we have an arrangement. What's your girl's name?"

"I don't have one."

"Ah come on! *You?*" A tempered laugh.

"I want you." Want the flesh but what else?

She finally said, "I have scotch at my place."

Unlike in New York, you cannot hail a taxicab on the street in Chicago any time and any place you want one. Only theoretically in New York. I stepped inside a phone booth and called a taxi.

Anita's key opened the door into a very colorful room, drenched in soft lights. The couch was a very simple affair, extremely orange in color, and the few lamps in the room were low, made of wood, while the coffee table was one round sweeping feature of oak with limbs of stud roots seen clearly beneath the varnished surface; the two armchairs heavy, simple, like the couch, one deep green, the other a screaming yellow, while the plush rug was gray in contrast with the Chinese white walls. "You like it?" She was watching my eyes. There was, nesting in one corner, a fifteen-thousand-dollar-looking TV/record player/tape recorder, dull finish.

"You've come close to it."

"What'd you say, Eli?"

"Forget it. This is beautiful."

Anita. There was the early marriage, big church wedding. Display in the *Defender*. The failure of it, the child that died at birth, the fussy parents at 86th and Drexel; their values she violently questioned. Her husband had turned out to be a big, empty, self-deceiving yella nigger. From a pretentious love for African culture to a confused cross between a radical socialist and a giggling pussyhappy clown. She had her problems, too. "I'll show you more."

I followed her into what turned out to be the bedroom, which was done in shades of blue, the furniture itself was early American, the color of the center of a sunflower. There was a spindle-backed rocker, like the one President Kennedy had owned and used so often; and there was a little writing table, a dresser with ruffles (sexy) around it, and a cherry (virgin) bench with its (hard) night stand.

I laughed. "Wow! *He* bought this stuff?"

She smiled. "It's all mine." Pretty pride.

Quickly and timidly. I kissed the corner of her mouth. Good Anita, who could have gone to the University of Chicago had she been able to pass the entrance exams; though for most of us at Roosevelt, it was an economic condition. I kept looking at her, trying to imagine what she'd look like without affectations, makeup, etc. Social habits, a different set of inhibitions, or none at all.

But she was bright! For her, Easter was a dress-up day but it was also simply the beginning of the planting season, which meant wearing fewer clothes, brighter clothes.

But she had no *black anger;* she was like any middle-class white girl. She could rave with anger about napalm and death under the buckram palm leaves in Vietnam, without having been there; she could demonstrate against the war, but she could still laugh.

The kitchen was ultramodern, L-shaped, with a thirteen-cubic-foot refrigerator, looking like a sterilized monster dedicated to a sparkling function. A note on the table said simply: "sugar toilet paper." The tile on the floor had a pattern which reminded me of syrup and butter whipped together. Fresh flowers on the table. Everything spotless. Anita's movements were studded with pride, as she directed this tour.

We went back to the front. The superglamour of this place floated into my senses, playing volleyball with my mind as I, against my will, measured its essence alongside the formation of artifacts (held together by warmth) I called home. The class struggle, said the May Day people.

She sat on the couch with her legs beneath her, running her

fingers through her hair, the grease. She had turned on the music. Soul volume, black magic.

"Ice?"

"Yes," she said.

I sat there silently drinking to and watching my lady of affections and melodrama so easily defined by her Calgon bath oil, her high school English teacher's way of smiling, or the sudden easy way she drops the information on the price tag of her latest apparel purchase, or by the fact that she buys Armour Bacon Longs . . . It was very sad to realize that I had come back to the wrong person—but there was no one else . . .

The bullwhip of time already driving the pain and joy of another journey into my giant gypsy soul . . .

Anita was not a black woman who emphasized the *blackness* of her beauty. I mean, she went to the beauty shop to have her hair fried, oiled, curled, or straightened to make it look like Lady Clairol; she was a shadow of a blonde, she believed blondes had more fun, once she even dyed her hair blonde; she used bleaching creams though she was already lighter than the average bear; she was a devoted reader of *Ebony*—she believed in its philosophy, especially its ads.

At the orphanage I didn't come in contact with very many girls. There were women. A thing like a woman, too: the Warden. There were Red Cross broads who used to come there, being nice. I dreamed of pussy a lot. Tried to see it under dresses. We all did, you know that. It's the way boys are. We had masturbating contests. We had visions, and there were hero shows. Anything to *prove* ourselves, into something.

A fantasy of a black grown woman with big muscles serving food in the chow hall, I could come a lot to her musical attention . . . Her breasts were like huge symbols of security.

They were also frightening.

Anita was a broad of some busy concern for material luxury; she was also the kind of chick who rapped: "Listen—you're the man, *you're supposed to do for me! I'm the woman . . ."* But she had no idea that I hated her attitude, felt that she was wrong in her choppy bullshit philosophy that that thought was unique. We didn't just eat each other, we went to all kinds of restaurants and shit, ate food and stuff. Had fun though. She dug window shopping too, *ate it up*. Loved to eye those garments; she had to see everything, especially *prices,* along the way.

But there was one thing she would not talk about: racial problems. She would not discuss civil rights or Black Power or riots. The realities in the world around us. She absolutely refused to become engaged in any kind of discussion even remotely related.

Later, in her wet grip, I rode . . .

Anita is whipping her tight pussy on me like mad! We are in her dark, beautiful apartment, with a little wine that has warmed her, I think, more than it has me. "I want the light on," I say, and get up; the shock of my sudden movement, leaving her, stuns her. I come back, the bright three-way lamp, a new dimension on her caramel-colored, firm, lean body. The taut little tits with their large rich dark *dark* red berries, some sweet nipples. The gentle yellow lights drive mathematical light sets, like beautiful *tupu* sounds of Coltrane. My spongy, sore, moist sword, as I come back to the bed, dripping her juice along the way, the sweet goodness of it all soothing my limbs; I happily pat my stomach, singing a couple of bars from something new by James Brown as I jump on the bed, over her now, growling like a dog, "GGRRRRRRRRRR," and imagining, even how it looks graphically in cartoons, or here, which is also a kind of cartoon of love, my soft black dick, by now completely stunted into a virginal softness, hanging there, and Anita goes, "Lazy nigger, you!" And her wide mouth, those big eyes, sparkling, her white *white* teeth glowing, spotless, virtuous teeth. "I'm dog—GRRRRRRRRR bow-wow! BOW-WOW! BOW-WOW WOW WOW WOW WOW!" I am in her face, and her head is turned sideways; she's looking with those big Lil Armstrong–jazzdays eyes at me, as if to say, "Who're you supposed to be *now*? What kinda new game is this, little boy? *My my,* men are always boys! Boastful, silly, self-centered little boys, who want somebody to jack them off all the time!"

She giggles, the unclear voice of Donovan carries its weight equal in space, timing our senses, from the FM radio. Her big red tongue shoots out, touches my nose. It is good that I am able to enjoy these moments with Anita, despite all the past contamination between us! She runs her long (she has an *extra* long, extra red, extra *active*) tongue around my cheeks, quickly licks my lips, but I am still a pompous dog ready to bark again, when her hard, long, firm hand intrudes in the soft, baggy, damp, hairy area of my semen-smelling fruit picker. The conduct of her dry hand always astonishes me, as it delights. She is still giggling. I am delighted, of course, whenever she touches my dick, I like it in a very civil way, not just a natural magnet, magic way. She puts me in large swimming pools of myself weighty with *supreme delight,* despite the slight roughness of her hand. Anita's hand is not rough because she's been washing dishes, sweeping floors, or ironing clothes—they're rough in a *natural* way. She is a creamy thing, *hard* all over. Her little tits are stiff cups that stand firmly, like prudent sentries, looking with dark steadiness in opposite directions. Her stomach is firmer than any stomach, male or female, that I've ever seen. There isn't one inch of fat on her anywhere unless we consider her earlobes fat. Donovan is doing "Mellow Yellow"; as I gently let myself down beside her, she's saying, "Lazzzy lazy nigger, *humhumhum,*" still holding my soft copper-headed dick with a kind of playful sense of disgust. For a moment I feel slightly ashamed that my bonanza detector remains, even in her active hand, serene. She is simply shaking it back and forth, and now asking, *"What's this?"* She smells clean, fleshy clean, she always does. So gently soapy-smelling, not strong with some overdose of peakily cheap perfume!

She is already on her elbow, looking down at me by now, smacking her lips, going, "Tut tut tut—What am I gonna do with you, nigger, huh? You're a mess—*won't* it get hard?" "*Be nice* to it, Anita, baby, it'll do anything you want it to do . . ." Yes, it has been a long time since she's given me that sacred rite she is such a master at performing. I'm thinking, Why should I torture poor Mr. ex-Perpendicular any longer, tonight, in her dry hole? She gets up to her knees, and I deliberately say nothing because I know from past experience that Anita does not like for me to ask her to suck it, though when she volunteers, she has proven to be unbeatable at getting to the essence of the act. I remember now as she is about to suck it, she knows that at least turning it around in her mouth, swiveling it, whirling it, rotating it with her thick, long tongue, makes it hard as bookends; and vigorous, so powerful, in fact, that I've rocked and almost unhinged her torso from such long, pithy, severe sessions of pure slippery fucking, pushing one juicy hour, to the rhythm of music, into another, right here in this bed. And I suspect now she thinks she'll get me hard and *then* stretch out on her back, her brittle pussy hairs twisting together there, damply, at the mouth of the jewel, hiding that ruthless, hungry, merciless gem! that gobbles and gobbles, eats at me—rather, lies more or less in repose, as *I,* out of deep meanings of the self, feel compelled to work myself to death, so to speak, to fill up its crater! But that ain't what's happening this time—she doesn't know it yet, but she's going to swivel it, rotate it, nibble it, lick it, gently chew on it, playfully bite it, turn and turn it in the spitkingdom of herself, dance it with her tongue, spank it with juice, excite it to huge precipices without bursting it out of its tense axis of delight; she's going to hold it in honor with both brown hands, as it dips, tosses, as it ascends, in all oh all ranges of mind states! Yes, it is my mind! Equal, that is, to every level of myself . . .

I know I can turn her *off* if I say One Word now. That's the last thing in the world I want to do now as I feel the weight of her knees adjusting between mine. "Put this pillow under you—" She's being clinical; OK, if she wants to be that way, it'll still be good. I feel how I deliberately relax every muscle I can consciously focus on with my mind. She wiggles her firm ass, adjusting it somewhere on her heels, her arms inside the warm soft area of my thighs, I feel the hairs of them. She takes a deep breath; I can smell the air of the ruby we drank drift up to my nostrils. Sound: the slow wet movement of her strong red tongue moving over her lips, mopping away the dryness. Like most of her body's exterior, her lips are usually very dry. Only two spots, exceptions, I can think of: the areas around the edges of her scalp, the crevices between her thighs and where the mound of her pussy begins to rise, are usually warm and moist. As I lift my narrow ass, holding myself in a loop, she slides the big pillow beneath me, I sink down into the conquering softness, her busy automatic-acting fingers tickle the rooty area at the base of this selfish generative Magic Flute of mine, pull and squeeze my sagging sensitive balls. She coughs, clears her throat.

I hear the smack of her tongue between her lips again. I have my eyes closed, soon I'll feel the slow, warm, nerve-wracking sweet fuck of the pensive mouth beginning . . .

This hesitation. I know it is coming. Her mouth has not yet touched the ruby head of my *dik.* The moment of waiting, the anxiety of it builds like musical improvisations in my bones, my membranes, the heat, blood energy in me; I continue to try to keep it all very still, cool, I am not even trying to concentrate on hardening up my ecstasy-weapon, this dear *uume* to the emissive glory of life itself! And for once Anita doesn't seem impatient, she isn't pumping it, bungling, and jacking it, trying to make it instantly hard—I suspect she's going to make it really great this time. She can be absolutely wonderful, when she wants to! The anticipation of these moments, of a kind of antagonism of sweet memory of the best times, is overpowering. It takes all the will in my being to lie here, still, the corporeality of myself, in the spit-slick heady memory of it . . .

(It is only at these moments, of course, that this particular "movement" of the symphony of life is so beautifully important, all-consuming . . . Equal to the working moments when I am excited by the energetic, rich growth of a concept I am able to articulate! Or my sudden ability to construct bookshelves, or create a silly wacky lovely painting, equal to anything that I do involving the full disclosure of myself! I hesitate to say equal to my ability to handle those firearms in Vietnam, against those nameless human collages that fell in the distance, like things, but maybe even equal to that, too . . .)

The hot nude hole of her mouth, *oh God it is so goooooood!!!* slides now, caressingly, dry at first, but she's excreting saliva, like cunt juice, her firm hands stretching out, in slow motion, sliding up my flat stomach, my gentle spongy dick blowing up, expanding at a pace equal to the tension in her lips behind the root of her tongue, getting hot as the crevices of her gums, the deliberately slow sinking of her mouth still coming down to the very base of my seed-giver, gently, but firmly engulfing it, in all of its lazy softness, the nerve-ends of my whole ass, my nuts, my thighs are fructifying! The meaty warmth of her velvety lined interior begins to climb just as slowly; Mr. Prick is anxious to quickly reach the full and painful proportion of its promise, but I fight that drive by applying more and more deliberation to my restraint, under the magic, almost weightless touch of her fingers as she adroitly glides them down, tripping through the hairs of my stomach. She need not hold my *uume* with her hands any longer. "He" is trying too hard to make headway in his headiness! He holds himself up; I refuse to let the progressive bastard gristle up to the prolific point where he is like some giant tendon, though Anita might (*if* she weren't unusually patient right now) *like* that; O motion, joy, oh *shit,* this is TOO MUCH! the still missiling motion of the circle of her tight mouth, restrainingly prolonged, up—up! I can feel the inelastic cords of my inner tissues pulling in a complex of nerves, pulling, as her strong big Black Woman, Mighty Nile, African energetic tough lips, the muscles in them quivering, the lengthy moist spongy-porous tongue gently milking the base of my valve, Mr. Hammer's underbelly, milks fruitfully, in a slow rhythm. My eyes are still closed, I am trying not to settle my mind anywhere, it tries for a moment to drift to the greasy magazine of a gun I was examining one day, sitting propped against another guy's back, at the edge of a rice paddy, and I don't know why. I want to *stay* right here, with her, focused on every protrusion, every cord, abstract circle of myself, of her every "feeling," every hurling, every fleshy spit-rich convexity, mentally centered in all the invisible "constructs" of myself, right here, where she and I now form, perform an orchestra she is conducting in juicy floodtides; stay *in* her woman's construction, her work, her togetherness, the rich procreating-like magic of her every touch as—more and more against my will—my *kok* protracts, *swells,* lengthens, perpetuatingly jumpy with fertility, as her permeable mouth decreases its gentle grip in exact ratio to Dick's eminent *strong* polarity. I love her for her reflective, melancholy approach to this fine art! So seldom does she take this much care to do it properly . . .

My serpent is just fatty-hard, but extra long, redundantly so! It is *best* this way, if I can manage to keep it from stiffening to the point where the nerves are minimized somehow. I feel the mouth-motions of her workings, the salivary warmth of her slow, pensive chewing at the *acutely sensitive head,* where the loose skin has slid back, the rich, thick nerve-ends in the thin layers of this loose skin, she lets spit run down slowly around this Bridegroom in his moment of heaven, the warm secreted water from the prolific glands of her taste bud–sensitive mouth, I feel these oh so slow careful and skillful movements, the deliberate soft scraping and raking of her beautiful strong teeth across the tender texture of the rim of the head, gently bathing with spit the prepuce's densely nerve-packed walls, which rub these ends of my luckily uninhibited penis. She is concentrating on the head of it, and she can do this for so long it drives me *mad* with porous, beautiful pleasure. She will nibble here, suck one or two times, stop, let it rest limp, aching, in the soft warm cave of her rich dark purple "construct," saliva mixing easily with the slow sebaceous secretion, my own male liquid lubricant, *smegma,* washing around in her grip—a gentle but well-controlled clasp! Then, she might take a gentle but playful plunge *down,* straight down, down, sinking down faster than she's so far moved, the dick head exploding up into all that wet, warm slime, it's running down, profusely, the tunnel-sinking sense of it, the sounds of the cool capful of wind speeding away giving way to this cravefeeding, just the hallelujah-warm, narcotic feeling of the drop, as my dick thickens, pushes out—the lengthy pole emitting into her muscles, and tonsils, the juicy soup of my penis glands, the sheath, now in this plunging motion stretched in this hymn of heat to frantic, mad ends! Two more strokes like this and she can finish me. I would shoot a hurricane of seeds into her, falling out convulsively, palmus, in nervous-twitching; *but* Anita isn't trying to finish me off this time, get it over. She's going to be good to me, but I *cannot* keep myself from the submissive fear that she might suddenly bring it to an end, and it can be very painful if it is done incorrectly. Instinctively, Anita knows this. This knowledge is in the very pores of her skin, she is the knowledgeable Mother of a deep wisdom, intrinsic in her every chromosome.

Yes.

God!!! Yes! She can sustain me, even as I lay pitched on this *brink,* she controls it all. The way I'm beginning to whimper, groan, beyond my own control, she controls it all. With her mouth, she is screwing the head of my dick, around and around. She is worrying it now, from side to side, clasping it, increasing and decreasing the pressure, the circles of my mind follow some rhythm she is leading, in this voracity. My ass already is beginning to throb under the acute, tremendous, mesmeric workings of her facsimile-pussy, which has the irresistible kind of skill the lower mouth of ecstatic agony, also a spicy feast, with good lips, does not have, because it lacks *this mobility.* I lie still, the rich body-pungency, the fuck-fragrance of ourselves in my senses, the dry taste of my tongue; as I lie here, my palms face up, the smell of rich black sweet cunt filling the room, the door of her mouth, the wet-smell of my own pungent body fluids that escape her jaws, dripping down into the hairs around this cylindrical, pendulous totem pole, Anita's rhythm upon it begins to increase . . .

I worry. Please, baby! Take it easy; but I am not speaking. A few muscles of fear harden in my stomach but I manipulate them back to peace. *Be quiet body,* but she now masculinely grips it, the excited columns of its interior pressed together, the cavernous tissues throbbing, like my head is throbbing, the roots of my hair, my toes are twitching, like this wonderful up-standing organ, she is holding in its wet harmony, as she treats the head like it's a popsicle. Anita has her hand just below the bulbo-cavernous muscle, wrapped in an amorous squeeze there, which serves as a kind of pump, and a restrainer. As she licks the edges of the dome now, lifting her mouth completely up, air currents rush in, refreshingly stimulating; her hand continues to milk my *coc,* setting a pace, otherwise the explosion would come. She knows. She rests. I rest it, I open just the slits of my eyes to see that she has herself in a very relaxed position, so that she can last, without getting tired. I whisper the first words thick like *cum* in the air, "Baby, it's great, beautiful, oh I can't tell you how much—" But I don't finish, I feel her mouth's downward movement, engulfing the bulb as it relaxes from some of its previous excitement. She can detect its state by its throbbing, meaning to be very perfect, she eases the pressure of her hand, the cylinder somewhat dried where her hand has been pressed. I can even feel the sperm, free, push up, the quickening exit, though it is still very slow, still under her control, I am helpless. I am almost unconscious with the pleasure of it. She rotates her heated seminal-stained mouth five times swiftly on this meaty pendulous organ, *uume* . . .

Fighting my tendency to explode, she plans to shift the pace of her work, she uses no method for more than one second, for fear of tipping me off the delicate whimpering thin-skinned "construct" I'm being balanced on. She chews at it, with the gentle crunching of her teeth, tongue working, like she's chewing the juicy texture of an apple, she does this three times—it is so effective, so deeply sinewy good, closing distance between us, a kind of suspended liquid oneness holds us, I am in her, I am one, in her . . .

Then, quickly she suspends that game, and seems to be trying to "drink" it, like she'd drink water from a fountain in the park, a kind of sucking-up conflicting feeling, almost accommodating an earthquake of an orgasm!—that she restrains with a downward connective lapping of her tongue, gently taking up each drop of juice as it comes up out of the hot, irritated eye, the umbilical, sweet, nexus-feeling of ME slowly, being milked, into her, slowly, she drinks ME, one drop, one rich corporeal swallow at a time. This is the only way to do it without having the orgasm so *powerful,* rushing up so swiftly that the action would be very painful, a struggle, all of it not being able to explode out the narrow head fast enough. She milks the tail, she goes very slowly, the harmony is perfect . . .

The symmetry of the way I'm coming is beautiful, this is the best I've ever had, the milking process she is using is a method she has perfected, developed on me (and probably on others I know nothing about), and it's great. With her mouth she fishes, ties knots with her tongue, around the bulb, she screws it as though she's using her pussy, she staples it quickly one or two times; then she rivets it, she hammers at it several times, she nails it down with stabs, it fights back in contraction, she puts a sash around it with her tongue, she seems to be padlocking it, linking it to her guts as she threatens to swallow it, the juices slowly draining out all along, the nexus deepening; now her mouth is thick with the creamy warm juice, slapping sounds of the pasty sperm from my swollen testicles, as the spermatic arteries are slowly being sweetly sucked up, slowly into this caramel beauty!

I will continue to come now until I am empty of semen, all of it that can come out, until my tubules are vacant, until the duct rests, without the nervous activity of excretion, I feel the careful building slim strength of her ligaments; now she seems to be throwing a lasso around my gun; suddenly she works it back toward herself, as though her mouth were reins, pulling at it, the spurts of semen thickening her pithy hole, still without hands; with her mouth she straightens it up, carefully, after swallowing most of the fluid, some of it sliding down the throbbing, nerve-racked pole, still holding up in this phallus rite of sensuous music; and with it straight, she makes some sudden strokes that seem to be some kind of effort to bridle it like she might bridle a horse or a dog; the dick is kicking, slimy with sperm, throbbing, nakedly buckling under so much tension, and she continues, keeping her grip just right, not finishing it; the juices continue to pour into her, she drinks them, and this is all done very slowly, now, with it standing nobly straight up again; her mouth seems to be working like ten busy fingers trying to button a button on a shirt, and my fluid is pumping up faster than ever—she detects this, puts her hands, both of them, on the upper part of the *kok,* and gently squeezes it as it bounces, punches, dibbles around in her cave. She has relaxed her connection. She doesn't make a move with her mouth, the dick is swollen bigger than ever, resting, robust bulbous thing, throbbing, oozing smoothly, with restraint, into her, under this efficient "tongue-lashing," teasing, and mouthing. This edifice of mine, this lucky stretched-out time-space harmony, feels the comfort of her hand loosen, and the continuation of pleasant effusion. She is controlling this orgasm so well, it may go on for more than an hour, I am percolating, oozing, dribbling at the dick like a river, but a slow river, being tapped by the mysterious rainfalls of Mother, voids, secrets, wet holes of the flesh world, carrying on an expedition to the ends of my self-conscious reality; at the floodgates of emergency, my dark, fleshy Anita, love, a gateway into which I exist, and erupt, enter; Oh! she frills it, gently, beginning again, now that the nerve-ends have stopped throbbing so . . .

She works at it like she's trimming corn off the cob, she skirts it, jerks it, confines it with quick frightening pressure, releases it, threads it, the juice gently secreting, Mr. Tail, ancient in his mighty moment; the sperm is just pouring out—but not the swift way it would in a "normal" explosive orgasm—as she nibbles at the edges of it, its prepuce slick with trimmings; the percolated head is so *swollen* the ejecting semen seems to feel choked in, but not painfully so, as it pushes, gushes, then trickles out, into her leaky hot mouth . . .

She ties a bowknot on it, making loud splash splash wet slappy sounds, zips up and down up down up down (faster than ever—) on the final up, grabs the head of the cable meat, squares it in her nest, locks it tightly, juices splashing, jumping, buckling into her thicker, hotter than ever, rich, oozing circuits of seedy fluid jamming into her; she takes them without blinking, still anchoring the dicker connectively, roped to her control, not allowed to empty, finish completely until she says so . . .

Huge emotional collisions in me, I had no idea I could ever generate so much fluid at one time. The padlock of her mouth now merely restrains it, but loosely, as she steadily holds it; it is like a wet electric meat god, cabling magic into her, screwing the tunnel of us close, stopping up the ends, to make us one rope.

I feel now the shift of her body. She adjusts herself for the Big Moment. She has planned to bring me into the finish. She is going to work it very carefully, make its *interconnection* so well bridged, so rich, *free low flowing,* consistent, to make it so complete and agreeable, tunneling into her, the flowing upbeat of the incessant cargo of fluid that completes the symphony. She is getting ready to start. I try *not* to brace myself.

I succeed in remaining as relaxed as I am, my wet *cokke* though has the sharp knowledge conveyed to it, and it stiffens, hard as a tendon, its prepuce slimy as the slick spongy head; I feel the top of her mouth slowly sinking down to rest on the protuberance of it. How do I know she is ready? She takes both my balls in one hand, and holds gently the belly of them but firmly, while they pout, my extremely bloated peninsula of a dickhead thickly tightens, "feeling" *her readiness* to work at it. She begins! She really goes! Until every drop of it is *gushing* out.

WHAM!

down

she comes, *zipping,* the antagonistic wet grip of her contracting, expanding mouth, is sucking, fucking it, chewing it, UP—DOWN! updown! . . . The dick is so shocked it stops even the slow corporeal leakage, stunned. But quickly the "shape" of it circles in, the magic excitement increases during this wild, twisting, collapsing moment; my dingdong begins to spit up semen again, responding to it—this *overwhelming impact,* this squeezing, sucking, and I hear the sloppy juices jumping, splashing around in her mouth; she is holding my balls and milking them of their substance, milking and milking, and *pumping,* jacking, fucking my cock with all she has, the contour of its working shapes against the round surface of my meat god, sucking him, sucking him, getting him UP, up—inelastic root-depth throbbings, I am almost out, with the rushing-pushing feelings pouring up out of me, up into her, bursting, *blind unconscious* (too much trying to come out at once)—She holds the balls, understanding what is happening, bringing modified rivers of seed juice out of my loins! She still controls his ebb, as she *pumps—now now now now blindly dead blind sweet sweeeeetly oh,* and I do groan, even shriek, this bonanza is so rich, it is *bursting*—

My senses stewing, fermented, quivering—I am breathless, unable to move, as she has it all out except for the last few drops, she hungrily sucks—

Oh how beautiful gentle she is with it as she licks it, the yeasty last drops, the end of the turmoil, how she mothers it, holds my stomach just above the line of my hair for a moment, then takes my prepuce with the other hand and holding just the head of this cherry-tipped, sore, nerve-wracked but happy *kok* pushes it back from the inhabitant beneath it, still throbbing, as he shrinks only theoretically, not actually, still too *tense*: he will stay hard, though empty, for a while yet; now, she gently sucks at it, like she's eating plums, pulling off the skins, and this brings out the tiniest of the tiny last drops of semen, the juices, and to make sure she has it all out, so that I am completely happy, she softly, rhythmically, masturbates it slowly; this is too taxing, the *pain* of it, I have to grip her hand, and stop her . . .

So, she knows she's done a beautiful job, and I try to open one eye enough to see her, and when I manage it, she's there, in the yellow light, big, soft red lips as she wipes them with the edge of the sheet, smelling spermy, and looking naked and ripe as a peach, and now I'm ready.

BASEMENT RITE

"What was the trouble?"

I sipped the black steaming hot coffee and waited. She smelled of Dove liquid and Ultra-Brite.

"That ol' guy who used to hang around . . . got killed out South . . ." Hilda said. "He was kinda crazy but I understand that at one time he was a song and dance man with a blackface routine in burlesque . . ."

I chose to say nothing. I had a view of the window: a blonde with green eyes in a Rolls Royce went by. A group of Boy Scouts at the next counter were going through a stack of summer camp snapshots, their Kodaks around their necks. Hilda's milky-white dress was a blast against her emerald greenish-brown sepia flesh-tones. The prismatic way she took the lights, her mouth moving: "He was always drunk, though; but he never bothered anybody, really. He was kinda smart; he could quote Shakespeare even. They used to let him out of the nuthouse pretty often; so he couldn't have been too dangerous." Her eye moved toward the flashy door each time it revolved.

Goldburg came over and sat down, tiredly; immediately I got up and went behind the counter and stood before him. He was a Jew who did seem self-righteous, and certainly obsolete because of his style; he argued with Brogan in degrees that turned out to be medical—like witchdoctor; we could hear their evil flamboyant rivalry often splattering the drugstore walls! "Just coffee."

I brought the coffee to him, returned to Hilda's plump sensuous chocolate presence, attracted by something mellow but too icy in her to want. I then had my own arctic problems. At this moment, a very tall, awkward white boy, who had been hired a day after my own employment came over and spoke to Hilda.

"How's Frank? Homesick, yet?"

He knitted his brow. "Naw! I'm all right." His white uniform soaked and stained with splashes of amethyst syrup, strawberry juice, grease from the grill; and his fingers were puckered from the water. There was so much sympathy seeping from Hilda toward him.

Ruth Kowalczyk came over and bluntly said to him: "Frank Engelmeyer, listen here kid, there's a sink full of dishes! You were hired *to work,* not to talk with customers!"

Frank couldn't conceal his unthinking angry reaction but he slowly, poutingly, returned to the pots and pans. Ruth was hard on dishwashers because if they didn't do their job she'd be compelled to sink elbow-deep into that steaming hot, greasy water, sweat dripping from her scarlet face. And her hands were already badly chapped from too many such times. Even I felt the threat of the pots and pans when the dishwasher wasn't taking care of business, or even just downstairs taking a shit. Like in the army, during basic training, the pots and pans always scared the living spectroscopic shit out of everybody!

Hilda said to me, "I guess you know he ran away from home. Told me about it yesterday. He'll go back . . ."

If you had a home to run away from it might be interesting, I thought. In neutral.

Jolene had a portable radio turned on, I could hear the precise voice of my main man, Brother Buckwheat Brownie, rapping: ". . . and Malcolm X, brothers and sisters, should live in our black hearts with the urgency that Jesus WASP Christ lives in Charles's gizzard. Oooops! I mean, *heart!*"

I looked at Goldburg's face to see if he was listening and what might be his reaction. A plastic face, he was deep in himself. But it wasn't his *schtick,* he had his own perspective. Hilda simply made a face.

"Got to run, Eli. Got a class."

As she went toward Mari, to pay, Goldburg winked at me. "Nice-looking chick."

Jolene's section was also now empty, and she rested against the counter, reading a racing form. She probably played every day through the bookies. I had been a chump, but always at the track itself, at Arlington, many times after coming back from overseas.

The hazardous wins, the filter of a fine race, the horses coming in, groups of mud faces taking program selections, the monkey, the luck-talk, the hunches, the little windows, win, place, show, and the daily double, all the magic of it. A customer came, sat at her counter, but she didn't notice right away. I saw Goldburg's halo melt, his rigid face shrink, his eyes jump into deep-freeze discord! I gave Jolene the signal, going, "Pssss!" Sometimes Jolene seemed too distant; I felt that I didn't and couldn't really know her—that she was only somebody who *looked like* a person I knew. And while I recognized the gambler in her not only did I make a mental note to talk to her on this score but I made one at the same time, checking out Sapphire Hilda's big whiplashing ass as it went out the front revolving door, to *talk to her* in reference to that *thang* of hers!

Brogan, with a chewed-up cigar jutting from his Jiggs-face comes down the steps, violently gasping and hissing, looking behind himself, as May Downs, the piggish, overly made-up, cheap-smelling loud-mouth chick, followed by a young broad, follow him down. I'm beneath the staircase, in the blue damp shadows, rubbing suntan lotion on Mari's stomach, and she's whimpering, scratching my arms, and I'm trying to get her to shut her fucking mouth before we're discovered and I'm fired, but Brogan and the females are creating too much noise coming down to hear the whimpering—she claims the peeling skin on her ass, stomach, thighs, all over, is really burning so bad she's dying . . .

The trio vanishes into the passageway leading to the lockers, their feet making splash-splash sounds in the water, and to that rhythm, I begin to stroke Mari's cunt; it's so good to her she props one foot up high on the staircase structure, so I can really get to her gushing trap without straining, twisting my wrists out of shape, when suddenly we hear these giant sounds of *pain,* screaming, and smell the fresh odor of blood, thick in the dampness . . .

I shoot back to the locker area and come to a screeching halt, where the scene jumps into my eyes, like acid, stinging, eating into my brain cells: Thick May Downs, who is naked down to stockings and high heels, holds a whip under her arm, and drinks wildly from a bottle of whiskey. Her gut hanging obscenely as her massive tits bounce around. She kind of absentmindedly does a few steps of the Watusi, to the music coming from the portable radio Wayne has left on the bench. The innocent-eyed girl looks fearfully over her shoulder, saying, "*Please* be gentle; won't you . . .?" But Brogan, who is naked, pink as a baby and just as chubby, just as pudgy as May Downs, is sitting on the bench, beside the radio, with his peter in his hand, pumping it, and it keeps folding up and slipping out of his grip, while he watched the girl's naked ass; she's tied to a pipe running from the ceiling to the floor . . . Mari, behind me, I suddenly notice, is about to scream at the horror of it, though we haven't yet been seen. I now notice that on the shaded side of the girl's ass there are large streaks of open skin emitting blood that runs down her painfully constricted hips. May lifts the whip and carries it wide, wrapping it around the young woman again, bringing out a shriek, and more fresh blood; at this moment Brogan focuses so intently on what is happening, as he struggles with his tiny meat, that neither he nor May nor the poor girl have noticed our arrival.

I simply go over, take the whip out of May's hand; she drunkenly grins at me, looking sheepish. "You should be ashamed of yourself! *Look* ashamed!" I demand, and she does instantly, but Brogan, I suddenly notice, has jumped up, snatched off his penis, and has thrown it on the floor, the tiny thing still very soft, and he is shouting, *"See what you've done? You've ruined everything!"* But the girl is looking over her shoulder toward me like Tarzan used to look at Boy when he'd come to secretly untie him where the natives had him bound while debating his future; so I begin to untie her and she's saying, *"I had no idea they wanted me for this, I really had no idea—"* And a slip of my tongue: "That's all right, mother. No one will ever know."

HILDA

Hilda—whom I met while at Roosevelt—was watching me too closely, I felt. My uneasiness. The look in her dark face promised something of the enemy.

But she was ardent-looking, a dark pepperiness. Only a few days ago I had thought it might be very good to screw her. Now, something was beginning to stalemate; something antagonistic loomed between us.

"The money," said she.

Her smile was crisp and unfriendly. Yet, for a moment she was the black woman in food service at the Paulson school, so suddenly propitious! She was clad in a silky blue summer dress, smelled of soap and simple perfume; her dark flexible face both attracted and repelled me.

We were in a downtown hotel room together at an empty hour.

I snapped the button at the door and the light on the ceiling shot weakly yellow through the room which was dusty, too small for the huge ancient bed and the big awkward armchair. The wallpaper was old and faded, colorless, like the rug on the floor, which was simply darker. The blinds were drawn tight against the sun's rays, and the dull picture, over the bed, of a forest. I saw the room as the wicked symbol of my unwillingness to meet Hilda's terms. So surprising to me!

"Well," she said without smiling, "this is it." There was something urgent, hot and liquid left in her eyes, but my private vision of a woman to love, to enjoy, was far from this belligerent bird.

So she wanted money? She had completely ruined my fantasy of her. She, not getting an answer, went into the washroom, opening the bathroom door roughly, mad, and standing there, studied its darkness. After finding the light switch, she took a deep breath, let it go. Maybe she was saying to herself, fuck the money! But even if she was, it was too late. I stood at a bleak angle behind her, looking over her shoulder. She seemed suspended in the pages of herself, then: "These strange washrooms make me sick just imagining how many thousands of people have been in them, sitting on the stool, taking a bath, maybe with syphilis, or pus sores, or diverticulitis of the asshole . . ." There was something so bitchy, so loathing in her voice it almost knocked me recumbent. I watched her as she carefully laid toilet paper thickly around the seat before sitting down on it.

(The taboo of excrement, the ritual surrounding it—how secret and ancient a hostility, what guilt for eating flesh was trapped here?)

How could I get an erection? I went back into the front. I could hear her flushing the toilet. The private moment of the shithouse, she had taken it without closing the door. I hated myself for hating her for her feces. The curtain was down on a bad show. She came out saying, "Well, what're we going to do?"

Hilda stood hideously innocent before me with her outstretched palm up. "Well?"

To see what price she placed on her fleshy castle I asked, "How much?"

"Anything you wanna *let me have*."

For some reason I can't explain, I suddenly had a vision of the dead child I saw lying on a roadside in Vietnam, caked with flies, two days after Moke had finished with her. The basement levels of my mind, the crude people moving through the subways, the loneliness, the hills and mountains of myself, the flesh of people, the ugly sickness of so much of it . . .

I stood up; I said, "I've got to go."

"Go where? You're not coming back?"

Disgustedly she flopped down on the bed, with a very dark, sad half-smile, like the one on the face of the young Vietnamese woman I tried to communicate with one morning, far up the side of a steep mountain, in the narrow front yard of her mountain goat–styled life, before the shack, etched into the rocks and palms, the short still trees. She tried desperately to tell me something, and I tried desperately to understand. I went away with the saddest heart. I felt that way now. For Hilda and I had failed to communicate, too.

As I was going out, I heard her voice, like an offended hostess: "What's wrong with giving somebody you want to sleep with money?"

I stopped. "I didn't say anything was wrong with it."

"But you *think* it is."

"How do you know what *I* think?"

My back was to her. I had been the first to turn away from the Vietnamese woman, too. I had climbed and climbed, the rocks beneath my boots, on the path, crumbling, falling down, the sand sliding, until I reached the clearing where my regiment waited for orders I never understood. I now went out, and down to the street.

The warm lake breeze sprinkled my face in the midday heat. I realized I was better off out three bucks for the flophouse room than I would have been had I lost some of myself, my balance. I couldn't afford to lose much more . . .

HILDA AND ANITA

I am in the Loop trying to find one of those little jukejoint tattooing places to have "MANTEIV" imprinted indelibly on my arm, the left, when I spot a familiar bouncy person sacked in a glossy red silk skirt: Anita! half a block ahead of me, and my first impulse is to run, catch her. I push the tattoo to the back of my mind, I begin to trot, but I am quickly brought to a hesitating pace when I see that Anita has stopped, up ahead, and is gaping into a shoe store showcase window. I come within two yards of her. There is something like a courtesan intensity in the dazzle of her eyes, they break the day with excitement, it's high noon. I move closer, I even *smell* her. She smells of sweat, and is throwing off beams, her mind is so loud it ticks the electric currents of her thoughts: "Oh my gooooooooooooodness!!!" People are going by, refracted; the sun is working optics on daytime neons, the window before Anita is a two-dimensional globe, illuminated with shoes that (I can see from the reflection in her eyes) are so sparkling, so breathtaking, so fleshlike, so resplendent that they might any minute flap up and walk on air, pure light, weightless, shimmerings in eternity! I am only three inches from her. The sexual odor she throws off is humorous, its characteristics I am more than familiar with. I knew the footlights of this odor before I was inducted, I used to simmer in it. I am so aroused by the funky gentility of it that I uncontrollably reach out, my mantlelike tongue scores; I lick her cheek upward, careful to get every bead of sweat. She responds to the craving of some inner voice, just beneath the surface of her mind; her hands, long brown consuming fangs, scratch desperately at the plate glass. Reflected on the mirror of it I suddenly notice Hilda, going up State Street, driving a new 1966 Cadillac; she has her hair up in pincurls, her face is streaked by the ghostly presence of cold cream, and she is shouting with more intensity than a jet breaking the speed of sound: "By outward show let's not be cheated. An ass should like an ass be treated." I recognize the cheap lines, from Gay's *Fables.* The traffic comes to a complete stop. I try to detect the flicker in Hilda's eye, the one I can see, but I get only her profile; and whose car? She certainly doesn't own a hog! Poor Anita, who has begun to blaze like a meteoric substance, is making the feline scratching and purring sounds of a kitten on glass. "Oh god, oh fuck!" she insists. I open whatever possibility of understanding I have, and watch it go out to her as on a puffy cloud, like the kind hanging over Little Lulu or Henry (in the cartoons of our American spirits). In my cloud, I am affectionately trying to hyphenate into Anita, who, though I begin to shake her arm gently but with persistence, is weeping the largest landmarking tears I believe I will ever witness as she nibbles without restraint at the glass that is keeping her from the beautiful shoes! She works with surgical skill, her teeth are cutting like a glass cutter. "Baby, these goddamn things ain't where it's at! Baby, *please, please!* control yourself! What about pure progress, what about psychology, knowledge, what about experimental methods, huh, and equality, and ideals, law and naturalism, what about peace, huh, what about optimism, revolution—what about revolution, huh, answer me that, willya, what about the universe, wisdom, words, what about curiosity and democracy, tell me, Anita, what about interaction and interdependence, huh? Huh, Anita, huh?" These words hover almost directly above my head so she'll know I am saying them. But she ain't got hip to my presence yet, and the cars, piled up ten miles south, jammed all the way to the viaduct where 63rd Street crosses State, just because Hilda has spotted us, she is shouting and waving. She has one of those big limp, *"How yawl doin'?"* grins. I suddenly feel sluggish, realizing that Anita has gotten her arm through the glass, without cutting the substance, without even ruffling the sleeve of her white blouse. She is groaning, hissing, gasping with admiration, as she picks up a pair of fashionable semi–high heel white pumps that reflect the showcase lights, as well as the gentle, natural phosphorescence. Anita murmurs as she lifts the shoes and holds them close to her womb, "Oh god, *oh* fuck!" Her eyes are shut.

I feel too clouded, I can't speak; Hilda's shouting jumps through the pause in the honking of horns but I do not realize that she is addressing Anita until I see the familiar words, lifted directly from Shakespeare's *Macbeth,* bounce off Anita's solar system, refusing to penetrate it. The words: "A dagger of the mind, a false creation, / Proceeding from the heat-oppressed brain?" And though I knew she was, in her dally-dally popular-quotations way, trying to warn her old college schoolmate of the danger of lust for clothes, because, before those words even hit the ground, to melt under the glorious energies of Shamash, Ormuzd, Merodach, Tezcatlipoca, Ra, or Helios, or whatever you call the source of life, the sounds became visible, like sound waves on the wing of a jet the moment it begins to break the sound barrier.

Before this instantaneous transformation can take place, Hilda shoots with flippant confidence the huge cliché from Cervantes: "All that glitters is not gold!" But the vapory quality of it bombards even my mass media–condensed sensibilities, as I find myself tugging at Anita's edges, any place I can get a grip. I'm almost climbing up on her like a zealous patriot lusting up the Statue of Liberty. As she's holding up the glossy white shoes, people continue to go by, passersby, Loop walkers, housewife shoppers; looking for the out-of-season white sales in all the department stores. Everything WHITE, electric WHITE, is being sold in pairs of seven—seven anything you can think of, seven shoes, three pairs and an extra one for the good luck seven brings—is on a huge LIMITED HURRY HURRY WHITE SALE WHITE SALE LADIES DAY TODAY FREE PARKING IN THE LOOP!!! The honking horns! Hilda's at my ear screaming, having left the white Cadillac still blocking traffic: *"Make her listen!"* But Anita's whimpering, as she licks the white-painted leather, murmuring, "Oooooooooh gosh."

Anita kicks off her shoes, Hilda begins to click her tongue, *"Tut tut—"* and she quotes Swift: "She looks as if butter wouldn't melt in her mouth." But I don't get it, at first, until I detect the critical look of one woman *at* another. Anita's wonderland-like solar system continues to protect her from communication as she wallows in the possessive lust for the new footwear she is slipping into, saliva dripping from her mouth. She stands on one bare foot, holding a shoe in each hand, her left leg bent, she forces the tight shoe on, drops her foot, stands on it, repeats the process with the other one, drooling as she steps back in order to see herself reflected in the showcase glass, and I simply stand here dumbfounded, watching also the footlights reflected in her eyes; but when I look at the actual display window I can't see anything theatrical.

People are pouring out of cars, coming toward Hilda. Time and space are being mastered—all this takes place twenty-one times faster than anyone is ready to think. "What's the matter with her, has she let all this whitewash advertising all this bullshit drive her insane?" snaps Hilda, looking more each minute like the great entertainer Pearl Bailey standing there with that "Now, ain't dat somethin'!" look on her bulletproof kisser. A man with UPPER-INCOME stamped on the front of his white shirt, unobstructed by his necktie, socks Hilda dead in the money signs in her eyes. Some of the stars are so phenomenal they crash into me, as they shoot out from the blow. It seems to be done in slow motion, because I can almost count the stars. And he's bitching: "Lady driver! Lady driver! Lady driver!" and right in rhythm to his words Hilda bounces, still on her feet, around and around like a punching bag, in a purple dress. Anita moves a little north on the pavement, just as the shoe salesman comes out, rubberneck style. His cry: *"How do you know they fit?"* But Anita, always on her p's and q's, seems tickled *chocolate* and privileged to inform him: "Because they fit." And I, like some kind of link in a fragment of conversation, say, "If." Meanwhile forty-two men with the same sign, UPPER-INCOME, attached to them, work in groups of seven, piledriving the weights of their frustrations from urban leisure, down, down, down on the beaten down purple, screeching form of what still looks like Hilda, despite the blood. I am outraged: I charge toward them. I hit an invisible wall, bounce off and fall on the sidewalk at Anita's new shoes, that, like twins, suddenly turn their toe-tips just enough to look me in my morally defeated eyes; seeing my tramp version of manhood, they say to me, "Motherfucker, we should kick you in yo ass-ss! Git over dah and help dat woman!" I feel deep shame, knowing the shoes are correct. "You jus gone lay dah and let dem hunkies strike lightnin' in dat sister's head?" Hilda, at my eye level, on the ground, only a few steps away, is calmly trying to pacify my four centuries of guilt, spitting out blood and teeth with her words, "Don't worry—*we shall overcome!* Remember the mighty words of

Wendell Philips: 'Physical bravery is an animal instinct; moral bravery is a much higher and truer courage.' " But it's no consolation. I even see Moke in one of the groups of seven, he's grinding his fist into his palm, impatiently waiting for his group's turn. I leap up, try to penetrate the wall again; but Anita's hand grabs my shoulder. "Listen, nigger, you're my nigger; where you think you're going? You gone pay for this shit, what'd you think you're for, anyway, *huh,* tell me, *huh*? You see this man standing here waiting for his money, *give* it to him. He ain't got all day, the stuff he wants makes the world go 'round." But my attention is split between Hilda's assassination and Anita's demand.

With one last, fleeting glance over my shoulder toward the ritual killing, I see that a young man—it's Frank Engelmeyer!—has a vending cart around his neck, walking among the groups of angry drivers who are purchasing armbands from a runaway boy. Anita has taken out my wallet; meanwhile, I see each group is getting a name, labeling itself. All the names seem to ring a bell but I don't know why. I have a mental block. The armbands are blazing and glowing in the daylight, in natural colors of red, blue, and yellow: names like *Seven Champions, Seven Sages of Greece, Seven Bishops, Seven Against Thebes, The Seven Wise Masters,* and so on; while police whistles and traditional police voices are blasting up and down State Street; I simply glance once, take it in—all of them have their backs turned to the seven years' war against Hilda, on the sidewalk in a pool of mysterious-looking blood that's beginning to clot into thousands of groups of corpuscles that jump around in a kind of war dance, chanting.

The shoe salesman meanwhile seems disgusted, waiting, facing Anita with his hand extended, palm up; trying again to be profound, saying, "It doesn't matter that they are not specifically meant to be *crutches,* but what kind of currency is this?" She, so fascinated by her new shoes, looking down at them, turning this way and that, trying to see them from all angles, hasn't glanced at the money she places in his hand. I slap myself upside the head—Wham! "I forgot to tell you, Anita—" *"Tell me what, nigger?"* she hisses. I scrape my feet and bow a little to her. She shoots these words at me, the ABCs clogging up my resistance. The shoe salesman says, "I think he's trying to tell you—" She chops off his sentence in midair: "Just shut the fuck up and let the nigger tell me himself! That's why he's standing here acting like a damn fool now, 'cause you white men are always trying to speak for him!" Now, specifically to me: "What is it, Eli, what'd you do wrong now, that you want me to forgive you for, huh?" Her mouth is twisted to the left side of her face as far as she can turn it. But the disgust, this time, isn't really as gigantic as I've seen it get in her, when I used to "stand her up" back in 1958, '59, '60, when I was a rather optomistic civil rights–minded student at Roosevelt and I wasn't shaping up to her image of what the TV told her a good potential husband ought to be. That mouth would twist, and that head would turn, and she'd growl viciously, speechless with rage.

"It's the money—" the shoe salesman says. He's holding it toward her. I suddenly feel exposed. "DIDN'T I JUST TELL YOU TO KEEP YOUR DAMN MOUTH SHUT? Huh, didn't I? *He can talk*—" I take a deep breath. The things of Hilda's resurrected blood, on the warpath, are seeping into the skin-pores of the groups of men standing around the remains of her body. They are bloodcurdling as they sting each one of these decent, upstanding, smart-looking, proficient assassins, with something instant-acting and deadly!

I'm trying to get my words out as the bodies behind me fall out, like tin cans from an overloaded garbage bin going *clang,* each one marked up as a "natural accident" by the score-keeping Cosmic Energy Platoon of the resurrected Blood of the Lamb. I'm really astonished that I can take all of this action in a glimpse. All the more amazing because I never went to perception school. Just took what came naturally. "Anita, I meant to tell you . . ." I hesitate, scratch my bushy hair. "I got my *own kinda* money." "*What? What* the fuck are you talking about, nigger?" She looks for the first time at the fourteen paper bills she had placed in the boot-sniffer's hand. *"What in hell is this?"* she shouts. *"Booker T. Washington!"* Old Booker's gentle face looks up at her from the one-dollar bill on top. Where George Washington used to be, Booker calmly occupies the half-oval of the center of the Federal Reserve note; across the top, just as usual, is THE UNITED STATES OF AMERICA, and to the left of the old mediator, "THIS NOTE IS LEGAL TENDER FOR ALL DEBTS, PUBLIC AND PRIVATE." Anita's eyes stretch! For one iota of a second I think she's going to scream, spit on, and tear up the little stack of money in her hand, the next instant, it's clear. She's going through the bills furiously: "Eli, what is this bullshit? Huh? Where'd you get all this shit from, baby, come on, tell me, I'm getting sick! Just look at this crap—George Washington Carver on a two-dollar bill! Little Black Sambo—I guess that's who this is, isn't it?—on a five-dollar bill. *This is too much!* When I get myself together and start laughing, I know I'll never stop! Now—who—is—this?" She looks up sharply. I try to duck the bullets of her eyes, but she shoots me, and her words too come like radioactive fallout, hitting me like a volley of doorknobs, squarely in the ears. She's holding the face of the paper note toward me. The white man is in shambles with gut-laughter, losing his, up until now, firmly maintained cool. He slows up, chokes himself a little, cocking his ear toward me, waiting for the name to drop off my tongue. "It's *Willie,* you know, the guy who used to be in the movies." The shoe salesman is kicking over, choked with laughter; he falls against the wall of the building, holding his gut, the graceless spirits of his amusement leaping up out of him, in the form of lumpy little devils like the clergy used to chase around in the Middle Ages with butterfly nets. Anita is overcome. She is trying to hold back the urge to crack up. But she isn't going to make it. At this very moment I notice a blind white man coming up State from the intersection of Canal, wearing a wooden display-board on his chest, suspended from his neck. The message, obviously printed with the care given to a majestic and precious keepsake:

HEAR YE! HEAR YE! HEAR YE!
——Get Your Favorite Tattoo——
TODAY!
Engraved handsomely on any part
of your body! No Holds Barred!
We Will Make Permanent Designs
Of Anything, Person, Or Place
On The Most Secret Parts of
Your Skin!!!
Come to:
JOE'S TATTOO SHOP
& Amusement Center

777 S. State
Open 9 A.M. til 5 P.M.
Suggestions:
1) Those who were born without
mothers, have your own favorite
mother *tatu*ed on your heart!
2) Those who survived Vietnam,
have the symbol of Patriotism
indelibly stamped on your forehead—
or if you prefer, Joe will
imprint his own original invention
of victory and national pride, the
word "MANTEIV"
Which really means Superman spelled
backwards, on one or both cheeks
of your posterior—
FOR THE LOW LOW PRICE
of just $7 per
etching!
****

WITHOUT DOUBT!!! THE LOWEST BEST
PRICE IN TOWN!! FAST WORK
BY A SKILLED ARTIST
62 years in
practice.
MONEY BACK GUARANTEED IF NOT
COMPLETELY SATISFIED!!!
****

***

PLEASE COME IN TODAY YOU WILL
NEVER REGRET THE MOVE!

!Surprise & Delight Your Friends!
——Endless Possibilities!——
"painless & fast healing, etc."

And as Anita goes insane with the wildest, bloodthirstiest kind of mad-mad scientist cackle I have ever heard, letting my new money float from her hand, I suddenly remember why I came downtown. I wanted to get a souvenir of my military pain, just a little token of my antiheroic commitment to what I was doing over there: just for myself, purely personal classified information. Anita and the shoe salesman are still laughing. I can see them, reflected in a trick mirror across the street on the side of the triple-deck Loop parking lot, and she's fat as the Tahitian whore who propositioned me at the foot of a hill in San Francisco the day before I shipped out for the Far East, in 1961.

I stoop, pick up my empty wallet, and bursting through the pack of side-walkers and traffic-gazers, weaving my way through the excitement-seekers, I catch up with the blind man with the advertisement. Several men from the Department of Sanitation are scraping up the last drops of Hilda, as whole squads of ambulances pull up and speed away in vain, with the stacked-up bodies of all those first-class citizens who died natural American deaths. I touch the old, smelly, white port–reeking fragment of a man who surprises the shit out of me when he turns, facing me, the whole surface of his face falling forward, a thin slab, dry and neat, like a little door, and it's actually on hinges. In it, on a flat, smooth, white slate-surface, printed neatly in black letters, are these words:

WHH BOP SH BAM
WHHBLYOP
WHH BOP SH BAM
WHHBLYOP

And though I was born through these sounds, the character of the message and the specific location of the scripture are still unknown.

COPS

There were always things coming to take my mind off Cathy.

I got home and found a business card between the door and the frame. The unimpressive odor of gum benzoin in the air. The holy smokers and the camouflage. My building was a 46th and Calumet collage of beautiful nameless people, but this fucking card! I took it into the light of my place.

James Harth. Detective. Chicago Police Department.

Scribbled on the back in an emotional style: "Would like to see you, Mr. Bolton, at your earliest convenience." There was a telephone number. The swift hard realization that troubles were *always* coming smashed into my intelligence and destroyed a few ounces of my youth. This shit! In spite of happiness there would always be the ripple in the water.

Recklessness, courage, and the anger of my youth guided my hand to the telephone.

A woman's sleepy, settled voice: "Harth's residence." In my fear, seeing elements that were possibly not there. This bullshit!

"Mr. Harth, please."

"Who's calling?"

Looking at, without seeing them, a bunch of dead flowers in a large blue vase on the coffee table.

"Eli Bolton."

"Just a moment."

I slid down on the couch now, wishing I had made a drink before dialing.

I heard his voice, husky, slow; "Mr. Harth, you left a card in—"

"Oh, yes, Mr. Bolton, I'd like to see you as soon as possible."

"About what, Mr. Harth?"

"I'd rather not discuss it on the phone."

"I'm free tomorrow until around one or two."

"Could I see you first thing in the morning—say nine o'clock?"

"Let's make it around noon, Mr. Harth."

"Of course, Mr. Bolton. At noon, at your place. And thanks for calling."

I could hear the *fireworks* outside.

He was a big handsome black man in a dark blue, perfectly cut suit. There was another man with him, brown skinned, shorter, well dressed also, and after Harth introduced himself, he introduced, "Joe Wills. We work together."

We shook hands. "Have a seat."

Wills sat in the armchair, Harth on the couch; I was at the other end. I felt very stable.

"Mr. Bolton," began Detective Harth, "we simply want to ask you a few questions. It won't take long."

How does a tightrope walker feel when he knows he cannot fall?

"Go right ahead."

"We understand that you work for Gould's Drugstore and Fountain Service."

"Yes."

"How long have you worked there, Mr. Bolton?"

"About a month."

"What did you do before that?"

"I was in service. Why?"

"Were you working there August fifteenth?"

"Yes—I think so . . . Yes, in fact that was the day I started."

"On that Wednesday night did you talk with a white man named James Sheraton?"

"Who?"

"James Sheraton."

"Did you talk with him?" asked Wills.

"I don't—*I mean*—are you asking me about a customer? I really don't know very many names."

"Have you read in the papers about the death of a white man out here on the South Side?" asked Harth.

"Oh yes. Yes, I did read that—"

"Did you ever meet that man?"

"If I have I couldn't say—I mean I couldn't say for sure. Thousands of faces, you know how it is."

"We have a report that you talked with this man while you were at work, on the night he was killed."

Now was the time to wade in, to really lend the show beauty. I said, "*Now* I remember! Yes—there was an old drunk man Brogan threw out that night. *And* it was on the night I started, too. Oh, I get the connection!" I acted really surprised. "That old man was the man the papers said got stabbed on 47th Street?"

"That's right."

"Did you talk long with him?" asked Wills.

"He was pretty drunk. He was raving, you know—almost fell off the stool two or three times."

"Uh huh." Harth went on: "Can you remember *anything* he said?"

"No. I don't think so. *Oh, yes!* He was saying something about his mother being a black woman. The druggist threw him out—"

"Yes, we know."

"Did you see Sheraton anytime *after* that?"

"No, I didn't."

"What time did you get off?"

"Twelve o'clock."

"According to the coroner's report the death took place around twelve-thirty in the morning."

"And incidentally, not far from *here*," said Wills. "Up the street, near the El station."

They sat silently watching me as I went across the room and fixed myself a scotch, without offering them any. Returned to the couch and sat on its arm.

Then the question that almost stopped my heart came: "Would you have any objections to coming with us to the station and having our witness take a look at you?"

Perhaps almost too quickly I stood up, trying to look both cheerful and innocent, but unable to hide my annoyance.

"Of course I'll come."

They stood up and both smiled twin, Tomish smiles, at the same time. However, Harth's face seemed kindly tolerating some huge personal misery, but Wills's was an abstract.

In the car I asked, "Wasn't there a confession?"

"You may have read that," Harth said.

The mystic squad car rolled with the punches. The metal congested jungle, a bitch! a whore!

Was a black man always a renegade or what in hell was going on in this society? I looked beyond the dirty automobile window at the tough black kids on the sidewalk, happy and jumping. Twenty years from now what would they be into? What would White America be into? *Darnu? Fataki? Moto?* The *kutia maji* was already on us!

The three of us went into a side room. Beside a white man who was writing behind a desk there was a pitiful little black woman with a sagging, worn-out face; she had the blue sightless fading eyes of an old dog. Her cotton dress was flowered and baggy, she wore old run-over flat shoes.

There was a malevolent air about this little room. The horrible rituals that must have taken place here! The quality of a human system of control designed to humanize itself, not succeeding. The room smelled of it.

Harth quickly stepped to her side.

"Mrs. Jones, is *this* the man—you saw standing near the body of the dead man, James Sheraton?"

Detective Wills was beside me, and for one wild moment out of the animalism of human nature I wanted to run. Somehow my cool was smothering the fear in my gutters, plus the scotch had me nice, so I stood still and looked her squarely in the mirror of her life without blinking an eye.

The men in the room all watched her as I watched her, and she slowly began shaking her head from side to side. "No," she said. "No, he was *bigger*—"

"Are you sure, Mrs. Jones?" the white man said.

"Yes, I'm sure he was a *larger* man," she said, thoughtfully sucking her gums. "Larger shoulders, and he was considerably darker than him. This man."

Perhaps a natural gambler, I had counted on this ambiguous moment of weird luck.

I pronounced my anger in my tone. "May I go now?"

"Sure, Mr. Bolton!" said Harth.

"Thank you, Mrs. Jones," said the seated man, who bent and continued to write. "One of the patrolmen will drive you home. See the sergeant at the front desk."

Harth and Wills followed me out, maintaining silence until we reached the front.

"Thank you for your trouble," Harth said. "Don't get lost, we may want to talk to you again, soon . . ."

That's what you think. I turned and walked out of the old building, the heat hitting me squarely in the face. This vicious place dripped with the spirit of too much of my blood. Fuck, I needed to be happy! I *wanna be happy* . . .

I hailed a taxi on Michigan Boulevard, fell back into the seat, loosened my tight shirt—feeling intensely free!

. . . and in need of Cathy!

CATHY

I was sitting in the window studying the minute texture of icicles hanging on the other side from the frame. A sparrow, on the ledge outside, was scratching down through the snow, possibly to pick a worm from the rotten wood. Everything outside was completely covered with a blanket of soft snow. In my hand was a glass of burgundy, and Cathy, dressed in a simple cotton shirt and jeans, sat on the floor with her face against my knee; her hand gently moving around my knee, her soft, chubby, snow-white pinkish fingers silently engaged in the secret writing of what I dreamed of as love codes.

Downstairs, we could hear Alma, another Volunteer in Service to America, singing and washing her click-clack-ting-a-ling dishes. She could hit the bottle all night, and never wake up with a hangover. We could also hear the TV spouting one of the midafternoon soap operas. The stillness. Such a lazy, beautiful, severe moment: emulsified by my happiness and intense love for Baby. She was already slightly tipsy; her empty glass with its mouth facing the door lay near her thigh. The colors in the dim room kept changing from greens to purples to deep reds to neutrals, and she affected each change—her brilliant, shimmering loveliness, her gentle silent, sometimes indigo sometimes ultramarine-charged-with-zinc white eyes!

I ached deep in my loins for the possession of her: to take her, truly enter her, to feel the walls of her softness cling to me, to slowly sink down into her compactness, to open her, release her, turn away her fears and doubts, chase out the drifting but frigid nightmares. To go beyond simply petting, giving in to her fears, to stop washing my psyche with booze, to stop getting high as a substitute.

"Cathy O?"

"Yes."

"Oh, baby . . ."

"What is it?" Her eyes became bright lazuli, charged with concern, as she got to her knees, closer.

"I want you so—the feeling is eating me up inside. I'm aching with the need."

She took a deep breath, and turned away. "I . . . I *told* you."

"You told me *what?*"

"I'm frigid." An expression as innocent as a bird's. "You wouldn't enjoy it; it would just frustrate you. Make you hate me."

We had been sleeping together for at least two weeks now and each night when I tried to penetrate her, she experienced *acute vaginismus!* She wanted to succeed, to have me make her feel, as Aretha Franklin would later sing, *"like a natural woman . . ."* And from the radio, softly, *"I've got sunshine . . . on a cloudy day . . . When it's cold outside . . . I've got the month of May,"* somebody sang.

"Baby—just *try,* that's all I ask."

"I have *tried.* You *know* I've tried."

I look outside—the bird stops clearing back the snow and looks up sideways, at me, to see if I plan to pull any shit on him. I am too happy to be disgusted, but the throbbing, oh the inner slow motion of my desire!

She continued, "You remember . . . I told you about the time when I was sixteen? The fifty-year-old man. Well, I really *wanted* him to. He couldn't get it in, and yet he came closer than anybody. Even closer than the boy I told you about, Willy, who I really think I used to love. Maybe I still love him, and that's why I'll have to go back to Berkeley, among other reasons—to find out. Do you believe it's possible to love two people at the same time?"

"Yes." I feel very helpless. "So, you're a virgin?"

"If you can call it that . . . When I was—I think I was seventeen—Willy tried. He came up to the house, it was a Saturday. They were gone; and I had finished feeding the chickens, and had put the horse out to pasture. I guess I told you—we always had animals. Our place is up in the mountains, a very small town. Anyway, Willy tried, he was very rough. He hurt me very badly—I couldn't walk for about a week, but he never got in; he just bruised me. I know I should have psychoanalysis, but . . . I don't know—maybe I'll end up a nun." Her smile is very self-deprecating. "You know, I used to dream of becoming a nun . . ."

"But not any more?"

The primary colors beneath the surface of her skin came intensely forward. "Sometimes . . . even now, I think about it . . ."

I stood up, forcing her to move; I sat deep in a sad corner of the faded couch. Cathy continued to stand there, on her knees, the swell of her maiden stomach so lovely it caused me to catch my breath quickly, while speculating on it. The finite risk in these moments, the stakes. Her fingers had come together, her arms a V, ending at the tightly covered area of her virgin vault. Something so hazy and yet so clear refracted all the way from the invisible sun, from the clouds, from the snow, brought out the precious accident of that moment; she turned slowly, a lull so casual and yet so crammed with *all* that she was, invited me adventitiously—she wasn't aware of it herself perhaps—into her, to sow, to instigate her first and finest harvest. I felt comfortable with my thoughts, they seemed so reliable. The best thoughts, like the best feelings, are always born passionately—especially compassion itself. I felt it for her, this moment profoundly, and later, and always.

"Come here, Cathy."

She came over slowly; obedient, quiet; her bare feet I watched. The big toe moved as she stood contingently, innocently before my patient judgment.

I was thinking, when she had talked about her stepfather it had always been with great reservation, spliced by superficial self-defensive arguments. To be completely fair, however, I have to admit that she was sometimes astonishingly objective and elegantly honest.

Her expression was ineffable.

I took her hands, and she settled—despite her awkwardness—very sumptuously at my knee, sitting on the floor; she rested her engaging face against my knee, again. The agreeable prodding of her symmetrical fingers dancing against the rough cloth of my wash 'n' wear trousers. In the simplicity of this affectionate incident I experienced an absorbing and comparatively bounteous reaction of compassion for her, as I have said—the quietness, the generosity of her modest beauty enriched my prodigal soul; I even knew, in those chaste and seemingly trivial, lazy moments together like this, that some of my own most buoyant, unparalleled, enormous and elongated memories of the most passionate happiness I have ever known and will ever know were being psychically inhaled, attained so naturally. We were now so quiet together; the delicate "sounds" of our silence, its intense message held the moment static: to make it last forever. Not even the sounds of traffic outside. The tweet-tweet of the bird outside the window, his pledge. Our promise to ourselves . . .

I stood, reached down and carefully picked her up, carried her easily slowly . . . through our musty old apartment to the chaotic bedroom and gently let her down onto the bed. I tried to unzip her pants but she held my hand. Her fearful eyes—so restful a moment ago—were filled with unreasonable diffidence. "I could never hurt you, baby; I love you." I felt dauntless. My voice was thick.

Finally, when I sat down, having given up, my mind sympathetic to her very real problem, I noticed her fumbling with her zipper until she took off her own jeans, and lay quietly trembling in the darkness. Her sobbing and gentle breathing, the waves of music from the radio. *"Whenever I'm afraid, I whistle a happy tune, so no one will suspect I'm afraid,"* sang some woman. This daytime darkness, its undertoned richness, was very common in our bedroom. I carefully stroked her stomach; then lower, running my electric-charged fingers through her damp, soft, already convulsive bush, feeling her currents and spasms, her wet substance. I parted her shadowed damp lips, but they retracted instantly; so, my fingers placidly stroked her also instantly but more violently alarmed clitoris. Her hands rested on her stomach, poised ready to push me away. I was on one elbow, only half on the bed.

Suddenly I stood up and undressed completely; beside her, I took off her blouse and bra.

Trying to enter her, as usual, was critical—seemingly impossible. She retracted *but! for the first time!* she seemed to be successfully relaxing, as I pampered her, coaxingly, lying on my side, I turned her on her side enough to see both her eyes. I prayed to myself that my own calmness was cogent medicine for her uneasiness. I parted her thighs—they were so stiff—so that I could move in closer; the woman smell of her, as I stroked her shoulder, the deep curve of her back down to the expandingly beautiful cheeks of her firm, but fantastically soft, cushiony ass, down the polarity of her equally sturdy, equally soft thighs; slowly, one at a time; meanwhile, listening to her breathing as a guideline, and a pacesetter; thinking about the slow, sensuous movements of her hips, her legs, the rhythms of her arms, the graceful tilt of her chin, the projection of her bust, that very subjective, beatific, and feminine mystic look in her eyes, when she was simply walking along at my side, the easiest, most natural thing in the world to do! She held very tightly to me. Her legs clutching my back. Her mouth, dry, opened, like a bird in the sun all day and finally, our tongues together, we bit gently at each other's flesh. Warm, radical, delectable colors rippling through my mind. I felt the beginning of *delirious* fulfillment. Waves of excitement mounted in me as I buried my face in the valley of her full warm breasts; her softness, her absorbing moisture, her genital mystery engulfed the thick swollen loneliness of myself. Shooing away the bats, the scarecrows, the Warden and everything! And my false impression of white pussy! and frigidity!

But she was still slightly tense. (She never got over it *completely*, except occasionally, when high, later in New York.)

Afterward, we looked at the bed with the light on. Amazed, she ran her fingers inside her cunt, and held them up to the light. *Blood!*

"It's not the same color as my period."

She went into the bathroom, and closed the door. This was an important moment for her. I lay there, listening and waiting for her to return. How really deeply satisfying her cunt had been!

The second time, when we finished, there was no blood . . .

I slept. A deer was jumping over a dead log. Had I seen that in *a movie?* Each time it jumped it paused directly over the log. Then, with the firearm I used in Vietnam I shot him, and like one of those toys you shoot at in a carnival to win a prize, he fell over, flat. A green substance, like chloride, dripped from the wound.

Two days later:

. . . For the first time I'm getting really into Cathy's delicate, tense, *ekundu-eupe* cunt, the sweet tight valley of its fruit, I taste with the strong end of my velvet-tipped, busy tongue, we are at last deep in a frenzy, slimy with our own juices, in the big bed, here in the darkness, the winter coolness, her large clean smooth cheeks, I hold wide apart, she is meanwhile nibbling at the glossy head of my screwdriver, this *bisifisi* object new in her mouth, in her virgin body. I have her going for *the* first time, really relaxing, her oven is tense with pleasure under the prodding of my persistent tongue, and she is twisting, her hole forming an O, it is so tense with the pleasure, the *shimo ma* of her so beautiful! I watch it, watch the pussy *bokoboko* flow out, a fruit ripe with the intensity of my expert masterwork, the nest of her—about to give birth to a vast!—choking—bubbling fluid *ass deluge!* I can tell, the outer lips are puckered, swollen tense, she is groaning—her other mouth accidentally biting my dick in excitement; her sheath is jerking in spasms!—her buttocks can't stay restful. She dislodges my member from her mouth. *Fimbo!* Too much for her, at last—!

I'm going very gently, now, knowing that it is too much to take lightly. I let my tongue simply glide over the silky surface of her stiff clitoris, the lips are still so tense that I know too much pressure from me would make her jump out of her golden age, her honey days, her palmy age.

I hold her ass (*punda*) as it is trembling in *so* much ecstasy.

Meanwhile, I am becoming irritated and annoyed with her because she has completely forgotten my selfish and lonely, throbbing *cokke*. The fluid flows smoothly down the pink crack of her *matako*; I'm not going to let her stop me *this* time—

I'm going to carry her—

carry her all the way—

all the way to the end. The end of herself. Into herself! Where she will empty into her first complete orgasm.

It continues to pour out: slow, steady, this surf, the streaming rapids; and naturally we are lying in a 69 position that allows me to enjoy the bubbling of her ebb. She is overflowing! I'm intensely happy for her! It delights me, though my serpent is down there near her cheek, not even caressed by her hand, hard as a bull's nose, neglected.

NOW!

It happens—her ass! It *jumps* out of control! She is kicking—

pushing me away, she is trembling, her feet are stabbing at my shoulders, an animal cry of unrefined and deep pleasure, of essence itself, lifts from her dry, choked mouth (I know what is happening, in a way, but can a man really know the nature of a female orgasm?).

The last of the suds, now stopping, just one drop, one more, her large pink ass fighting me away, as I hold gently but firmly to finish her, as she fights and pumps, the hard muscles of her stomach flexing; I feel them, getting it all out, down to the last soft, silent stream, and now—I move my dripping tongue back just a little, to watch her whole pussy, the hair, the lips, moving in and out like the gills of some water creature, and her soft ass still jumping—jerky—from the nervous exhaustion . . .

I lie down, in the still coolness of the morning, upon the dark bed beside Cathy, who is sleeping very soundly. It is almost daybreak; the worst hour in the world has gone by, and I survived it: I am still breathing. I am *not* lonely. I feel the comfort of her closeness. There are only the sounds of the night, muffled. The city out there, being milked by the mystic revolutionaries, despite God's coming, for collateral.

Our lovemaking was like a rite in a hungry hour of ritual. A cycle we needed. Grateful, now: we are transformed. The entrance behind us, yet before us.

Gently, I take her into my arms, and she, like a comfortable babe not even waking up while she's handled, comes in her sleep snug against me. Her hot sleeping lips part, the kiss. The taste of night. Of Cathy, her warm sturdy flesh. Our legs lock, our sex coming together, hot.

I know I will go mad when she leaves me.

We've made a home, of sorts. Also, we've made plans to fly to New York, to live on the Lower East Side, among the hippies. We're both sick of this big hick town. We ache to get to New York! Right now, Cathy is at Father Flexner's parish, explaining that she is resigning from VISTA; tonight she will write to Washington to make it official. I've been very happy possessing her here. I love even the sour taste in her mouth in the morning; I love her untidiness—even the holes in her shoes. She never upstages me during lovemaking, and there isn't a woman alive who cannot upstage a man. We make love a lot, I sleep a lot and dream a lot.

I hear the music of a sad room, it has a telescreen in it, like in George Orwell's *1984*. I twist the knob, the wall slides back, and back. Then, a garden with peach trees appears, blossoms falling, and the screen holds, for a moment, Cathy's eyes; the screws in the side of the slot are slowly working their way out of the threads. In the wrong direction. Now, the wall closes on her—and the peach tree goes up in smoke. Like a jinni. I take things to measure other things with. Sometimes I have to laugh at myself. I can imagine giving Cathy a child, and she'd kill it, but if she *weren't* successful, I can hear her out there in the impartial spaces of the future reading *Winnie the Pooh* to him, or to her, while I'd speak to him, saying, "The time will come when even little animals will be poisoned, the trees will die, the ground will cave in, and the air you and I breathe will kill us"; he will laugh and ask, "Will we be dead then, Daddy? Really dead, like bad guys on TV?" and I will speak softly of the myths, and of manhood, and especially of his black history; but what is it, he will ask, "What *is* death?" And I will be able to think of nothing but the fact that there is more water on earth than there is land, and not know the answer to anything. Last night, again, I dreamed of my mother, Elizabeth Mamzazi; poor Liz, she stood on a rooftop in these slums and sang a madwoman's song, clad in a large black Spanish hat, with Renaissance jewelry, in the summer warmth, the day choked by industrialism, and they took her away in a wagon, and she was screaming at the sculptures along Michigan Boulevard. Her voice was very husky. When I was a very lonely child, very small for my age, when I was six years old, she used to talk to me about all the majestic cities she had visited, how they had sprawled out at her feet, all those friendly people laughing and enjoying her presence, her velvet silk voice, her beautiful clothes; the way she joined them in their native dances in the streets, all night, how she clapped to the music in their coliseums, how she strolled through thousands of gardens of trillions of beautiful ochre, lapis lazuli, vivid red, lilac, gaudy *vert*, snow white and brilliant red flowers all over those treasured cities in the classic days of her youth before the injustice, the penal presence of me, a fetus, in her no-longer-free womb. She used to make me very sad, narrating such sweet stories; nevertheless, I liked her best then. She could laugh very beautifully, with snow white teeth. Against her rich dark brown complexion, her mouth, like her blazing dark eyes, was so perfect. She would rub my stomach with her nose, and grunt, saying, "Who is a sad snorkeler, when I am a happy snorkeler?" The colors of my memory break, reshape. I don't like to remember the time she became impatient, screaming, "I wish you were dead! I wish you'd never been born! I'm in a prison because of you!" And the time she stuck me with thorns she had saved from one of the gardens she visited. I allowed them to carry her away, though, for a long time, and I didn't think about her. Cathy was enough. I don't think about her now, not seriously. The dreams don't really bother me: she's harmless, unless I feel very low. She doesn't try to hurt me unless I hurt myself. My father never comes at the same time Mamzazi does. They are not in harmony. Black Ouranous? I could see him less clearly. Once, Steve, the boy who ran away from the orphanage, was with me, leading me to my father. Somehow, Cathy catches up with us. Her feet are wet, holes in her shoes, and the first thing she says is, "I don't deserve your love; I'm just coming along for the ride. Tell me to go back, and I'll return . . ." But before I can say anything we're overwhelmed by the presence of a gloomy house, at the edge of a forest. Strange—it is in Vietnam. The hills, I recognize, right away. Cathy is *shrinking* from fright. She's wearing the type of lace-up boots tiny *Alice* wore. Steve and I peer into the window of the spooky house; there is an old man who is saying, "Correct, correct, correct, correct"; he sounds like the keys of a typewriter. Meanwhile, Cathy has vanished. Strange that I thought nothing of her sudden transformation. Almost as though I had always known it would happen. The old man is in a wheelchair. "He's your father," says Steve. "Oh, no," I hiss, wheeling back from the window. "*My* father is young—handsome—strong—you forget I'm Kronos!" Steve says, 'I don't give a gnat's ass if you're the man in the moon; you asked me to lead you to your old man, and this is the cat—" and the paralyzed old man sings, "Correct, correct, correct, correct." I turn away. I push Steve, knocking him against a bush. He falls as I skid across the grass, jumping, my arms outstretched, my shirt blowing behind me in the wind the way it used to do, running track at Paulson. I run straight through progressions of space into Chicago, into the basement of the restaurant in which I took a job in August, smack into a brick wall. BLAM! The very white nude form of this woman screams, then realizes that I'm blind, rushes to me, throws her arms around me; I think, *"Mother!"* A cold-turkey trembling, how did I get goofed down here? trapped beneath the gray cement, the pavement, with no exit? What is going on up there? I feel her hands struggling with my eyelids, trying to open them, and she's sobbing. *"Oh, you poor black bastard, oh you poor poor thing you, I love you I love you I love you I love you I love you."* But I can't see her, nor even smell her breath, the odor of the fungus basement is too rich everywhere. And yet, I'm happy that my sight is coming back. Cracks, already, to peek from. I run my hands over her soft naked body. I know the curves, they're my woman's curves. Her breathing is close. She's grabbing painfully at my face, her fingernails are stubs, they are gentle. She is insanely blowing her breath into my mouth, trying to create man. The lights come on; I am *in* Cathy: our mouths are together. "It's too hot to sleep, baby; I'm going out." She never answers, so I won't wait for her answer. Down to ol' Roosevelt University I go; it is three o'clock in the morning, and I am not sure why I am here but shit I must have lost something. Something I thought I needed. I have busted open a dozen or more lockers before I wheel around and—spaces with sounds, objects in them, moving as my ax still echoes through the building; running down the hall, three nude girls investigating the night. They are nameless witches, playing games with me. Yet, I know them, they move in my context; I can even, at this distance, smell their pussies. Have known those odors. Now—they are singing from some room into which they've just sunk. I put down the ax. *"Here we go 'round the mulberry bush the mulberry bush the mulberry bush so early—"* The gas lines everywhere have busted, the swivel of the flood into new gutters being swiftly dug to combat it. But what really puzzles me is, Who are these moonstruck bitches? I'm aware suddenly that I must get my black ass to work, or else. I'm in the basement, again, *Alice's* Wonderland; I open my fly, exposing my "flower" to Wayne, here in the dark dampness, and the water is steadily rising. My feet are soaking wet in my shoes; I sneeze every minute but Wayne's large, powerful purple lips carefully engulf all of me, the entire length of my silky black dictator and both of my balls, rolling the appendage skillfully around in his powerful muscular orifice, before me on his knees, unconcerned that he is soaking from his thighs down; I'm constantly being distracted from the thrills he's causing to move in shock waves all through me, by the large cracking sounds of flames licking at walls, miscellaneous basement walls of the psyche; people don't know it, but the riots are in full session in the streets; the recorders of the *action* think the fight is still at a normal pace. I hear the dicks shooting with the phenomenal authority of the Foggy Bottom; the suicide of ideas jumps into affirmative graves; popular quotations jump out of squad cars with submachine guns and fire stolen *akido akido akido* into EVERYBODY! Wayne isn't going to get my nut—I'm too far from his action. Cathy and I really drink a lot, mostly wine. When we can, we smoke, for those kinds of rhythms. But the booze, gushing into our thirsty mouths, like the water out there, flooding everything, coming into the mind from the oceans of the world, fermented; the baptism of holy wine water, the distortions of our wet perceptions; I see my own body stand up from the deep hole of her scared cunt and fall headlong, splashingly into endless drunks, dropping down through structures, bottles, we fall over so many empty wine bottles; I am a moist animal, hairless like an alley rat worn from scraping in and out of holes; I fall blind, intoxicated, sick, happy sick, screaming joy and love, down through open mouths, booze gushing out, mouths that come; girls who suddenly come out of these bottles, our DTs, are sour mash striptease dancers like the soul sister we saw not long ago, infiltrating the juicy minds of night people with broken eyes, and flaming skulls; I also dream of fucking Cathy's roommate, if I'm drunk. The three of us—maybe it wouldn't shock Cathy, really. But as I begin to screw skinny Beth, in her own bed, she starts crying, and her sobs are so heartbreaking as she hugs a teddy bear to her side, obstructing my rhythm and hold on her, I cannot tolerate her tears. She throws me off; her pelvis bangs up at the wrong time, and destroys my pace. I have a weak, premature orgasm, and Cathy is holding my rod, trying to keep it hard, but makes no headway. Beth lifts up her swollen face, and asks, "What happened?" Why should we explain? But Baby says to Beth: "Watch this—" We demonstrate. I am trying to hump Baby in her milky snow white rump but the worldly head of my totem pole will not penetrate the circle of her sphincter. I feel like I'm high on something *really* forbidden! Tomorrow—is it tomorrow?—we're leaving for the coitus beach. White eyes will surely be murdered by our presence on the shadows of the moon. I am a missile, very fecundative—with Baby's feces left from the failure to demonstrate something new to Beth. I go into deep wells of rapid streams, into ocean bottoms, to wash the head of my dick. When I come back into the room, Beth is a big Diesel, humping a mighty piston to Baby, who's going, "Oh oh ah ah oh oh ah ah—" I sit down, alarmed and jealous. "What am I supposed to do—?" Beth looks at me, and very mechanically says, "I knew her first. Anyway, just to be nice I'll dress up very pretty and masturbate you with toothpaste in my mouth." Waiting for them to finish, I fall asleep and dream of Greta Garbo. Sometimes Cathy O looks like her. When is she to return? I am tempted to go to the track: to try to hit the Daily Double. Everything has gone wacky here at the track, the horses are being corralled, and injected intravenously with something that is changing them, because each one they release after the corralling dashes out onto the track like an insane animal, no, like a wild human being: that's it precisely. But I am here to win, so to hell with this sideshow. What is going on anyway, how come the third race hasn't started? A voice blurts over the loudspeaker: "A SHOW EQUAL IN GENTILITY TO THOSE STAGED BY THE GREEKS WILL NOW BEGIN. PLEASE DO NOT MISS THIS. THE THIRD RACE WILL IMMEDIATELY FOLLOW. MEANWHILE, WE NEED FEMALE VOLUNTEERS TO JOIN THE HORSES IN THE TRACK." I notice little guys in baggy suits are grabbing women at random and throwing them over the fence. Husbands and boyfriends are using their racing forms as baseball bats, weapons, in an effort to fight off the body snatchers, to retain their wives. I'm suddenly happy *I* didn't bring Cathy! "WE TRUST THAT MOST OF YOU PEOPLE KNOW WHAT A VIRILITY POTION IS? HEEHEEHEE," the voice snickers. "THIS NEW ABSOLUTELY REVOLUTIONARY DRUG EXTRACT CREATES IN ANIMALS HUMAN-ORIENTED DRIVE! IT IS THE MYSTERIOUS REVEREND SHEEN'S MOST DARING SCIENTIFIC DISCOVERY

TO DATE. HOWEVER, WE UNDERSTAND THAT HE IS ALSO BUSY, LIKE THE GOOD LITTLE MAD SCIENTIST THAT HE IS, WORKING ON SOMETHING THAT IS SUPPOSED TO CHANGE YOUR NOODLES FOR THE BETTER." People are stampeding the grandstand, the lower levels are also repetitions of furious bright discontent, fist fights, jabs, screaming, stabbings, and occasional shootings; thousands are trying to climb the gate, many have crossed the track and are wandering like fading spots across the grass. Yet, people are standing here, where I am trapped by the immobility of the mob, *watching* what is going on! I think about the poor horses, who have no marine biological information to rely on, the poor creatures do not know how to utilize helium, and are really going to be up shits creek very soon. Look how muddy the track is already: and rain is simply what is soaked up from the ocean by the sun. I see Jolene sailing through the air, her fat vein-streaked brown thighs working desperately for ground while lecherous gamblers lust at the sight that she has on no drawers, as she shrieks, indistinguishable from the other suddenly enslaved women. Well, women thought they were free: all this time, now the truth comes out. The stallions are tearing at the flesh of the human females, rolling them in the chunks of freshly turned earth. I see an exceptionally fine-looking horse, "Roy of Troy," who is using his long massive and slick pink piledriver in . . . *what? Who's that?!* It's impossible! It's Cathy! on hands and knees, hideously alarmed, trying to get up out of the mud as Roy of Troy whams it to her, straight into her bottom, prancing along, keeping pace with her revulsive and sad rhythms, as she vigorously tries to shake the mud and stand up; but Roy of Troy's industrious piston has a cadence that would break her back if she tried to stand! I jump straight up—with more stamina than I ever dreamed I had—without even wondering for one moment *how* Cathy got here. Or what Roy of Troy meant to me, to her, if anything. I must rescue her! The beast has ripped the backside of her jeans open; her snow white ass is completely black with mud as it trembles, activated by the sledgehammer. Up close, I hear Baby screaming like a male dog stuck in a bitch who is running wildly, being chased by a pack of wolves. Suddenly I realize I have no weapon. It would mean nothing to beat the horse with my fists. A lightbulb blinks above my head; *an idea!* I take off my belt and lasso the horse's firearm;

I buckle it, get a good grip and pull with all the strength I have—sliding through the mud, falling on my ass—furious. And when I realize that a strand of Cathy's hair is around my dick, causing the pressure that wakes me, this moment that I drift into sleep, in her, my meat going soft. But I am *not* asleep: Roy of Troy has a strange but familiar rider who has a mule face. Could it really be Churchy? I rib Jolene, standing beside me spotless and consumed by the gambler's itch, "He was in Vietnam with me." A pause. "The first splib I've seen working as a jockey." Jolene says, "He ain't no spook, baaa! What're you talking about? He's been racing in Florida." I suddenly hear little Bud Lemon's voice close to my ear: "Don't jump outta your skin—but it's me, your main man, lay it there—" His choppers are so twisted by bliss they look like an old-fashioned plow. We go—SLAP!—the palms of our hands together. "What's happening, Doosy, baby? Great seeing you—shit, this is really a moment to celebrate!" He chuckles. "Nice! Nice! But you better get over to the Daily Double window and put everything you got on Roy of Troy and this other horse, right here." The horse is called "Pal Black." "This is the only chance you'll ever have to play spades—two of them that's gonna cop the double in the first race, and pay like a motherfucker!" I really can't believe Bud's prediction. I'm sick of hunches. I introduce Jolene and Bud, and they begin to chew the rag as I go into the shoulders, between the skulls with sunglasses, peering at racing forms. Theoretically to buy a ticket, but Cathy shakes me and says, "Wake up—Eli, wake up." I turn into the pillow. "We're supposed to go to Orchestra Hall, to hear that lecture, remember?" Now, I sit up. I look at her, she *is* real. "When did you get back? How did Father Flexner react to your announcement?" Cathy goes and sits on a chair, turning completely red, just thinking about, confronting this question. Something so simple as this defeats her. Looking at her there, a pink dilemma in the greenish shadows of our stuffy room.

HAROLD

The suddenness of it was unsettling.

Anita stood up, a little nervous. I remained where I was sitting on the couch, watching his eyes. He had let himself in with a key and the metal was still in his hand.

"Hello Harold," Anita said.

He didn't answer but continued to gape at me as he closed the door. He seemed rapidly reaching a state of derangement. His big wet eyes enlarged. He was breathing with irregular force.

I could feel Anita's sudden tension, shock.

Blown up out of shape he came over; while looking at me he said to her, "Could I see you in the next room . . . for a minute?"

In her hesitation she looked at me; I could see her out of the corners of my eyes while watching him.

In an out-of-style hippydippy strut he went into the bedroom.

Slowly she went to the doorway of her chic bedroom and looked in, and even slower, after a complete theatrical stop she, like a death subject, vanished. Suddenly this grave triangle, myself, a reluctant spoke. I heard his voice subdued, demanding. Her sounds were weak, frightful. Then, the unending cracking flesh words scream *sock!* together.

I shot in.

Anita was on the rich floor holding her cracked face in her hands and sobbing. This weak Sambo half stood, was about to slap her. On his knees holding up her face.

"You bastard!"

By the time I had my arms locked under his and had him off the floor, I realized he had a switchblade knife out and was striking at my back but couldn't reach it. The motherfucker. I carried him, because I had to keep the knife in sight. I didn't want to get cut, naturally. I had him from the front. I took my chances and threw him outward but the blade got me on the side, across the ear and lower cheek; but it wasn't a very nasty cut after all.

He hit the floor and I rushed him, put one knee in his chest and one on the arm that extended into a weapon. Niggers fighting each other, always this shit I was thinking, sad shit. Briefly though. I took the wrist and twisted the arm around backward until the pain was too much; he dropped the streamlined light green object; the screaming of an exotic bird.

"*Quick!* Anita GET THE KNIFE!"

She already had it.

My fist broke the skin (possibly a bone) of the nose and opened the right eye. He struggled with his hands toward my throat. Blinded.

Anita somewhere near going, "Oh God!"

He got up hitting his head on the bed. I lost my balance too but got it back just in time. He was coming up ass-end facing me; I decided not to damage his nuts, so aimed my blow higher on his ass. A sense of humanity.

His head went floorward.

I had kicked a boy's ass when I was twelve years old on the Paulson playground, and I had had my ass kicked there, too; but this was the first naked primitive fistfight I had had since then.

From the floor I picked up Anita's key and stumbled over to her, placing it in her hand.

With excessive energy I took the cat by the back of his suit coat and dragged him out of the bedroom, across the plush living room carpet. He struggled but not much, he was exhausted, trying to catch his breath. It was running away.

I left him in a pile and opened the front door, then got a hold on his ass again, while Anita was still going, "Oh God!" and dragged him out into the hallway. My own clothes blood-smeared.

But in the hallway he tried for my legs with some luck and threw me down. His fist got my stomach, but it wasn't bad. It just pissed me off. His chest was still going up and down dangerously.

He got up on his knees and elbows. He looked up. He was trying to say something.

I went inside and locked the door.

Harold is coming through the door, shit, rasping, without having opened it, the rasping turns into a husky grizzling; Anita and I are on the floor, wrestling playfully; she shifts, sees him first, her wet mouth hangs slightly, corpulent juicy cinnamon.

But I thought I'd gotten rid of this imbecile!

He dashes over—picks me up as though I'm a feather. One becomes the word, the name very quickly. Like a cunt or a flirt. I am almost weightless in his vengeful disposition. My idealistic weapon still sticky with Anita's spit, curved, pointing toward the ceiling. A conceited impressionistic bardistic, looming bastard! He runs over to the sudden French windows, and throws me—a tiresome grunt emitting from his offended face. Throws me out. Out, into the squares of the sidewalk, the disconnected hearing-aided sounds of the South Side.

All my teeth remain.

I get up brush off go up and . . . Harold, this big monster who looks like he'd never sound like a faggot, comes rushing in straight through the wall, with his rod in his hand, flying with a cape attached to his neck, screaming like a girl waylaid wag in a prosaic voice: "Reeely now this is rawthuh nasty of you two! *Oi weh!*" And Anita, whom I have bent over, with her ass stretched capriciously before my poker, turns her head around like a cow and hisses to Harold: "SHH-EEE-IT!" And James Brown from wax on the turntable doing his thing like, "Hey mama why don't you come here quick, bring your licking stick . . ."

Harold crashes into the opposite wall, having come into the room with a force too gargantuan—

As he slides down, like a cracked egg, his blood is instantly sniffed by thousands of tiny things that never stop coming—

And Anita opens her purple mouth, like O, and in Marilyn Monroe's voice says, "Oh, my!"

While Harold, with blue jays circling around his skull, abased, murmuring, "Ah turds ah turds ah turds!" sounding like Jimmy Durante!

It was late and I was in the front room alone with the almost empty bottle of scotch.

Anita, with her black eye, appeared in the doorway of her bedroom, clad in a nightgown. "Can't sleep?" the classic three-o'clock-in-the-morning question.

I threw down a copy of *Ebony*. "No."

"Me neither."

"A drink?" Also a very classic question that gets a very classic answer.

"Yes, thanks." She came toward me, blue shades of flimsy transparency against the dark richness of her skin texture. "I still have a headache . . . I never dreamed he could be so violent . . . so jealous."

My fists and muscles were still aching from the fight with Harold. At one level of my mind the act had become pointless: yet somewhere else in me it was valuable and left a good feeling, because I won.

She sat on the couch beside me with her arms folded across her stomach.

"I hope I did the right thing by whipping his ass."

"You *did*." But sadly.

"Glad you approve. Makes me *feel* better."

The phone rang, we looked at each other.

"You answer it, honey."

I went and picked up the receiver. "Yes?"

Except for human breathing, there was silence at the other end. The volleyball of this urban game.

I hung up and laughed. "Heap mystery man."

"Nobody?"

"Not a word, just halitosis."

"It was him, I *know* it," she insisted.

She moved closer to me. I finished the drink and sat down my glass, as she lay her face against my chest. I disliked her somewhat, now, but heard myself saying, "I don't know why I ever let you get away from me in the first place. So he's the guy you fix fine meals for?"

"You didn't have *time* for me. School, your friends, everything. You went away."

And it's ending. "I remember." Really ending. I'd miss her strong lips on me, all over me. Her spit. I'd miss the protection of her flesh against the meanness of the aqueous age! Things move into each other, die.

I didn't want to hear any more.

I had already pushed my thoughts ahead to tomorrow. I would go to the track to try my luck.

My luck? Out of the sacrificially deep psychic past of my history a thin fur rabbit dashes meaningfully from left to right across my lucky path . . . I feel—how do I feel? Strangely similar to the way I felt about the unnerving presence of the rigid enamel bridgework dentally inserted into my mouth—its false presence sometimes touched deep into my soul striking the most uncanny and alarming animal fear I had felt in years—Yes; luck was still a very mysterious land untouched by science—

Already I was more or less living with Cathy—we had met at Jerry Ginsberg's house one afternoon. Jerry and I were sitting in the living room drinking beer when she came in wet in a green raincoat. She had such a beautiful shy face, she affected me right away. We talked about . . . everything, for hours, after the beer ran out. That had been early in October—now, more than ever I realized that Anita was truly a relic of my past. I was also wise to her now: she believed religiously in the values of the White Knight Ajax cleaner Kraft Foods Wildcat and Impala cars, the existential reality of Aerowax and the divinity of jet-age plastic Sperry Rand Frank Sinatra George Burns Maxwell House coffee Jack Benny and Texaco gasoline; she thought the Hully Gully was a game invented by Jewish kids in Israel, that who Stagger Lee shot was his mama, that a Blood was an Indian, and that C. C. Rider was a civil service technician.

I was in a cab on my way to see Anita.

I had the cab wait while I picked up liquor. In the store I bumped into Wayne Fisher. He reeled back and looked at me and we both laughed.

"My main man," he exclaimed. We slapped hands.

"What's going on, man?" I asked.

"I guess you heard what happened last night."

"No, what d'you mean?"

"Well, man, a whole lot of mess. Step over here to the side and I'll tell you."

The cab, I thought.

"Judy got shot, man."

"What?"

"Yeah. She's on the critical list at the county hospital. They don't expect her to live."

"No shit! What happened?"

"David came home early. Took off against Ruth's will. So he's fired. Jolene and Judy got permission.

"And after you left last night he got drunk. Judy got drunk, too. She started accusing David and Jolene of secretly going together, behind her back. Indignant, Jolene called her a 'dirty lying bitch' and Judy got some kind of little pistol and tried to shoot Jolene, but she got the gun from Judy. The thing went off while they were wrestling over it. Judy got it in the belly."

"In the belly?"

"Right here." He patted beneath his heart.

"Ain't that a bitch!"

"Sure is, my man."

"I've got to split, Wayne. Got a cab waiting outside."

"Oh, all right, I'll dig you later, Eli."

I bought a bottle of good scotch and returned to my cab at the curb.

Wayne drove off with a wave of his hand. I gave the driver Anita's address.

For some reason, sitting there in the taxi, I was thinking about Steve—when we were all very young—who used to run away from the orphanage. They would bring him back and every time they did he'd come back to the bay telling us long stories about his adventures in the outside world, a fantastic place in our imaginations. I used to envy him; I thought he was the greatest, bravest boy I knew, except for Leroy . . . But why Steve came to my mind now, these years later, I can't say. Was my memory of him some gauge for the future?

Anita was clad in her pink robe and had a cigarette burning in her hand. I went in past her, without kissing her, and put down the scotch.

She too seemed preoccupied as she brought in two glasses. She was close, now, but just physically "What's the matter?"

"Ah, every damn thing."

She put my drink into my hand and holding her own carefully, sat down close.

"Like what, baby?"

"I just came from the police station."

"Oh?"

I told her about Jimmy Sheraton, the "Warriors," the stabbing, the newspapers. "Oh, you must have read about it, Anita!"

"I did. So, how did they find out about you?"

"I wish I knew."

"What did they want precisely?"

"They wanted to know if I had seen him after work that night."

"What did you tell them?"

"Nothing."

"But why didn't you tell the truth?"

"Anita, be reasonable!" I jumped up. Very irritated. "The truth? *What is truth?*" I snapped. "And especially in a situation like this, what would it get me—?"

"Peace of mind, Eli."

"I see you don't know shit about policemen."

"Won't they believe—"

"Hell, no! I'm leaving."

"Going to see Cathy?"

I went out without answering and as I banged the door I heard her scream: *"I know you're living with her!"*

COPS

Just a few days before I left Chicago, they led me into a small room. The cops.

"Sit down if you like."

"I'll stand."

Meanwhile Harth and Wills took seats on hard chairs, facing me.

The white man (a fat one this time) was fumbling with papers on the desk. Seated behind the desk. He spoke first: "Mr. Bolton, we have something we want to read to you. No—better still—you read it yourself."

I took it. I read: "We saw a brother being attacked by a whitey with a knife and we ran to stop the devil from his murdering. The whitey had a big knife and he looked crazy. We thought it was unfair for him to attack a brother who did not have a knife. We was just passing along the street and saw this happening. The brother was trying to defend himself against the whitey who was crazy. We meant only to help and do what is right for our black brother. Whitey tried to kill us so we had to defend ourselves. The guy almost did stab Tim. I got the knife out of his hand and defended myself. I hit the white man because he hit me. The knife stuck him by accident while I tried to defend myself. He meant to kill us. Then we ran and left the black man there. But we did not know that the whitey was hurt bad or let lone dead."

I silently passed it back to him, as he was saying, "It's a confession by Charles Donald Jackson. A member of the Warriors."

"Worse than the Blackstone Rangers," said Harth. "But Mr. Bolton—"

"Let me do this my way, Harth," said the white man, with a sigh. Lighting a cigar.

I waited. My thoughts on my plane ticket. I couldn't wait to get away. Cathy was waiting for me right now. This stupid shit detaining me!

"You're the mystery man, aren't you, Bolton?" asked the fat man, with a cynical smile.

Why not admit it? Why hide it?

He said to Wills, "Go bring in the boy."

Wills went out of the room and came back very quickly with a skinny black boy.

"This is Jackson, Mr. Bolton."

The boy's eyes were large and resentful.

"Jackson, is this the man who was there?" the cigar smoker asked.

Jackson hesitated, then spoke. "I . . . I'm not sure. Could be. It all . . . ah . . . happened so fast."

"We don't know for sure Bolton, but Brogan saw you and Sheraton walking together after you got off that night. He saw you from the window. If you know anything, we'd like to hear your side of the story. These boys may be going to prison for life because of your silence."

I sighed, sat down and lit a cigarette and told them the story. When I finished, Jackson said, "That's what happened."

The secular silence hung a moment.

"Take the kid back to the lockup, Wills."

Wills, without a word, stood and took the handcuffed boy out, holding the skinny arm. I looked at the back of the young man's neck.

CATHY

We were in her old car and stopped at a place called Al's Bar, a blues singer (was he Joe Williams?) featured. She was the only white broad in the joint. We were packed into a corner, her cherry pink cheeks caricatured under the trick blue-yellow lights, her fluffy ruffled bright dress provoked colorless by the electric outburst. She downed one whiskey after another—straight whiskey with ice. I couldn't believe it. We had to strain in order to see the exaggerated transgressive face of the howling singer enravishing the cramped nightclub audience. Afterward, at the wheel of the car in the parking lot, her face fell forward on her arms and she groaned. "You want me to drive, Catherine?" I don't know why her name came out of me that way. Occasionally it would happen. "I'm all right." She looked up—vampire eyes in the sweetest almost perfect face. I kissed her then. This way enkindled. She drove south on Michigan Boulevard, her profile, the smooth fervency of her neckline, intense chin, her quarrelsome bottom lip wanting to tigerishly poke but impetuously sucking in under the more tamed range of her gentle reliable top one that begins a curve inward and up to where her short small nose toots the bridge, firm smooth sensuous, and climbs to her liquid playful eyes. I wanted to touch her carefree short rich hair, the color of the floorbed of the hilly Appalachian woods in late fall; she threw her head to one side, the texture of her enriched voice, the booze in her, Cathy O puffed up trying to sound gruffy: "HAA-RUMP HAA-RUMP . . . HAA-RUMP HAA-RUMP!" My empress looked absolutely blandishable! What a great night of fragile elopement—my everloving Cathy with me! "What was that all about?" I asked. Her eyes on the horizon before us. "Didn't you ever read *Winnie the Pooh?*" she said. "No." Her alarmed eyes turned to me. *"You never read* Winnie the Pooh?" Her face a fissure of amazement! I saw the dismayed shapes of

Katherinna's definition of me crack against the swift tides of this new information.

We had possibly encountered each other three times since the sleazy rainy afternoon in Jerry Ginsberg's barrackslike rented house on 45th and Langley. The first time I ever touched Cathy O was at the end of her long deliciously followed monologue on what she had learned from a dissective course on John Milton's *Paradise Lost* and *Paradise Regained*. She was reciting some lines from memory: "What in me is dark, Illumine; what is low, raise and support; That to the height of this great argument I may assert eternal Providence, And justify the ways of God to men . . ." At this point I took her hands into mine and pulled her up from the couch. She came easily into my lap; we both were very high on Jerry's grass, boss shit. While Jerry himself sat stiff withdrawn at the other end of the couch. My mouth clung to hers, we judiciously filled the room with the first warm silence suddenly split by Jerry's shriek: "Wow! man! Wow! *What is this?!* You want I should just leave my own house, Eli?" He had jumped up, was red furious boiling, throwing his hands out, his soft eyes behind his glasses now very narrow and mean. His curly hair hanging in his face. His hawk-nose was an arrogant compass. I loved the way Cathy's ass filled out her Levi's, holding her smoothly against me, her arms so natural around my neck, ordained to be there, and Jerry too close, angry, obstructing our sweet levels. "I've seen it all now man—Wow!" Jer was pacing the floor, furious! Masochistically he whined: "Why don't you just tell me to leave, huh, Eli? . . . You want privacy don't you, huh?" Obviously the pot hadn't had a soothing effect on him. "Well, Jerry," I said very fatherly-like, "if you must leave, I guess we'll be all right." Cathy burst into giggles.

I remember when I first met Jer: he came up to me in the hallway at Roosevelt, had been kicked out of several better schools. He was from Cleveland, I think. He wanted to know how it felt to be black and to have fought in Vietnam. I thought, Oh another bright-eyed kid looking for a cause. We had coffee together, sometimes talks, and he had given me no hint that he was romantically attracted to Cathy.

I walked her home that inner revolutionary night westward on

45th Street past the towering structure of the Catholic church on Forestville where Father Flexner, to whom she was responsible, held forth. We were followed by playfully menacing tiny half-hungry multicolored kids with whom Cathy O spent her daytime hours. Affectionately they touched her thighs called her name: "Kathe, Kaathey, Katti, Cat, Caathe . . ." I wanted to be invited in but she only reluctantly allowed me to kiss her briefly at the door and Cat whispered, "Goodnight . . ." with the door opened. I saw Beth's lean fretful face straining to see me, heard her shrill superfluous voice: "Cathy who was that—" and the door, where it was, the square of darkness, then down the stairs—O Kathelee Z! O Catherina! I felt infinite happiness! My lovely blue-eyed Empress Catherine I of California! I felt weightless! The beautiful protracted night so good, so coated with Caathi wonders, O Katti love! These streets that had seemed so ugly night after night rushed me with depths of loveliness. I was levitating along South Parkway whistling and riffing the then popular "Up Tight" by Stevie Wonder. I even affected a couple of teenyboppers coming by who pitched in like a chorus doing their own *mishugah shtick* with the footwork like bop one two bop three four bop one two three bop!

When I saw Anita the next day before going to work she asked, "So who's Cathy?" Yes Jerry G had turned vengeful but it didn't matter, something so real, so beautiful was happening in me that Anita too was rapidly eclipsed. For days I went over the eminence of each second we had spent together. Only one who has known the profoundest most unselfish love, an overwhelming consuming voluptuousness of love—only this person knows the luxury of such a selfless outpouring of so much that is beautiful in the loving of someone. I was delighted with myself for the first time in my life! I couldn't see anybody couldn't hear anybody. Hilda came into the restaurant. I forgot to speak as I placed coffee before her. She murmured: "A man must get a thing before he can *forget* it." "What d'you mean?" "Nothing: just a line from Holmes." "Sherlock?" "No; Oliver." Aside from the fact that Anita was the first and possibly the most deeply affected by the change, Judy, Jolene, Ruth, David, Wayne, May Downs, all kinda stood back with: "Well!"

And for the time being Jerry Ginsberg still came to my apartment as usual, maybe once, twice a week to talk books or politics but he was always now somewhat moody. I often felt that he danced to my "lament"; he would put himself in my service. I tried not to abuse his industrious tendency . . . A clue to who he was was dropped one day after I had known him only a few short weeks, having met him quite by accident since both of us were former students who happened to have been in the building that day for one reason or another. Anyway, this particular time I refer to now we were sitting in Walgreen's on the corner of Washington and State having coffee and he said, "I guess . . . well, I guess you know I *admire* you. I read your poetry and your short stories in the school anthology when I first came to Roosevelt. They still talk about you in the English department. I was envious, until I heard that you were in Vietnam." He chuckled. "I believe you're a genius." He lowered his eyes. His head, his hands, his fingers met on the counter. Then he turned, looked at me briefly, his gentle hands offered like centers—like keynotes or seedcases for his own self-deprecation—a moment of victory I hadn't asked for drove the rivulets of poison in himself deeper, like fatal accidents in a nation after an internal *coup de grâce,* following the acknowledgment of the victor, the almost masochistic love of seeing his flag or his mentality go up on your most respected building and the inquisition of the self stops as the bloodletting and bootlapping begins. I knew Jerry was unappeasable in this approach to our relationship. Unlike some former white hangers-on he didn't worship me as the noble savage, the black vanguard of the future of America, except incidentally, supplementally. So after driving me home one Saturday after chauffeuring me nearly all over Chicago fulfilling one errand after another, at the curb, in a defeated acquiescence, he said, "I'd probably suck your prick if you asked me to. I'm reeelly a *schlemiel.* Oh boy! am I a *schlemiel!*" He got into his car, slammed the door, and drove away.

This incident left me deeply depressed. Any step he took to shipwreck the hardly formed romance between my baby Katty and me proved specifically to be a setback for himself and an ironic log-on-the-fire for this difficult to ignite love affair . . . How many times did I call Cathee O Catherina asking her out only to hear her stammer something like: "We're making kites for the kids tonight and I'll be at the nursery school until very late . . ."? I would say, "Listen, I've got to *see* you. How about tomorrow afternoon? . . ." "Well, I really can't say—" and in the background behind her voice, Sonny and Cher singing "I Got You Babe." And Beth asking, "Is that Eli?" So one Tuesday afternoon I simply didn't go to work. I went over and knocked; Beth stood there, her mouth like a fistula, behind her Katti O her entire face a cleft of surprise mazed with all kinds of minute mental rivers of godly devilish passions. Both of them in jeans, the apartment in shambles. "If you can stand it," said Beth, "come in—" I entered deliriously pissed off but concealing it because Cathee had not been the one to invite me in, but I soon learned that Caathe always took "second place" out of a deep feeling of being inferior in her relationships with anybody; even small children in the neighborhood sensed this in her and often treated her accordingly: they sensed that she was a victim like themselves. But they loved and respected her. I sat in a corner watching Cathy fumble in a frenzy over the arrangement of several books on a table. Nervously she shifted them around avoiding my eyes, avoiding me. Beth from the kitchen shrilly informed us: "Jeremiah is coming to take me to a drive-in theater tonight to see *Who's Afraid of Virginia Woolf*. Cathy why don't you and Eli come with us?"

Well, we didn't go. I spent five hours trying to break through into Catherine of California, O my frostbitten Katherina! The next night I didn't go to work again. We drove around in her car. I drove a while, she drove, we stopped at several spots but finally discovered Mickey's, downtown near LaSalle. A young white crowd dancing to Benny Goodman, Paul Whiteman–oriented takes in large scowling unbalanced doses, disguised as the new frenetic sounds since the Beatles. To drive nails into the eardrums. Chicago was such a segregated city! I was the only black man here. I was bored until a jellyassed soul sister working off her booty as a striptease dancer showing all those pretty sardonic white teeth jumped out onto the stage and shook her tits and tooted her tooting ass all over the joint, coming down off the stage her G-string unable to cover the bushy hair of her cunt as she saucily wiggled it in all those secretly satirized minds. I remembered being in a dance hall in Detroit in 1965 where a sapphire loaded on booze and something a little bit smoother stood before my table and slowly finger-lifted her short flimsy silk dress, working her belly and all that bushy cunt hair around around around in my face until I was seasick knowing she wouldn't fuck because *this* itself was her way. Cathy sipped bourbon and was impressed by the stripper. Our relationship remained at this level for four or five weeks and each time I saw her just to kiss her or to touch her breasts through her clothes sustained me leanly.

Meanwhile, accidentally or perhaps not so accidentally, Anita "bumped" into us one afternoon. Cathy and I were sitting at a window-table in Walgreen's restaurant on the corner of 47th and South Parkway having lunch. No appetite but I played with a hamburger while I delighted in her eating French fries and a tuna sandwich. The movement of her throat, her eyelids, the pressure of her fingers, how they bent their curves on the bread, the clean white line of her smooth teeth when her red lips were lifted back, her pink tongue moist, anticipating the next bite. Watching Kat—my private kitten!—I could almost taste her, loving every crevice and ripple of her; *she* was *my* food! The hasty but neat stroke of the side of her pale folded index finger extracting a bread crumb from the pink adhesive outer lining of her delicate neat mouth. My sustaining nectar was the glow from her speckled ocean blue eyes—eyes as blue as *Bahia de Banderas* in Mexico!—so subjectively paused as she swallowed, also causing the lifting of her breastline, the dropping of her long fluttering eyelids. I could almost hear the next word in the sentence she had been weaving.

"But I don't really hold anything against him—I mean, as a matter of fact, I probably love him better than I do my real father . . ."

I was wondering many things as I asked: "Do you mean—romantically?" Idly I picked up a dusty green pickle and pushed it lazily around in a complete circle of heavy dark yellow mustard watching my own action, avoiding her eyes to give her confessional comfort. It was difficult to avoid Kathela's incandescently spirited face

"Romantically?" She seemed to mind-chew on the word. Like a bird, Katheo's head turned slightly as if to listen for the combustion of spring waterfalls. I was not really truly aware of the tides of heavy Negro middle-class chatter bobbing around us, the clacking of commercial spoons against thick coffee cups, the whisking-sounds of quick passing waitresses with minds agitated by long lists of menu items. I well know this psychology and often studied waitresses but not now, they didn't exist, nobody but Cathea, glorious Kathi, gentle Caathy, sacred Katheas, my empress, Cato Katheus, my princess, Catti my whore, divine Kathee, my angel Cathela! Cathy was finishing the tuna sandwich with obvious enjoyment but her forehead knitted thoughtfully, her tongue sensitive and adroit was now a glossy beautiful rich strawberry color, the pink undertones still there like the natural colors of land sea and sky. Her mouth in the way it hesitated and closed had many of the characteristics of her other mouth.

"I . . . I don't know—" she started. I didn't want to press her on this point: it was certainly too delicate if she wasn't *ready* to examine beneath the surface shrubbery of her motivations. Her affections. I would have to let her take her *Kathi* sweet time! "I never thought about it *in* that way." The left side of her face—she flung her hair back from where it had fallen too close to her eye. In and across the mountainous terrains of her mind she was working it out. But would she bring it out, share it? Her mouth opened. I waited. The lids of her eyes dropped twice and lifted, finally sublimely. Her alto voice reached out:

"You know, *you* remind me of him—my stepfather." Having gotten that out she sucked her lungs full of stale air and released it, her jaws moving where her tongue inside was busy, perhaps at embedded food between the crevices of her teeth.

It might have been at this point that Anita made her entrance but it would be quite a few moments before she would come over to us . . . I asked Cathica: "*How* do I remind you of him?" From what she had told me of him he seemed to be a monster. I was offended but beginning to realize that Cathangel's own vision, her own attitude toward him was a very complex and tedious riddle; also I realized that this was the second time she had expressed a part of this idea. On another occasion, over the phone I think it was, she said, "You sound like my father: I mean the *way* you talk, what you say." Cathquel called him either Father or Dad. Now, she said, ". . . Maybe that's why I like you—I mean—*you know* . . ."

I testily challenged Cathadilla, asking: "Do I remind you of him in the way I make love to you?" She flushed noticeably; her eyelids were butterflies of a priceless summer. I had butted into a foible. I watched her fingers, busy now extracting a cigarette from her pack, the match, how its flame curved up the oblong orange-colored intense structure of the fire, what it did to her vivid emotional face. She took my question carefully, almost gloomily into herself, weighing it and I had expected her to be offended by it, to throw it back into me like a trickbag foisted on her. She sat there dragging deeply on her mild, filtered cigarette. The cupolas of her bust for a moment captured me as they moved beneath her many-times-washed suit. It was a thin cotton with yellowish-white printed clusters of purple flowers all over it, so sensuously out of season.

"No," she began, "*I told you* he never *actually* made love to me." Her voice dropped at the end. Blood rushed beneath the surface of her face; the cigarette smoke was swiftly scattering between us. She went on stammeringly: ". . . You see, he used . . . well, he would wait until she . . . you know . . . until she was out of the house and she always had plenty of social events to keep her occupied then . . . he'd start taking a shower . . . then he'd call me . . . to bring him a towel. Well, when I'd come into the bathroom with the towel, you see he'd tell me that I too needed a shower. Why didn't I take showers more often. And I'd—" Poor Cathette caught her breath, got her breathing controlled, then: ". . . and I'd *have to* undress and get into the shower with him. Then, he'd have me soap his body . . . I'd rub soap all over his body, avoiding his privates, of course . . . I didn't *like* touching him—down there."

Her eyes were focused absently on the burning tip of the cigarette. Then she stole a glance up at me; momentarily she seemed concerned about my reaction. Didn't Cathero know that I couldn't hold her guilty? She put down the cigarette in an ashtray, the palms of her hands came together, the friction of their bright pink surfaces, the tips hesitating, looking at me. Her curious lost sad blue eyes, her head turned, and she looked beyond the window, her face in profile, a classic natural work of art. ". . . But . . . he'd get—very angry . . ." she paused, her fingers moving through her hair; "*extremely* angry! at me . . ." Still looking beyond the window perhaps at the stark gasolined trees in the park lane. ". . . He was so . . . so *in*satiable!"

She suddenly looked at me, her face so filled with gorgeous colors beneath the snow milkiness, banana yellow streaks, with an interplay of scarlet red touches, of gold yellow around her temples, tinges of emerald green, of her blood veins, the washes of cinnabar, new oranges, flowing transparent tones of ultramarine blue, pinches of indigo, intense vermilion reds, all charged with furious coatings of zinc snow-milk and lilac whites! All of those tones, washes, tints, blends, were always there in the raw and warm structure of her face, but it was only at this moment that the kaleidoscope of it hit me; deepening levels of my own sensibilities for some sudden unconscious reason, expanding and enhancing her essence as well as my own. "No—I don't—I don't understand," I told her.

She nervously took up her cigarette. "You know . . . you know how men are. All men want to be touched *there.* So, he used to make me soap him there." She caught her breath, her tension was flowing into me. I couldn't resist the lewd temptation; I asked: "Did he become . . . *excited?*" She said: "Of course he became excited." I asked: "When did it first happen—how old were you?" She inhaled exhaled smoke and gently held the cigarette to the side of her face. "Well, before any of *that* started, he used to . . . *beat* me."

I felt the shame of prying so, my imagination working back to those dark ages of her enslavement, but I consoled myself by believing this personal disclosure good for her; I pushed on: "How?" "Well, he used to strip me . . . I was only—let's see—I must have been—" She ran the fingers of her left hand through her reddish hair, again looking away from me; ". . . I was eight when he married my mother. The beatings went on up until I was fourteen or fifteen. Then—it was *then* that he . . . well, you know . . ." She looked straight at me."Do you think I'm bad?"

My heart almost fell out of my body, the penitent quality in her eyes, in her rich pleading face. I instantly reached for her hands that came—after she put down the cigarette—gently into mine. "Baby, baby—oh, baby! How could you ever be bad?" I saw relief, the passion that was pinched and stuffed deep into the corners of her psyche come forth, trustingly toward me to be accepted to be understood to be loved loved loved. Her hands responded to the pressure of mine. I was so possessed by Cathnosa not only was I not normally conscious of the world around me, I was blissfully almost unaware of myself! "I *love* you," I told her, "there's—there *just isn't any way* to fully convey how much—" In the middle of my sentence her face contracted; I hesitated, stopped: she spoke urgently: "But *how* can you be sure? How do you *know*—I mean, *really* know? Can you tell me . . .?"

Trapped in levels of unworking human media I shook my head negatively. ". . . I just know . . . I know it—all through everything that I am!" A dreamy look flowed from the back of her eyes and innocently she overflowed absently: "He used to say the *same* words." I was baffled and damaged like a man chained to a wall forced to watch his beloved woman begin to enjoy, to respond to being fucked by a mercenary soldier or prison guard in a war-torn country. It was that dreamy look in her eyes when she spoke that caused me to throb with love pain, to give her ugly names, running in the playful yards of my secrets, names like Cathon, Cathpez, Cathale, Cathlima, Cathmos.

"You mean—he talked *that way* to you?" She seemed surprised by my question. "Yes. He used to say that he couldn't live without me, that he'd kill himself if I left. He wouldn't let me date: I never had a date before I went away to Berkeley. He said he'd be nothing without me. He was planning to leave *her,* and take me away—just the two of us. He *is* really a very sensitive man, and he has suffered a lot. During the war, as I told you, he was in a prison camp, and they tortured him. As a matter of fact, he's almost blind from the blows on the head he received . . ." Impatient for her to continue as she mashed out her cigarette very ceremoniously, I pushed out the question: "Did you *love* him?" She obviously was prepared for the likelihood of the question. Her answer was calm, was undeformed. "Yes, I think I did." She shook her head thoughtfully. "I honestly loved him *in a way*." I immediately jumped on the tail end of her statement: "What d'you mean by *'in a way'*?" "I mean I felt . . . uh . . ." She stopped completely. I pressed: *"Uh—what?"* I felt betrayed. I felt like the man who has discovered that his wife not only *enjoyed* being raped before his very tortured eyes but has begun to love the raper!

Something formal, something self-defensive eased into her tone: "Well, it obviously didn't make sense. He was my own mother's husband, and in almost every sense of the word, he was my father. I certainly never knew my uh—other father." I was hot angry—she was ugly Cathfonso or Cathecasolano or—I said: "Tell me, when he began approaching you when you were a little girl, why didn't you tell your mother?" The possibility of this question also was obviously no unsettling proposition for her. "I've thought about *that* a lot . . . recently . . ." Her eyes were downcast as she spoke; "You see—from the very beginning . . . from the time when—" A sad smile swept her face. "I had a very *bad* relationship with my mother." She paused. "I used to . . . well, there was a time, not long ago—I couldn't talk about this, any of this. I've really come a long way. When I . . . when I was home, before I went away to Berkeley, I didn't realize how really screwed up I was . . . OK, I'll try to explain . . ." Suddenly her eyes were filled with pain. "Are you sure you want to *hear* all of this?"

My entire body moved forward against the counter with the tension of my positive response. "Yes, every bit of it." She continued: "My mother and my real father—well, probably they married because she was pregnant. I think I've probably known that a long time, but only recently I've been able to face it. He obviously didn't love her. I think . . . she possibly loved him but—anyway, it doesn't matter . . . and I'm not too sure about any of that . . . The fact is, in Rhode Island where I was born, my mother's family really gave her hell for having anything to do with my father. You know, he was from a family they didn't approve of. He was German and Swedish and my mother's people were English and Irish . . . there was this whole big lineal question . . . Well, that was bad enough, and after nine months of abuse from him, while carrying me—" She was desperately trying to sound lighthearted about it. "I don't know if he left *before* I was born or right afterwards. In any case, I became a kind of Achilles' heel to her . . . We moved around a lot, because she didn't want to live at home with her parents and every day have to listen to that ol' song, *I told you so*. So, she dragged me all over the country. Up until I was eight, I don't think we stayed in one place more than a few weeks . . . I suppose she had a hard time—anyway, I really find it very difficult to sympathize with her because she's such a callous stupid woman and so brutally indifferent—so insensitive to everybody except herself. Oh, she *pretends* to be interested *and* concerned—oh, she's really great at pretending—her whole life has been one great long act of pretending. When we had nothing, she used to pretend that we were rich. She lives in *such* a fantasy world. Well—of course, she blamed me for everything: my very presence in her life was, to say the least, was ah—"

Baby seemed desperately agitated, in search of a word. I offered: "Liability?" She shook her head no, she didn't want that word especially, then she said, "I was a constant reminder of him—he had done her wrong, see. She actually *hated me* from the very beginning . . ." Her bright face was suddenly a vivid lost child's, oh my baby Cathica! Trust yourself! You are very strong, sang the wisdom of my heart. "She used to tell me all the time how much I looked like him, how I sounded like him. She tortured me with it up until she found Bob Daily, and tricked him into marrying her . . . I'm *sure* she was pregnant with my little brother, Tony, when they got married." She seemed to go on deep into herself for a moment. I said: "Did *she* beat you, too?" "Up until she married him, yes—she did; then, he started—"

A heavy painful silence enveloped our presence, then she said: "I guess I make it all sound *very* bad. It isn't really all so bad; he loves *his* children: Trudy and Tony are very beautiful children . . ." "I suppose you felt like an outsider in the family, huh?" Cathy answered this gently: "Yes, yes I did." But she was growing deeply silent, she looked at me suddenly as though I had cheated her out of something, and almost a little too self-consciously and glibly I said, "Well, at least you didn't have to grow up in the impersonality of an orphanage . . ." But I don't think she really heard me, she was so remote from my words. And could I really give her the comfort of knowing that I suffered deeper and greater than she?

I was thinking when Anita walked before us. And it took me almost a complete second to recognize her, so deep was I still in the severely emotionally confusing inclemency of Cathy's unburdening which in itself was a transferral of some of the weight of it to me, to carry like a scapegoat or priest. ". . . and imagine seeing *you* here!" Anita was saying. But she could hardly take her secretly pained eyes from Cathy long enough to focus on me. She was stunningly dressed. She stood awkwardly for a moment; seeing that I wasn't going to ask her to sit down she pretended it was her wish to move on. Even before I could introduce Cathy, she said: "Toot-a-loo! Got to run . . ."

The next day when I went to my apartment for a change of clothes, Anita was there. She had gotten in with the key I gave her after Harold's attack. Her severe ochre-colored face challenged me right away with a viscid poisonous rage as her voice hurled: "You sure have gone crazy over that white pussy haven't you? Yeah, you're just a typical, dumb-ass nigger! That white pussy has you so blind so stupid you've even quit your job!" Still fully dressed she sat up from the bed—obviously she had slept in her clothes. I was beginning to undress, to take a shower, to change and to leave as soon as possible. She went on: "I really thought you of all people—considering all the shit white people have thrown in your face all your life—I really thought you were *all right!* You really fooled me!" She followed me every step I made, standing at my shoulder speaking close to my ear. Full of pain, hurt very deeply, she had plenty to say. "That little young dumb country-looking bitch! I swear *I can't see* what *you see* in her. But you must see something . . ." She gave a pathetic laugh. "She walks like a fucking bear—and that raggedy coat she was wearing needs to be thrown in the garbage . . . I wouldn't use that funky coat for a dog to sleep on."

I couldn't look at Anita: I knew tears were blazing in her eyes. And yet I had my own existence to handle and she wasn't going to be a part of it. With resignation she said, "But that's the way you colored men are, though: if it's *white* no matter how skunky it is it's *right* . . . Tell me, Eli, *what* do you see in her?" I was undressed to my underwear and went into the bathroom, the tile beneath my bare feet, a bright coldness; I dropped my shorts to the floor to have something to step out on, then stepped inside the shower stall, turning on the water only a little, waiting for it to warm up. She followed me naturally. "You don't have to answer. It's really none of my business, I guess. I don't *own* you. I don't have any papers on you, and it looks like I'm not going to ever get any, either . . ." I turned briefly to see her tear-stained face, her smile was sarcastic. "I suppose that makes you happy, doesn't it? . . . I know the answer already. You never really wanted me. I've always been the one chasing you. If you had wanted me you would have come back to Chicago when you got out of service—but no, you went galloping all over—everywhere. I know you have a lot of deep resentments toward me. You just can't forgive, can you? Just because I didn't write to you when you were in Vietnam—I think, I *really* think you still hold that against me . . . I know my excuses sound weak—anyway, it doesn't matter anymore . . . You've got what you want, and I really hope you're happy, Eli. I really hope she makes you happy . . . I sincerely mean that . . ." Tears poured down her cheeks. I could hear her heaving sobs: cramped by psychic collisions of the heart. She was silent a moment, I soaped my armpits, my shoulders, my chest, turned up the water full blast. Anita went on: ". . . I'm just standing here talking . . . and I *know* it doesn't matter . . . I *know* that you don't care . . . I feel very foolish; *I am* a fool . . . I guess you really want me to leave, don't you? I guess you won't answer that, either . . ." My back was to her now. She had stopped talking and when I turned around she wasn't there . . .

JUDGMENT DAY

It is Christmas Day.

I catch a clear snatch of the blasting sound from Alma's TV: "BECAUSE OF THE LARGE INFLUX OF OUT-OF-TOWNERS—MANY ARE FROM STRANGE COUNTRIES—AND BECAUSE OF THE QUALITY OF THE EVENT ITSELF . . ." the media voice pauses before pushing on, "MANY EXPERTS, INCLUDING REVEREND SHEEN, HAVE SUGGESTED THE ELIMINATION OF MONEY, NOT ONLY AS A SIGN OF GOOD WILL AND BROTHERHOOD BUT ALSO TO DEMONSTRATE IF NOT TO OURSELVES AT LEAST TO THE BACKWARDS PEOPLE OF THE WORLD THAT WE HAVE CREATED A TRULY DEMOCRATIC SOCIETY. SOME ARE SAYING WE SHOULD OPEN ALL PUBLIC PLACES TO ALL PEOPLE; THAT EVERY PERSON SHOULD BELONG TO EVERY OTHER PERSON, AND THAT ALL IDEAS AND FEELINGS SHOULD GO UNCENSORED: BUT LET US NOT FORGET IN THE FURY AND JOY OF THIS OCCASION THAT THIS IS OUR CITY AND WE ARE RESPONSIBLE FOR IT. WE MUST KEEP IT CLEAN: DO NOT THROW CIGARETTE BUTTS CANDY WRAPPERS SOGGY ICE CREAM CONES POPCORN CRACKER JACK BOXES ON OUR STREETS. THIS CAN BE A CLEAN BRAVE OCCASION NOT ONLY FOR OUR ALL-NIGHT VISITORS BUT FOR US CHICAGOANS AS WELL . . . SO FROM MY HEART . . ." I look at Cathy's distressed face. What is happening? At the same time, in the same breath, occupying the same space, our radio challenges the TV downstairs: "We must be mindful that the resurrection is a one-day affair while the fires and floods go on forever . . ." I sit up, deeply alarmed, my toe kicks over a wine bottle. Cathy is standing dead still against the light from the kitchen. ". . . who, by the way, next week, will receive the Nobel Prize for the most important scientific discovery in this decade: a chemical substance to sustain the briskness in noodles . . ." "Who're they talking about now?" I ask Cathy. "Reverend Sheen," she answers.

I go to the doorway not at all sure I believe it is good that space and time are being mastered. Now coming up I hear Buckwheat Brownie's voice. "This is your man on the street . . ." he is saying. Our door is ajar. I smell the sickening odor of rubber burning as I dash down, Cathy saying something I miss. Alma's door is open. Flash: I see Cathy at the top her mouth forming to the sound *swali*. Alma, a fat black woman with a boss natural, a discreet brave chubby face clad in a faded smock, worn-out slippers, sits with a bottle of good scotch whiskey on the nearby lamp table. "Hi, Eli. Where's Cathy?" I can't answer. I'm transformed to shock: are doors open all over the world? "We're coming to you . . ." says the black announcer, "direct from the spot in which it has been said he will appear . . . As you can see, it's raining here in Jackson Park, downtown Chicago. Just behind me, to my left, which would be to your right, is the famous Buckingham Fountain. In about an hour it will be in lights." Buckwheat is handsome in his trench coat. Cathy comes into the dim TV-lit daytime room. "Hi, Ace!" snaps Alma. "Have a seat!" A pause. "Both of you!" I shoot a glance toward Cathy, my baby, whose top button is open and the pushy presence of her breasts cross-index my eyes a moment. With a deep sigh my baby sits down. Alma asks her, "Did you tell Father you're leaving today?" "I told him twelve days ago." A sigh of relief, *and* something else. For me the nasty rubber fumes were causing breathing discomfort. The announcer was saying, ". . . we're actually covering two sites. As I'm sure you must know by now the experts have all this year predicted he will appear somewhere in this area or somewhere in the area of 63rd and Stoney Island. Jack Beanstalk will give you a play-by-play account of what develops out there . . ." He clears his throat. "Certainly, we have a crowd here that breaks all records in the history of public events." A white boy brings a handful of envelopes to him, he quickly opens three of them. "All day we've been receiving thousands of telegrams from people *everywhere*! Naturally we can't possibly read them all, but I've just been handed several rather interesting ones. Here's one from Mao Tse-tung: 'Once man has eliminated capitalism he will reach the age of permanent peace and will never again desire war.' Here's one signed Ulysses S. Grant: 'Let us have peace.' Here's one in Latin, as nearly as I can make out it says: 'Ye immortal gods! where in the world are we?' and it's signed Cicero. This one, torn a little at the bottom, says, 'Pray as if everything depended on God . . .' It's signed Francis Cardinal Spellman . . ." He hands the telegrams to the boy at his side.

I feel weak in the knees. Cathy and I have been upstairs eating drinking screwing blind and deaf to the world for the last forty-eight hours.

". . . And the entire city is jampacked, except for several side streets here and there. Even the North Side, where he is not expected to appear, is crammed. You home viewers are the luckiest of all: certainly the TV eye will be him—I mean *see* him . . ." Alma cuts in: "Shoooot! Cathy, girl, I've been thinking—I'm gone quit this jive game, *too.* This just ain't getting it for me." Baby's face shows sympathy. ". . . I just might be coming to New York, right on you all's tail. I'm sick of Chicago, *and* VISTA," Alma groans. "Where you from, Alma?" I ask. "Texas, honey." While we talk we all are still mainly captivated by the TV screen, not really focusing on each other. "I guess you know—" Alma pauses, her voice becoming almost inaudible like a lip-splitter's after blowing all night; she motions with her eyes toward me: "I guess you know Jerry Ginsberg, your ol' trusty friend, was the one who screamed on you." I can see that Cathy doesn't understand. Alma sees it too; she rephrases: "He told Father a man was living with you." Jerry! our one-time friend! The priest apparently hadn't believed it.

I do a kinda cakewalk in the center of the room at the discovery. "Is he still in town?" I ask Alma. "Honey, that boy got his ass out of this city so fast—last week I think it was—the minute he got wind that somebody had squealed to Father on *him.* Guess he thought father would go to the cops. You know he kept his stash right under Father's nose, in parish, which was pretty smart. Who would ever look for pot in a Catholic church?" Yeah, we know the whole story.

Brother Buckwheat, I notice, is interviewing at random. I'm not even vaguely surprised to see Brogan's bulldog face before the hand microphone. "What'd you do for a living?" the interviewer asks. Brogan removes the cigar from his mouth. "Medicine." "A medicine man?" "I didn't say that!" I can tell Brogan's hot. Buckwheat asks, "Why're you here, sir?" "I just don't believe any of this hocus-pocus—I've got to see it for myself, that's why." He put the cigar back into his mouth and clamped down on it with firmness. "Thank you sir—" says Buckwheat, who sneezes—AH-HA-CHEW AH-HA-CHEW; rivulets of rainwater run down his trench coat, he begins to look soggy. Brogan tugs at Buckwheat who shows by the expression on his face his distaste for Brogan's improper outburst: "I just . . . I just want to say that that . . . uh if he shows I'm going back to my drugstore and take a baseball bat to those shelves of bottles." Buckwheat trying to conceal his annoyance throws a shoulder in front of Brogan's head and speaks to the camera: "In case you've just tuned us in this is Brother Buckwheat Brownie direct from Jackson Park." Behind him a microcosm of black and white faces roped back.

As the TV newsman strolls down the police line I remember hearing on the radio several days ago that we were being watched by the CIA. But I didn't catch why. Suddenly I see May Downs waving madly, jumping up and down with a placard on a stick. The message is: "IF HE COMES THERE WILL BE SUMMER REVIVALS & ALL-DAY SINGING!" She's also shouting something not transmitted. Alma says, "Eli, why don't you and Cathy get some glasses and have a drink that mess's been on TV all day all night it's gone be on all night again and probably all day tomorrow just like when President Kennedy was shot." She sips coolly from her glass. "So, why don't you guys sit down and drink and be merry and everything . . .?"

People are waving flags, carrying all kinds of placards with all kinds of messages. The camera moves along the line of people swiftly: I see Clara with two beautiful dark babies, one in each arm; both look like the huge creature that is a man standing to her right. The camera moves swiftly on. Anita's face suddenly snaps around into the camera. Harold stands beside her lovingly. I see the two dicks, both in plainclothes; Harth is carrying a placard: "AIN'T GONE STUDY WAR NO MORE." Buckwheat moves on through the rain looking for a talkable face.

So many of the faces are bloated with the excitement of the occasion. Still the rubber stink is more extravagant. I see Ruth Kowalczyk briefly peering around Marvin Goldburg. Buckwheat stops before Brogan's partner. "Your name and occupation, sir?" "Don't care for personal publicity," Goldburg says. "But in reference to this absurd situation I'll quote one of my famous ancestors—Oliver Goldsmith—who simply changed the last part of his name from -burg to -smith to escape sixteenth century English anti-Semitism. He said: 'Every absurdity has a champion to defend it.' " Buckwheat says, "That's a strange statement—" Goldburg cuts in: "Not really—you think about it. Though you're a Negro you should know what I'm talking about."

Buckwheat moves on. Already I've spotted Mari who is holding . . . hay what's this! Frank Engelmeyer's arm and he looks older, surer. Buckwheat breaks, stops to interview Mari. "And what occupies most of your time, Miss?" Her large smile is pumped full of urgency. Me?" she snaps, "*I* do—I occupy it!"

She kinda throws her hip for emphasis. I hear Alma shaking her head, the crusty collar of her smock scrubbing her neck. "Lord, she sounds like she's trying to become a piece of cheesecake—famous." I leave the room fighting the temptation to laugh.

I come back from the kitchen with two glasses knowing that I shouldn't admit knowing Mari. I fix the drinks, the first swallow opens Cathy's already latent intoxication. Her neck snaps back, she closes her eyes tightly, goes: "Whew!"

Me and Cathy all last night 'til early this morning consumed burgundy. Now to drink whiskey? We weren't nervous any longer about the bottles all over our apartment—like that previous early-November morn. We heard a female voice outside calling: "*Cathy! Cathy!*" Baby jumped out of bed. "Oh God! it's Margarita Holborn!" she stammered. "I forgot she was coming this morning—" I sat up sleepily on my elbows still slightly drunk even a wine bottle on the foot of the bed the taste in my mouth and Cathy's taste also in my mouth.

The gloomy dusty stuffed room with her books everywhere and always falling, never being picked up, falling out of closets, off the dresser, off tables, her panties with bloodstains and cum spots on the seat, her dirty slips, her old jeans and dirty socks and various dresses never worn; the dirty towels we used night or day to dry our love sweat; the thousands of trinkets on the incredibly disorganized dresser excited my imagination. I rambled through it and found a postcard from her childhood sweetheart, Willy, that said simply, "How about a letter?" There were many letters Cathy had written to her parents and never mailed.

Now she was jumping around scared, half crazy ready to cry. "Who's Mugger-rita Hobo?" I wanted to know. Outside the voice lifted on the wind: *"Cathy Cathy—"* Hobo climbed the bleak, never-used rickety stairway outside—which was, considering Cathy's obvious fear, the best of possible things Mugger could have done. The real way up was through the hall past Alma's door. Baby was flying through the apartment, her blue faded terry cloth robe half on as she collected wine bottles; at the same time she was insanely snatching down from the walls sketches and poems we both had done for each other.

I leaped from the bed with a mighty erection. Dashed into the front. Cathy wheeled around, her arms crammed with bottles and notebook paper, her face incited. She dropped several bottles on the old rug; they didn't make much of a sound. I tipped to the window and could see a young woman with a pinched, frosty face, trembling in a cheap fur coat, standing impatiently. I knew she couldn't see into the apartment, as she continued to bang on the door, shouting: *"Cathy! Cathy!"* I stepped back easily, yawned and scratched my balls, when I saw Baby shift into a strange rhythm, dropping everything in her arms. Her head rolled to the side and she sunk to the rug *ploobp*! The soft vibration shook the wood-frame house but I could hear the woman descending the staircase. I remembered Cathy telling me that this reaction to a pressing situation was common to her. I got a damp cranberry-colored face towel from the flooded, messy bathroom, drenched it in icy water, the only kind at this hour of the morning, and gently soaked her forehead and temples while holding her on my knee. My knees bent.

Alma downstairs saying: "She sleeps very sound. It is important Miss Holborn?" The woman says: "Well, yes, we're supposed to take the Baptist Church kindergarten kids to the museum today. We've chartered a bus. I told her I'd be by early, maybe she forgot to set the clock. Can I get up by this stairway . . .?"

Meanwhile Cathy was coming back to consciousness. "I'll go up," said Alma, "and see if I can wake her. Why don't you wait in my place . . .?" The woman reluctantly said, "Well . . . all right . . ."

Alma coming up, I opened the door then dashed back to Baby, picked her up and carried her to the couch. Alma closed the door behind herself. Hair coated with lint and in her shapeless red-and-blue-plaid housecoat; her morning breath, as unkind as my own, as she whispered into my nose: "What happened to her, she faint? Is she okay?"

Cathy opens her eyes. "Father's girl Friday is downstairs, Ace. I'll tell her you're sick. I'll get rid of her." Alma turned to leave as Baby fretfully sat up. "But—if you tell her *that* she'll suspect something. Maybe I'd better get dressed . . ."

"Horseshit!" said Alma. Shame seeping through the ventilations of Cathy's expression. So often that mistreated child–like look I saw in her. How I wanted to lead her to the mirror!

Alma, a cross between a palpitating nanny and an eager dyke, bent, kissed Cathy on the head. "Don't worry—" As Alma eased out Baby on her elbows said, "But . . . but . . ." I stood outside her field of vision. Her disarrayed hair! How I had trimmed it, loved it, loved every inch of her!

Alma went down and shooed the woman away. The woman's horsepower kicked off outside. No, we certainly won't worry about surprise visits anymore.

The whiskey is too sour, the hour is unfit for scotch whiskey and Alma's apartment has the sharp odor of armpits challenging the fumes of burning rubber somewhere. I say, "I'm going for cigarettes," but my intention is to bring home a bottle of burgundy, the blood of the mission. My arteries, the lucid temporary state of my body's wine-captivated soul, feels the precious, painful stampede of psychic buffaloes through the nerves to the ends of my private zodiac as I put down the glass, stand up, stretch my arms, the soul weight of myself.

"One of mine?" says Alma. She has Winstons, my brand.

"No. I want some air, anyway. I'll walk."

As I go out I notice Buckwheat interviewing Judy, her husband David sheepishly behind her—her mink coat hides half of him from the camera. "Well, for one thing," Judy was saying, pulling her coat back and opening her blouse, exposing her naked fat belly, "if he comes I'll forgive my husband for this—" Buckwheat peers closely at the embossed bullet-wound while Judy gives David the evil eye.

Alma is chuckling. "Now, how come she had to go pulling off her clothes like that?" I go out as she asks: "Eli, what you gone do with *your* folks?"

I'm wearing no coat against the frontline urgency of the Hawk of Lake Michigan. The neighborhood has sunk to near-zero. I vaguely notice three young rangers milling around a parked car; now my mind is somewhere else; the moment I pivot and start toward Calumet I run into a blanket of dense eye-burning fumes of . . . what? Rubber. I try to open my eyes to see my way out but I'm permeated by the substance, my skin burns as though exposed to pure peroxide. As from a deep permutation, I howl: it's my longest profound cry of panic. I feel my knees grow weak—my stomach contracts. I am aware that I'm screaming. Am I turning to dust?

I become aware of *something* . . . I perceive it not through my senses: before me is the levitated body of an unborn child. The "person" is hermaphroditic. It is suspended upside down in the fetal position and is the size of a five-month-old fetus. I fall to my knees. I *see* it clearer, smell it: it is like rubber burning or . . . perhaps the nose-blistering substance of human carrion the rancid underbelly reek of every human death in the universe since the beginning!

I can even taste its liquid fleshy fumes. It comes flawless in motion directly before me. I recognize the huge flaccid black penis which like all the other parts has a speaking mouth; on either side of it each flabby hairy testicle has a large bloodshot ocular crevice with irises that are ornamented by some strange spirit or radar.

The sense of myself has almost totally vanished into it. At the bottom the relatively huge skull has three modestly garnished faces beneath the rich wine red color; lying dormant in a spermy embroidery all six eyes are shut but I sense instantly that the middle one is less static than the two on either side. It possesses half (*elli*) of the universe; the one to the left (I am left-handed) is the guilt-consumed primal "I"; the one to the right is the third stage of self: that is the I sense of Me seeing You. The You is also Me. Each tit is a bouquet-like "surface." The face on the left is less wreathy; it is surely Elizabeth Mamzazi's essence Gaia, to put it another way.

She packs so much mystery between me and the confused child I once was.

My father is here, certainly—the sickle of psychic steel for profit, from the enslavement of his balls. It is representative of my own death already prematurely in me. I turn my perception from my mother; I feel such a flourishing of pain. I know the warden dwells here in the spirit of Scylla as from a damp ill cave of the heart.

There are six tiny heads projecting from it on six necks each has three rows of vicious she-dog teeth identical to Gypsy's; dangling from the lower curve of the tit are twelve tiny legs complete with feet and toes; just above them, the upside-down face of the stomach is unmistakably that of the primordial giant of confusion, Jimmy Sheraton, who radiates from his ruby-colored, fatty-surface, also a sense of vagueness.

This thing's two feet are textured with the nameless faces of Vietnamese I killed in self-defense or by accident. My father is (my own penis) erect with Gaia's fretful, contracting vagina beneath him. Her eyes are frightening, they are moving; all the eyes all over the body begin to shift; I hear breathing; the odor thickens.

I am strongly attracted to the presence of Liz's abandoned vagina, almost tempted to touch it; the taboo holds me back; one of my father's testicles begins to shrink into the body, crowding the crevice cunt. Repeat after me begins the orotund voice of my father that I recognize as my own hoarse: "WHH BOP SH BAM WHHBLYOP WHH BOP SH BAM WHHBLYOP . . ."

The head, a crown, contains five very flat and magnificent faces of Leroy who forced Junior's energy into Gypsy's death. It is also reeking with the spirit of my brother Krios-Junior himself; is a freakish combination of my brother Iapetus and my sister (memory) Mnemosyne; Calvin is none other than classical Coeus, Buddy looms forth as Hyperion; he's grinning with emerald teeth; Steve, who looks like he wants to run to be free as the ocean, is mysterious and obviously Oceanus. They all chant in unison with me: "WHH BOP SH BAM WHHBLYOP WHH BOP SH BAM WHHBLYOP . . ."

I am melancholy but resonant as I ask Elizabeth: "Why did you not love me, why did you leave me?" Instantly she answers: "WHH

BOP SH BAM WHHBLYOP WHH BOP SH BAM WHHBLYOP . . ." sounding a little like the early Ella Fitzgerald.

I ask Leroy: "Why did you kill Gypsy—and leave our hearts heavy with murder?" Gypsy barks out of her twelve mouths seven times looking down at Leroy who answers: "You take this spinning top and spin it around. Do you get it now?" His eyes close forever.

I look at Moke. I ask simply: "Why—?" He growls: "I'll kill you before I let you break the spell and expose me."

I shift to the warden. I find myself speechless. Her Anglo face opens; she speaks: "Everything I did was meant to interrupt noises in your silence."

My attention to Sheraton: "What a different state—" he cuts in: "Yes, yes I was on the stage—" I can't psych out the pleas of the Vietnamese. I'd go insane.

I know *it* is about to take me into itself: it is me. So the ceremonial visitation of myself to the altar of myself comes to an end and this is what all those TV faces standing in the rain downtown and everywhere are waiting for again and again, the riddle, the birth and the rebirth.

The burnt-rubber smell clears away by currents as I go past three dudes, possibly the ones who danced with Sheraton to his death. They are watching the interior and tires of a car burn. Flames curl upward. The car bears the words "OFFICIAL BUSINESS."

Returning with the wine I have the pleasant knowledge that at 4:15 this afternoon me and Cathy will jet to the mecca. A car explodes as I enter the house. Alma and Cathy are so intent on TV they don't hear the explosion.

Baby stands and yawns. She begins to uncork the bottle. I sit down in her chair. Alma screams: *"Cathy look! It's Beth!"*

Cathy jumps fearfully almost dropping the glass of wine she is placing in my hand. Beth leans toward Buckwheat's microphone as though it were magnetic. ". . . other things more important than this," Beth is saying, and Buckwheat asks: "Like what?" To the left of Beth I see Bud Lemon elbowing his way through to the police line. Beth clears her throat: "Like, for example, what this uh ex-roommate of mine did . . . She was about to fly away to be trained for VISTA social work. Her parents were driving her to the airport and having this big argument like they always have at least once a day, and Cathy for the very first time in her life spoke up, said to them quite simply why don't you two shut your goddamn mouths and just drive me to the airport in silence for God's sake do I have to go away listening to *this*?"

Slowly Buckwheat with his eyes crossing turns to face the camera and lifts his index finger. He points it straight as he can toward his forehead and pulls the trigger. He goes "BANG!" The strain of it is too much for him.

Cathy is blushing. Alma seems stunned.

Buckwheat approaches Bud Hophead. "Here's a brother—you want to say something, brother?" He holds the microphone beneath Bud's mouth. "I been saying it all along but you didn't listen . . ." Bud grins slowly. "Well, say it again, brother—make it loud and clear!"

Alma recovers from the shock of Beth's statement. She stands up, beginning a long-gutted laugh that pushes and rocks her in spasms out of the room. Cathy seems puzzled but I know why Alma is cracking up.

With a ruffian face Bud says: "I wanta say two thangs and they both connected. I just come from the other site where this cat, you know—you'll call the maker—is s'pose to appear and already he done come disguised sixty-nine motherfucking times while you down here talking trash . . ."

Buckwheat can't repress his chuckle but retorts: "I'm sure we'd have had word on it if—"

Cocaine cuts him off with: "Listen I ain't got no reason to lie to you, baby."

Alma comes back, the corners of her mouth turned down: Medusa. I wonder why Jack Beanstalk hasn't been TV-ed yet. Bud seems up but maybe he's telling facts. ". . . you ain't got *all* the information Jack! Their system ain't gone give it all to you either!" Bud slams his fist into his palm. "The dude came disguised sixty-nine different ways and each time he got busted no shit."

Buckwheat frowns. "Could you describe him?"

Lemon Head proceeds: "The first time he showed up he was strolling across the grass sipping pluck from a bottle of Thunderbird and he had three of his disciples with him all 'em drinking from the same bottle like equals you dig a groovy boss dude—"

Here, Buckwheat cuts in: "But how was he dressed was he wearing the long robe and the—"

"HELL NAW MAN WAKE UP: this dude was just like *you* and me!!" snaps Bud.

"You mean . . ." stammers Buckwheat. "You mean uh . . . he was *black*?"

"How could he be anything else *but* black; *damn*! Buckwheat! what's wrong, baby? I been digging you for years I thought you had *it together*! You still under the murphy of Sylvester's yeast and prat in that damn okee doke game all that muckety-muck! Shit baby I'm beginning to thank you is just a trick Sylvester yourself." Bud chuckles all to himself way upstairs! Madison Avenue First Lieutenant Brinkerhoff and one or two other whities used to call O Dossy "The Lemonade Viet Bubble Cong" for some reason and for the first time now watching Bud this name sounds funny. Suddenly I laugh. Bud was unzipped beautifully, getting his energy from such abuse!

Buckwheat was speaking through Bud's mirth: "But if the gentleman—all sixty-nine versions of him—you refer to is the real—"

Bud cuts in: "HERE! I'll prove it to you!" He snatches from his coat pocket a snapshot and hands it to Buckwheat. "I took this pix myself!"

Buckwheat is carefully examining it. "Well," the announcer says, "all I see is seven policemen escorting three drunk men from the park."

He looks up sharply at Bud who's groaning, "Yeah yeah yeah—*that's all you see*!" Then abruptly a station break; I take a sip of wine and the clock says it's *one-thirty-five*. In order to get to O'Hare Field in time for our flight we'll have to split in about an hour and a half from now; our luggage is already packed upstairs.

Cathy is pouring herself more wine. "You two drink so much of that mess it must be good let me try some," says Alma. She pours some into her own glass as Cathy almost falls off the arm of the chair I'm sitting in.

THE ESCAPE

The TV-eye has switched to the white-faced Jack Beanstalk who is lean, tall, and movie star–like. He's standing in soggy grass at the police line holding the microphone before Anita's face. ". . . I *said* I got married yesterday and my husband and I have been trying to get home—to my apartment. And we haven't been able to make it." Beanstalk suddenly laughs, as he turns to us: "Did you hear that folks? Here's a newlywed couple—" Harold's face, directly behind Anita's, comes into focus. "This couple has been trying to get home from—where? City Hall? Yes, from City Hall, in the Loop, since yesterday . . ." He whistles. "That'll give you home viewers some indication of how many people are in the streets . . ." Beyond the media announcer stands a sea of black faces intercepted by the immobile white faces of very serious-looking cops. I notice by the clock that Cathy O and I are running out of time. "Baby, we better split." Cathy snaps out of her stupor, she stands up. *Then.* Suddenly. This is the point: Now something is happening! but the TV camera is not properly picking it up. This moment is charged with the consecrated hostility and disorder of the slaying of

Lee Harvey Oswald. Gratuitously or perhaps not. The three of us watch with candor: the hot activity of our eye for Its eye. I can *feel* our minds clutch the horror, the holiness of what is our need for ritual and for cleansing, for redemption. The camera picks swift, strange compositions, throwing them at us: is somebody knocking the shit out of the technician, destroying his camera? A hoard of dashing hodgepodge black people momentarily becomes a cone-shaped mirage that bounces into the El track beams supporting the end of the line.

This is such a hysterical moment Cathy suddenly throws her hand over her heart, laughing her beautiful musical laugh, and recites: "I pledge allegiance to the flag of . . ." God! What about our flight?!!!

Now Jack Beanstalk is being focused on as he stands before us his shirt collar open, his topcoat ripped; he looks dazed. Alma chuckles sardonically. "Now, you know them niggers didn't have to tear that man's clothes off like that. Honest to God, they make me 'shame to be a splib sometimes!"

The three of us are standing before the set. I don't dare jump to conclusions—Beanstalk is shouting into the microphone but nothing is coming through the video soundtrack. I feel the tiny pressure of Cathy's fingers against my own.

Beanstalk seems possessed by devils as he persists; for a moment a little Negro boy who's under a big-billed cap that shades his winter eyes pins his paws to the announcer's leg, obviously trying to get Beanstalk to look up. Without even looking down Beanstalk slaps the boy's hand away as though a fly were annoying him.

Alma drunkenly begins to giggle as she falls deliberately back on the couch, screaming now with laughter. *"Shit let's do anything the world's come to an end . . ."* Her faithful inner response to media madness, I chuckle at it.

"What is the boy trying to tell him?" Cathy wants to know.

"It's obvious, Baby."

Alma, all eyes, jumps up as the camera begins to search the sky. We still have no "voice" yet while Alma throws her hand upside her forehead in an improper lazy salute. "We hold these truths to be self-evident: that . . ." She rocks on her toes as she goes on: ". . . that all men are created equal; that they are endowed by their Creator with certain unalienable rights; that among these are life, liberty, and the pursuit of happiness."

Cathy, who is almost as intoxicated as Alma, stands at puffed-up attention reciting: "Fourscore and seven years ago our fathers brought forth on this continent a new nation, conceived in liberty and dedicated to the proposition that all men are created equal." She's trying to keep a straight face: not to laugh.

And the camera finally picks up a moving object way up in the sky: it's a bird! it's a plane! no wait a minute! The camera returns to Beanstalk, his mouth moves to something like: "Good grief!" He holds his head and his eyes are big as Chattanooga stoplights.

Very quickly the camera again picks up the thing in the sky. It looks like a monkey suspended on a toy parachute. Alma is hoarse with laughter falling all over Cathy, knocking her down to the floor. Alma climbs to her knees and piously clasps her hands together.

I look at the clock—*shit*! we have less than an hour to make it to the airport. I feel hoodooed by frustration. I take a quick drink from Alma's bottle and Cathy caves in from laughter at the sight of Alma on the floor babbling: "Oh Allah, I didn't mean to do it! I swear Allah I didn't mean to do it! Please Papa Allah give me one more chance—just one more chance I swear I won't mess up no more. Don't jinx me this time, Allah. If you let me slide just this once I swear you'll never have any more trouble out of me as long as I live—"

The monkey on the parachute is still slowly descending while they try to get a better closeup. I tighten a grip on Cathy's arm. "Let's go."

She says to Alma: "We are leaving . . ." We go toward the door, Alma is trying to say something but I have Cathy's arm and upstairs I call O'Hare Field, *yes* flight 777 gate four is still scheduled. I'm conclusive—I grab the luggage—two suitcases, leaving the third for Cathy.

"We're going to make it!" I predict, going out almost falling down the stairs with the bags, Cathy struggling behind me.

Alma rushes out—faces us. "Y'all are missing the BEST part—" We drop the luggage. Dash back into her place. Meanwhile trying to get into our coats. Beanstalk, standing up in a jeep holding his microphone, is being faithfully followed by the camera to the spot where the . . . well, where God is going to land. I step two inches closer. They flash a closeup of the "thing." Beanstalk's coattails are flapping in the brisk wind and his hair is blowing movie star–style while a more or less imperfectly kept police line is threatened by a growing mixture of black and white people. Jack Beanstalk, a confessed "poontang" eater and friend of Everybody, even the pope and president, jumps off the jeep where several men dressed like Standard Oil station servicemen are frantically pulling the parachute from God's tiny form that is completely snowed by his own descent. As they get it off Beanstalk waits talking bullshit to the

TV audience but we're not listening to him; we're watching the closeup now.

Suddenly it is *clear*! Beanstalk says: "Ladies and gentlemen, as you can see on your TV screen it's . . . just a rubber tarbaby about three feet high bearing a likeness to . . . my guess would be Mickey Mouse . . ."

"This manila envelope attached to its neck," the announcer says, as he dislodges and opens it, "looks like it might . . . might contain something important . . ." Beanstalk clears his throat. "I'm . . . I'm frankly . . . uh dismayed . . . by this . . . by this entire event—as I'm sure all of us must be. I . . . well, let's see, what have we here . . .?" With the manila envelope open, a sheet of paper 8 × 12 is extracted and he reads it silently first then murmurs: ". . . I'm frankly . . . uh dismayed, to say the least, but, as you can see, I have the contents of the envelope in my hand . . . uh . . . I suppose the proper thing to do is to read it—it's an announcement, and since I'm an announcer I will announce it—" He looks toward the cameraman, asking: "Are we ready . . .? Can you get a closeup of this as I read it?" We see the face of the page. Beanstalk reads: "FOR IMMEDIATE RELEASE. Office of the Mayor. THIS IS AN OFFICIAL PUBLIC NOTICE OF GREAT URGENCY. A General Curfew is hereby declared at 4:00 this day, December 25, 1967."

I looked at the clock—it was already three-thirty! Beanstalk was reading: "Everybody without exception must clear the streets immediately. Go to your homes; do not under any conditions risk returning to the streets. We stress that it might be extremely hazardous or even fatal. Only authorized officers of the law are exempt from this curfew. Those who violate this curfew will automatically be handled by the proper authorities and in the proper manner. I personally hereby and otherwise give my full consent to the chief of police to use the full force of his department to strongly urge his men to shoot to kill any and all violators of this order. WE WILL MAINTAIN LAW AND ORDER AT ANY COST. We act with the full approval of every level of the government in our great fine Christian nation. Yours Truly, Viajes S. Knovak, the Mayor of the City of Chicago, Cook County, Illinois."

I can't react to any of this right away: it is too much so I grab Cathy's hand and make a mad dash for the doorway, feeling for my wallet reassured that it has folded inside a small sheaf of traveler's checks purchased with the bread won at the track a few days ago. I grab the two suitcases from the hallway floor and command Cathy: "Grab that one, Baby!" and like in those 1940 lighthearted American movies starring Jimmy Stewart or Gary Cooper I conject: "I don't know how we—gonna—do it—but we're gonna—make that flight!" She picks up the suitcase, her face turns red from the strain, perhaps she has the really heavy one containing our dreams and secrets and the unborn remains of all those babies nature promised us.

But just before embarking on the grand final chase Alma comes out and blocks the exit. She is very drunk with a vertical palm against the wall. "Just one last word . . . *to you*!" she says trying to look very profound but sisterly with her housecoat hanging halfway off, the pink slip showing beneath it; "this is *not* for you, Ace!!" she's speaking over my shoulder.

My heart is pounding from carrying the luggage and from excitement. I shout: *"Let me by Alma we've got to go—we'll miss our flight!!!"*

Alma lifts her mighty matriarchal bullhorn voice above mine: "I can say what I have to say in one second: I just want to tell you right now so I won't have to tell it to you in a different way, later; that this girl—standing behind you . . . she's yours, right? OK, that's all right. That's yours and her business, but . . . I just want to say that of all the people and breezy dippydips I've met since I joined this so-called domestic peace corps, she's the only one who's been a *real* human being. I mean *for real*; do you dig me? So listen carefully 'cause like I say I'd hate to have to go to war against you . . . Don't—I repeat; *do not* get her up there in New York and start acting like ah—" The corners of her mouth twist upward and her knowing expression lingers; she goes on: ". . . You know what I mean . . . 'cause if you do I shit you not: me and you will lock asses and do the Rumble the Jerk the Fox Trot the Watusi the Monkey and the Dog from the moment I get to your behind on through sunset sunrise winter summer fall and spring 'til one of us takes care of businesssssss . . ." The corners of her mouth fall as she skids on the *s*'s.

"Alma—" I cry out but she cuts in: "I know—I know! I just

wanted to tell you that even though you've been a perfect gentleman. I mean I ain't heard you knocking her head up against the wall trying to bust her brains out. But *you know* what happens when so many brothers and white girls get together . . ."

I am trying to move her to the side. She says, "OK," and moves from the doorway to hug Cathy and to kiss her somewhere near her mouth.

Now . . . on the burnt rubber–smelling street, Cathy trailing struggling with the suitcase behind me; I have no idea how we'll get a taxi on a day like this. This street is relatively empty of people but South Parkway is jammed with so many people running into and knocking each other out and just as we reach the intersection one of the bags I'm carrying pops open and Cathy's torn panties, my mismatched socks, a fake wedding ring, and a douche bag fall out; I stuff the stuff back in. I've never been a quitter. We will make it, even if I have to pay a motorist—any motorist!—a hundred dollars or more to drive us there.

I see a Sambo cop coming across the triple-lane street swinging his billystick. He's just gotten out of a squad car, there's something in his gait that is very familiar yes damnit it's Jumpy Eyes himself sloe-black Wayne Fisher but what is he doing in a keystone suit . . . He comes non-stop to us, singing: "my man my man—" and cacklingly says, "Gimme some skin!" He extends his hard-worked crusty right hand so I slap it.

"Dig man—I'm trying to make a four-fifteen flight from O'Hare to—"

Wayne snaps: "Forget about it! Ain't nothing going on out there—hehehehe! You just gone have to stay right here with us as the shit does down . . ." He looks to Cathy for approval. She's silently baffled—she has *that* look.

". . . I'm talking straight!" I tell him; "I've GOT to make that flight—it's still scheduled. We checked . . ." He drops the smile. He's very serious now. Absently I say: "I'd be willing to pay anybody *anything* they ask just to drive us there . . ."

Wayne clicks his heels together and salutes. "At your service, Doctor! My lemon-zane is parked in yonder parking lane!"

"Are you serious?" I try to further contaminate him with the urgency of my mission by the tone of my voice.

He jacks up his arm, pulling back his sleeve looking at his wristwatch. "It's five minutes to four—I'll have you there in exactly twenty minutes!" He starts off. "This way Miss Ann—you too, boy!"

In the police car going west Wayne opens the siren as we pick up speed going full force cars ahead are pulling over to the side out of the way. The siren sounds like an inelegant dying beast. Our luggage in the front seat, we numbly watch the back of my pal's head. Wayne shouts back to us: *"I got the spotlight on, too!* We're looking good brother Eli we're looking good!"

I sit back trying to relax. I say to Wayne: "Thought you were in business, man—didn't know you'd become a cop!"

He calls: "I ain't a cop!"

"What?" I cry and Cathy looks at me, unable to be shocked anymore. "Then how'd you get this car, the uniform?"

He chuckled. "Ah shit! man, *every*body's doing it: that's easy! I just dressed up like Li'l Red Ridin' Hood, den picked me out a li'l bitty policeman—one I could handle—I just skipped up to 'im sweet-like and stuck my finger in my mouth and asked him if he'd play hopscotch with me—you know how they like to play hopscotch with pretty li'l girls—"

"Then—what happened?"

"Well, when he got to Kingdom Come he turned his back on me—that's when I let 'im have it. Nice fit, ain't it?" he asked hunching his shoulders.

"It's a perfect uniform, Wayne . . ."

Cathy wasn't with this humor: she sat looking beyond the window.

"By the way," I inquired, "how much are you charging me for this trip?"

We go sweeping through scarlet red stoplights at Wentworth, as he answers: "See—da you go da you go! Take it easy shit we can talk about dat later. Haven't I always took care of you, huh? What about last August when you needed a job who told you *how* to *talk* to the white folks, huh, answer me dat?"

I notice Cathy is suddenly nervously busy tying a string to a hairpin. "You doing that damn juju trick again . . .?" My nerves are shot but a gentle touch of my hand tells her I'm sorry to have spoken so gruffly. I look beyond the icicle-lined window at shivering dudes in makeshift self-defense guerilla suits pounding the cement their jellyjelly faces moving under the badass command of their chattering teeth.

"Do you have a radio in the car?" Cathy asks Wayne timidly.

"Sho nuff, I do, Miss Ann . . ." But he keeps right on wheeling with a fab smile reaching all the way around his face.

Baby seems more agitated as she whispers to me: "Does he have a radio or doesn't he—?" He's hunched at the wheel riffing. I lean forward to see his snowflake-white teeth working like glaciers against the bars of a Sam Cooke song.

"Do you do or do you don't got a radio, man?"

"Oh," he says, reaching out, snapping it on; "you want to *hear* it?" At that moment I see an arctic-dressed joker galloping on horseback, his tiny round burnt-sienna face and his snowdrift eyes peeping out from under his huge parka. The gold engraved name on his saddlebag is "Ellison," he's being chased by a pack of stormtroopers across a vacant lot; up ahead suddenly a building blows sky-high, the colors so mellow and varied it looks like fun—fireworks—the blizzard-torn street we're taking looks like Germany after World War II. So much action it's like looking at paramecia through a microscope.

"Boy!" sang Cathy O, "how long does it take the radio to warm up?"

Wayne starts slowly his voice spiraling: "*Uhhhhhhhhhhh-Uh!* Eli, my man . . . I think I feel a draft!"

"No you don't you paranoid nigger—she was just making an exclamation—she wasn't addressing you!!"

Cathy, puzzled, turns questioningly to me. I murmur, "Forget it."

The radio is speaking to us: "Good afternoon my dear friends, this is Buckwheat Brownie coming to you from Cook County Jail—"

"Ah shit!" cried Wayne, "they done arrested my main man!"

"Shut up!!" I command, "maybe he's only interviewing somebody . . ." We suddenly zap through a whiz of hailstones and hoarfrost cakes, the cool blazing semiliquid tension of a middle-class suburban neighborhood.

God! we're getting there. We have maybe three minutes to make it. Buckwheat, in his usual coherent and rich-toned voice is saying: "Needless to say, I've been arrested. The charges aren't yet defined, the network refuses to act in my defense. I can't have a lawyer, but I was allowed to keep my microphone . . ."

"You hear that shit, man?!" cries Wayne looking back at me and almost running over a little Mother Hubbard–dressed woman in hightop boots who lands on her butt. It's Mrs. Jones.

Meanwhile Cathy is juggling the hairpin on the string. "What did you ask it this time, Cat?"

"Oh, just questions."

"Is it really legitimate, Baby?"

"It's a proven scientific fact—you just ask the question silently to yourself while holding it completely still if it goes this way the answer is no—that way the answer is yes . . . A group of scientists at Harvard proved it—"

"Gimme—" I reach for it; "Let me see it—"

Cathy moves back clinging protectively to her piece of string with the dangling hairpin.

"*Oh no*! you have to make your *own*—this one wouldn't work for you, anyway. I've trained this one to work for me, and if I let you touch it . . . Well, it's best not to let anyone touch yours *after* you've trained it."

I repress a strong urge to burst out in coldblooded laughter. I lean forward and ask Wayne: "How we doing?"

He confides: "Fat city, baby! Fat city!" Now we're here—Wayne enters the gates full blast with siren and lights on, meanwhile asking: "Which kinda airline is it, Doctor?"

"American Airlines." He skids to a piercing headsplitting stop.

"Here we is! American Airlines at your service!" He looks back, sweat dripping from his face.

"Looks like you've been in a steam-bath!"

"No, Eli, just a deep-freeze. It's exactly four-fifteen . . ."

Wayne carries one of the bags—the airport looks pretty normal—the wintry brilliance of the place with its chrome and the velvet-covered ladies everywhere perched or moving slowly like sacred birds.

Over the intercom system a patient, well-trained voice is kindly saying: "Will Mr. Maxim Gorky please go to gate four, please . . ."

"What's our gate number, Eli?" Cathy asks.

"Ah shit, I can't remember—" I set the suitcase down and it cracks open and some of "my own" money falls out with pictures of Willie, Booker T. Washington, George Washington Carver, and a new addition to the family—that hoarse cat who used to run around serving Jack Benny. I look at the tickets. "It's gate four, Baby!" I quickly gather my scattered bills but Wayne manages to pick up the new-currency note.

"Man, is this my uncle you got here on this play money?"

"It's not play money," I say, moving fast now toward our gate while the intercom says: "Passengers now loading for flight seven seventy-seven at . . ."

Cathy and Wayne tagging behind. "I *ast* you a question, Eli—" whines Wayne; "Is dis my uncle—?"

"It's not your uncle dumdum it's . . . Oh, never mind!" Cathy, who has seen the money before, begins to chuckle. Presently we reach gate four. The pilot is taking tickets; we fall into line behind the escapees, the classy-looking gents with gray temples, the flatass women standing in gray suits with their eyebrows eternally lifted, the ridges of their noses slightly gaped as though trying to determine precisely what it is that they smell that is so goddamn unfavorable.

Wayne stands to my side pushing the suitcases along the floor as the line moves, intently examining the movie star on the currency note. *"Man you lying to me this is uncle Emmanuel the good shepherd messenger of the Messiah—"*

All those lined-up people are turning around to try to psych out what's going on. In a somewhat lower voice Wayne continues: "*I know* my own uncle when I see him! Shit! Look at that smile! Look at those eyes!" Wayne seems very earnest. "I'm sure you must have heard of him, he's pastor of *Holy Trinity in Unity God the Father God the Son the Annointed Savior Prince of Peace Holy Ghost Church for Armed Black Self-Defense and Liberation, Incorporated . . ."*

"Look man—" I snap, "how much do I owe you?" Meanwhile smartly whipping out my book of American Express traveler's checks and my Parker pen, poised waiting for him to tell me his fee so I can start signing the checks to meet his figure; but he seems dumbfounded by the business in my hand. He turns blankly to Cathy, his bottom lip hanging; she is embarrassed by the sudden attention from him.

"What's he doing?" Wayne asks her.

"Those are checks," Cathy explains, turning red as she sees how many eyes are on her.

"Let me see those things—" Challenge in his voice, I turn over the booklet of checks to him; he holds it out at arm's length alongside my new money then very impudently throws the sheaf of checks into my fumbling hands—but I catch it.

"You mean to tell me you planned to pay me with them things?"

"That's right. These checks are good all over the world, man. Movie stars use them . . ." I retort.

The line is moving too slowly. "This may be only a dollar, man, but it's got *my uncle* on it, you dig! This is all the pay I want . . ." He pauses. "Can I keep it?"

"Sure," I snap, "if I had time I'd run you off a thousand—"

"You got the plate with you?"

"You bet—right here." I kick the suitcase, it pops open and the black metal plate falls out between Wayne's pointed-toe green alligator shoes.

He screams: "HALLELUJAH!" Picks it up and begins running down the slick-floored hallway—suddenly he stops, turns around and comes halfway back, that is, in earshot and calls: "You'll be good, now—hear?" Then he boots it out of sight.

And the ticket-taker is reaching for our tickets and smiling pleasantly. "You will have to check your luggage. We have a minute or two yet."

Wow! How could we have forgotten? Cathy and I struggling furiously back down the long hallway to check the luggage through the proper channels at the ticket-sales counter; then trotting the distance back and the ticket-taker is taking the very last ticket from the last ticket-holder who . . . *Oh, God, no!* is Mokus Dokus stuffed into a suit with a necktie around his neck. We go across the erected bridge from the lobby into the plane and the stewardess just inside the jet smiles. The skin of her silver-red lips stretches beautifully back from the top row of her zinc-white bunnyrabbit teeth as she checks our seat numbers which are 6 and 7 and points the way to the coach seats.

I look back and catch the evil eye of Mississippi Moke. The stewardess rushes up the aisle with a very motherly look on her brow and she holds under Moke's mouth a large paper cup, the kind they give you to throw up in if you get airsick. Hastily Moke elbows her out of his way and takes a seat in the first-class section. We find our seats in the coach section and soon the jet is taxiing out to the runway where for a second it pauses as if to get on its mark—then we're off; the aircraft lifting, finally; the moment it takes to the air, I feel Cathy's hand grip my knee. She's beside the window, we're both looking out.

HITTING THE APPLE

We were spurting in fumes of gas and metal from JFK through the complex night. Colored objects dashing zooming by. This ground-level entrance was so sensuous and ritual-like! Up ahead, over the faceless driver's shoulder, through the window, a huge billboard:

THE VERY BEST AT AMAZING DISCOUNTS

you can trust us with your very life!!!

But how about this driver? Could we trust him? I kept looking at his audacious name: *Gunman.* A warped scheme in his mind? Apparently—because I certainly hadn't given him any address; and it possibly didn't make much difference to *him*—a man of routine, simply doing his job, dead work—like an evildoer playing everything by ear but with compassion, an address, a destiny so far, hadn't pulled any trigger in my impolite mind. And Baby, from the very beginning, injured like a lonely ovary in a vacant woman, simply refused to think, to make decisions—which left me not only with the colossal load of my mismanaged self, but slightly cringing, restless and pummeled under the load of her spirit—though I wasn't fully aware of it yet—I was too happy, wildly so!

The cabbie gave a quick boorish laugh and called over his shoulder, "Popular impulses at special human rates!"

"What'd he say?"

"Baby, listen—" I began, slightly weary, showing my ill breeding already—and we had been together only since October 28, and this was like the day after the Plot, I mean the Sacrifice, December 26; but I decided to control my usually unveiled but mystifying tongue, which, in any case, was tired.

"What were you going to say?"

But the cabbie thought Cathy was addressing him and retorted:

"I only was trying to remind you folks that I haven't the slightest idea where I should take you. How about Brooklyn?"

I thought of asking several questions at once but all of them jammed up in me and nothing came out for a moment anyway. "You see," I began, "the problem, Mack—" and I threw my weight forward, elbows on my knees so that he could catch the body of each word in at least the ear on *this* side of his head, over the roar of the expressway traffic, the heavy groaning of trucks and buses and the swift oozing metal sounds of the glittering modern buggy-wagons that still had horsepower for some mysterious reason: ". . . the problem is *this*—" Suddenly, while still focusing his cumbersome head forward like any good driver he shamelessly cut into my sentence.

"The only reason I suggested Brooklyn is there's a lot of superstitious people in other parts of the city. I live in Brooklyn myself; you'd never know it, though, because I don't have a Brooklyn accent—did you notice? Well, you folks are obviously from outta town so you didn't notice. Even grew up there, and I don't talk like an ordinary taxicab driver—if you know what I mean . . ."

Cathy, in a furiously cheerful voice, broke his monologue, announcing: "Didn't you use the word superstitious?"

"Yeah, lady, that's what I said—but I'll explain to you what I mean by that, if you give me a moment—*can you both hear me*?" A little too loudly, we assured him and he cranked up his voice and pumped on: "Like the gentleman called me *Mack*—" and now, directly to me: "I know you didn't mean nothing by doing that, but it just proves a point; the same thing I'm talking about, the way I talk. I mean, I never call people Mack, you know what I mean?" I could feel his passionate desire to turn around to witness my reaction to his clouded question; but he didn't and because he was obviously such an excellent driver I never saw his face. After a while it was like his voice was coming out of the rear end of his head and it seemed so natural for him. "That's the way cab drivers talk, you know—hey Mack, Mack this and Mack that." His pause was very stingy. "Well—the young lady asked me about superstitions, now, I ain't—I mean *am not*—no expert on the real nature of these kinds of things, and I don't know anything about you people—I mean whether or not you two are married, or just friends or what have you, but I know this, that—except for Brooklyn—a mixed couple, and as I say, I don't know if you are a mixed couple, I mean if you two are . . . you know what I mean, married or going together—for all I know, you could be a couple of civil rights workers—right? Right! And I really don't care, I mean I don't even care to know, but in case you are in some way romantic—" For the quickest and most tense moment of his speech he suddenly and automatically took his fat, reddened hands from the wheel to form the beautiful word romantic; he just threw his palms up, facing each other, as though he were holding something round and invisible—"then, I'd suggest Brooklyn, because there's less hard feelings there against . . . Well, you know what I mean. In Brooklyn, you'll never find people going around using bedbugs, for example, as a cure for sore eyes. But in Manhattan—oh Christ! there're folks who do this kind of thing: actually mix bedbugs—all crushed up—with salt and the human milk of a pregnant woman, if they can find one, and not only for sore eyes but the poorer people, in the ghetto—you know, they're even dumber than just the average guy—they even take it internally, they claim it cures urban hysteria. It's witchcraft, is what it is . . ."

Oh mercy wrathful God I was too tired to laugh but this was about to get to me and to make matters worse, Cathy, in her usual innocent manner flatly stated: "Are you saying that this is generally true of *every*body who lives in Manhattan—"

And the driver, really excited now, defensively snapped: "Do you know what *literal* means, young lady? Yeah, you do, huh—well, that's the way I mean it. I wouldn't tell you anything that isn't true." He hunched his shoulders. I was still leaning forward, to hear better. Cathy now anxiously joined me. I was looking straight ahead, fearful but trying to keep my composure. I must have been peering for some indication of our destiny, or at least my own, as I listened to the sovereign voice of our volunteer tour guide. "There certainly ain't nothing in it for me, I mean for me to lie to you, deliberately. Ask yourself, What could I get out of it? Just trying to be a decent fellow and tell you—since you both are obviously from no parts of New York—how it *is* in places like Manhattan, the Bronx, even in Queens and Staten Island, you find some kind of superstitious practices, but to a lesser degree, because, well, those people out there they've had a little more education, but Manhattan is the worst of all!" I could feel Cathy's excitement and frustration and confusion; she obviously wanted to argue with the man but didn't know how to begin. His voice was so coolly antiseptic, so sure: "My son-in-law, he's a lawyer, told me just the other day, believe it or not, that a Manhattan lady came to him to file for a divorce from her husband. Want to hear the reason she wanted a divorce?"

"By all means," I smoothly assured him.

"This husband of hers, the poor guy, he dropped a black ace of spades—accidentally—while just playing a normal game of cards, in their living room . . . You know, just sitting around, with the fellows. That's *why* she wanted a divorce, and before you call me a liar, I'll tell you this, my son-in-law is, first: a good Catholic, a Harvard man, a responsible gentleman who maintains his ethics, and a decent husband to my daughter—they're even buying a home in Brooklyn Heights, and if you knew anything about the city here at all you would know what *that* means—"

"Mister Lawman," Cathy shot, "you *must* be putting us on—"

This of course steamed him up again. *I* wanted to hear what he had to say; I was ready to believe anything—and everything he said, so far, sounded perfectly logical to me.

"Look—" he snapped ambitiously, "do you know anybody, in your hometown, where you come from, who hangs garlic around in their home—I mean to keep evil spirits away?"

"No," Cathy admitted.

"Do you know—or have you ever heard of—people who go around rubbing baldheaded old helpless men on their heads just to try to improve *their own* memory? Or how about this theory that water is fattening? Well, there's a lot of Manhattaners who are right now, I mean this very minute! who're on a water diet—I mean a lot of them don't drink the stuff at all, and nothing that contains it, not even liquor! And furthermore, all over Manhattan there are like thousands and thousands of voodoo rites. And I don't mean concealed in some basement—right out in the open! Certain people are put under spells by certain other people for certain reasons, and they're actually held like that, as victims. They use everything from rotten apple-roots to certain kinds of perfumes to get certain effects, cause people to go insane or walk around crazy-like, you know—restless, can't sit down or nothing, just going on and on until they drop dead—you've heard of the hippies, haven't you? Sure you have—that's what's happened to those poor kids—they're all under a spell. They've been hexed. And, believe me, I'm not trying to scare you folks, I'm just trying to inform you . . . Actually, there're a lot of cab drivers who won't even go into Manhattan, especially way uptown, the farther you get uptown the worse it is—" He coughed, and now speaking directly to me: "Nothing personal to you sir, but the colored people are the worst of all; but it's not just *them*—I don't want to give you that impression—it's all of New York City; like I say, except for Brooklyn. It's really funny sometimes; you can be driving around in Manhattan and see people strutting and just ah strolling along and everybody—I mean *everybody*—is carrying an umbrella—"

Cathy cut in: "But why?"

"Well, you see, they have this belief, it's like part of Manhattan culture, you know—they believe that if you carry an umbrella that *that* will forestall rain—"

"But what have they got *against* rain?" asked Cathy, about to lose her temper.

"Search me!" His shoulders lifted and fell again. "All I can tell you is what I see!"

I cut in: "So, where're we headed now? Where does that leave us?"

He pondered the hugely serious question for several moments. "You see, it's a long drive in, and right now you still got a chance to choose. Like they say on television, when they're talking politics, you have an *alternative*—" He chuckled. His shoulders rocking. "That's a nice big word, huh?" He stopped laughing, then said: "I don't mean to dwell on this subject—if anything I hate is somebody who dwells on a subject—but while you're making up your minds, let me ask you a question. You sir, *or* the lady. Have either one of you heard of the art of capnomancy?"

"The art of what?" I cleared my throat, hoping my mind would also defog.

"It's an evil force that's practiced, very commonly practiced, in Manhattan; some people call it pollution—"

Cathy cut in: "But how about the Village, certainly, the Village—"

He cut her off: "The Village is no different; of course you may find some people there—you know, they're all weird down there—really weird people, and as I say, some of them might call it pollution, but the true name of it is capnomancy—it's an art. It's done with smoke, and it's very deadly; so, if you decide on Manhattan *anyway,* remember that—because you're going to come up againt it—"

"But if it's smoke, certainly it would drift to Brooklyn, too—" Cathy pleaded.

He answered her swiftly, very curtly: "Nope—we don't have that sort of thing in Brooklyn . . ." His tone was absolutely self-righteous.

I said, after a moment of silence, "I won't ask you what *do* you have in Brooklyn—" This statement obviously bewildered and confused him.

He asked, *"But why not?—"*

"Because," I said pleasantly, "I've heard that, aside from other more private reasons, they haven't started body-snatching yet, in that area . . ."

We were going straight ahead eighty-six miles per hour on the expressway and for the first time he turned completely around, he was so perplexed he looked like an ambassador of confusion—aside from the fact that he also looked somewhat like Jackie Gleason—*"What're you talking about?"*

Well, I was a little surprised that he hadn't heard but I faked more astonishment than I felt: "You mean—you haven't heard?"

"No, but I'm all ears—"

I relaxed more when he turned back to the business of driving and I quietly cleared up his confusion: "Don't go around talking about this to anybody you don't know, because you could easily get into trouble but, already . . . already, in certain parts of the world—I'm not saying where—people are being snatched off the streets, under the shadowy cover of night, and taken to certain places—usually hospitals, where very rich or important people who have heart trouble are in critical conditions, about to die—they call these captured people, the ones they snatch, who're always poor and defenseless people, especially pregnant women because their hearts are in better shape than anybody's—they are especially sought after! Anyway, they take these people and change their names, you know what I mean—?"

"No—" the cab driver said, "but I'm listening—" He chuckled, obviously not taking me very seriously. Cathy, by the way, was listening intently—and, of course, she should have been because I had never before told her about this secret information that had come my way, quite by accident (and even now, I'm not at liberty to reveal the source!).

"They all get the same name, they're called *donors*—"

"What?" He was truly puzzled and seemingly more seriously intent on what I was saying.

"You know, one who donates." I paused, to let that slip into his head. "You see, the only way the operation can succeed is if you catch a person who is healthy, walking around with good blood circulation—and you have to *act* swiftly, like they say where I come from—*you have to be swift*—and use very sharp instruments, have everything all ready, get your little team together, then *shhhhhhhhh*! cut out the donor's ticker, and get it into this other person's chest—everything depends on how quickly and skillfully it's done . . ."

"Holy Christ! in heaven! what *are* you talking about?" he asked. For the first time since we'd left Wayne at the airport in Chicago, Cathy laughed, though it wasn't a happy laugh.

As an afterthought I thought it only fair to add: "Of course, they use antiseptics and all kinds of—"

He cut me off: "Just hold on a second will you? Answer me this—what has this got to do with Manhattan?"

"Nothing—" I said, so thrilled that he finally got the point: "That's *why* I've decided we're going to Manhattan—just head toward the Village, and I'll decide where you can let us out at when we get down there—"

"Look!" the driver said in an offended tone of voice: "If you're talking about what I *think* you're talking about, which is murder, *and* if you think for one moment that we have that sort of hanky-panky stuff in Brooklyn—then you're dead wrong!"

It always makes me feel joyful to know what I'm going to do

next; so, by now, I was quite overjoyed when I reached up and gave our friend a friendly slap on the shoulder; "Well, I certainly wasn't referring to Brooklyn and I'm mighty happy to have your word that Brooklyn is still safe, at least to that degree—"

I could see the huge mouth of Midtown Tunnel up ahead, speckled with yellow light. I had the distinct feeling that we were making an exit rather than an entrance!

BON VOYAGE

She was now in the front room tying a rope around her suitcase. I could hear the girl from across the hall saying, "I envy you, Cathy. Wish *I* was going to California. Last time I was in San Francisco, two years ago, I really loved it . . ."

I lay in the semidark room, my naked temperate body like a crucifix beneath the dirty damp sheet, where, all day, all afternoon, into the night, up until this nosy bitch, our neighbor, came over, we were in bed, off and on, making love.

I had never really faced the disquieting fact that she, a kind of pivot point in my life, from the very beginning of our relationship back in Chicago, even then was scheduled on some undetermined day to leave me. Now, that day had come: February 18, 1967. What time was it? I couldn't keep my eyes off the clock beside the bed. It was three o'clock in the morning. Her flight time was 6:15.

Wish that neighbor bitch would go home. I wanted these last minutes with her for myself. For a moment I felt enough anger and frustration to get up, go out there, and tell her to go home! But I was too hung in my own private lamentation. *"Cathy!"*

Cathy came through the dusty wool curtain, her silhouette before me.

"Yes?"

"Come here." With a tired sigh, she came over to the bed and sat down like a child, her heavy hinges, a beautiful pressure against my thigh. "Spend this time with me, baby. Get rid of that bitch!"

I could see the outline of her face, her smooth neck. The Adam's apple moving. I *felt* her thoughts. Her sympathy. I began to stroke beneath the blue faded terry cloth bathrobe. Her flesh was still damp from the electric screwing twenty-five minutes ago, before the neighbor came with her unflavorful *"Bon voyage."*

I lay smooth, pleasant, empty. Only for a moment, the quarter of the pleasure, the aftermath.

Then, the mounting dread, the reality of the sounds of the ticking clock beside me, inscrutable in its relationship to *real* time, though I couldn't yet accept her leaving, to face alone the unconcealed inhumanity of this city, I had somehow already, in the most secret part of myself, moved beyond the pain. Its bamboozling structure.

It was five o'clock. Our neighbor had gone home two hours and thirty minutes ago. Cathy and I had been asleep, in each other's arms, until this moment; the clock was ringing: BRIIIIIIIIIIIIIING! I slammed it off.

CATHY

I am depressed, evil, I feel the crushing weight of her departure; I hardly know what to say to her; it is five o'clock already, the superstitious hour of birth and death, and this bright electric luminous frenzy I feel, the ebb of my dishonorable condition, is too much! But I cannot let Cathy know that I am desperately insane with the sickness I feel at her leaving me; the bewitching entanglement of all the luxuriant feelings she has constructed in me leaves me charmed and ensnared in myself, ugly with craziness; yes, I am "dying," this moment, as she avoids my eyes, too chubby but still shapely, still teenage-looking in her too-tight-fitting gray suit she hasn't worn all the while we've been here; I feel the huge lure of her, the sense of her, and yet I know she has her back to me, busy with her shabby suitcase, checking the strength of the rope precisely because of the delicate fortune, the almost somehow risibility of this incident—her leaving; I almost hate her for the sneaky excitement I know she feels. How can she *want* to leave? I go over to the window; the blood-colored fire, streaked with rich butter-yellow fission lines, smacks its lips eating at the routine structure of the building across the street; tiny hydrogen-oriented little men in colorless suits on a hypothetical payroll dedicated to proving that they and all the rest of mankind are not merely tentative and temporary; they are shooting their polluted liquid, like hypodermic injections from the supreme pusher himself, up into the hysteria of flames; this activity has become so common almost nobody in any of these ghettos except the people in the particular buildings that are burning even bother to stand up, husky with shock, to the excitability of this gigantic moment in which surgical-like perfected social forces, born out of the system of slavery and lies in which we have hustled or pimped so long are bringing down all the bridges, all the prisons, all the stockyards of the self, of the nation. I can hear her behind me, sighing, standing up from the rope. And now the echoes of her five-o'clock-in-the-morning tiredness, as she is saying, "I'm ready," and I thought of ambushing her prowling soul, so that my furious loneliness can feed on it.

"So you're ready," I say, going to her, taking her, her body in the tight suit, into my lean arms; I am shabby, I have hastily dressed in an old blue work shirt and worn-out jeans, I have only to put on my coat, a hooded parka that is thick with the heavy warmth of man-made fabrics, imitation animal hair. I look down into the blue undeluded eyes of her mind, the repressed luminous joy in each hole frustrates me; nothing from her tranquilizes me now.

"Yes—and *Oh God!!!* look at the *time!!!*" she says, having just dashed over to the entrance to the bedroom, looking into the semi-darkness at the *makina* mystery of the moving minute-hand, prevailing. Her pink cheeks are turning red. I must be a mentally somersaulting sleepwalker—I am trembling as I climb into my parka, watching her as she pulls on her shabby frayed-at-the-edges, three-quarter-length coat, which assaults her gentle young beauty; I've noticed this in the past—it hardly is meaningful to me now, except that I wish I had been rich enough to have bought her everything possible to enhance her natural loveliness.

She is trying to pick up the suitcase; I haven't moved from the prints of my heavy-booted footprints. "Baby, I'll carry that."

I go down the steep steps, the blistering coldness of the blue-black–tinted morning greets my face; I feel the concerted effort of gravity take the sonofabitching suitcase out of my hand, and embrace it to the face of the earth, its body. The frosty slabs of the wind that zoom along the street like suspended two-ton slidedoors bump my body back into Cathy's, as she trails behind me toward Avenue A. The frozen snow coughs, barks, crunches beneath our pedestrian strides. The odor of garbage isn't so heavy at this hour, frostbitten, perhaps still hiding around the inside edge of these beaten-up old cans, sentries of the sidewalk, gracing the ghetto buildings from one end to the next.

Three-fourths of the block south on Avenue A, three artless PRs are hustling an inebriated and uncommunicative, short, obese, old PR into the blank, metal interior of a double-parked car; I see the silhouettes of two heads already in the vehicle, arms grasping for this corpulent victim.

BELLEVUE

What decided me to move into a hotel, finally, in June, was simply the monsters and inner flying bats I had to put up with in my bellyaching skull, a kinda haunted castle of the planet Lamentation, filled with unrefined, though nobly born visions of who I had become. After Cathy left, even the walls began to grumble. The place became my disordered Castle Bibliomania—but books didn't relieve the pithy burst of mournful loco-motion, *non compus mentis,* the howlingly silent soft walls of myself. I stopped eating. When I tried to sleep things jumped through the pain, vulgar: tickled to death at my disorder. I walked, lonely, the Lower East Side streets. I knew I had to get out of the apartment. Or else. I took the ashes of my soul, in search of some beatitude I had once touched, the intrigue of Cathy, to try to cultivate it again. The day I decided to move, I was crossing at First Avenue. The screwy taxicab traffic was pissing me off: I couldn't cross for a devil's length-of-breath; then, when I did step out (stoplights didn't mean anything at an intersection like this), everything inside began to go black . . .

I remembered while I was dropping down through all those levels of illogically smooth barricades of the self, I had a clear though dimming view of fellow New Yorkers, all around me, continuing, unmoved by the fact that a man was dropping dead next to them. They moved as if to an ominous, gasoline-smelling funeral march! I heard rubber in friction with pavement. The June heat, though it was only eleven in the morning, baked my stuffed ears. But nothing happened. The dizziness was malleable, and I was hammering it into the natural shape of my life: I jumped. The taxi driver swore: "WHATA AH FUCK YA TRYING TA DO HUH GET MY LICENSE TAKEN FROM ME?" He shook his fist. His vindictive face was a playground for obscure ranting, touched by a crackbrain spirit so comforting (to him), a Pioneer, Heap-Big-Bad Cowboy, Lone-Ranger, Germanic Superman with a monopoly on monomania! Then his face explained itself: *he was a Moke!* Who else? Back on the curb, I tried to shake myself straight, I still felt dizzy. As Moke or maybe just a man who looked like him, shot away, his message was flung back: "IF YOU WANNA COMMIT HARAKIRI GET OFFUV DA STREET WILLYA FOR CHRISSAKES—"

I went to Bellevue Hospital. I was a moth sitting on a bench, a number, waiting. I had never been here before: *so this* was the place Cathy used to come to for her birth-control pills. Endless lines of Puerto Rican mothers. The big walls. I was sent up to the second floor, sardined between two plaintive old men. Both were murmuring intercommunications of mutual hypochondriacal pain across me impolitely, to each other. I had been here more than two hours already, yet hadn't seen even the edge of a doctor or an intern. Someone on the bench of dying men would mew, or growl, or whimper every so often; the nurses and orderlies strolled by without the slightest indication of compassion, their eyes flesh-engravings for another world. At the very end of the bench of men in front of the one I was on, a tiny old man who couldn't stand it any longer sniveled and coughed until he fell off, his head bouncing. *O tempora! O mores!* A small boy, from the ladies' section, skipped over and squatted down to examine the musty little "sackcloth and ashes." A colored woman from the women's section jumped up, coming over, saying: *"Dat's what I say about this place; the peoples will let you die before they'll do something for you!"* None of us dying creeps on the benches moved anything, except possibly our eyelids; but the man on my right, when I became so curious about the strange smell of bleach, stale milk, and urine that he emitted, received a slight clamoring from my eyes, and he calmly responded: "I just got out of a sanitarium," because he had *really heard* me ask a question but knowing that he himself was "blind" to all but huge sounds, put the incoherence down to himself.

A big-titty white nurse and two black orderlies came slowly up from the other end of the building. Before even bending her back, the nurse, who looked like Ruth Kowalczyk, indifferently yawned, holding her big fist before her mouth, her eyes scanning us, while the two brothers, who were looking down philosophically at the man on the marble, seemed to wait for her lead. Finally she said: "All right, pick him up and follow me."

Five minutes later another old man, about six kneecaps and twelve wrinkled-old-knuckles down, began to blubber so loud a white orderly opened a door that had been closed all this time and came out, took him by the shoulder. "What's your problem?" he asked the old man, standing him up. But the man only smacked his lips and held out a pink slip of paper for the orderly, who said: "Pops, you're just going to have to wait like everybody else until we finish our lunch." A voice from the back row rambled up distractingly eccentric, high-pitched and equally maniacal: *"We been waiting forever!"*

Finally when an intern confronted me, after an orderly weighed me and took my temperature, I was kindly asked to strip. He was young, with a headful of fussy curls, and serious but uncertain eyes. The first thing he noticed, of course, as he began to examine me by poking here and there on my body, were the embossed markings on the lower left side of my stomach where Vietcong shrapnel left a visible token for the totem pole of my mind to always remember those lonely, insane days in which I was trapped behind the busy ACK-ACK-ACK-ACK ackackackack—ack—ack—ack ackack! sounds of antiaircraft on both sides of the gun. He wanted to know about the operation. He even wanted to know the doctor's name. What I thought of "these Vietniks demonstrating against the war . . ." What about those Victor Charlies; how many guerrillas did I kill; how did I like that baby, the Willie Fudd, WF-2, propeller-driven mobile radar station; but I couldn't answer him. I wanted to know why I felt dizzy. He didn't know. A staff doctor, intense with indifference, came in and also poked around on my stomach.

"What color is your stool?"

"Black."

"Hhhhh."

He motioned for the intern to follow him out. A moment or two later one of the black orderlies and the white one came, peeped in with blank faces, then split.

The staff doctor came back and for the first time he looked at me. "I don't know how to tell you this, but you ain't got enough blood in your veins to hold out another six hours. Unless of course, you immediately start receiving transfusions . . ."

Sitting there naked on the table I felt no conscious fear of the final ride to the psychic demolition dump. All of the backside of my mentality had been shellacked by the silent and grand stillness of my loss of Cathy. I had finally stopped sending desperate telegrams, stopped writing long pleading letters, I was sinking into the horizontal lethargy of death. A scientific fact.

I got dressed, and the white boy wheeled a chair in and the intern held one arm as I sat down into it: remembering the American Hospital in Vietnam. The long Saigon rest. The unspeakable loneliness. Unutterably stupid chatter of the young metal-surfaced brains of my fellow soldiers, mostly white, verbally worshipping aircraft, firearms, particular kinds of jeeps, trucks, cars, daggers, motorcycles; and because I was propped up abed reading one book after another the whole while I was there I earned the name of overstudiousness: "The Tool." Formality, ritual, now, here in Bellevue, while the attendant wheeled me toward the elevator, going down in it, at the Emergency desk, being stamped CRITICAL, and finally wheeled into the Emergency ward, the intern was, in his way, I suppose, trying to distract me, and thereby to theoretically comfort me by asking an endless tapestry of questions about *things* like "thud" incidents, that is, hits made against U.S. aircraft by enemy forces or antiaircraft; like, What does that baby, the Thunderchief fighter, the F-105 look like up close; did I know any pilots victimized by "angels"; what? Hadn't I heard of an angel incident? They're like misleading images, blind spots. He had a buddy, a second lieutenant somebody who was rescued from the wreckage of his jet after crashing because of faulty radar circuit warnings. What was the ARVN outfit really like, huh? Did I think the "birdfarms" in use now were any better than those used in World War II? Had I seen any pilots get "boltered"? Being an infantryman, how many "oil-spot" takeovers had I been involved in; and how about those Vietnamese bunnies, did they have, you know (a wink of the eye), any of that *zaftig* quality? But seriously, since he himself was a draftee who already had word that he was going to be practicing in a hospital close to the currently publicized

DMZ, he was naturally interested in what it was like over there. Did I mind the questions? It was OK that I couldn't tell him much about anything, he understood, having been just a "leg," hahaha. That's what his buddy, this second lieuty, calls infantrymen. This one buddy was in the paratroopers, but the second buddy of his was in the air force and in just a few months had already a hundred and thirty-seven flight missions under his belt; a great driver, but calls infantrymen everything but children of God. A pack of dumb "choi oys." Oh, yes, here we are. In the Emergency ward. How did I feel? It was good that I felt all right, because that would make it easier.

Anyway, after three units of blood, periodic blood counts, phenobarbitals, Darvons, milk of magnesia, urine and feces analyses, tests for anemia, for possible leukemia, or infections, for possible hemophilia, liver disease, jaundice; a series of verbal question-and-answer sessions with one intern or staff doctor or visiting stomach-doctor after another; after watching two men die, one in the bed next to me whose bones were crushed and broken in three hundred and thirty-two separate places, and the other, a very *very* old shrunken guy in a coma, on the other side of the room; after all this, and the sweet-pussy interruptions of objective, detached nurses who woke me in the middle of the night to help me take a leak, holding a pan between my legs, while I stood on my knees, with the bloodline tube still attached to my arm and the O-positive type slowly, silently entering me, from the bag resembling those that Mexicans in the desert carry water in; anyway, they see that I'm not going to hemorrhage, and the next morning the white Baptist preacher comes just to say hello, nothing serious, and I see him looking at my "Castro" and I think I know what he's thinking; after he's gone, and the tube from my arm is gone, and my blood count is back to normal and I'm taken up to a room for the beginning of a two-day GI series of tests for an ulcer; after they discover that I have some of the symptoms of one with a peptic ulcer in the duodenum, of the esophagus, and that my pepsin isn't in proper proportion to aid digestion, that my metabolic process has been recently affected by not eating; after they confirm that I have none of the symptoms of the dumping syndrome, or weakness, rapid heartbeats, or nausea, but do have a very ulcerating condition, after strongly suspecting that it is ulcerated colitis, because of, among other things, my recent loss of weight, they want to know if I eat well, am I worried about anything, how about a job, am I working, after the X-rays *show nothing* like an ulcer except some irritated areas caused by, if you don't consider the fact that ulcers root from neurosis, excessive acidity, I am transferred from the Emergency ward to a regular one; after a rubdown by a beautiful soul sister, and later, the same night, by a blonde chick with a thousand freckles on her cheeks and nose, who told me her life in slow strokes, all about Harmon, New York, and her parents; after living through a drop of ice cream, or a turd of farina or a tiny carton of milk; after a doctor comes to warn me against abusing my stomach; after running into Charlotte Williams in the hallway, daughter of Mr. and Mrs. Williams whom I lived with briefly in Chicago, ten years before, after seeing her bloated, yellow, toothless, murky face, and listening to her tell me everything that had happened to her, the two husbands, the six children, the problems, the illness, all of it; after the doctors stopped coming so often, on the fourth day, though they wanted me to hang around for further observation; I get up and go through the process of checking out; an orderly escorting me downstairs to pick up my clothes, and murmuring a dry farewell; I go into the dreary toilet, get dressed, and feeling very sober and detached—even from myself—I go out, the daylight stinging my eyes.

And I checked into a hotel.

THE OTHER SIDE

We were standing in front of the hotel, a hangout. "Got a smoke on you, kid?" Old man Bob Whatmough—that was the name on the registration book—with the wooden leg was sitting stiffly in a straight-backed chair against the wall. Bad leg out. Double-breasted suit, twenty years old. Old wrinkled hat, weather-beaten face. I put a cigarette beneath his nose. Little chubby black Ann was watching from the sunken world of her junkie nod. Drifting into it and snapping back. "Don't pay me no 'tention, honey." Now she was saying it silently, words no longer calendars.

"If them damn welfare people don't hurry and send out them checks even Mr. Whatmough'll be out on the streets trying to sell some ass. Ain't that right, Mr. Whatmough?" Two visiting junkies waiting to score from Horace McLeod, along with everybody else, cracked up. Technically I was supposed to chase these renegade drifters from the unholy doorway but I couldn't have cared less. I gave the old man a cigarette. At a forty-five-degree angle beneath and beside him on a single stoop to an abandoned doorway just next door, with her arms locked around her lean bone-white knees, was white-haired, cultured Mrs. Guptill, the drinker. She too was giggling.

Whatmough ignored Ann's comment, the satirical question. His hard face twisted toward mine; I stood in the doorway facing nodding-Ann blocking the free passage of pedestrians. A special crusty broad, hung in urban madness. The deep junkie blues. "How'd you like working that desk? It's a bitch, ain't it?" His Brooklyn accent grabbed the words.

"Not really bad."

"Not bad, hell!" he barked. "They should destroy all dese old places like this! There's just no reason why people should have to live like dogs and rats in pissy places like this!"

Mrs. Guptill, no teeth in her head, went quack-quack-quack, and finished up with a sharp cackle. "Go fight city city city hall!"

Ann was laughing to herself. "You people is too much!" A chubby sapphire in a starched summer print.

"I'm telling you, this is a lousy city. Like I'm thinking of going down to Florida, but I just don't like the South—"

"That's 'cause you is really a nigger at heart, Mr. Whatmough. Watson always told you that, now, didn't he?"

Whatmough laughed a little. "Maybe I am, maybe I am." Then his face contracted as he looked up at me. "What chance has a guy like me got of getting a decent place to live, huh? I can't work because of this bum leg. And the welfare check ain't enough to keep a kitten in milk. How in hell can a grown man live on forty dollars a week, huh? You tell me! You work the desk, you know how high the rent is even for this flophouse!"

"But can you *imagine* how disconcerting it must be *for me*" asked Mrs. Guptill quickly. "I was once modestly wealthy. My ex-husband was a general in World War II. Highly decorated. Only problem was he came back to civilian life and couldn't leave military mannerisms *behind* him. He tried to make us, me and the children, live like soldiers, and you can't run a family *that* way! Just imagine! I had anything I wanted! Material luxury was no problem, but because of his attitude I became a wreck, *a spiritual wreck.* Now here I am." Quack quack quack. "I never had to think in such small terms in my life. I get forty-two dollars a week."

But Whatmough wasn't listening to her. He seemed, in fact, annoyed by her voice, with *her*. He focused on me. "A young man like you, why are you here? You just ain't the type to be in a place like this. You're educated, intelligent, and being colored ain't no handicap these days. The colored people are changing things for the better, for all of us! You could make something of yourself. You don't have to be working that desk! A two-cents job like that!" Fury beating in his voice. "Sure, I run my mouth. What good does it do? Your people fight back, and they're getting what they want!"

"Human nature," said Guptill.

Whatmough ignored her still.

"Eli," the old woman said, looking sadly at me, "You agree with that?"

"With what?"

"That it's human nature."

"I do."

"Well, y'all go right on and solve the world's problems," groaned Ann, scratching her neck patiently.

Jody, a new whore around here, was coming up the street with a trick, so I quit the doorway and went behind the desk. Her trick was an old man, drunk, his suit hanging half off his body. She might roll him, of course. That was the price a drunk often had to pay.

Standing before me the fat whore hissed to the trick, "Give him five for the room, and give him the ten for me." Her voice was brassy, dry drunk. But what was this bullshit?

Meanwhile the trick was, despite his drunkenness, suspicious and looked at us both as though we were monster spiders waiting to trap him. And we were. Eli Bolton, the unconscious monster spider! See Eli, see Eli run, run Eli, run! "No, no no! None of that shit!" He turned toward the door. "Ain't gonna get me fucked up! I know what you two are up to! Forget it, forget it! Forget it!"

She had blown her trick but it didn't bother her (she was young) like it would have destroyed, for a few moments, an older bitch. Seen older bitches go to pieces behind a loss like that. Jody Horn wasn't a junkie, but a carefree drunk. Trying to get tight with me. New entries. Everybody knew she needed a companion. She sat down on the bottom step, and waved her hand to his exit. "Good-bye motherfucker." Her fat thighs hanging like slabs of pork, her miniskirt stretched tightly across the massiveness.

Ann, worried like a nigger mammy, came in and, motherly, asked, "What happened honey, you lost him?"

She groaned. "Look, I'm not worried about a trick. To hell with that dude." She looked Italian, the long black hair.

"He thought we were trying to take him off," I explained to Ann. Her mouth hanging, dead eyes on mine.

"Baby," Ann said to Jody, "don't you know you don't suppose to do no irregular shit? These motherfuckers are scared to death of us in the first place, and the first out-of-the-way thing you come up with just runs them away. So what happened?"

Jody ran it down to her.

"Yeah. I tried to get a bastard one night to go to a hotel with me. The motherfucker was drunk, see," said Ann, beginning to go off into the deeper layers of her trance but still talking smoothly, "*and loaded!* I was racking my brains trying to figure out how to take him off. He had about five hundred dollars in cash and some checks and shit, and the fucker had the money stuffed all in his socks, in his underwear. He was one of them little old-fashioned dudes you see around looking in garbage cans. You'd never suspect he had any money. Anyway, he didn't want to go to a hotel. I hassled and hassled with him for at least an hour. He wanted to fuck, he wanted some knowledge box, he wanted *everything,* but he wanted me to go to *his* place. I couldn't talk him out of it, and it was cold as hell that night; I was broke. Didn't look like I was going to get another trick. So, I finally went with the dude to his place. We took a cab. There I was sitting there—" She knitted her eyebrows. "I was mad as hell. He lived way the hell up in the Bronx! You know I didn't go for no shit like that, wasting all that time, and I was just trying to get enough money to get myself straight, see. How could I get *to* this motherfucker, I kept asking myself. He opens his door, and I'm right behind him. I tried to get his wallet even before he took off his pants. It didn't work, so I had to wait. He was really drunk out of his mind, but I knew once I got him to lay down I could operate. He'd go to sleep the minute he hit the sack. So I was talking nice to him, even helped him undress. I had already seen the money, see—by accident; but I didn't know he had *so much* of it until later . . ."

Jody's laughter was infectious; I started too.

"I even gave him some knowledge box right away, really socking it to him—" Ann's laughter between words was muffled, "Put him out of his mind! Really knocked him out—"

"Did you get it?" snapped Jody.

"You damn right! I walked out of there, baby, *within* ten minutes." She threw her head back proudly. "Shit, baby, it was cold outside. Below zero! And I walked out of that motherfucker's place and got me a cab and came back downtown and got my shit from Horace and went to my room, and shot up and was nice. All the bitches still out on the scene freezing their asses off; but I was cooling it, and honey let me tell you, I didn't turn another trick for a whole month." She cackled and slapped her thighs and did a quick one-two step. "I stayed nice and got me some nice clothes and the bitches couldn't understand what was going on. You never seen so much jealousy in all your life! You weren't around here then, Jody."

"I used to work Forty-Second Street."

"You don't see spade bitches up there, do you?"

"Sure, Ann. Lots of them."

"Well, it must be a recent thing because members ain't never hustled Forty-Second Street, to my knowledge."

I went back to the doorway. Mrs. Guptill and Mr. Whatmough were sitting there stranded in their individual silence, disappointments. Across the street, a chic lady was walking a poodle. A truck with huge letters: "A Truck" printed on it, rumbled by. The poodle was now taking a crap. The lady looked away.

Linda came in with a big black dude, a trick. Soul brothers were seldom tricks, but here was one. After the business ritual I said, "Take room eight."

Mrs. Guptill came creeping in holding onto the wall, and when she got to the stairway she paused and Linda and everybody else looked at her. "Go right ahead, I'm very slow." They side-stepped Jody, who stood up at that instant, and went up. The old woman looked at me, the flabby wrinkles of her face stretching into a bunny-rabbit smile. "It takes me twenty-five minutes to get to the first floor; so can you imagine a couple behind me in heat for the bed?"

An old colored woman who lived on the first floor of the Other Side was away five days. Her rent was two weeks unpaid and nobody had heard from her. This was unusual because she usually came in every night, and if she didn't, she'd call and say she was "sleeping in." She was a domestic for white folks in the mini-meadows.

During the day, Dan and Salomon (my fellow workers) moved her shoddy personal items from the room and rented it to Clark and Linda; it was bigger than the one they left. The old woman came in around eleven thirty. Hoyt, the white boy, was working the desk. She wobbled grandly over and said to him: "I want to pay my rent." I was sitting in the chair beside the soda-pop machine, reading a sick comic book. The Parliaments, from a portable radio, were singing "I Wanna Testify." Over her shoulder, the old woman said to the carrier, "Can't you turn down that blasted radio, young man?"

His huge red eyes getting into something meek; he turned it down with, "Yes, ma'am."

"Your room has been rented out, Mrs. Mullin," said Hoyt, his bright queer eyes waiting for her, a reaction. He looked sideways at the woman; behind her grandma-glasses, she was fumbling in her big cloth bag. For her wallet? Her hair pulled back in a bun, like *my* (imaginary) grandma, my father's mother. All the dead. I felt close to her. I was on her side.

"What *right* did you have to rent my room?" she snapped. "I didn't give notice!"

"You were gone—nobody knew what was on your mind! We can't hold a room like that! Sorry, Mrs. Mullin. Besides, you owe two weeks' rent."

"I have it right here!"

"I don't know if I can accept it. You won't have the same room, anyway."

My grandmother, and from there to my father. In the bleak shadow of *his* mother, getting "nigger rich," and buying a restaurant, going into all kinds of shady businesses—a new Cadillac, a hog, every year? A richly mean life. He might have put a pistol to his skull but he didn't. Mrs. Mullin was my heritage before my eyes, confronting a brash white boy who suddenly said: "I'll call Mr. Bard to see what *he* says."

"You better *do that,* young man!" She was clearly angry. Her heavy-looking shopping bag rested on the floor at the hem of her long hurdy-gurdy dress.

"Hello, Seymour, Hoyt. OK. I've had only seven since you left. Listen. There's that woman, Mrs. Mullin. She came back, wants her room. I told her. She wants to pay it. No. Clark and Linda have it already. Another room? I'll—"

Meanwhile fat bearded angry black Watson (another desk clerk from across the street) walked in, in his bermuda shorts, copping it all, the quick spy.

Hoyt was talking into the thing: "I'll ask the broad, hold on a minute." He put his hand over the mouthpiece. Facing Mrs. Mullin he asked, "Say, would you be willing to accept another room?"

But Watson had already exploded. *"What did you say to this woman, you little white punk?"*

I could imagine Seymour on the other end of the line in his comfort, wondering desperately what was going on. Hoyt simply stood there dumbfounded; he couldn't speak. Something abstract was struggling to break out as talk. A deadlock held. Watson: *"Do you know this woman is old enough to be your grandmother? You owe her the respect she's entitled to, I want to hear you apologize to this lady!"* Hoyt pretended to ignore Watson, talking to the thing in his hand. Then it happened, *Blam!* The dull thud of flesh and bone against flesh, the plastic of the phone bouncing against the wall, when Watson slapped it, and in the same motion, slapped Hoyt across the face. The phone fell on its string, dancing, while the boy wiped a blazing tear from his red eye.

Mrs. Mullin had stepped back to the doorway and was sobbing without tears. I stood up. My arms went out, but to whom? One frame of reference was being tossed headlong into another. I went over to the woman and touched her. The shoulder. What could I say? She saw me as part of this awful hotel and its staff. She turned and went out. I watched her go across the street, stop at a lamp pole and stand there with her head against it. I wanted to scream to her, *I am not who you think I am!*

Behind me Watson's mouth was going a mile a minute. And I was simply waiting for Eunice to call.

I had been behind the desk about ten minutes when Linda came wiggling in straight to me.

"Hi, Eli."

The office-girl look because of her eyeglasses.

"What's happening, Linda?"

"You're working the desk?"

"You see me."

"Could you do me a favor?"

It was difficult to drop your guard here. Nobody in the hustling world of Third Avenue did it. Such a risky thing to do. "What?"

"I have a trick outside. Just a young kid." She paused, looked over her shoulder to make sure we were alone. We were. "He hasn't got much money. Uh uh," she stuttered, "W-would *would* you let me take him up to a room? I mean without signing the book." Her eyes measured mine. She also was using her charm. I liked her. "I'll give you three, for yourself I mean." I'd risk it, not because I wanted the bread, but because I dug her so. Despite her being a whore. A lot of people were whores, but she was just this particular kind. I had become very cynical about this place. It was for Seymour's profit, not mine, and I had no love to lose on him.

I put the money in my pocket and watched Linda's massive rump as she climbed the stairway, the skinny farm boy stumbling up behind her. They were up there maybe seven minutes, a quick start and finish. The time element.

As fox Linda was coming down, a black cop, a sergeant, came in grinning, saying smack-style: "Hello hello hello—How's the house of infamous deeds?"

"What?"

Linda laughed, going by with the sheepish-looking tall gaunt white boy following her out, looking leery at the sight of the uniform.

A delayed response: "You heard me." Cynically, the grin was gone. He took out his long impressive leather notebook, leaning on the desktop, his eyes faded but were glowing, sparkling. "You want to be behind bars?"

"What d'you mean?"

"Come now, Mister—uh . . . Your name?"

I told him; he wrote it down.

"You see, Mr. Bolton, it's just a matter of *time* before this place will be closed. Now, what with all this shady business going on here, surely you realize we can't just sit by and not say something. Neighbors are complaining, Mr. Bolton. And when neighbors complain . . ." He ran on, grinning slickly with his smack, "your friendly police department acts."

"Maybe you should talk to the boss."

"You're his agent. You're responsible for this place as long as you're behind the desk. Aren't you?"

I didn't answer. Who was he? Simply a shit-shooter of a different complexion from the common variety! His smile changed its contour on his comic heart-shaped smack face.

"When we get enough facts and complaints against your little place here we'll just come in and throw handcuffs on you . . . By the way, I haven't seen you here before." He paused, but said nothing. "How long have *you* been here?"

"Not long . . ."

Over his shoulder out on the street was a dark green cruiser and a yellow-pink cop at the wheel.

"Just a warning," he said on the way out. "Just a warning, and remember: the clerk goes, too!"

Seymour Bard, a fat red-faced New Yorker with a money nervous tic at the edge of his pushy puffy mouth and jumpy liquid eyes, came sprightly in, clad in a dapper blue suit, and in a surprised voice asked while checking the record book: "Is *this* the total number of transients you took in today?"

"Right."

He sighed deeply with urban-crusted disgust, with prankish drama playing his own emotional game principally for himself. "A guy can go broke around here, for Christ's sake!" He rubbed his neck. "Is Hoyt around?"

"No—he went home."

"You mean Long Island?"

"Yes. An emergency." I lit a cigarette not really wanting one. "A cop was here, but it wasn't anything serious."

His reaction was mild. "What'd he say?"

"He was playing games, man; it wasn't serious. He stopped in to talk with me, probably nothing to do."

Jumpy jumpy eyes. "No calls . . .?"

"Nothing for you since I've been on."

"All right, see you later. Gotta go downtown. Argue with these Wall Street tycoons . . ." And that was the way the boss came: like a burning cigarette.

A few moments after Seymour left two pasty-faced men in dark suits came in. ". . . The manager?"

"Not in."

"The owner of the building . . .?"

"Not around."

The speaker began taking out papers and placing them before me and out of his flabby secular mouth: "We're here from the city to inspect this building for any possible violations." Pause. "Could you show us around? Fire escape windows plumbing sprinklers, things like that. A question or two . . ."

The other man was silent but watched me intently; a big-assed whore came in and gruntingly climbed the steps. Not that there was any money around except in my pocket but it was not a good idea to leave the desk unattended. I shouted up for Dan. He came to the head of the spiral, and looked down into my mouth. "Could ya come down . . .?"

Sleepily and with a yawn he said, ". . . Yeah, go on . . ."

He went behind the desk and began studying the transient book. "I'll hold the desk for you . . ."

They followed me up to the first floor. "These rooms on this floor are all vacant . . . Let's go up to the second—"

"Why are they vacant?"

There was no point in answering such a question. We continued up. We knocked at a few doors getting no response and finally when we did hear a voice answer at one stop it was Whatmough's. He slept a lot during the day; I knew he was pissed off by the gruffy tone of his: ". . . *Yeah?*"

Arrogantly, one of the chumps shouted: "BUILDING INSPECTOR!" And he cocked an ear toward the door.

There was silence until the inspector knocked again. "Hello, hello? We want to just look at your room. Just a routine inspection. We're from the Department . . ."

"*Go away!* I'm sleeping! You guys are just heartless bastards—aren't you?" groaned Whatmough.

"*Would you open this door fella?!*" commanded the until-now silent, shifty-eyed inspector.

"*Listen—*" shouted Whatmough, "*you goddamn privacy invaders*—GO SOMEWHERE ELSE WITH YOUR BULLSHIT AND LEAVE ME ALONE!"

Beautiful, Whatmough, *beautiful* . . .

Shifty-eyes was red with fury. He turned to me. Restraining himself. "Do you have a key to this door?"

"I couldn't open it if I had. It would be unethical."

He turned deep purple with rage, with frustration. He was so furious he couldn't speak. His dull urban eyes suspended in his skull like broken watches without hands.

The other chump said, "Let's just make a note of it, McNamara . . . and come back another time."

"Yes! And we'll bring a policeman, too!"

I led them down.

They went out, looking from the rear like twins.

Already Dan was grinning, waiting for me to amuse him with the story.

Linda had gone to the Vera Institute of Justice, a private organization, to try it. She was also kidding herself, as it turned out. She didn't want to kick drugs. She stayed away two weeks, then came back.

"When'd you get out?"

Standing on the corner of Third Avenue and 11th Street. She looked fatter, happier.

"Yesterday. Damn," she said, laughing. "This is something else!" A letter opened in her hands.

"Who's it from?"

"Read it. It's from a friend I met at Vera's."

I read: "Dear darling, I miss you very much. I'm so lonely since you went away, I could die. The nights are empty here without you. I need you desperately. I can't wait until we're together again. Please write to me, and let me know everything you're thinking. Love, Pat."

Cracking her sides. She was really having a great laugh. It was good to see her so happy. The last time I had seen her she was so uptight and desperate for money.

"A dyke?"

"Yeah, she's a dyke. She loves me. Isn't that funny?" She spoke between spurts of laughter.

Linda was breathtakingly stacked. A totally sensuous-looking woman.

"Eli, I bet you'd like to join in with me and my dyke sometime, wouldn't you? We'd make you feel greater than you've ever felt in your life! We really would have a ball, man! I'll invite you down the next time we get together."

"I'm counting on you."

Watson strolled up and said, "What're you niggers standing here giggling about?"

"She ain't no nigger, man."

"I am too!"

Watson, his pink tongue hanging out of his mouth like Dizzy's, fat and turning darker from the sun, held out his palm for five from Linda. A private black ritual.

Clark walked up and jokingly asked, "What's with you niggers standing around yakking with my mother, wasting her time when she's supposed to be out here getting the bread together?"

"Your *mother*?" Watson shot.

"That's right: she's my mother, sister, wife, everything, man. My baby, my whore, everything. Ain't that right, sugar?" He kissed her rosy cheek.

"That's right, Daddy."

I had just come up out of the subway at Third when I saw three Puerto Ricans jump Horace McLeod on 14th Street, in front of the orange-juice stand. One held him while the other two thugs worked him over in the face and stomach. When they turned him loose he staggered and held himself up against the restaurant, gasping for breath, blood pouring out of his nose. People quickly collected around him while the three PRs swooped. Their ducktail hairdos in the wind, their heels clicking on the concrete, jetting out of sight. Saturday night in the thick of a crowd, this happened. I gave in to wonderment: had he burned them?

The dealer, pusher, after all. In fact one morning I was working the desk and four sick-eyed junkies came into the place and one stepped forward, the mighty spokesman. He was a black dude; one was a seedy-looking ex-hippie gone desperate and the other two were PRs. "Man, we'd like to see Horace. Is he here?" A rudeness. Without anchor. Wow! "No," I said. I was somewhere else. In fact I was busy reading Malinowski's *Magic, Science, and Religion.* "Look, man, he *just* left," I said sympathetically, smelling their desperation—like nothing else on earth. Gut-hunger for drugs.

Wild eyes, despite the New York State Criminal Code, God, and Commissioner Howard R. Leary. Meanwhile a PR shot upstairs ignoring the whole conversation. The whitey danced out quickly to the street and looked up to Horace's window, calling, "HORACE HORACE!" Despair deep in his tone. I went up double-time behind the PR trying to grab him by his reckless ass! I caught the cat in the hallway and confronted him without touching him; *to touch* is sometimes fatal. "Look man, *come on downstairs*." I was out of breath. "I will! I will!" he whined. "All I want to do is just knock at his door once, just once!" "He's not in, man, I told you . . ." We were a few steps from the door. "OK," I said, "go and knock." The PR stood there five minutes knocking, his eyes blazing with tears, disruption with loss. I watched him in amazement.

So here was Horace with the living green shit beat out of him. He was a chubby fatherly dark Negro who sported glasses and sloppy shirts and slacks. Soft-spoken, and always had that quiet suspicious look on his face. People had to prove themselves first. People were buzzing. A cop was coming through the crowd but Horace straightened himself up and stumbled away before the cop got to him. Cops were the most dangerous people on earth. "Hey," the policeman called, "What happened to you?"

"NOTHING NOTHING!"

And he split.

They loomed unseen as a threat to dark breathing, the uptight money-grabbing rhythms. You saw them creeping in cars, and huddled together on corners in twos or threes, putting in the hours, like anybody else. Thinking of the pensions, the stomachs of wives. Their guns and their dream of the Great American Chase. The thieves, thugs, and fakirs and bunko-steerers of the streets, the pockmarked, hypothetical black Billy the Kids of poor life.

Jody, the whore, was standing there watching everything, her mouth hanging open. Once I was settled down behind the desk again, she said, "Do you have any rubber bands, Eli?"

"No."

"Then, could you lend me some typing paper?"

"I'd have to go all the way up to the top floor to my room for that."

"I'll come up with you."

Dan was standing outside, so I figured it would be all right to leave the desk for a few minutes.

She led the way up. Her fat buttocks struggling before my eyes. And she was only nineteen years old. She smelled clean, for a whore.

She stood beside the doorway as I unlocked the door. Her large dark eyes on my profile.

"I really go for you, you know."

"I didn't know."

"Well, I do."

We went in and I opened my desk drawer and took out the ream of typing paper.

"I don't want *that*, I want you."

I looked at her. Her eyes fell away, floorward. There were sweat circles under her arms. She was wearing too much makeup. Suddenly she moved closer, stroking my chest.

"Look, baby . . ."

"What?"

"Come on now, be nice. I don't have time." I didn't want her. I also didn't want to hurt her feelings.

"What's the matter? Did you lose your dick in Vietnam?"

I put down the paper and started for the door. "Come on, Jody, let's go."

"Fuck you!"

She went out and down the hall. I locked the room, went back down to my work: the book I was reading.

An hour later I was feeling very unhappy about the incident, because a girl like Jody *had to give,* she had things to give. It was the way of her life. She wanted to give to black men. Money. There were many who would take her money. Strike it sad.

He asked, "Where'd they go?"

"Where'd who go?"

The PR shot upstairs and I heard Dan shout: *"What the fuck's goin' on here?"*

And the woman screamed: "CALL THE POLICE!"

The dyke echoed: *"Call the police!"*

I started upstairs. I wouldn't call the cops if I could get around it.

When I got to the second floor I saw Dan wrestling with the drunk Puerto Rican who had small red eyes and slick black hair. Dan twisted his arm and took the gun from him. He was leaning against the door of the toilet where the dyke and her whore were locked in for safety.

Dan was really the backbone of this hotel. He *cared*. A tough stupid hard good nigger from the deep turnipgreens-and-chitlings South. He didn't trust "nobody" and didn't especially like "nobody."

Dan carried the little guy down the steps and I carried the gun. Going down, I unloaded the pistol, and once we were in the lobby, Dan turned the bitching man loose. He was jabbering away in Spanish, angry as hell, his eyes blazing. His drunk yo-yo mind probably spinning.

Dan, who was extra hard on PRs anyway, shouted, *"Now get your ass outta here and never let me see you anywhere near here again as long as you live. I mean don't even come walking by this doorway. I'll put my foot in your ass."*

I gave him his gun.

. . . I said, "Where you been?"

The old white man scratched his rough face, looked away toward Third and said, "Oh, hell, up there hassling with them sonofbitches!"

"Who? The welfare people?"

Bob Whatmough said, "Yeah, *those* bastards! They starve a guy half to death, then you have to go there, kill a whole day just hassling with them about a little crummy check that don't last you one day after your rent's paid . . ."

At that very moment, clown Salomon ran up shouting, *"Watson's in trouble—"*

Clark Webster, who had just come outside, heard the full cry. I had started out, across the street with Salomon. Dan was working the desk. Clark called, "Wait up!" and followed in a trot.

We shot up the stairs of the Countess Hotel to the office. Four colored women sitting on the bench outside the office door, waiting, hung in dark mystery.

From the window I could see The Other Side Hotel and the drift of the old man, outside. Ann had joined him. She was clean and shaking a finger in his face.

"What's going on?" I shot at Watson.

"Oh, man, this stupid motherfucker just accused me of robbing him! The girls outside, too. He accused them! The drunk motherfucker's out of his mind!"

Cops were on the way upstairs. We could hear their crisp voices. Coming madly.

The Spanish hombre was old with a bald head and he *was* drunk.

"True, true. You rob me. The colored girls, they rob me, too. I have three hundred dollars. I have no three hundred now. I have nothing. Empty." He was angry and holding up his wallet.

The girls were on the way out by now but the two big cops stopped them. We could see the action through the office window.

"What's going on?"

"Nothing!" snapped Watson, a heavy stud with a light brown bearded angry face, "Except this—this detestable drunk—"

"What's the problem?" the cop asked the PR.

"He rob me! The girls rob me! Three hundred dollars they take!"

The cop looked at Watson. "Did you take his money?"

"Hell no—I haven't been near the stinking sloppy bastard!"

"You lie! You came in room and girls give you my wallet while I sleep. See? Wallet empty."

The cop asked Watson, "You in charge here?"

"That's right."

"What's your name?"

"None of your motherfucking business."

I felt Clark's elbow in my side, gently. Salomon's eyes rolled around Uncle Tomishly in his head.

The other cop had the girls blocked. But one eased away toward the stairway. The cop heard the floorboard squeaking. "I wouldn't do that if I were you." She came back. A deep painful sigh. As if to say, Ah shit.

The cop by now (you could see) had made up his mind about

who was *guilty*. Watson suddenly had the title of villain, and would be forced to act like one. It wasn't simple enough to hate the system that gave the authority. He looked at the sweating desk clerk, wedged in between his desk and the window, and said to the shirtless young man in shower clogs, "Again—*your name*."

Meanwhile the PR was murmuring to himself, looking accusingly at the girls, who, too, were mad as hell. One girl said, "I've got some place to go, officer—"

"Just shut your goddamn mouth!"

We all looked at each other. We knew what was happening.

"I'm going to ask you one more time: your name?" He stepped menacingly close to Watson, now leaning against the desk. The white cop was big, beefy, and very dumb-looking.

"Watson Jones."

It was quickly written down on a pad. He then rapidly took everybody's given name. Names bounced off the walls. Names names names.

"You gals sit down," the other cop said.

They came in from the office doorway and sat down in the vacant chairs.

The first cop picked up Watson's phone.

"I didn't hear you ask if you could use the phone!" cried the desk clerk.

"I don't *have* to ask!"

Watson turned to us. "This dumb flatfoot motherfucker wants another Watts on his hands, I can see that!"

"You goddamn right, you black bastard!" Then into the phone: "Send a patrol wagon." He gave the address.

Watson said, "So you guys see what we have working in the public service?"

As the cop hung up he bit the air: *"What?"*

"I was just asking my friends here to take a good look at the sort of beast the city hires to protect white folks' safety: you people must really feel—"

The cop slapped him with the back of his hand. The other Keystone fellow rushed forward and slapped handcuffs on Watson. At that moment three more uniformed cops came up. Weapons dragging them down. Big, red, beefy faces, narrow blues eyes. I almost looked to see if they had comic tails wagging behind them. They wanted to know what was happening.

"Seems the desk clerk and these prostitutes robbed this man of three hundred dollars."

A very authoritative-looking cop said, "OK, everybody empty his pockets and put the contents right here on this desk." He banged his fist on the desk. "You have to treat these niggers and spics like little children. Didn't you know that, Joe?" He was laughing with a great deal of gentle ease. Self-contentment hung deep in him. This new arrival.

"OK, girls, that means you too. Everything you got goes on the table."

The other cops laughed.

Nobody, meanwhile, moved.

"Pussies on the table!" cried one cop back in the crowd of law enforcement agents. More laughter.

The women, used to being harassed by cops, got up and placed what money they had on the desk.

"I'll have to *help* you, big boy," said the first cop to Watson. And he went into Watson's pockets and brought out the rolls of money. Seymour's money. Watson's hands twitched in their confinement.

"I've never seen a more barbarous group of animals than you dull-minded ghosts in my entire life." Watson shook his head sadly.

Suddenly all four cops were working like a demolition team on Watson's head, and when they backed off him, he was purple with rage. His eyes seeming to pop out. They pulled back, and he was in the now slightly busted desk chair. Looking up. "I could kill each one of you motherfuckers with my bare hands, you brave nasty honkies! Take off your guns all you brave fuckfaces and put down your sticks and take this steel off my arms and I'll beat your asses into the next world."

They smoothly laughed at his words.

When finally everybody's pockets had been emptied, the total amount of bread didn't come to much more than fifty dollars.

Watson cried, "Why don't you make that *lying* drunk empty his pockets, too?"

Seymour walked in. "What's the trouble?"

"Who are you?" the cop asked.

"I own this place."
"Your name?"
"Seymour Bard. How come my desk clerk's in handcuffs?"
Watson spoke first. "Because this dumb flatfoot is a racist! That's the reason, Seymour!"
"Oh Jesus Christ!" whined Seymour, pushing his stocky way through the crowd of New York's finest to sit on the edge of his desk. "Will somebody *please* tell me what this is all about?"
"They rob me!" snapped the PR.
I looked at the black women. Beautiful, I saw a dignity born of astonishment and pitfalls.
Seymour was very doleful, his face generated piteousness. This expensive trouble wouldn't slide off so easily. It would cost, and that was bad.
"Three hundred dollars," said the PR.
"You *do* want to press charges?" the most talkative cop said.
"Charges, yes. He'll go to jail. Jail," he hissed pointing at the women. "Robbing me, *the nerve!*"
The woman who wanted to leave finally couldn't contain herself any longer. She shouted: *"You're a damn drunk fool, we ain't took nothin' from you!"* She had a snappy voice.
Another cop came up and looked through the window into the office: "The wagon's here."
"OK. OUT OUT OUT. The women and you, buster!"
"Man," said Watson, "take these damn handcuffs off me."
"Keep your mouth shut and march outta here."
"Fuck you," bit Watson.
"We'll see who gets fucked. Move!"
The horde of policemen shuffled Watson and the four women out.
Seymour stood. "I'm coming, too."
"Good idea," said the cop.
"Would you take over here, Eli?" asked Seymour. His face in deep pain.
"All right."

"THERE'S A FIRE UPSTAIRS!"
Right away I shot up there. The second floor was choked with smoke—it was coming from Mrs. Guptill's room. I couldn't get close it was so thick. I banged on the door with my shoulder until

it danced on the hinges, busted. Going down I shouted and knocked on all the doors I passed. The spectre doors began to flip, hardship-shocked faces emerging. When I got downstairs to the lobby the guy who originally alerted me was on the phone but he couldn't make the operator understand what he wanted.

Out of breath I ran two blocks to the fire department, my Charlie Chaplin trot, a track star—and they got my out-of-breath message: "Fire . . . Other Side . . ." By the time I walked back a radiant magic lily-white crew was working against the consuming smoke. A thudding crowd outside. Mrs. Guptill came up the street, stunned, and sat on an orange crate to watch. Watson, Salomon, Linda, Clark, Ann, everybody oblique phantoms, watching.

Seymour came hot running up, straightening out his luminous red tie. "What's going on?"

The firemen were going and coming, in and out. A burnt dresser came flying out the window: BLAM! on the street. "Wow!" somebody said. Black smoky rags were dropped down to the broken sidewalk.

"OOOOOOOOOOH."

Angrily Seymour asked: "Who called the firemen?"

"I got them."

"What'd you do a thing like that for . . .?"

"What'd you expect?"

He chuckled. "Should've let the whole place burn down first. Look at the insurance you knocked me outta . . ."

Seymour went over to the firemen, and after a while I went upstairs to see the wet crisp burnt room that was the black charred remains of Mrs. Guptill's personal life. I asked a fireman: "How d'you think it started?"

"See that lamp?"

"Yeah."

"The bulb was touching the shade."

"How can you tell?"

"I study dese things—that's how!" he said.

Carefully stepping over the debris, Seymour came into the room and laughingly said, "This is pretty good—better than I thought! Christ! Look at the damage! I'll get something out of this, I kid you not . . ."

EUNICE

My door was open, as usual. I saw big cops going back and forth. No, I wasn't dreaming nor was it a nightmare. Dan, the desk clerk, had called them I guessed, though we who worked the desk always tried to avoid calling cops unless absolutely necessary. But a woman who was in room 23 for two days hung herself from the light fixture with a stocking. You know, very much like in the movies; I couldn't get to the tragedy of it but I kept thinking about her . . . I remembered the hopeless look in her eyes that evening when I checked her in; but *that look* was so common here. Now, the cops no longer around I was stretched out in the dark, with the door still opened for air, and some freak was walking on the roof again. Suddenly I heard Dan, up on the roof, shout: *"I got you—you sonofabitch!"* I didn't bother to move. Dan knocked the man down in the space between the buildings. He didn't die. Death being an intrinsic part of life I was getting to it, when somebody—oh, Ann, I think—called me, saying, "TELEPHONE!"

I went out in the hall in my swimming trunks, sweating. It was Eunice. "Eli?"

"Hi, baby. How are you?"

"What're you doing?"

"Lying down."

"I just came in from class. I had three exams today. I just know I flunked them all."

"How do you know?"

"*You* know how you know a thing like that. I feel like going off some place and blowing my brains out."

I laughed. "Poor Eunice. I love you."

"Love you too."

"I want to see you, baby."

"Tonight?"

"Yes."

"OK, but I don't want to go out anywhere," she said with a sigh, and we hung up.

Eunice? The most sophisticated unpretentious girl I had ever loved. Loosely used term, bear with it. She occupied a sweet place in my mind, like Cathy. Like Anita, before both. And she was an intellectual, Eunice the Brain! Thoughts for her ears: a sign on an ocean front, blue untold merging depths between us. We came to know it. Her slim legs going against the sky to the Atlantic. Sea gull came in low and snatched a crumb near her toe in the sand. Still, it was a surprise. Pools of her warmth, saint girl, in her communications. The summer program kids beating drums in the bus and her smile! We took them out to the beach, Eunice tapping her finger on the edge of the seat. I felt her hip against me while we walked, her mouth searching for mine, urgently. I had thought the world was coming close to a prison of the self until she, the accident, the circle completed in sperm, came. Tall, lean, graceful she was. Graceful summer, soft city girl with India in her. Deep in her, in a dirty Now. Quietly teaching her the rhythm of the future . . .

In all the months since Cathy left, I have not been happier; more keenly stimulated, more beautifully frustrated in my relation to another person. We are standing by the rails, on the lower level of the Museum of Modern Art. We have just come in a few minutes ago from the liquidity of the outside air. (She was waiting outside when I came and her ears were being "folded" by the impressive, baffling wisdom of a self-educated young black man who had apparently come up to her, seeing her a lone girl standing there in the roughness of no company, and tried to make her mind a part of his menu to dine from.) We have been strolling around inside the coolness of this often camp, centralized and furrowed assemblage of exhibition rooms, airing, even verbalizing our mutual interest and agitation, inspired by the two-dimensional spumings, paintbirths, brainstorms of people who are often just names glib on snappy tongues; but Eunice has no such pleats, fancy ruffles of falseness, bogging down her smooth, gliding mind, nurtured by her elegance. These moments are going to be very festive to me, forever; her presence is already a kind of intense and necessary ration of symbolic passion and human nutrition.

We are climbing the steps, I feel her slender fingers ease into mine, dispatches of summer romance; I do not necessarily want to take this lightly but do not dare foretaste anything like the firmness of a gutty, sustained relationship, I *want* to urgently but—

I am distracted by the sight of her toe jutting through the stiff but comfortable-looking structures of her water-buffalo sandals.

She is tall, rather she seems tall, she is a proud, upstanding girl with inborn dignity; her simple summer dress, Indian print, hangs on her with ease and obstinate magnificence! I can smell, almost taste and hear the involuntary gentility of her sad extrinsic presence in my life, the innate fragrance of her clean, self-assured mentality. She is wearing the fashionable large, dark blue sunglasses, her strong, luringly sightful, classic face, which I am digging dogmatically, out of the corners of my scheming and unhappy eyes, is focused on the impactful presence of a huge subjective canvas that we are now approaching on the main floor. We stop before the Jackson Pollock. I watch the intricate patterns of her reception demonstrated by her feminine sighs, the busy presence of her obvious sensitivity to the construct before us. I look at the canvas: It is nothing that I should bother to put a name to. Just a formation of pigment that somehow does something extrasensorial through me—I try to see what it is doing to Eunice. Intrigue in her dimple, in her chin.

Everything is intact, the world is not disobedient until twenty minutes later, we are side by side on Fifth Avenue, walking like proud breakers of icons from the submerged levels of the society, figures of infraction, tabooed in the mechanically produced minds of these passersby; but I hardly concern myself with them until suddenly I notice that the sky is darkening, the tall mystic kronos-power of these buildings is bursting with a hot but camouflaged violence, the insularity of man-made fires secretly started by financially insulted big gamblers who wish to get back on their feet by way of payoffs from insurance companies; also I notice that all kinds of unassociated shit, messy specks of garments and promiscuous lumps of the most private artifacts from people's lives, are floating along in the gutter-water that, for over twenty-four months now, has been steadily exorcising everything from the underpassages of all the big cities of this land; it is nothing these days to witness huge green or reddish and gloomy turds drifting easily along Fifth Avenue. I suppose we have all gotten used to it. Our dislocation is so complete.

The restaurant we choose is on the main floor of one of the finest hotels in New York City; we stand just inside the doorway, waiting for the headwaiter, who eyes us but does not come; an old man governed by so much pride in his profession that his nose, the tips of his eyelids, the beefy edges of his lips, the rolls of his soft white neck, all glimmer with the sexuality of his self-esteem; I am digging the agitation in his face as he fumbles with a pencil, pretending to write something on a pad; his head is like a two-winged giant insect, the smooth polished dome of it, graced by weak hedges of white fuzz around the sides, faces us, but his eyes are also secretly evaluating every inch of us, my shoes, Eunice's casual grandeur. He is unaware that the pencil in his hand isn't even touching the pad. His stiff black suit is a perfect fit; the collar seems to be white metal, the sagging layers of flesh pushing desperately out over formality of style. When he relaxes at home he must surely be a soft, puffy, disproportioned bulk of an animal with female tits, have a gut that hides his eyedropper-sized sexual adornment. I look at Eunice; she is looking around. The people, all middle-aged, rich-looking, easy in their splendid manners, dining in the soft lights off the deep mahogany of the walls and chairs, in the thick comfort of the expensive dark green carpet, the even more resplendent strut of the waiters, who, I suddenly notice, go by with trays of picturesque and sweet-smelling meats, stews, violently appetizing roasts and rich spicy soups.

As the old man comes toward us, the evil in his encroached face causes him to suddenly blow up with the kind of force behind an earthquake. The vast immodest sound, the liquids of his body, the spermy-substance of his brains shoot out, his eyeballs, rebellious question-marks, hang down suspended on long slimy patheticus strings from his sockets; Eunice's hand, inside mine, tightens; "Oh damn—look at that! That poor man—He's having a heart attack!" The gooey stuff splashes in nearby plates of food, customers jump back in their chairs, an old woman with a bust as big as a bathtub drops her monocle, falls over backward in her chair, her floor-length gown flying over her head, her broomstick-sized legs, juggling frantically for some balance, her rich, pink Playtex girdle is even drenched with the juices from the explosion—I wonder why some of the folks are beginning to hold their noses: then it hits me, the odor of the substance from the waiter's skull smells like shit. He is a lump of slimy flesh and starched garments, on the floor. Eunice is pulling at my sleeve; "Please, let's go, I'm getting sick. I can't eat here." Eunice, even before we reach the street, is gagging.

We are slightly drunk from the consumption of vodka, our footfalls slow and abbreviated as we drift toward the intersection of 14th Street and First Avenue where we will stand and wave for cabs that will not stop; it is close to three o'clock in the fumigated morning. We are fresh from a perfumed party with faces bathed in voluptuous lights of psychedelic rhythms, where girls had sensitive mouths like vulvas, where a few soft-spoken white boys took the symbolic sexual autographs of these virile girls (Eunice's former schoolmates) seriously while dancing, impressed only by the achievements of their oldest, closest friends; I was soaked by the odors of their gracefulness. There must have been thirty chicks, busy mouths, lusty ticklish nymphs and expressive dykes, colorful, their mouths, tongues raking through the affairs of everybody they knew. Two of the girls were very high and babbling something like Arabic at each other, sitting face to face on the floor, at my foot: One plump, dark-haired broad, who smoked a cigarette with exquisite brutality, had a warm, soft-looking blonde, quilted by shadows, in the corner between the piano and the wall, where she kept pampered the girl's slit, not openly, through the cloth of her garment; another girl, so banged on *ups* and cocaine she fell out on the floor, after a long sexy masturbatory dance, her miniskirt around her hips; her rosy biter winking its hairy eye at me where I sat, wallflower-style, on the couch, wolfing down delicious cheeses, crackers, and chopped liver on slabs of breadsticks, all on a tray at my elbow; the girl was still wiggling flat on her back, and Eunice, amused at my inability to take my eyes from the passionate cherry sunk between her neatly protruding lower lips, playfully, jealously, kissed me to distract me.

The swells, throbbings, the projections of the party are still pithy in me, my lust pushes all the way to erect fantasy! I can hardly keep my hands off Eunice. She knows that I want to make love to her, and it amuses her. The dimple in her chin seems to wink at me.

We stand waiting, ten cabs go by until a brother stops, picks us up and—

Eunice lived on 106th Street, between Amsterdam and Broadway, in a huge comfortable apartment on the fourteenth floor, which she shared with two colored broads, one she had spent last summer with in Italy, the other, a social worker and student from Boston. Baby had graduated from Sarah Lawrence not long before I met her, and had won a scholarship to Harvard's school for the study of Eastern religions. The way she smiled, her big beautiful eyes, the dimple in her chin, got so deeply to me, dug in so truly, I will never forget her, though there was a gulf between us: my silence. I was, then, still brooding over the loss of Cathy, and Chicago was also still heavy in me, dragging me.

We had spent the morning and early part of the evening at Fire Island, on the sand, on a blanket, with about thirty of the kids, along with several other instructors and helpers. I rubbed suntan lotion on her back, getting sand mixed in it. We ate fried chicken and potato salad. It was a clear day, the children running with their portable radios turned up full blast. That was the beginning, in a way, though to her it began the day we stopped in an Indian restaurant on 110th and Lenox Avenue, some other adults from the program with us. "You looked at me *with* desire." Maybe that was it, the beginning. It probably really began when first I spied her, unconsciously, during a staff meeting in a Spanish church, before the public school that housed our project was opened.

Anyway, after Fire Island that evening, we took the bus up to Broadway, she bought a six-pack of beer (refusing to let me pay for it), and we went up to her apartment. Drank a couple, kissed, soon I was on top of her, kissing her neck. She lifted my face. "Let's go to my bedroom." So we did. Slim, flat-assed, shades of a vague image of my mother. We fucked sweetly for about an hour. She was impressed. Afterward she said, "My breasts are too small, aren't they?" "No, I love them." I kissed each nipple. "I love them very much." We lay side by side, and made love again.

Later we went to a Japanese restaurant on Broadway; ate with chopsticks. She talked. Her activity, her existence. It wasn't so much *what* she was saying, but the wide-eyed immoderation of her charm. I could have kissed her warm neck, bit into her soft stomach, done anything to forestall the day our summer of frenzied elation would end. I could not consciously buy the fact that this affair was just a sweetly brief, tremulously quiet liaison for her, like so many others she had fed herself on in Italy, Paris, Mexico, anywhere.

At Lincoln Center, among the tourists, in the massive heat, her eyes on the rivulets of water going up, STOP—straight up, STOP, fall! How natural it was! We had to take a piss in this "very human" (her words) place of American culture. Her head on my shoulder in the caged darkness of a poor flick. A Harold Pinter. Her eyes were often so clear I could see the deep modest rivers of my motionless self there as we love-fucked in the stretched-out unruffled comfort of her fourteenth-floor bedroom. Her long lustrous brown hair was silk-soft, wet in my violently sensitive hand, I felt her querulous torso struggle often beneath mine for the elusive orgasm. Her white hand, desperately reinserting my question-mark penis from the disconnection caused by her rapid hip-banging!

And in Chinese restaurants and regular American cheeseburger joints we talked out our possessions. Our claims. In subways, taxis, buses, on crowded streets we seldom lost the depth and limitation of our contact. But sometimes, I went directly to the guzzling center of her, no need for provisional bridges. No words, a warm restful idea. No need for the abstract crises of things crowding us. I told her, "Your pussy looks like an oyster," and she held onto my ramrod of existence. Her warm edible marine mollusk engulfed me through those long sleepless sweet nights. The accident of her words: "Strange how quickly we have come together." Strange? She had never had a black man before. Beautiful rhythms of love were washing into our tides of dark gold, pink light flesh.

We walked after breakfast quietly Sunday morning down Riverside Drive, heat coming into our skins, into the dirt of the city, the love itself. I felt tired and comfortable, at peace with her. She suddenly was excited at the sight of trees in black action against an unclean blue skyline. The deep retreat of beauty into each measure of things.

Well, right now Eunice was my life away from the Lower East Side's Other Side Hotel, and its strung-out people. I was some kind of perpetual *picaro* with an uptown chick, a downtown bank account. She was dressed casually, as usual. The smile, sad, gentle. We kissed.

I had arrived.

I closed the door behind myself. Her wide, clear forehead. I kissed it. Those huge Joan Crawford eyes going over and over my face, liquid rims.

On the couch, her Buddhist ceremony music album on the turntable, the monks chanting. "I'll take it off, if you like."

"Leave it on."

"You like it?"

Eunice was especially very deep into Zen Buddhism; had spent four years in India between the ages of fourteen and seventeen, where her father was teaching Christianity in a university. The whole family, I gathered, after I met her mother and brother, had a missionary complex, with a premise like: What right did we have to try to convert them? Hatred for her father. "It's not bitterness, it's simply that I don't like what he *stands* for." She laughed. "The point is, he *doesn't* stand."

In bed that morning her long hair all over me, the phone to her ear, talking to her father, up the island, saying, "Dad, I'll come out there but gosh Dad I don't want to just sit around! There's nothing to do out there, Dad! Can't you meet me at the station and drive me to the beach, leave me, then come back for me and drive me to the station again? That way we'd still have a chance to see each other." A cold shot for the old man and when she hung up she lay in my arms saying, "He's a little meek man, stooped, very henpecked. You met my mother and I'm sure you can imagine—I mean understand why. We sort of take out our grudges on him."

Eunice is here but she is a cloud, she has flesh that is weightless, she moves around without making sounds, it is possible to see that her eyes are still her eyes, her words, somehow come out, and in some strange context, make sounds that I understand, finally, yes, Eunice is here and she dances in melancholy rhythm, her thin flesh I touch but I do not really feel it, it turns white as notebook paper, but it is possible to now hear the high, sweet ring of her summer laughter, and to feel the long, graceful genital depths of her, the erotic rhythms of her features, moments in my arms, nights together.

THE OTHER SIDE

Some young dudes were on my floor skin popping and giggling and listening to Redd Foxx while I was busy trying to type my report on the progress of my workshop at the summer school. I gave up, went downstairs to the hot street, tired and mean. My phenobarbital had run out.

I was frustrated—I wanted to loaf. Why not go downstairs and listen to the prostitutes complain about being slapped with a Section 887(4)(a) and (c) of the Criminal Code . . .? or any kind of shit . . . It was a hot August afternoon . . .

Linda, in her instant see-through dress, said to me, "Finally got off that typewriter, huh, Eli?"

"Yeah, baby."

Ha Ha. She laughed with joy, real fun. Her gray eyes. An all right woman nothing phony about her! Together all the way through. She didn't turn many tricks, nor was her habit very heavy. She had done some time in prison in Jersey but she had done her graduate work hanging out with niggers; she called herself an "honorary nigger." "Why don't you write a book about prostitution, Eli: Now, man, that would really be a gas—"

Clark, her man, black as night, the calmest junkie in the world, standing at junkie's attention to keep from nodding, said, "Eli'd have to know a lotta *inside shit he just don't know,* ain't got access to, Linda."

Skinny black Salomon slapped his fat white boss on the shoulder, cracking up at the new information. I laughed at the clown. Not Clark.

She wouldn't challenge him. If anything, she would cry. She had been through a lot but she was still a soft woman. Not like Ann or Jody: hard prostitutes.

He went on: "Shit, he'd have to know shit like *why* tricks buy pussy. He'd have to know that this money is used to throw up a wall between himself—the trick—and the woman. That's what the money is all about: it's protection. It says, 'Don't touch me, don't touch my emotions, my mind. Just be a body, be ass.' "

Seymour, red as ever, leaning in the doorway, said, "Gosh, professor, may I enroll in your class next term?"

There was something gentle and intelligent in Clark; he was forty but he looked twenty-five. He maintained that junk had kept him together, young.

And Linda, insecure, shy, and heartbroken, was completely under his power.

I was remembering the time she came to my room, desperately silent for a few moments. Her skin, milk-white, damp. Sick. The sudden carelessness about her: she had always been so neat. "Sit down," I said, "What's the matter?" Meanwhile, I offered her a cigarette, forgetting that she didn't smoke. "Eli, I need six dollars. Could you let me have it, please? I promise I'll pay you back this evening as soon as I turn a trick, I promise." I had twice lent her money I never got back. She had stopped trying to kiss me. I always turned away from her mouth. She couldn't win me *that* way. I liked her in another way. For something else. I held out a bottle of soda, she took it and sipped. "Why can't you turn a trick *now,* baby?"

"I'm sick, Eli." In her pitifulness, there was a touch of disgust. But she *was* down. I had only about seven dollars. The bank was closed. And she didn't mean all *that much* to me. "I got this habit, Eli, you know that. You know I can't do anything, sick like this. Please lend me the six, please. I promise—"

I suddenly remembered a white boy over on 11th Street between A and B who asked me if I'd turn him on to one of the girls. I had said no, really insulted by the question. Now, looking at Linda, I thought about him. As a trick for her. After we were out of sight of the Third Avenue people we knew, she took my hand. "I'm your woman while we're walking, okay?"

"Sure baby."

"I'm your whore, okay?" She had meaty hips but her waistline was narrow. Wearing a miniskirt of polka dots, sandals and a warm, joyous smile. Suddenly she was no longer depressed. She was rapping during the long walk: ". . . so my mother wanted to see what

Clark looked like. She decided to meet us to see what Clark looked like. She decided to meet us at Grand Central. But she wouldn't come over to shake his hand or anything. She's very funny about colored people. She says they're all right, but not to get too friendly with. I went to talk with her and Clark stood off at a distance. It was so silly. She said, 'God, he's black!' " "Was that *all* she said?" "That's all!"

We knocked at the door and it opened; no one was there. Except the cat. "He leaves his door open?" she asked.

"I guess so." Linda picked up the black cat and stroked the creature. A quick snapping mouthful of tiny teeth took a bit of her flesh away. She instantly cried out. The animal licked his tongue. His eyes glowing, changing. Like diamonds. It happened so quickly. The cat leaped from her arms and, with his fur bristled and tail straight like a walking stick, circled her legs. Jumped and bit into her tender flesh. Linda was too shocked to move. She couldn't cry a second time. I quickly kicked at the animal. He moved to avoid my foot. *"Scat!"* I kept moving him back with my foot. "But what did I do? What did I do, Eli? What's wrong with him, Eli? Animals always love me. What did I do?" Tears were beginning to come.

I whispered, "He's crazy."

"Maybe he doesn't like me."

"He's just crazy. He scratched me once."

"But he *bit* me!"

"Let's go," I said.

She sidestepped, keeping behind me, and we went out. Some trick, huh?

GERRI

She called herself Gerri. She had simply taken advantage of my open door and walked in with a sheet wrapped around her. She was sitting on the side of the bed; I sat in the chair at the desk.

Ann walked in and came to a halt. "*Damn, bitch*! Every time I turn around you're in a different room!"

Gerri's little pink nose twitched as she spoke: "Ann how *old* are you?"

Ann walked away.

I looked at Gerri. A face, a voice. I had never talked with her before.

The radio's music paused and a newsman said, "*Racial unrest continues today in Detroit . . .*"

Her voice riffed over his, saying, "I'm so sick of all that hate, hate, hate, hate." She groaned. I was that close to her, the room was small. An uptight room. "It's all so silly."

She was stroking my thigh, then she stopped, stood up, and said, "I'll close the door. All I need is for Ann to start running her big mouth about what I'm doing. It's not that I care so much about Salomon—I don't. He's an ignorant nigger, a clown. I'd stay here with you if you'd let me. My girlfriend, Paula—do you know her?—No? Well, you've probably seen her. I live with her down the hall, but this guy Salomon. You know Salomon? Well, he wants me to stay with him. I bet you don't want a woman staying with you, do you?"

I had no desire for her, I could not imagine working up an erection for her. What vision could I form looking into her eyes? She would cry, I felt sure.

"I've got to go out."

"Where?"

I sighed. "Out."

"I'll go with you."

"If you want to." A way of getting her out of my room.

On the street she managed to talk me into playing a game of pool with her. OK, just one. Then I have work to do. We went to the bar around the corner on Third Avenue. She bought a beer for herself and a ginger ale for me. I was worried about my sensitive stomach and was no longer drinking booze. The game of pool was enough, so I wasn't about to play a mental game with her by letting her win. I won quickly and put my stick down. "Just one more . . ."

"No," I said. I wanted to laugh but I couldn't. Clouds were moving over New York as I walked out on the sidewalk, looking up at the black blanket of smog hanging over the city.

REALITY

I am making love to the daughter of a river god; can you believe it, she turns and calls her father, Inachus, but this doesn't frighten me, I know she's really the girl way back in my blue moons, Anita, for a moment she *is* Anita, then she's surely a female deity who swims through the green thickness of the water I'm submerged in, to take my arm, first the fingers, the hand, into her mouth, to suck; steadily, more girls pop up from the nectar-thick solution—I see Clara, Linda, even beautiful Cathy and Eunice embracing and swimming toward me; my student, Lucille, is swimming around in a circle, like a duck; Ann Fennmore and Jody are trying to do the Monkey right in the water—they are giggling and knocking elbows; Cathy's ex-roommate Beth and good-time Alma keep trying to come to the surface, clad in one-piece, 1920s swimsuits, but can't make the grade; where're all these bats coming from—I see Ruth Kowalczyk with a toilet plunger stuck on her nose, swimming toward me, too; and I'm stuck like a dog in this bitch—and don't know who she is! The green water is slowly turning blue. This girl has fins. Shit, she's as slick as a fish, they way she—

O Lord! can it really be Liz?

Linda is working her soft soft wet mouth gently against mine, letting me dream her tongue and meanwhile, below, she cups Mr. Genital in her hands and gives the triangle a firm squeeze, a rockabye side-to-side shake. We stand secretly in the hallway of this whorehouse, dripping with drugs, the used skulls of wishes, the fellatio-queens of songs to the "great" white "father," like: *"Gimme dat money first and I'll eat anything you say, dat's right—even yo shit, you blue-eyed moth!"* Drugs make Linda and Ann think this way. Linda has nothing on beneath her pink dress, her tits stand up firm like sixteen-year-old things, her mouth still, without pressure, plays movie star against mine, straight out of flicks. Remember she once rapped to me: "When I was in the joint I was the hottest pussy—all the dykes were after me. They fought like sapsuckers to get to me, Eli . . . You shoulda seen 'em! One jasper even cut another one over me!" And I understand *why*, 'cause I ain't never seen a woman better put together than Linda!

It doesn't make sense—but what does?—Ann comes up the hallway, and Cathy is on the bed naked; naturally I have my door open it's so fucking hot and this bitch, Ann, who is in her thang again, you dig, fella, and that makes her even nosier than usual, she stops, and just lets her EYES take in everything, so slowly she spies Cathy on the bed; I can imagine how the wires in her mind are getting all crossed 'cause she ain't never seen Cathy before (even I can't remember when she came in, or how she got here, but—). Ann means to really check her out in detail, her droopy eyes, like swollen hognuts: hanging over her bloodshot peeps. Miss Knowledge Box, sometimes known as Wisdom Tooth, Miss Derby, or simply Head Queen, can't even shake the H a moment to get words out of her mouth, she stands here, I hear the abstracts of what she's rapping, shit like: "Damn, man, you mean to tell me you got a woman, and I thought you was all by yourself, and me feeling sorry for you, shit, and here you is with mo' snatch than anybody got. Shit, dat snatch looks so good I could go for a little taste uv it myself!" Quickly Cathy covers her body, embarrassed. The sheet is damp. Ann, who's gone completely to sleep standing there, drops her works, the hypodermic kit, the eyedropper rolls all the way into my room and stops at my foot; the sounds wake her; and she drops her bottom lip again trying to get out another word but the only thing that comes out is: "Shit, ah thought you up—" and she goes top-heavy off down the hallway to her room . . .

. . . I even screwed a winged monster who had the body of a lion, the head and breasts of a woman, and the greatest loving in the world; but this woman swore upanddown that she was named "Cathy" and in the bar where I met her she was popping riddles, one after another, at me, but couldn't hear any of my answers, though I had them all slamming right back at her as fast as she whipped out the riddles. Didn't you know? That's the way you treat all diseases.

I even ran into a monkey strutting down Eighth Avenue in the West Village, all dressed up and whistling "I got plenty of nothin' / and nothin's plenty for me—"

WEEKEND AWAY

She was a redhead who was about forty-two years old, but I knew she was just waiting for me to say something. So she invited me to stay on a ninety-acre estate for a weekend. The drive up was in a heavy warm rain of big splashy drops. The fluffy dogs and cats greeted us at the back door the minute we dashed in from the station wagon parked in the driveway. Light on, her blue-veined (varicose) legs dumped into the light. "I'll make you a whiskey!" The screen door banging, the dog wagging its ass: no tail. The other one, jealous, scrambling for my attention. The majestic feline creatures digging it. The expensive comfort of the kitchen rested me as I drank the whiskey, looking around at the push-button gadgets. I meant only to be friendly. Later, after a shower, I ran into her in the hallway without her teeth and wearing her thick reading glasses. I smiled. Good lady. I went to the room she had pointed out as mine for the night. The fluffy dogs were with me. Tomorrow she would drive me from Port Jefferson, up to the beautiful wavering forces of the rich woods of Peekskill down a longingly narrow but branch-covered, lonely road of silence, fog, and to a lake with soggy boats, rotten wood with snails occupying an endless struggle in space. For my alien eyes. Timeless as roaches.

Standing by the harbor up there in the night fog on the platform of the abandoned radar site, I felt the overwhelming relief from the city's merciless gas, and a formidable peace.

Peekskill's beautiful isolation, the equilibrium it offered, the honored impression it left. The collective silence here obtained, I needed badly; then the chilled easy night on wool and the crack of an already faded dawn—a trite sky without promise. My heart insane.

I walked through the thick rich grass wetting those precious tennis shoes. Despite the beauty and peace, even here I felt the whimpering uneasiness of the interconnection of people, for a few moments, somewhere. I saw Moke's face come up out of the lake, eyeless. There was, a few yards down, half into the water, Sheraton's body. I could even hear the scintillation of fire in distant trees, the head swam across the water to my dark face. So much magic fervor!

Sunday afternoon blasted with new sunlight and carefree pink children in blue, green, yellow swimsuits came. They swam out to the red boat. They were laughing (those small voices bouncing off the water!) while a teenage blonde sat on a stone near me telling my ear, "I'm young, I'm lonely." The kids turned over the boat. The caretaker, a sensitive-looking, withdrawn boy of nineteen, swam out to the capsized artifact. It took him a good hour to get it up again. Meanwhile the girl's words filtering into my sensibilities. Belle, the liberal, fumbled around like a flustered hen until she finally chased the girl away from me.

I will always remember the peace of that morning, reading a book by Richard Wright, the quiet, the tiny sounds of bugs near my ears, the bite of insects, the harbor, and the ducks drifting on the pond. A moment difficult to communicate.

That night, with the caretaker: He was barefoot, I felt dusty from the city. We were coming from the radar site when he said, "I'm white, you're black: but at this silent moment on this road, we're simply two human beings way out here miles away from everything, everybody."

By midmorning I went for a swim, and afterward, still in my swimming trunks, sat out in the thin sunrays on a swing from a tree and continued Richard Wright.

I had a daydream of a man's arm washing up on the shore. Where had that come from? A cluster of motionless boats on the horizon, birds crying over them. The lyrical words of the black master writer who saw the *human* condition as a poet, embracing me! There would be no breakfast, I knew. I wasn't out here for formal things like that. The peace, the quiet existence of growing things standing or moving in their time. That was why I was here. Maybe I could find an apple somewhere for lunch. Belle had gone back, and that was good.

By the time I got back to the urban haven the city was flooded to the point of an emergency. And the rain had the subways at a standstill. I made it to my room and listened to the rain outside.

BAP BAP DO-BAP

BAP BAP DO-BAP

EUNICE

We got dressed that Sunday and went to Long Island Beach. Me in my white tennis shoes. We walked down the street with the blanket over our heads. People going by in cars waved to us. The world was beautiful! everybody knew we were in love and loved us for it. I had my notebook with me. It was a foggy day.

In the notebook I quoted Eunice: "You have a headful of pubic hair." And my answer: "So now I'm a sex symbol, huh?" Eunice: "In a way, yes." Her yum-yum was white inside like the belly of a fish. This is in my notebook, also.

We stretched out on the sand, the wind racing over us; later, I walked back to the hot-dog stand and bought two. We ate, and laughed together, under the blanket.

On the way back to the train station, we stopped and had steaks, salads, tea, at a very cozy little restaurant. Her eyes, diamond crystals.

She had her hair pulled back in a simple bun; plain like that. Face clean, bright; I kissed her nose. The Eastern music on the turntable. The heavy lingering odor of marijuana. Certainly not to create a feeling of adequacy! Eunice didn't need a medium like that *for that reason*. It opened for her vital windows to other levels of reality.

It was again a dreary evening. I went immediately over to the windows and looked down on the rooftops of upper Manhattan, the skyline in mist, the sounds of Puerto Rican children fourteen flights below, screaming. There was a large piano in the far corner. A thickly carpeted floor; two huge armchairs facing each other, like old men, talking. Eunice sat across the room on the couch with her slim legs beneath her. I turned and saw her soft eyes playing with the lights, and in misty green shadows, I went to her, sat down, and kissed her fully.

"Do you want to get stoned?"

"I don't think so. Not in the right mood."

She stroked my chest gently, looking up into my face, resting her cheek against my shoulder. Faintly in another section of the apartment I could hear one of her roommates typing on a quiet typewriter, the other singing and possibly washing dishes. The music. I felt the beginning of some vague disappointment. A nameless quality.

"Miss Hemp."

"Wilson," she corrected.

No games with Eunice.

The shrill cry of the oriental instrumental music was sparkling. I casually stretched out on the couch and began flipping through one of her notebooks. She often recorded her thoughts while high. I stopped at an interesting looking page and read: "If my oriental soul clashed with my occidental origin, it is the latter that must be reconciled to the former."

We went out for hamburgers to a place where the "football types" at Columbia hang out; the waitress came and asked, "May I help you?" She was pretty in a small way like a special bird; red-head, big blue Irish eyes; a very heavy brogue. She brought a quaint charm.

When she went away Eunice said, "I like her. In fact, I have *a crush* on her. She lives in a basement apartment not far from here. I was at party there not long ago. A boy, just a friend, took me. He made her, I didn't."

"Were you jealous?"

"Of course not! He said she was very efficient in bed. I liked her even more."

"Would you like to try her?"

"I'm not a lesbian, Eli."

I laughed.

"Haven't you seen *men* you felt attracted to?"

"They always look like beautiful women."

"There's something masculine about her. Here she comes now, *look* at her."

There was a certain peasant-hardness about her, in the prettiness. She put down the burgers. "Two mugs of bear, too." The place smelled of heavy stale beer, sawdust, the strong odors of cooking. The place was jam-packed with young men in sweaters and a few women, deep in booths or standing, chatting. I watched Eunice drag one french fry after another around in catsup. "Do you see what I mean?"

I grunted; I was remembering how Eunice and I one night went down to the Bowery in the crowded cab we took at 125th Street and Lenox Avenue. Two female teachers from the summer school where we worked were with us. We were going to see "our" kids in our band play in a competition with the kids of another program's band. We got downtown early and went to an old Russian restaurant, where a fat woman and a little man sang and played two strange hand-instruments. We drank wine and ate American bouillon. We laughed a lot and talked. Eunice was excited about going to Harvard; she was also frightened by the prospect. As it turned dark we walked over to the playground where the competition was to be held. She drew close to me as it began to rain. The two bands were already there. The other group was in the middle of a Latin number. They were doing all right. The kids were dancing in the rain. Neighborhood people had come out to listen and to watch. We had a crowd. I felt very happy. A man came from somewhere with keys and opened the recreation house and we all poured into it, soaked and full of music. Our band's turn came. We were clapping and urging them on. They were doing great. They got right into a jazz number with bluesy overtones. I took Eunice's hand and led her out to the center of the floor where the kids were working out. We cut swiftly into the Monkey and some of the other older people quickly joined in. The vast amount of laughter, clapping, and foot-stomping was invigorating. Afterward, Eunice and I stopped at a bar in the East Village for a drink. Whiskey Alexanders. We got very high, I think, and kissed a lot, in the relative privacy of our booth. The next day we went to the Museum of Modern Art, casually strolling through the galleries discussing the pictures. We were together all day that day. We ended up at a party that night, getting quite drunk and listening to psychedelic music.

The Irish waitress came back. "Anything else?" She put down the beers. I sipped the cold heavy liquid. It was good.

"No," said Eunice, and to me: "Eli, there's so much about you I love. You're so oriental in so many ways. Your wisdom. You haven't read a lot of Zen, have you? I didn't think so. So, it's natural wisdom you have." She paused. "I'm just thinking of the things you say from time to time. Like the time I asked you about God, and you described God as the deepest element in man, and religion as a system of man's ideals of his society."

"God, I never realized I had ever said anything that profound. Sounds good." A little laughter.

"I'll miss you. Will you write to me?"

"In detail."

With my little finger, I touched the very tips of hers.

A WALK IN THE PARK

"Eli, I might be pregnant."

"Eunice!—Ah come on—how *could* you know?"

"*Of course* I'm not sure, but, but I'm late, very late." She sighed and lit another cigarette. We were in a booth in the bar across from Columbia where she was taking one course this summer preparing for Harvard.

"I have some pills a doctor once gave me. I don't want to take them, but I think I might—if nothing happens tomorrow—" She sipped the Bud. A fan was humming. Soft male voices threaded the enclosure; good to be in out of the hot August sunlight, the congestion of New York City. A girl in knee-high boots went by like a lion tamer.

I took Eunice's long fingers into my hands. The eye-level. "Baby, let's go make love."

She wasn't for it. Frustrated and she was afraid of being pregnant. How could I suggest such a thing at a trying time like this? Was I out of my cotton-picking mind? She hesitated. She almost spoke. Her mouth held a silent word; but it dropped back into space, dangling. The unconscious resentment toward me mounted. It was understandable. But not then in my lust. My own frustration, selfishness. The last time we made love had been the night after returning from a party given by a music critic who worked with us in Harlem. On the way to her place in the cab, looking with her dewdrop face sadly at me, "I felt *so* far away from you tonight." I *had* been pretty much out of it. I wasn't in a party mood that night; I was simply in a mood *for her*. My party days were behind me, in a way. I had refused to dance. That had annoyed her. The weights and measures of human hassling.

And that dream. There was a tall white man, though not the professor, and yet he was. He walks across a stage, and as he progresses, he gradually gets smaller, and darker, so that by the time he reaches the other side of the stage, he is a tiny black man; though not me, still me all the same. The black man starts the journey back across the stage, getting even smaller, so that when he reaches the starting point he vanishes.

Still she hesitated; she pulled herself to the word, "No." And she repeated it, "No, Eli. I *can't*."

I was containing my fury like a riot squad controlling a mass of underclassed victims scrambling for exotic valueless relics.

"I don't *want* to be frivolous."

"You're not."

"I mean if . . . if, oh, if so much wasn't so futile. Oh, I can't explain what I mean, Eli. I love you though." She hesitated again. "Okay, why not? Let's make love."

"Not with that attitude."

"Yes, you're right. I'm not for it. *I* have to want it. Don't you want me to want it, too?"

"Yes."

"And I have things on my mind, now."

"I know."

"You really don't know."

Her face was wide, clear; the bright eyes. Easy beauty. A lean, endless but calm sadness in that brightness, in the clearness; as the heavy volume of beer floated up into my senses. Her smoke also pinching my nose.

I looked down at my own hands. Anita was behind me. Cathy was in the past. Eunice was flying away, now. I had left Anita. Bets hanging in my heart, throbbing with the little teeth of werewolves. Angles of iron shooting up in my memory. And Jimmy Sheraton's killer brought out into a blasting light, examined. But still I felt strong, in a good spirit. No more crutches! An excellent clear spring, a renewal. Cathy had been a crutch.

She wanted to walk over to the park; and I had a tug-of-war with myself at the corner; take the subway downtown or her hand and stroll. Simply together, or not. For instance, we never fucked but made love, like that, in essence. Side by side, no one being more aggressive than the other. But she could *wham* and *bang* when she wanted to. "Let me rest," I once said. "Put your leg up here." Across my hip. "My, you're very clinical," she said. Now, I almost left her in selfishness, in anger. But the action was below me, too cheap.

We sat on the brick wall, looking down the hillside into a Chinese landscape straight out of an ancient etching, large trees crowding the foreground, numbing the eyes; a disarming simplicity and her powerful reaction to it all.

"What was Anita like?"

"Did I ever tell you about her?"

"Don't you remember?"

"I guess I've told you a lot. She was nice. Very ambitious. She wanted *things*."

"Did she love you?"

"I think so."

"You never told me much about Cathy."

"She was very shy and . . . Well, I loved her very much." For some reason my tongue wouldn't move.

"Why didn't you marry her?"

"She had to go back to school. It's a very complicated story, Eunice."

She was trying to help an ant with a broken leg move along near her foot; she was captivated. Little old men walked dogs that looked like themselves, children played on the grass. A sunny clear day in the park. A couple of lovers strolled by. These things made the moment.

"Why did you never marry, Eli?"

"I have married, a few times, but not legally. And then there are so many things I want to do."

She was still tugging at the ant with a tiny twig. I looked out at a boat moving along slowly in the sun. An old man behind us was coughing his chest out.

"What do you want more than anything else in the world, Eli?"

"I don't know."

The tremendous sadness in her smile.

"Nothing?"

"A woman to love." I looked away because I knew at this instant that she wasn't that woman. "One who loves me."

"I'd better go home and study. I'll be *so* stupid when I go to Cambridge."

We got down.

"You'll never be stupid."

She took my hand and we found the path.

EUNICE

After a while it is not strange that for a time I cannot measure I am consciously trapped but oddly freed inside *Eunice's mind* she is using me as a symbol in a dream she is having. I realize that she is frustrated, afraid of being pregnant, her period hasn't come, a deficient cycle fills her with ageless anxiety, I talk gobbledygook from the wish-fulfilling structure she had me projected in. She externalizes me in her most private workings. I have no control over myself except to the extent that I know I am here, feeding some of her deeper desires contesting deltas of her most lewd fears.

She knows I detect her though her anxiety is superficial and she proceeds compulsively unconscious repressed segments of Wilson—the will *of the* son *will be done on earth as it is in heaven Daddy you displacement Dad I love you no you don't tell the truth you didn't tell me that I could freeze to death that I your first-born your favorite could suffer, you gave me repressive moralized crap Dad. That I could come out here to the beach pregnant with a Negro baby inside your hallucinations yes I like the warm sand of the beach the smell of the ocean water, like Mexico and all of its blues its pinks and greens and Italy. I love all the sand and the water oh so much the Spanish have a better word for it,* agua. *The* océano *is my womb the synonym of the universe. You say Eunice you must pray ask the Lord to restore your faith come on Dad come on just look at yourself why are you on the beach in that dark hot suit and that ridiculous tight collar come down off your high horse here beside me this black man and you can't even see his hand stroking my sides good feelings oh good feelings! You can't see his face and I know the nature of your deferment on his humanity. Eunice I am a man of God a good citizen I believe all men are brothers I see the boy but who is he. I am*

Eli speaking out of Eunice. Come out Dad has decided to shake your hand. Breaking the chorion that is holding me the uterine muscle dragging behind me in Eunice I am the baby. Eighteen days I look like a peanut when I lie outside her in the sand between her thighs. Her anxiety-ridden father who stands brisk, sturdy cannot see my hands. They are bricks to build the future. But they are here: I am stroking his daughter. I run my deeply burned hands along Eunice's stomach. I'm bitter toward the ol' man I bar him from my frame of reference rather I try but he stands there against the tides of my mind I turn Eunice over and pull down her flimsy swimsuit I run my finger into her all the way to the uterus I take off my sunglasses I feel very handsome in my new pale green swim trunks I am the rich color of the earth I say to the old man . . . She is sleeping she bears my child look his stunned face strains his eyes provoked he looks down with excitement between my hands I am holding Eunice open all and I notice his eyes fearfully sinfully watching and he is at the same time disgusted and consumed by rage. Go on I tell him reach in there shake hands with the son I am in there shake my hand I am the father. He murmurs I can't can't do this it's too new. Try I say you can do it. I see my hand a gentle friendly object lifting out of Eunice dripping the residue of our love. I am watching the poor old man who has such a tumorous-looking face whose right hand makes a jerky move the fingers twitching they grip the cloth of his trousers his mouth both eyes are swiftly shrinking closing the muscles are pulling in deep lines. His face has become bloodless white wrinkled. Eunice's voice contralto shocks me. Dad you're procrastinating again. She goes tut-tut-tut with her tongue against the roof of her mouth. He's only a little Negro fetus perfectly harmless creature Dad and your hand is paralyzed by the prospect. He is beginning to sit up and I look down I'm suddenly bored with playing games with her father it's easy enough to tolerate him at a distance. Eunice speaks: Isn't that right Dad? What did you say? I don't bother to answer as I pull up my swimsuit realizing that he actually pulled it down because nobody else was here when I dozed off. Dad be a sweety and drive me back to the station won't you how can he say no he is nothing without me and Ma I Eli should explain that Eunice has no reason or inclination to mention to her southern-born father that she makes love all through this urban summer to a black man beneath him her body sweating calling Daddy Daddy Daddy O Daddy! Maybe there isn't a black fetus with beautiful nappy hair forming. The feeling of relief comes the moment she sits down in her father's car. She sits down on the sofa and in the apartment on 106th Street rubs her eyes. She yawns and stretches out.

Last time I saw Eunice was a day early in September in her plush Upper West Side apartment. It was also the last day of school, and I had just taken the bus from there up to say good-bye.

But I felt extremely happy. I threw her back on the soft couch, tickling her—we kissed. On top of her I said, "Exit love."

"But there are ways. You," she said.

"You," I said.

A dreary and rainy day, the wet streets of New York. She was waiting for her father to come to pick up the heavy trunks. One of her roommates had this morning flown to Greece where she would continue her schooling; the other one had taken a smaller apartment nearby. For Eunice there would be a brief fellowship conference somewhere, I think in Philadelphia, then she would go on to Boston, to a new life, to an intellectual life that she found so necessary. Perhaps to sanction all that she already knew. Wasn't this principally what these college sessions were all about . . .?

". . . Well, you know tomorrow, baby, I've got to be in Mass. to see that the apartment is ready for my roommate and me." I loved the dimple in her chin, especially when she talked. O Eunice! We embraced. "I'm coming back to New York, baby!—the world isn't coming to an end—not just yet anyway!"

"I'll have to trust in that."

I kissed her neck.

But what did I have to go to now?

MAMA MAMA

I'm sitting in dark, warm Pee Wee's, Tammy at my elbow, greasy with barbecue, her defiant face bloated in the spirited shadows; I'm really only putting up with her for this one final night maybe because it's been three lonely weeks since I've had a touchable heroine to correspond to my gallant journey through this animated plight; she is living out in Queens, kept by her boss, a textile manufacturer's foreman, a creep who hired her on the basis of her youth, her ass, legs, his ungraceful fifty-year-old lust, a chicken-hearted little guy, who came, moved her few busted shopping bags of pell-mell personal effects from my narrow apartment twenty-one historical days ago. He's cursed by a hatred of Negroes. When she first blindly started gigging for him she used to come back red in the face telling me conversations, dull office incidents, how his words put down niggers as dumb animals, inferior creatures, how she confessed her pride in having me the person, though not telling my skin color, her sick lies endless, internally trapped confusion; she was sometimes sleeping elsewhere even then but with me like two three nights per week putting dusty U.S. currency on me—I had no job—the ol' government-sponsored poverty program in celebrated Harlem was washed up, I was abject, lying around noodle-style watching my secondhand idiot box TV and she was the funniest thing you ever saw, coming in grotesque in her ill-chosen assortment of new expensive garments her boss had bought her and rapping a storm of lies:

"Guess what!" "What?" "I'm rich now! Sol gave me a thousand dollars to put in the bank." "Did you put it in?" "He put it in *for* me." "In his or your name?" "In mine." And later: "Why did you have to lie about it?" Sadly, the nervous little-girl face, the twitching corners of her unhappy mouth. The big, desperate eyes when I said something like: "Tammy, you're really a pathological liar."

But the lies kept coming: "Guess what?" "What?" "Sol took me to Café A-Go-Go, Cheetah, The Village Gate, Peppermint Lounge, The Waldorf-Astoria, Max's Kansas City; every night this week we went someplace! He spent five hundred dollars on me. He's a real swinger. But he has other girls, they're older than me. He likes me because I'm young. I met one of his girlfriends. She's nice, has a little boy. We were at her apartment last night, guess what? He made love to her while I watched." "Why did you watch?" "Shhh, I didn't really watch—*he* watched me and Carol play around." *"Play around?"* "You know, belly rub." She giggled. "And don't go thinking I'm a lesbian either."

So I am remembering all those sorrowful moments of the distorted codes and dispatches of herself to me, how she invented the world, so deeply hurt by the index, the terms of the one presented her, when she insults me in the grandest possible way: "Sol asked me to ask you if you'd pose (for money, of course) with me so he can take some pictures of us."

"What d'you mean?!" "You know, of us just playing around. We don't have to be really doing anything. I can hold your thing, pretending to suck it. Things like that." The vivid red-light horror of the carnival-like request hasn't fully penetrated my sensibilities, psyche, intellect, I cannot believe my eardrums! I am only blandly surprised at the growing violence of my reaction, though I haven't yet shown an iota of response. I'm stunned. Finally, I decide not to show her how shocked, how pissed off I am; she is still explaining Sol's dissipated and deviant request as I no longer acknowledge her existence. I walk out, the sawdust gentle beneath my footfalls.

A thunderstorm outside!

It was four o'clock in the morning. I couldn't stand it anymore and I got up. The Puerto Rican woman was crying again in the hallway, the shuffling feet of her seven children, the stifled painful sounds, the gruffy vocal music of her husband's self-destructive jabbering down the staircase, his Spanish dissatisfaction had echoed through the building since ten. I couldn't make out what he was recommending that she do but now the pregnant woman stood outside my door; I sat up on the side of the bed, the ruffling slabs of wind that ebbed in through the cracks of the windows of this old turn-of-the-century, noninsulated but expressive hand-me-down building showered me and caused me to bristle.

At this point her ancient pain reached its apex, her sobbing was so low, so private, the ritual quality of it pulled me respectfully to my shaky feet. I could see by the light beneath the door the shadows of many feet. Hear the sweet fearful voice of a tiny child: *"Mama mama mama . . ."* and something in me shifted, trying to become commensurate to my loneliness; I was truly alone, even Tammy had stopped coming around. I put on my pants, tiptoed over to the two-dimensional protection against unmeasured shadows, my door, and stood there, my heart insinuating something extremely new coming to the copious surface of my up-until-now usually sweltering mind!

The husband's voice from upstairs sailed shatteringly down: *". . . y si tu vuelves te mataré!"* The Spanish so different from the kind I had lived with in Mexico after returning from Vietnam. Something about murdering her. The door banged, echoing rafts through everything; my hungry mind, almost sultry as it tried to extend to the sounds of the children's voices, only a few inches from me. *"Mama, mama, donde dormimos esta noche?" "Mama, mama por qué no llamas la policia para llevar papa?"* But the mother's sobbing continued, as modest, and somehow selfless, as an ancient river beneath our nourishing earth. The hippies in the apartment upstairs over me were giggling, a girl's voice screaming, "*Put me down! Larry!* PUT ME DOWN!!!" The child in the hall; *"Mama, necesito a pee!"* The mildew odor of my unwashed, damp socks and underwear, pell-mell on the toilet floor, only a few feet from my suspicious nose, surrounded me, a board of the floor squeaked as I shifted my soon-to-be twenty-eight-year-old assemblage of 145 pounds of human pyramidal essence.

Through the peephole, I could see only dark edges of the woman's hair. I had stood there only a psychic inch into a moment of apprehension, the kind New Yorkers have about getting into other folks' business; the kind that lets people, bereaved, die on the windy, storm-swept sidewalks, being stepped over, like litter, when I realized that I could not rationalize my way out of my human responsibility to those ageless sounds of pain that were expropriating this mother from a kind of blemished but necessary social security, the tangible reality of herself simply in the world. *Her* dispossession was my responsibility, despite her husband. Who he was socially. Though the Warden may have helped arouse within me a streak of cruelty, my bitterness was imperfected; I was no victim of complete inner blindness, subjective corruption.

I opened the door as a flock of honorable-looking hippies, three girls, five boys, all high, behind stalemated sunglasses, came down the stairs. I stood directly behind the woman, looking over her trembling shoulder, as the hippies filed around and down the next flight of stairs, in an untarnished silence. One bright girl, however, did look back, but because of the photogenic (say "Cheese") smile pirating around the lovely corners of her extremely young mouth, I knew the woman, to her, was only as valuable as a figure in a film. "Lady—uh, *Señora—Y* . . . you and uh . . . *y* . . . your . . . uh *niños*—come in?—Out of the uh—cold? No?"

My Spanish was awful. But I was possessed by now by her face; a skinny dark surface of impecuniousness, with two occupants empty of anything but fear and pain, her large, instinctive mother-eyes; her initial reaction to me was perforated with social fear, the impoverishment of everything our relationship—the lack of a communal relationship, rather, had been reduced to. But something drove me on, despite her shrinking away. The child in her arms, wrapped in a thin raggedy red and green faded blanket, had a round, stately face that looked quizzically toward me without focusing, the smallest of the five girls, tugging at her mother's shabby black woolen coat, was whimpering. *"Mama, tengo hambre."* And the tallest girl, who looked about ten years old, murmured sleepily; *"Mama, tengo frio."* The woman said, *"Silencio!"* She was such a thin but sturdy-looking woman. I knew that her husband had lived upstairs, long before I moved into the building, but she and the seven children had only recently come here from Puerto Rico. I had first begun seeing the children playing in the hallway, and in front of the building, and knew that neither the mother nor any of them spoke English.

In my desperation, I tried to get beyond the verandas of my mind to find the proper move, the correct Spanish word or nuance, sign, anything to convey to her my interest in helping her, the children. "My *casa—? Por favor?*" I saw the light of understanding divide her uncertain mind, begin to harbor my idea. I was holding out my hand, limply, toward the dark interior of the apartment. *"Mama, necesito a pee." "Mama, mama, tengo hambre."* And I stood aside, as she entered, the seven stark children, with dark porcelain, starving eyes, followed her. A little stream of urine ran down the leg of the last girl, leaving a thin, spotty trail along the floor. I closed the door, turned on the light. Instantly, I went to the refrigerator, opened it and brought out the hardly touched platter of fried chicken I had picked up at the deli on 14th and Avenue A. I placed it on the coffee table near the bed. "Uh—let me see: *niños, por favor!*"

The eight of them were very motionless, watching me. One child, snot running down to the finger in her mouth, stepped toward the chicken. *"Por favor!"* I said again. The mother said, pointing to herself, *"Maria Vega, gracias." "Niños?"* I pointed toward the children, trying to smile. She touched their heads as she spoke, between deep painful breathing. *"Rosetta, nació* 1957; *Rosalia, nació* 1959; *Jose, nació* 1960; *Maria, nació* 1961; *Angelina, nació* 1962; *Lolita, nació* 1963." And the weak but proud smile of this good mother shone portly through her air. Then looking down to the baby in her arm, *"Josefa, nació Agosto,* 1967." I could hear the huge thunderclaps slamming and sliding through space, outside: the city seemed shaken by the powerful strokes. But I had one narrow bed, and it was to be hers and her babies' which was the least that I could do. I put on my shoes, shirt, and parka, and unable to formulate a simple word like *adios,* I smiled foolishly, almost stumbling. Going out, I heard her emphatic *"Gracias."*

I stood inside a doorway down the street, vibrantly alive, watching the rivers of water wash along the street, the giant dynamite-streaks of lightning pulverize the sky and I stood there till daybreak.

ACKNOWLEDGMENTS

An abridged hardcover version of this novel was first published by the Olympia Press in 1969, and a paperback version appeared in 1970. Hardcover German and Italian editions were published that same year.

Several other portions were subsequently published in periodicals and anthologies as follows.

"Capricorn," as "Eli," *Lotus* 1, no. 3 (1972).

"Induction," "Honey Locust," and "The Future," in *Ten Times Black,* edited by Julian Mayfield (New York: Bantam Pathfinder Editions, 1972).

"Dossy O," *Black Creation* 3, no. 4 (1972). Reprinted in *Writing under Fire: Stories of the Vietnam War,* edited by Jerome Klinkowitz (New York: Delta Books, 1978).

"Hilda and Anita," as "Tattoo," *Massachusetts Review* 22, no. 4 (1981).

"The Other Side" and "Reality," *Alcatraz* 2 (1982).

"The Escape," as "TV," *Callaloo* 7, no. 3 (1984), special issue edited by Charles Johnson.

"Hitting the Apple," as "Scat," in *Calling the Wind: Twentieth-Century African American Short Stories,* edited by Clarence Major (New York: HarperCollins, 1993).